Sawbones

William W. Johnstone
with J. A. Johnstone

WHEELER PUBLISHING
A part of Gale, a Cengage Company

GALE
A Cengage Company

Farmington Hills, Mich • San Francisco • New York • Waterville, Maine
Meriden, Conn • Mason, Ohio • Chicago

Copyright © 2017 by J.A. Johnstone.
The WWJ steer head logo is a Reg. U.S. Pat. & TM Off.
Wheeler Publishing, a part of Gale, a Cengage Company.

ALL RIGHTS RESERVED
Wheeler Publishing Large Print Western.
The text of this Large Print edition is unabridged.
Other aspects of the book may vary from the original edition.
Set in 16 pt. Plantin.

LIBRARY OF CONGRESS CIP DATA ON FILE.
CATALOGUING IN PUBLICATION FOR THIS BOOK
IS AVAILABLE FROM THE LIBRARY OF CONGRESS

ISBN-13: 978-1-4328-6182-7 (softcover)

Published in 2019 by arrangement with Pinnacle Books, an imprint of Kensington Publishing Corp.

Printed in Mexico
1 2 3 4 5 6 7 23 22 21 20 19

SAWBONES

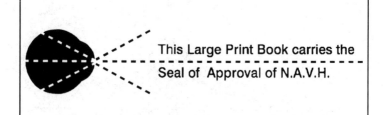

This Large Print Book carries the
Seal of Approval of N.A.V.H.

SAWBONES

CHAPTER 1

Dr. Samuel Knight doubled over as pain drove into his belly, worse than any knife wound. He forced himself to stand upright. Sweat beaded his forehead, and it wasn't from the sultry late spring day in East Texas. He was used to such weather. He had grown up in the Piney Woods. The agony came from the void in his stomach from lack of food.

Or maybe he had poisoned himself with the weeds he had eaten the day before. His time spent in the Yankee prison camp at Elmira, New York — Hellmira, the starving, disease-ridden inmates had called it — had hardly been as bad. There the tainted food caused different symptoms. Diarrhea. Vomiting.

He gasped when stomach pain doubled him over again.

"Must have been hemlock and not wild carrot I ate." Desperation had made him careless. Wild carrot leaves looked fuzzy, hemlock didn't. But with his vision blurred at times from lack of food, making such a mistake was all too easy because the leaves were similar. The only luck he had was being alive. Hemlock killed as surely as a Yankee minié ball to the head.

He talked to himself to get his mind on something other than the pain threatening to swamp him. It worked, concentrating on his wife and the homecoming she would give him when he got to Pine Knob. How they would celebrate! All night. For a week!

It had been years since he had seen Victoria and almost as long since he had written her a letter. The Yankees hadn't permitted their prisoners to send or receive letters, even if Victoria had known where to write him. The more he thought of her, the better he felt. The brutal pain died down enough to let him keep walking along the muddy road. He had no particular destination in mind today. But soon, soon he would be back in Pine Knob and home. All he had to do was to keep putting one foot in front of the other.

Home. Where he had grown up. The house. His wife, Victoria. His heart beat faster as he concentrated on his mental image of her. The pocket watch case with her picture had been stolen by a bluecoat the first day he had been taken prisoner after the Battle of the Wilderness. The watch had never kept good time, but her picture was the real reason he kept the battered gold case.

Closing his eyes, he pictured her waving weakly to him the day he had ridden from Pine Knob on his way to Richmond and the Louisiana Hospital located there. He had begun as an assistant surgeon and quickly found himself teaching classes to first-year medical students. Too few of them had any aptitude, but Surgeon General Samuel Preston Moore had assigned most of them to forward units under the Bonnie Blue flag. Attrition in medical ranks proved almost as great as among those on the front lines.

Disease ran rampant, not caring if a doctor or private or butternut-uniformed general suffered.

His feet moved a little faster. He knew what he'd left behind back East, and he knew what lay ahead. Home and hearth and Victoria.

Hunger pangs tore at him again when a tantalizing odor made his nostrils flare. Without realizing it, he left the road, cut across a grassy yard and found a game trail leading through the pines to a small, well-kept house. His mouth watered. It had been too long — a lifetime — since he had tasted freshly baked peach pie. Knight stumbled forward, ignoring everything around him but the pie set on the windowsill to cool.

He braced himself, hands on either side of the window, as he leaned forward, closed his eyes and took a deep whiff. He turned giddy with anticipation. Eyes popping open, he looked around. Stealing a pie was wrong. *Stealing* was wrong, but starving to death had to be a sin of some sort, too. Hands trembling, he picked up the pie. The pain as heat stung his fingers proved far less than the knife thrusts of hunger in his belly.

He turned to steal away with his booty. Not ten feet away a girl, hardly six years old, looking all pert and small, dressed in a plain brown gingham dress, gazed up at him. Her stricken look froze him in place.

"That's for my birthday party," she said in a choked voice. "Please, mister, don't take it. I ain't got anything else." She shuffled her bare feet and looked at the ground. Her shoulders shook as she tried to hold back sobs.

"I just wanted to get a better look at it. It smells wonderful." He held out the pie. His belly grumbled.

"Mama made it special for me. She got the peaches fresh from Mr. Frost. He's got an orchard of fruit trees. Apple, pear. Peaches are my favorite." She took a step back.

He knew what she saw. Knight might have been a scarecrow come to life. Standing almost six feet tall, he was down to a hundred and twenty pounds, ribs poking out, face gaunt, his long, unkempt dark hair greasy and pushed back out of his feverish eyes. Scarecrows in the field were dressed better, too. His trousers hung in tatters, his shirt had more holes than a woodpecker's dinner, and his coat would fall apart if he dared to remove it. He wished for the first time in months that he still wore his Confederate uniform. It had been presentable, but it had rotted away in the harsh winter spent at the prison camp.

She stared into his eyes and took another step back. Her small hand covered her mouth in horror. He knew his blue eyes were sunken and bloodshot, turning him into a bogeyman.

A bogeyman stealing her birthday pie.

"It's a mighty fine-looking pie." Knight turned and placed the pie back on the windowsill. "Happy birthday." His hands shook, as much from emotion as from hunger. Not daring to look back, he hurried away, found the path through the woods and got onto the road again.

Tears ran down his cadaverous cheeks. "I'm reduced to stealing from a little girl. No, no, no."

He stumbled on, trying to convince himself he was a good man, only driven to desperate acts by all that had happened to him. Life in the prison camp had been harsh. When the Confederacy finally capitulated, they had no resources to help those prisoners kept by the Federals. He and all the others had been turned out, put on trains going south, and then abandoned in Richmond without food, money, or hope. Those civilians in the onetime Confederate capital were hardly better off. They certainly did not want diseased ex-prisoners in their city.

"I'm better than that," he told himself aloud. "I am."

"Reckon you might be, if I knowed what you was talkin' 'bout."

Knight took a few more steps before he realized the voice was not coming from inside his own head. He stopped and looked around. Undergrowth started only a few feet from the road. Sparse trees quickly grew into a dense forest blocking his view after more than a dozen yards. A rustling made him home in on the short, tattered man emerging from behind a barberry bush.

Knight knew he wasn't the only one down on his luck. This man, with his scratched face and tangled, sandy hair, was in no better condition. As he hobbled out, Knight realized he was in even worse shape. The right leg twisted outward so the foot plowed up the dirt as he came forward.

"You don't look like no threat to me," the stranger said. "Are you?"

Knight shook his head and immediately regretted it. Dizziness hit him from the simple movement. Surprisingly strong arms circled his shoulders and held him upright.

"Sorry. Been a while since I had anything to eat."

"You got the look of a soldier about you, but not exactly. Hard to put my finger on it." The man steered Knight to the side of the road and a stump, where he collapsed. "You some kind of officer for the Rebs?"

"Captain," Knight said, seeing no reason to hide it. "I was a doctor attached to Jeb Stuart's cavalry unit."

"You're nuthin' but skin and bones. You ain't sick now, are you?"

"Hungry. Can't get anyone to give me the time of day, much less a decent meal. I've walked most of the way from Richmond. A few gave me rides in a wagon, but not many. Not enough." He thrust out his stickthin legs.

The man came around and put his foot up against the sole of Knight's shoe, then bent and got a closer look.

"Our feet's 'bout the same size, but you got a hole in that shoe big enough to shove a silver dollar through." He reached over and poked with his finger. "That anything more'n old, rottin' newspaper you got shoved in there?"

"All I could find."

"You are truly a man down on his luck, Doctor . . . ?"

"Dr. Samuel Knight from Pine Knob. That's where I'm heading."

"Pleased to make your acquaintance, Doc. I'm Jake — Jacobs. Leonard Jacobs. Folks just call me Jake, though." He hobbled around and sank down on a log next to Knight's stump.

"Thank you for your kindness, Jake. You . . . you got any food?"

"Reckon I'm in a similar situation as you, Doc. Nobody wants to help out a gimp." He thrust out his left leg and rubbed it. "Too many soldiers returnin' for me to find a decent job. And the Federals, curse 'em

14

all, they moved in with Reconstruction blowin' at their backs, and took over 'bout everything. No spare food for any son of the South."

"You?"

"Me and you, from the sound of it, Doc. But I got an idea, only there's nuthin' I can do for it."

"Food?"

"More'n just food. All we can eat and a few dollars, to boot. Likely only them damned Federal greenbacks but what good's a hunnerd-dollar bill with Lucy Pickens's fine portrait on it? Or even a five-hunnerd piece of scrip sportin' that great general, Stonewall Jackson?" Jake tipped his head to the side and squinted in Knight's direction. "You ever see Confederate money with denominations that large?"

Knight shook his head.

"Well, sir, I did and am proud of it. Only them Federals stole it all away and left me with a bad leg and nothing more'n the clothes on my back."

"What of food?" It was all Knight could think of, right at the moment. "How do we get food?"

"You ain't adverse to doin' a little thievin', now are you? If it's from turncoats cozyin' up with the carpetbaggers?"

"I was tempted to steal a peach pie from a little girl. Anyone helping the Yankees is fair game."

"That's the spirit!" Jake slapped him on the back and almost knocked him off the stump. "Now, I got me a plan, but with my bad leg and all, I can't rightly do much by myself. The two of us workin' as a fine Rebel team, now, we have a chance."

Knight turned slightly to face Jake. The man rubbed his leg as if it hurt him.

"I'm not going to be much help. I'm so weak. My eyes don't focus all the time."

"You don't have to see too good. That's the beauty of my plan. We're not a half hour's walk from a town." Jake looked hard at him. "Call it an hour away, what with your shoe and that hole and all. It'll be dark when we get there. I'll keep an eye peeled for the marshal or the owner comin' round all unexpectedlike while you break in and scoop up food for the pair of us."

"It's a store?"

"A restaurant. Best of all, the damn fool owner keeps all the money he takes in hidden behind his stove. We get food *and* money, money from carpetbaggers eatin' their fine meals all in style while the rest of the town starves 'cuz there ain't no money. The Yankees have sucked the townspeople dry with taxes and fines and levies."

Knight had to speak up over his growling stomach. He rubbed it until it subsided. "I swear, I can feel my backbone when I press in like this."

"You say you're on your way to Pine Knob? That's another hunnerd miles to the west. A long walk, but a couple days' hard ride iffen you set astride a horse. Maybe three or four days if you take it easy. You could be in the bed next to your lovin' wife 'fore you know it. What's her name again?"

"Victoria."

"You and the missus must have a lot of catchin' up to do. Get the money from the damned carpetbaggers and you can buy a horse, a good one, and let it run. As featherlight as you are, you can gallop it all the way and it won't feel nuthin' but the saddle."

Knight closed his eyes and imagined himself home. It seemed like a fantasy to him, a dream he had given up on. *Victoria. Home. Bed and food and Victoria.*

The thought of his lovely wife kept him moving. They reached the small town a little after midnight, if Knight judged the position of the stars right. The streets were deserted. He looked around for the saloon, but even it had shut down.

"Why isn't it open? The saloon?"

Jake laughed harshly and shook his head. "It don't open on Sundays. They got some religious feelin' in this town, even if it is overrun by damned Yankees."

"Sunday?" Knight said dully. He had lost track of time, how long he had been walking, the day of the week. All that had mattered was taking one more step to get back to Pine Knob.

Victoria. He had to be with his wife again, but the impact of what he was about to do crashed in on him. "I can't rob a store on the Sabbath."

"You don't have to. By now it's past midnight. It's Monday, not Sunday. We got to hurry. The proprietors will be in there soon to start the day's cookin." Jake spat. "Cookin' for the carpetbaggers. They line up and make all kinds of nasty remarks about us, about us Rebs and Southerners. They especially hate Texans."

Knight felt adrenaline pumping through his veins. He straightened. Everything Jake said was likely true. He had met with little charity as he crossed the country. The towns run by the Reconstruction judges and lawmen were the worst. He had almost gotten lynched for nothing more than passing through one town in Louisiana.

"That's the place. You get on 'round back and break in. I'll keep watch. The deputy makes rounds whenever he wakes up."

"What'll you do if he comes? He's likely armed. Do you have a gun?"

Jake laughed harshly, took hold of the tails of his coat and pulled them away from his body to show nothing but his suspender buttons.

"If I'd had a six-gun, I would've hocked it for a square meal. Listen for a mockingbird. You hear one, that's me warning you." Jake came over and slapped him on the shoulder. "You're a good man, Doc. I know I can trust you. What'd I say about the money box?"

"Behind the stove."

"Get going. I'm gonna find a lookout spot."

Knight watched Jake hurry off. Something was wrong, but he couldn't focus well enough to figure out what it was. Then he forced everything but the robbery from his mind. The restaurant stood in a simple wood-frame building. Around back he found a locked door. He tried it, but it had been barred on the inside. Trying to force it open wouldn't do him any good. Even if he had strength enough to kick in the door or slam it open with his shoulder, that would cause too much of a ruckus. The town slept peacefully. Sudden noise like that would awaken the dead.

Or worse, the deputy marshal.

He pressed his hand against the door and applied a little pressure, only to give up trying to push it inward. Running his fingers down the poorly fitted frame he found a spot that yielded when he pulled outward. Sitting on the ground, shoving his feet against the wall, and pulling with what strength remained to him caused one panel to pop free. He landed flat on his back, staring up at the stars. Clouds moved in from down south, coming off the Gulf of Mexico and bringing a spring storm.

He sat up and ran his arm through the opening, then slowly worked his way up until his fingers brushed the locking bar. Heaving, he lifted the bar and let it drop to the floor inside. The door opened on well-oiled hinges. He was in.

Knight tumbled forward and almost passed out from the odors in the kitchen. *Food. Fresh and wonderful.* Mouth watering, belly rumbling, he crawled forward and pulled himself up to a table. Greedily stuffing stale bread into his mouth caused him to choke. Common sense took over. Eating more slowly, he let the bread make its way down his constricted esophagus into his belly. New rumblings told him he might puke. His stomach and food had been strangers for too long. A dipper of water helped ease the complaints.

More bread gave him reason to continue. As he scavenged for food that would go into a flour sack, he kept eating. Cheese. A bit of beef so tough that his teeth wobbled as he gnawed on it. Pickles from a jar. Okra. He ate anything and everything until he felt bloated.

He turned to filling the flour sack for Jake and his meals later rather than eating. When the sack weighed him down, he went to the cast-iron stove and reached behind it. He cut his fingers on a sharp-edged metal box. Fumbling it out and dropping it on the kitchen floor, he saw that a small padlock held it shut. He hunted until he found a knife and tried to force open the lock. Before he applied enough leverage, a warbling sound came from outside.

The noise puzzled him for a moment, then he realized Jake sounded a very poor mockingbird's call. He stuffed the metal box into the top of the food-laden flour sack, tucked the knife into his waistband and went to the door. A quick look out made him catch his breath. A dark figure stalked along.

The clouds moved away from the moon enough to cause a glint off a badge. Worse, the deputy carried a shotgun in the crook of his arm and he came directly for the opened door. Knight touched the knife, then knew facing down an armed lawman with a butcher knife was suicidal. He closed the door, then lifted the locking bar. It fell into place just as the deputy reached the outside.

"You in there, Gus? That you? Open up. Gus? Augustus!"

The deputy began banging on the barred door with the shotgun's stock.

Knight caught his breath, wondering what to do. Then he realized the only way out was through the main dining room and out the front of the restaurant. The energy given him by the food heightened his senses and put spring into his step. He felt better than he had in weeks. He dodged through the red-and-white checked cloth-draped tables to the front door held shut by a lock. Without thinking, he slid the knife between the hasp and door and pulled down with every ounce of strength he had. The nails holding the hasp ripped free. He burst out into the street and looked around frantically. Jake's plan had ended with them leaving the restaurant undetected.

"Don't just stand there. Come along." Jake motioned to him from the corner of the building.

"What about the deputy?"

"Don't worry your head none 'bout him. Just hightail it."

Knight had considered asking if they could go to a livery stable and steal a horse. That was a damned sight worse than stealing food and some money. Men got their necks stretched for such a crime, but he wasn't sure how far and fast he could run, even with his belly full.

Besides, was it really a crime stealing a Yankee's horse? After all they had done to him and the other prisoners in Elmira? They owed him more than a horse. They owed him a life.

"No time to dawdle. We might have the whole town comin' down on our heads." Jake scuttled away, moving fast for a man with a bum leg and forcing Knight to trail behind. He found himself hard put to keep up with the man.

They left the town and plunged into a wooded area darker than the inside of a cow. Somehow, Jake found his way through the stygian night. Knight wasn't as skilled at avoiding low branches or even tree trunks. He bounced from one to the next, following his partner in crime more by sound than sight. After what seemed an eternity he popped out into a clearing.

Jake stood at the edge, hands on his knees, bent over and panting harshly. He looked up as Knight approached. "You hang onto the loot? Lemme see." Jake grabbed the flour sack from his feeble grasp and held it open. The tin box tumbled out to the ground. "You got it! I'm rich!"

"I got us enough food to last a few days. If we use some of the money to buy horses, we can be in Pine Knob real soon."

"Pine Knob? Oh, yeah, Pine Knob." Jake looked around, found a rock, and smashed the small lock. "Lookee here. There must be a hunnerd dollars inside. I knew that son of a bitch was rich, but I never thought he had this much salted away." He looked up and danced a little jig.

Knight stepped closer. The stacks of greenbacks might amount to that much. A few silver cartwheels rattled about in the box. Jake grabbed them and stuffed them into his coat pockets.

"Is your leg all right? You seemed mighty spry after the way you were dragging it around when we met."

"My leg? Oh, it's hurtin' something fierce, Doc. We got the time. You think you can do something about it for me?"

Knight went to him and knelt, then looked up. "Which leg was it? You've been limping on both legs . . . and neither."

"It comes and goes, the pain does. It's my right leg. See?"

As Knight looked down, Jake launched a kick that caught his benefactor under the chin. Knight's head snapped back, and he sat heavily, stunned. Through blurred eyes he saw Jake lifting the rock he had used to break the lock. Then the world went dark all around him.

CHAPTER 2

Samuel Knight smiled and rolled over, pulled the pillow tightly under his head, and settled down. He was home. Back in his own bed. Warm and safe.

"Victoria?" He reached out for his wife and recoiled when his hand smashed into a rock wall.

He worked hard to open his eyes against the crusted gunk gluing the eyelids together. A quick swipe broke the seal and let him stare directly into an unfamiliar wall. Struggling, he sat up, swung around, and dropped his feet to the cell floor. *Cell?* He panicked. In front of him rose iron bars. He was in a cage again, just as he had been at Elmira every time he tried to help his fellow prisoners of war.

"You finally decided to wake up, huh?" A portly man came from the shadows on the far side of the cage. He pushed his face forward until his chubby cheeks pressed into the bars to get a better look at Knight. "You don't look like you got the strength to do the dirty deed."

"What are you talking about?"

"Go on, play innocent. That won't cut it when you get to court. We're on the circuit for Karl Lassiter, the toughest judge ever to come to Texas, or so folks claim. Don't know about that, but he has sentenced three men from town to hang since the end of the war."

"A Reconstruction judge?" Knight spit out the words.

"He's from Wisconsin, that's true, and he was an elector for Abe Lincoln. Ain't sayin' that's how he got this job, but the way things are these days it didn't hurt none."

"You're going to hang me?"

"Not me. Judge Lassiter. And a jury of your peers." The man pulled back from the bars. For the first time Knight saw the marshal's badge pinned on the taut cloth of a vest. "I'd say you deserve it, if Slowpoke dies."

"Slowpoke? Dies?" Knight held his head and winced when he touched the large lump where Jake had clobbered him.

"Don't reckon you'd know my deputy's name. We call him Slowpoke. Slowpoke Bennet. Now that I think on it, I'm not sure

27

I ever heard his real name. Might be Clarence. If I have to make up a tombstone, it'd be proper to put his Christian name on it." The marshal mumbled to himself.

"I was attacked. A man named Jake. Leonard Jacobs, I think was his full name."

"Now, don't go lyin' just to save your neck, mister. You hit Slowpoke with a rock and put him into a coma. Doc Phillips ain't sure he'll ever come out of his stupor, though it's hard to tell the difference between him layin' in bed now and when he was sleepin' on my desk while he was on duty." The marshal chuckled, shook his head, then sobered. "I ain't got no call jokin' about him. He was a decent man. Not too bright, but he did his job, such as it was. If it was left to me, you'd swing for ambushin' him, no matter if he dies."

"I never touched your deputy. Jake hit *me*. It's Jake you want."

"You denyin' you broke into Gus's restaurant and stole his money? Where'd you stash it? The money box was empty when we found it. And don't you go tryin' to say one of my posse stole it. They were all family. Two brothers and a cousin. Honest as the day is long, the lot of them, even if Cousin David did stray a mite when he stole that scrawny calf, but that was when he was

28

younger and full of piss and vinegar . . . and a considerable amount of 'shine."

Knight put his head in his hands and leaned forward, trying to think. Jake had hit him. The man had set him up. The reason he limped first on one leg and then the other was that neither was injured. It had all been a ruse to get a sucker to take the risk of breaking in and stealing the money from the restaurant owner. His hunger and weakened condition had made him easy to hoodwink.

Now he was going to swing for a crime Jake committed.

"Is your doctor well trained?"

"Now, why do you ask that? Doc Phillips is a good man."

"I'm a doctor and saw too many wounds during the war. Traumatic injuries can be treated, and I have the experience."

"Well, now, Doc Phillips ain't a medical doctor. He's a vet. Damn good one. He saved Ramon Zamora's prize bull last year when nobody thought it was possible. Then he did a good job on —"

"I can help. Let me see what I can do for your deputy."

"Anything to bamboozle me into lettin' you out of that iron cage? No, siree. You ain't gettin' me to turn the key in the lock.

Not today, not until Judge Lassiter orders you to appear in court to stand trial."

The marshal lumbered off, puffing from the exertion. A door leading into the outer office closed, followed by a metallic click as a key turned in a lock. Knight was doubly locked into the cell. Even if he escaped from the cage, he had another door to open before confronting the marshal in his office.

He got to his feet, wobbled a bit and began examining his predicament. Some of the bars were rusty — but not rusted through enough to make escape possible. The hard-packed dirt floor was almost as good as concrete for preventing a prisoner from digging out. The outer wall he had banged his hand into had been constructed with imprisonment in mind. A barred window set high in the wall was too small to squeeze through, even in his emaciated condition, even if he pried off the bars, even if he jumped high enough to get out. Elmira had been mostly large, tattered tents to house the prisoners, with sheet-iron cages and pits dug deep into the ground for extra punishment. A few days spent in both had given Knight experience in sizing up the chances to escape.

The Yankees had been good at making escape-proof cells. This marshal's jail matched anything he had endured during his incarceration, in spite of its superficial look of disrepair.

Frustrated, he rattled the bars. For all the rust, the door was solid. He rested his forehead against the cool metal and shook as if he had the ague. Being too trusting — gullible! — had landed him in a world of trouble. Jake had duped him and then made off with the money and a bag full of food. Knight smiled wryly. Of all the troubles, he missed the flour sack filled with food the most. His belly still churned and grumbled in spite of the bread and other food he had eaten while robbing the restaurant.

"Marshal! Are you going to feed me? You can't let me starve." He glanced up at the tiny window. Pale dawn seeped through. "It's breakfast. Bring me some eggs and ham. Maybe some cornbread to go with it. Or biscuits and gravy."

"Shut yer yap. I'll get around to feedin' you when I danged well feel like it. Right now I'm going to see if Slowpoke's still among us or if you don't get fed at all 'cause he died."

The outer door slammed. Knight had the sense of being completely alone. He sank onto the cot and considered curling up to grab a few more minutes of sleep. Whether the deputy lived or died had little effect on what they would do to him. Even if they didn't stretch his neck, he was bound for prison due to the assault and robbery.

As that thought sunk in, Knight turned cold all over. He had endured so much in Elmira. Never again. Better to die than be caged like an animal. He stood, pulled the blanket from the cot and began tearing it into long strips wide enough to support his weight. It took him the better part of fifteen minutes to get a noose made and to fasten the free end of his crude rope through the bars in the window where he couldn't even look out to see the new day.

"Jumpin' Jehoshaphat!" The marshal slammed back the door leading into his office, turned and grabbed the keys, and rushed to the cell door. He stared up at Knight dangling from the rude noose, unmoving. He fumbled and finally got the cell door open. A quick step took him to the dangling body. Strong arms circled Knight's thighs and lifted to get him down.

The marshal expected deadweight. Instead he caught an elbow to the top of his skull. He staggered back and released Knight. For a moment, Knight kicked and then got free of the harness he had made from the blanket. Landing on his feet, he stepped forward, then dropped as hard as he could to drive his knee into the marshal's big gut. Air whistled from the lawman's body. He gagged, turned purple, and rolled onto his side. As he gasped for air, Knight acted.

Like a cowboy during branding, he whipped a length of blanket around, caught the man's wrists and bound them. A second strip fastened the marshal's hands to his ankles. Grunting with exertion, Knight pulled his victim into the cell and looked down on his handiwork.

"Sorry, Marshal. I didn't want to do this."

"I'll have the army after you. I'll —"

Before he got another word out, Knight whipped a third piece of the threadbare blanket around his head and tightened it into a gag. Only then did he exit the cell and slam the door. A quick turn locked the marshal up.

"Believe me, I hope the deputy is going to be all right. I might have robbed the restaurant, but I never touched him. If anything, I went out of my way to avoid him. The one you want is named Leonard Jacobs."

Knight closed the door between the cells and the marshal's office, turning the key in that lock, too. The lawman was as secure as Knight had been only a few minutes earlier.

He tossed the keys onto the desk, then hesitated when he saw a stack of wanted posters. His likeness would be among them soon enough if he didn't clear out. Wasting time pawing through the pile made it all the more likely he would get caught, but he did it anyway. Halfway down he saw a smeared picture of a fugitive who might be Jake. The crimes were all robbery and swindling. He was a known confidence man. Knight found a pencil, scribbled a hasty note to the marshal letting him know this was who he really wanted for the assault on the deputy and then started out the door.

He again hesitated.

Hanging on a peg beside the door was a gun belt with a revolver thrust into a holster. Hand shaking, he took it down, drew the pistol and looked at it. He had seen plenty of six-guns in the army. This was a Colt Navy cap-and-ball. He thrust it back into the holster and slung the belt around his meager middle. It almost went around him twice, given the marshal's girth and his own lack. He fastened the buckle and slung it over his shoulder, then grabbed a leather pouch with two loaded cylinders and more slugs, caps and powder. Only then did he venture out into the street.

The sun had risen high enough to hang

above the pine trees at the far end of town. Commerce proceeded and the town's citizens went about their chores. They had no idea that a desperate outlaw joined them as they conducted their business.

The town was small enough that Knight found the livery stable quickly without asking anyone for directions. He hesitated to enter. From the street he saw four horses stabled there, a towheaded youngster of eight or nine dutifully giving each a nosebag of feed. His hemming and hawing saved him. Two men came from the rear of the stable. Both carried rifles but didn't wear sidearms. He spun away and pressed against the rough-hewn wall as he overheard them.

"He's a damned cheapskate. We caught that varmint. We deserve more than a shot of whiskey for our trouble."

"Yeah, Cousin Ned, you're right. We coulda got our heads blowed off. We didn't know what to expect after Slowpoke got all bashed up like that other than we was on the trail of a real desperado. Being summoned to ride with the posse interrupted my sleep. We shoulda got paid at least a dollar, like any other time."

"If you ask me, the marshal kept the posse money for hisself. The mayor puts up ten dollars a month, silver, not any of that worthless Yankee greenback scrip, just for such things, and it shouldn't matter if we was out a minute or a day. The rules say a posse member gets a dollar a day."

"We did get a drink."

"Yeah, but it was trade whiskey. It's still chewin' holes in my gut."

Knight slid the Colt Navy from the holster and held it down at his side. Cocking it would draw attention. He kept his thumb on the hammer, just in case he had to get off a quick round. The thought of shooting it out with the two who had been in the posse that caught him the night before made him slump. The first report from his pistol — or their rifles — would bring the rest of the town running. He would be caught for sure.

"What are you doin', mister?"

Knight jumped a foot. He swung the six-gun around and hid it behind him as he stared down at the boy who had been working in the stalls.

"I . . . I'm looking for Doc Phillips."

"Ain't got no sick animals here. Not today. They's all healthy and, well, as strong as horses." The boy smirked at this small joke. "You want the doc, go on to the end of the street until you see a sign carved to look like a horse. Or if you kin read, his name's on it."

"Much obliged."

Knight backed off, kept the drawn six-shooter out of sight, and tried not to make it look as if he fled from the two men just emerging from the stables. He walked with shoulders pulled back and spine straight . . . as if he had every right to be out and about as a free man. If those two had gotten a good look at him the night before, he might find himself exchanging lead with them. The hairs on the back of his neck rippled, then settled down the farther he got from the stables.

Before his heart stopped pounding from the close call with the posse, he saw the horse-shaped sign swinging in the sultry wind. Knight slowed and finally stopped. What he intended was crazy. If not outright *insane,* then reckless and not a little bit stupid. With a deep breath, he opened the low wooden gate and went to the veterinarian's door. Two quick taps almost convinced him to leave. Before he could, the door opened and a young man, hardly in his twenties, with mussed sandy hair and blood-shot eyes, confronted him.

"What is it?"

"You're Dr. Phillips?"

"Am. And you are?"

"I came to see how your patient is doing."

"The four-legged one or the deputy?"

"Slowpoke. How's he feeling?"

"Can't say since he hasn't recovered consciousness yet. You a friend? I don't remember seeing you around town before." The vet's eyes fixed on the gun belt slung over Knight's shoulder.

"Passing through when I heard. His family and mine . . ." Knight let the sentence trail off so the vet could draw his own conclusion.

"Come on in. I've got him in the back room."

Knight followed the young man to a small room outfitted like a medical doctor's surgery. He saw bottles of carbolic acid and a few surgical instruments next to a small library of books on large animal anatomy. One lay open. Knight stood on tiptoe and scanned the pages. The vet hunted for ways he might help the deputy.

"He's not a sheep, you know." Knight went to a cot where a pale, unmoving man stretched out under a thin sheet.

"I don't know squat about fixing people, and he needs help of some sort. I'm trying to figure out what."

Knight turned Slowpoke's head slowly

and saw how the back of his head had been bashed in. "I've seen a wound similar to this. A man was grazed by a cannonball. You've got to relieve the pressure from the bone fragments or he will die." He reached for a sharp knife on the table.

"Not so fast. I can't let you operate on him. Who the hell are you?"

"The one who's trying to save his life." Knight shoved the vet, causing him to stumble. As he tried to right himself, Knight drew the Colt Navy and pointed it squarely at him. "Do I tie you up or do you help me?"

"You can't take that knife to him. You —"

Moving faster than he thought possible in his condition, Knight stepped up and swung the pistol, laying the barrel alongside Dr. Phillips's temple. Stunned, the man dropped to his knees. In that condition, Knight easily tied him up with cord he found on the table. Before the vet regained his senses, Knight picked up the knife, tested its tip, and then sloshed carbolic acid over it.

"Don't. You'll kill him."

"I might, but he's going to die if I don't do something fast." Knight dabbed away caked blood, cleansed the wound, and scraped away all the hair on the deputy's scalp that might get into the wound.

He sucked in his breath and held it as he slipped the knife's tip under a bone fragment and applied outward pressure. The bit of skull popped free. Pressure using a bandage stanched some blood flow enough to let him get to a second, more dangerous piece of bone driven into the brain. "Do you have forceps?"

"In my kit bag. Behind the table."

Knight relaxed the pressure on the bandage. Blood flowed. If the vet had helped, the deputy would have a better chance of not bleeding to death. He found the bag and dragged it beside the cot. After a few seconds of rummaging around, he found the forceps similar to those he had used to good effect during the war. Applying them to the edge of the bone, he withdrew it with steady pressure, then tossed it onto the floor. Only then did he work to stop the bleeding. After several minutes, he sank back on his heels. His hands shook.

"I think he'll make it now. He might not be as sharp as he once was but —"

"They call him Slowpoke for a reason," Phillips said. "You really got the fragments out of his brain?"

"They weren't too deeply embedded."

"Who the hell are you?"

"Someone who is going to take your

horse, the one I see tethered out back." Knight wiped blood from his hands, slung the gun belt over his shoulder, then climbed through the window. "Don't let him thrash about too much. If you have to, give him whiskey to kill the pain if he ever wakes up. That's all right."

"If? You mean he might still die?"

"There're never any easy operations or outcomes with head wounds." Knight kicked over the ledge and dropped to the ground.

In the small surgery he heard Dr. Phillips thrashing about, trying to get to the knife to free himself. It wouldn't take such a young, vital, well-fed man long. Knight wanted to be a mile away on the stolen horse when Phillips went to report to the marshal all that had happened — and found out how the town's lawman had been locked up in his own jail.

CHAPTER 3

Sam Knight shifted uneasily as the horse trotted along the muddy road. He wiped sweat from his forehead, turned to see if anyone pursued and finally settled down, letting the animal set the pace. He had stolen food on his way home, but being a horse thief was new for him. He closed his eyes and forced away the memory of almost stealing a peach pie from a little girl. It had hardly been better breaking into the restaurant to gobble up food and steal money, but that wasn't a moral low. Not like trying to swipe the cooling pie from the windowsill.

He had done the right thing once. Now he would pay a severe price for what he considered lesser crimes if the marshal caught him.

"Doctor? Nope, horse thief." He slumped in despair. What had he become? All he wanted was to return home to his wife.

Knight almost turned the horse's face

about to return to the scene of his heinous crimes. Slowpoke needed more help after the crude surgery he had performed. The vet might do just fine with that care now that the danger had passed, but he wasn't a medical doctor. Complications often arose needing an educated doctor's skill. Dr. Samuel Knight. Savior.

He owed it to the deputy to give of his experience and battlefield training, but he realized the chance would never happen if he showed his face back there. He'd be stuffed into the jail cell and never allowed out until they strung him up for stealing Dr. Phillips's horse.

He straightened in resolve. Return to Pine Knob, reunite with Victoria, then he might consider what could be done for the deputy. There was no need for him to personally attend Slowpoke. With some luck, he could find another doctor passing through, perhaps one in dire straits such as he found himself in now, to volunteer a quick checkup of the deputy. The towns were only a hundred miles apart.

Knight found himself smiling and then whistling as he rode. Depression lifted as his plans took form. There was no need to abandon the deputy and —

"I'll blow yer damn Johnny Reb head off

if you don't stop whistlin' that song. I *hate* that song."

Knight drew rein and looked around in panic. The demand came from thin air.

"It's 'Eating Goober Peas.' There's nothing wrong with the tune."

"I was in a battle where the entire damned Reb line came marchin' at me singin' that song. I got shot up and my cousin got hisself kilt dead."

Knight found himself staring down a rifle barrel almost at eye level poking out from leaves in a tree. Looking carefully, he made out the man holding the rifle squatting on the oak tree's strong lowest limb. Mixed with the greenery came flashes of brass buttons and a blue woolen uniform.

A Federal's uniform.

"I didn't mean anything by it."

"Were you in the Confederate Army?"

The leaves rustled and then parted to give a better view of the grizzled man drawing a bead on him. Scars crisscrossed the weather-beaten face like lines in a tic-tac-toe game. The left eyelid drooped, giving an eternally sad, hangdog look. The soldier's garrison cap had been pushed back, showing a receding hairline. Knight tried to figure out the color of the man's hair and failed. The top of his head was hidden by shadow. The soldier, in spite of his obvious age, was only a private.

"I can sing something more to your liking? 'Battle Hymn of the Republic'?" Knight kept from spitting out the name. The words would burn his tongue, but if it got him on his way, he was willing to belt out whatever this blue devil wanted, at the top of his lungs if that was necessary.

"Climb on down from that there horse so I kin git a better look at you."

Knight considered his chances. To duck low and put his heels to the horse's flanks spelled his death. The stolen animal had been hitched to a wagon most of its life and wasn't suited to riding, much less galloping with a rider hanging onto its neck for dear life.

"Down!"

"I'm getting down. I am."

Knight made his decision. The soldier had been in the tree for some time. He had no idea about any horse thief coming this way. Whatever mischief was afoot, it had nothing to do with any crime Knight had committed. Considering this was a Union soldier, he probably robbed every traveler who rode past.

A small chuckle escaped his lips.

"What's so damned funny?"

"I don't have any money for you to steal. There's nothing I have, other than the horse, worth anything."

"You ain't the sharpest dressed man I ever did see, that's for certain sure. You jist wait fer me to climb down."

Knight thought he had finally caught a ray of luck. The soldier fell from the tree rather than shinnying down, but he shook himself and got to his feet. In addition to the sagging left side of his face, he dragged his left foot a mite. A hasty evaluation suggested the soldier had endured a minor stroke. So why was he still in the army? Knight asked.

"What do you know 'bout my troubles? Captain Norwood didn't send you out here, now did he? Him and my brother, they don't git along none."

"Your brother?"

"Shut up. Head out that way. Into the woods. There's a clearing beyond the tree line."

"What would it take to just let me go? There's nothing I can do or give you — or your brother — that'd amount to a hill of beans."

"I got my orders. If I want to stay in the army and collect my pay, skimpy as it is, I have to obey."

Knight got a better idea of the power structure but had no idea how that would benefit him. The man's brother had managed to prevent the officer, Norwood, from mustering him out because he wouldn't receive any pension for what many considered a nonexistent injury. The private had no visible wounds, just the impairment to his left side.

"Did you get shot in the head? On the right side?"

"You shut yer tater trap. Keep walkin'."

Before Knight could figure out a way to convince the private he meant no harm, he stepped out of the woods into the clearing. He sucked in his breath. He thought he had been captured by a wounded soldier who was part of a small detachment, maybe not even a full squad. Two companies' garrison banners stirred in the sluggish wind. More bluecoats than he had seen since hiking south of the Mason-Dixon line bivouacked here.

"That tent yonder. Hurry up. I gotta git back to my post."

Aware of the soldier keeping his rifle trained on the middle of his back, Knight marched forward. He tried not to panic when two more soldiers came from inside the tent, rifles rising to cover him. One gestured with his weapon for him to enter the tent. He had to duck. When he got inside, the roof was hardly an inch over his head. Shadows moved endlessly there, remnants of the sun shining past thick treetop leaves.

The officer, a lieutenant, looked up. Knight saw the resemblance to the private and guessed this was the brother. A younger brother who looked after an injured older sibling?

"Stop staring," the officer snapped. "Why were you brought in?"

"I was out on the road when the sentry stopped me. I don't know why." He bit back a denunciation of Federals overstepping the bounds of the constitution and denying rights to the South. That would only land him in irons. "I haven't seen anything and I'm poor as a church mouse." He patted his pockets.

"You got yourself a six-gun. We got orders to interrogate anyone packing an iron."

Knight started to reach for the gun at his hip. He yelped when two rifle muzzles poked into his back. The guards weren't going to let him touch the six-shooter.

"Take his piece. Check it to see if it's been fired."

One bluecoat plucked the six-gun from

the holster. Knight had to grab to keep the gunbelt from sliding off around his hips and dropping to his ankles. He needed to punch an extra hole far up into the leather so he could cinch it down tight to accommodate his scrawny frame. Taking time for that had been a luxury he dared not enjoy, since getting away from the marshal and any posse on his trail mattered more.

"Ain't been fired, sir. Not recently. In fact, it's got a spot of rust disgracin' the barrel and needin' to be polished off."

"So how is it you are dressed like that, without any money or gear so you ride along bareback, but you still have a six-shooter?"

"It's a family heirloom. My pa's," he lied. "It's all I got left to remember him by now that he's gone."

"Killed in the war?"

Knight held back the easy lie. He shook his head.

"He got kicked in the head by our jenny mule." If he had claimed it was a war relic, the lieutenant would have accused him of being a rebel soldier. That was true, but not the way the officer would accept. They were looking for outlaws, probably former Rebs.

"You see anybody else on the road today?"

"It's been mighty lonely out there, sir." Knight wanted to bite off his tongue for giving that small bit of respect. The guards at Hellmira had given no respect, either to captured enlisted men or officers. Their leaders had been the worst.

The lieutenant sniffed, shuffled through papers spread on a wooden plank resting on his knees, then finally looked up as if seeing Knight for the first time.

"You look familiar."

"I —" Knight clamped his mouth shut before he blurted out that he was just passing through. Anything that aroused suspicion meant his chances of getting away unscathed were diminished. "I work for a farmer down the road a ways. I had delivered a message for him and am on my way back. Chores pile up when I'm not there because there's no one else to help out." Knight knew he ought to let the lie stop there but nerves kept him babbling. "His entire family's dead. All his boys, at least. He needs me to help out."

"He doesn't feed you too well, from the look of it." The officer pawed through a stack of papers. Without looking up again he asked, "What's the farmer's name?"

"Johnson." It was the first name that came to mind.

"I don't see any farmers named Johnson on the list of land deeds."

"He just —"

"Corporal!" The lieutenant looked up, his eyes flinty. "Let's investigate this matter further. Lock him up, find out where Mr. Johnson's farm is, and verify his employment."

"Yes, sir!"

Before he could protest, Knight found himself herded out of the tent toward a small corral at the edge of the clearing. He balked when he saw how the Federals had nailed shackles to tree trunks. They intended to chain him up like an animal while they investigated his lie.

"There's no need for this. I —"

He staggered when the soldier slammed the rifle butt into the middle of his back. A few stumbling steps took him to the crude prison. The sun was setting, and the camp plunged into darkness. Here and there cooking fires flared. Otherwise, they were cloaked in darkness. Knight knew he had to act now or remain a prisoner. Even if there had been a farmer Johnson nearby who vouched for him, he imagined he heard the thunder of a posse closing in on him. He had to keep riding or the law would catch up with him. Either was bad, but at the moment the town marshal was more likely to string him up.

"Set yerse'f down whilst I fasten the cuffs on your wrists."

"You know where the farm is, then?"

"Whatcha mean?"

"I need to draw you a map so you can ask my boss about me. Finding the farm's going to be hard without a map. There aren't many landmarks to help you get there."

"Draw it in the dirt. Use a stick."

The guard stayed back. Knight picked up a twig and slipped a large rock into his left hand.

"See here? This is where we are. The road runs like this. Now the farm's about here, down by the river."

"There ain't no river nearby. We scouted the area. There's a lake."

"You're wrong. See? Here's the lake, but the river comes along like this to feed it." Knight made a muddled mess of the fake map. The corporal stepped closer to see in the twilight. As he bent over, Knight swung his left hand as hard as he could. The shock of the rock hitting the man's head jolted all the way to his shoulder. He cocked back for a second blow, but there wasn't any call for it. The soldier lay facedown in the dirt.

For a horrified second, Knight worried he had killed the man. A quick check of the artery in his neck showed a strong pulse.

Relieved, he rolled the man over a couple times and got him to the shackles. The work of an instant fastened the iron manacles around his wrists. For good measure, Knight fastened another set to his ankles, stretching him out between two trees. Then he gagged the man.

He plucked his six-shooter from the soldier's belt — he thought of the stolen gun as *his.* Having the corporal take it felt as if he had lost his personal property. It felt right weighing down his hip. With the soldier's rifle in hand, he set out to find his horse, then realized he had no way of finding it in the encampment. Going on foot made no sense. He would be caught quickly.

Then the solution to his problem rode slowly by. A horse soldier nodded off. Whether he returned from scouting or had been instructed to make a circuit of the camp to watch for intruders hardly mattered. Knight walked quickly until he paced the horse, then jumped, grabbed, and pulled the man from his saddle.

The attack should have been easy. It went wrong immediately. The soldier turned slightly as he tumbled down and tangled his foot in the stirrup, spooking the horse. It took off at a trot, dragging the soldier behind. The bluecoat let out a yelp and began thrashing around, unable to kick free of the stirrup as he was bounced along.

Knight put his head down and sprinted for all he was worth. As exhausted and starved as he was, that wasn't much. But it was enough. The horse burst into the woods, making a straight run impossible. As it swerved to avoid an elm, Knight got his arms around its neck. The horse fought and almost kicked free. Knight clung for dear life, his own as well as that of the soldier still trapped in the stirrup.

He finally calmed the horse enough to let it stand. Front hooves pawed at the ground, and it tried to rear. He found the reins and kept its head down to prevent that. A full minute of fighting brought Knight out as victor.

"Let me get you free." He worked on the soldier's leg. A cursory examination showed nothing broken. "Don't walk on it for a day or two, and you'll be all right."

"Can't stand," the soldier said, trying and falling.

"Don't put any weight on it, or you'll hurt yourself. You might even give yourself a permanent limp."

The soldier looked up at him and rubbed his leg. "You're mighty helpful for an escaping prisoner."

"How'd you know that?"

"You're not in uniform. Ain't never seen you before with the scouts."

"I just hired on. The lieutenant wanted me to go . . . scout." Knight remembered how he had talked himself into a corner by his nervous babbling. He needed to control that.

"You sure my leg's going to be all right? It feels like it's on fire and is throbbing like a drummer's banging on it."

"I checked it. You'll be fine."

"You a doctor?"

"I'll go fetch some help from the camp." Knight swung into the saddle, ducked under a limb, and headed into the forest. "You stay here all quiet and don't move until they come to get you."

He angled away from the Union encampment until he found the road. Taking it might be dangerous if he passed other sentries. He had no other course of action. He knew where Pine Knob lay and was less inclined to go out of his way now that he had stolen a second horse, this one from the US Cavalry. He brought the horse to a canter and rode into the night, jumping at every sound around him, sure that the lieutenant's entire company rode after him.

CHAPTER 4

He fell out of the saddle and crashed hard enough to the ground to stun him. Knight shook his head. Nothing rattled loose, but the shooting pains in his neck told him he might have seriously hurt himself. Common sense dictated that he move slowly, examine himself the best he could, and then — only then — get to his feet.

The horse galloped away, taking with it his chance of reaching Pine Knob and staying ahead of any possible pursuit.

He twisted about, winced at the fiery jab down his spine, then sat upright. He turned his head from side to side and didn't pass out. That was the best examination he could afford at the moment. Knight levered himself to his feet and stumbled along. The horse was long gone, vanished in the pale dawn light. He had ridden all night long, risking Yankee patrols and the possibility the horse would die from exhaustion under him. Instead, he had nodded off and landed hard enough to jar himself.

Carefully stretching as he walked told him all he had done was strain some muscles. That any remained after his near starvation and deprivation on his way back home counted as a minor miracle. He tried to remember the taste of the food he had stolen in the restaurant. That theft had become a distant echo in his memory and belly. He plodded along, wondering if the Yankees would have fed him. That fanciful notion evaporated. Better to starve to death than be chained up again as he had been too many times in the Union's prison camp.

He had tried to erase the bitterness he felt by replacing it with hope of returning home to Victoria. It had come as a dispiriting surprise that he entertained both at the same time. He touched the six-shooter at his hip and half drew the weapon. During his entire enlistment in the C.S.A. never once had he strapped on a pistol or carried a rifle. The need for his surgical skills had been too great. He also suspected the number of rifles and ammunition had been so limited only soldiers on the front lines had been armed, but he wished he'd had something more than a scalpel when the Federals had swarmed over his surgical tent after the Battle of the Wilderness and taken him prisoner.

They had pulled him away from an operation. He never knew his patient's fate, but considering his condition, the extent of cutting where Knight had been in the operation, and the chances for recovery on his own, the Yankees had pretty much signed the man's death certificate. Knight turned even more morose as that thought crossed his mind. There wouldn't have been a proper burial. The Union troopers had been piling bodies high and burning them. No attempt at identification had been made.

Knight realized his pace had slackened. His legs throbbed and sleep tried to turn him into a walking corpse. He felt the sun already hot on his back. The heat sapped his strength further, forcing him to stop to get his breath. The break from hiking saved him. Over the thumping of his pulse in his ears came a distant pounding. Hoofbeats. More than one horse galloped down the road from behind.

Knowing that only trouble came from that direction, he got off the road and flung himself into a ditch in time for the squad of Union cavalry to thunder past. Knight's usual caution failed him. He stood too soon.

A straggler caught sight of him, pulled to

a halt, and shouted at him. "You, drop that gun!" The young soldier fumbled to pull his carbine from its saddle scabbard. "Don't you go nowhere!"

Knight drew the Colt Navy, cocked it, and thought pointing it at the Yankee would end the affair. He underestimated the youth's fervor, or perhaps he simply didn't understand that anyone would shoot at him. The troopers in the cavalry command seemed split between battle-hardened veterans weary of the war and greenhorns who had missed service and yearned for what they thought was adventure.

"Ride on," Knight called. When he saw the soldier would do no such thing, he fired. The .36 caliber six-shooter bucked in his hand.

Growing up, he had been a decent shot with both shotgun and rifle, but the opportunity to fire a handgun had never presented itself. The report didn't unsettle him. The puff of white smoke meant nothing after all the battles he had been through during the war where choking smoke draped the fields for hours after the last shot. But the feel of the butt in his grip was unusual. His bullet went wide.

He had no intention of killing the soldier, but he had not thought through what he did want from the shot. The horse reared as the slug tore through its shoulder, then bolted. The rider's finger slipped, and he triggered a round from his carbine that added to the horse's panic. Knight watched the chaos for a moment, then realized both shots and the frantic neighing attracted attention from the patrol that had galloped by only a minute earlier.

Running for the woods, he tried to come up with a plan that ended with his escape. When tiny plumes of dirt rose around him as the patrol opened fire, he found new energy to speed himself along. A single round came close enough to make him duck involuntarily. It unbalanced him, and Knight crashed facedown to the ground, stunned. By the time he recovered enough to get back to his feet, the patrol had covered the distance between the road and the woods. The soldiers fanned out fast and he found himself in the center of a half circle of riders, all with their carbines out.

"Surrender or die!"

Knight swung around to face the officer giving the command and stumbled backwards. The air filled with lead as the soldiers opened fire on him. He hit the ground and avoided the hail of bullets. More out of reaction than intent, he started firing the Colt.

His slugs tore along at knee level for the horses. He hit one and caused two others to rear. One rider was thrown. Confusion spread rapidly, giving him the chance to scuttle like a crab into the woods. He let the thick undergrowth swallow him up.

From the sound of bullets ripping through the bushes around him, the soldiers had no idea where he had gone. Without giving any thought to an escape plan, he plowed on deeper into the forest, getting his feet under him and dodging around the trees. In seconds he passed the sparse perimeter and plunged into denser vegetation and more numerous trees. Behind he heard the officer bellowing commands. Some troopers tried to enter the copse on horseback. They didn't get far.

He put his head down and pumped his legs harder when the soldiers dismounted and came after him on foot. They had to advance cautiously, fearing an ambush. All he had to do was get the hell away.

That proved harder than he hoped. His physical condition betrayed him. Less than a mile into the woods, he couldn't take another step. Knight looked up and considered climbing a tree, lying along a limb and praying that the soldiers missed him. Few horse troopers had any woodsman's skills, unless they had been recruited from the backwoods. If they were mostly Yankees, chances were that they knew Herald Square better than a sweet gum tree.

Scrambling up into the limbs proved beyond his strength. Knight collapsed, then rolled between the broad roots holding a large oak tree upright. He pulled what detritus as he could over him in a camouflaging blanket. He sagged back when he heard two soldiers calling to each other.

"Over here, Zeke. I got the trail."

"What do you know?" came the immediate reply. "You thought that rabbit was him, too."

"It coulda been. The rustlin' in the bush coulda fooled anybody."

"Not me."

Knight held his breath as the voices passed on either side of where he hid. He closed his eyes, thinking this might help. He had noticed how staring at someone across a room caused them to become uneasy and finally look around to see what was wrong. A faint smile came to his lips. He had stared so hard at Victoria at the barn dance that she had batted her fan faster and faster and finally, aware someone watched her but not sure who, had studied the others in at the dance. When their eyes had locked, both knew they were destined to be together. Like a lodestone drew iron, they had become an inseparable couple that night, then married a month later.

"You move a muscle and I'll plug you, I swear I will."

Knight opened his eyes to a bore the size of a fire hose. The carbine shook slightly as the boy poked at him with it, as if it were a pitchfork and not a rifle.

"Got him, Zeke. I got him. Over here!"

"There's no call to shoot," Knight said. "I'm out of ammo." That wasn't true. He had two loaded cylinders. All he had to do was pop out the one with its spent chambers and click in another. He wanted to calm the obviously anxious soldier.

"You just don't move a muscle. No, sir, not a twitch." The soldier poked at him again with the carbine.

Knight surged upward when the second soldier came crashing through the woods and startled his captor. The young soldier spooked. A round ripped through the spot where Knight had lain only a second before. More from luck than intent, Knight threw his arms around the soldier and drove him back. The youth hit the ground hard. The rifle sprang from his hands. As if by magic, it ended up in Knight's.

He worked the lever, got a new round chambered and swung to meet the second soldier. Not even realizing he did so, he fired. The slug went high and tore off the second soldier's cap. Surprised, the soldier threw up his hands to his head. His rifle crashed to the ground.

"Both of you, give up." Knight stepped away and covered the pair of them.

The one whose rifle he held sat on the ground and thrust his hands high in the air. The second soldier was slower to respond, but he, too, put his hands up.

"You ain't got no call to murder us," the one named Zeke said.

Knight motioned for him to get on the ground next to his partner. He snared the fallen rifle and began backing away.

"You boys count to one hundred. Then you can do all the shouting you want. Try anything before that and I might just shoot you with your own rifle."

"They'll be counting to one hundred in the stockade, if they can count that high. If they don't know now, they'll be locked up long enough to learn." The voice behind Knight came with a mocking superiority he had learned to associate with officers, mostly those who had never been in combat.

He feinted right, spun left and froze. The

officer wasn't alone. Flanking him were a half dozen soldiers. Without being told, he dropped both rifles and lifted his hands. He was caught good and proper.

"Now that's a real shame, you giving up so easy, you damned Johnny Reb. I wanted you to keep shooting so I could ventilate you myself." The officer lifted the pistol he had leveled on Knight. "I haven't had a chance to try it out yet, except for shooting at airtights and bottles put on fence posts."

"This is all a big mistake. Your soldier tried to shoot me. I —"

"You shot Private Rendell in the foot."

"Check the wound. He likely shot himself with his own rifle."

Two soldiers behind the officer snickered.

"Shut up or you'll be walking punishment duty for a year!" The officer stepped up so a single ray of sunlight angled down through the canopy of leaves above and highlighted him as if he were an actor at center stage. Captain's bars shone like sunlight on train track rails. The sharp creases in his uniform, the immaculate scarf and polished brass testified he had an overworked servant and valued doing everything by the book.

Knight cursed his bad luck facing an officer like this, much less a Union officer. "It's all a misunderstanding, sir."

He gasped when a soldier punched him in the kidney. He fell to his knees and tried to suck in his breath.

"You'll speak to Captain Norwood only when he tells you."

Knight wasn't able to speak, even if he wanted. The liquid feel inside his body told him things had been bruised, if not ruptured. He kept the blood in his mouth from choking him, in spite of wanting to spit it out on Norwood's mirror-polished boots. He bent over and let the blood ooze onto the ground.

"Get him back to camp. I need to move my company out immediately to my new command. Tend to him, Lieutenant, then return to your patrol along the road."

Knight saw boots moving about but hardly focused. Strong hands pulled him to his feet. His toes cut furrows in the forest floor as they dragged him along. By the time they reached the road, he had regained his feet and walked without support.

"All yours, Private." The declaration was given along with Knight's gun belt, six-shooter, and spare cylinders. The soldier sagged a little as he slung the belt around his shoulder and juggled his rifle to keep it ready for action.

Knight was shoved forward. He kept from

falling only through dint of will. When he looked up, he realized his new captor was the soldier whose horse he had stolen. "How's your leg? Not too sore, I hope."

"Reckoned they would run you down. The lieutenant gets angry when he loses a horse, no matter the cause. And the captain?" He shook his head sadly. "That man's a fanatic when it comes to discipline. He's got me on extra sentry duty for the next month."

"Sorry to hear that. It wasn't your fault your foot got tangled and you were dragged along."

The soldier sighed. "I wish your word carried weight with them, but it don't."

"What are you taking me back to?" Knight held his breath. He still feared that the town marshal and a posse had followed him this far, though stealing a cavalry horse was likely enough to get him put in front of a firing squad.

"Not for me to say."

"But you know, don't you?"

The soldier nodded, then motioned for Knight to start walking. Neither of them were given mounts. The rest of the squad had already mounted and left on patrol.

"Are you going to make it on your leg? You shouldn't put any weight on it, not after it got all twisted up like it did."

The soldier frowned as he studied Knight. "I don't know if you're a snake-oil salesman or if you really do give a damn about me."

"Does it matter? You know how your leg feels. Even a tinkerer can be respectful of your injury."

"I'm ordered to get you on back to camp, and that's what I'll do. It's my duty."

"I respect that."

"Are you giving me your parole?"

"That's only good for soldiers, and I'm not a soldier. No uniform." Knight looked at his rags. Even when he had been in uniform, the cloth hadn't been much better. For all the cotton plantations and textile mills in the South, the uniforms had been poor. Most of the better quality cloth had been smuggled to Europe in trade for arms and manufactured goods otherwise unavailable.

"You sound like an educated man. Not a lawyer. The way you looked me over, I'd take you to be a doctor. Maybe a rebel doctor?"

"The war's over." Knight plodded along, one foot in front of the other. Getting back to the cavalry encampment would take them most of the day at this pace. It might even be dark before they trooped into the camp.

"It's purty near lunchtime. I got some rations I'll share with you."

"Much obliged. I need water, too. My mouth's so dry it feels like the inside of a cotton bale."

The soldier cocked his head to one side and turned in a full circle, snuffling loudly. He stopped, pointed to the south away from the road, and said, "River's that way. Or a lake. I can smell it."

"You part bloodhound? I never heard of anyone who could sniff out water. Once, I saw a woman use dowsing rods to find where to sink a well, but everyone thought she was crazy as a loon."

"Seen that, too. My pa could use a dowsing rod that way. Where he said there was water, there was. Always. And I don't need a stick to tug in the right direction." He pointed. "Water's down there a ways."

They left the road and cut across increasingly rugged land, finally coming to the shore of a lake that stretched off into the distance so far Knight couldn't see the far side.

"We might get lucky and catch a fish to go along with the hardtack. That and some moldy jerked beef's all I got for rations."

"Will this get you in trouble with Captain Norwood? Taking so long to get back to camp?"

"There you go again, sounding like you give two hoots and a holler 'bout me."

"You should soak your foot in the lake. The cool will ease the pain."

They made their way down to a rocky beach. From the tracks leading to this point, cattle used the lake as a stock pond. Other animals likely did as well, though they didn't leave tracks like the cows. The two of them eased to the edge, found rocks to sit on and shucked off their boots. Knight had to be careful. The newspaper he had stuffed into his shoe threatened to come apart. Some of it stuck to his foot in a wet lump. He peeled it away and stuck it back into his boot. Only then did he soak his feet.

The soldier laid out what he carried in way of food, dividing it down the middle. Knight tried not to wolf it down. There wasn't much. He wanted it to last so he could taste every morsel, no matter how tough the beef or stale the hardtack. Water helped it all go down where it formed a lump in his belly. A week or two of regular eating would keep his stomach from rebelling against whatever he swallowed. Knight turned glum because he wasn't likely to last that long after the captain handed down the death sentence for horse theft.

"I'm all tuckered out. We can tickle some

fish after a nap. That all right with you?"

Knight opened his mouth, then clamped it shut.

"I'm going to stretch out up on the bank, under one of those shade trees. You find one that suits you and don't go waking me none." The soldier hiked up to the tree he had pointed out, sank down and rested his rifle against the trunk.

He dropped Knight's gun belt with the Colt Navy and spare cylinders onto the ground some distance away, then settled down. He pulled his garrison cap over his eyes, dropped his chin to his chest and slipped into a noisy sleep in seconds.

Knight stared at the young soldier. Did he expect an escape so he could shoot his prisoner? Or did he offer the chance for a prisoner to get away and avoid a certain firing squad?

Knight eased over, lifted the gun belt with its heavy pistol tucked in. He replaced the empty cylinder with a loaded one. What kind of trouble the soldier got himself into letting his prisoner escape Knight could not know. The young soldier might face jail time up in Fort Leavenworth. Or maybe he knew something no one else did. With Captain Norwood riding on to his new garrison, no one back in camp might know the soldier had been ordered to deliver a prisoner. If that was true, Knight had only to walk away.

He hoped it was so. There was no way in hell the soldier thought he would simply lie down and meekly return to a fate that would put him in a shallow grave.

Knight looked back once and thought the soldier had pushed up the garrison cap to watch, but he couldn't be sure. He started hiking around the lake, heading for the far side. From there he could get his bearings and get back on the road to Pine Knob. To Pine Knob and lovely Victoria.

CHAPTER 5

By the time he had fired all but three rounds from the Colt Navy's loaded cylinders, Knight had become a crack shot. No rabbit was safe. He even considered trying to bring down a deer, but the small caliber and need to creep up on the skittish animals kept him from trying. If he got close enough for a clean shot, he could as easily swing the six-shooter and club the deer. It was good enough to fill his gut with meat from rabbits and whatever plants he found growing in the increasingly familiar woods.

Two weeks had passed since he had escaped from the Union soldiers. His thoughts still turned to the soldier who had let him escape so easily. Resting his hand on the six-gun's oak butt reminded him how the young private had simply laid the gun belt and revolver to one side and slept. Or pretended to sleep. The more Knight thought on it, the more he realized his crime would have put him in front of a firing squad. The soldier either had no stomach for such an execution or had a spark of decency deep inside burning brightly enough to give him some sympathy for another's sorry plight.

Knight wondered if the soldier would have been as willing to look the other way if he had known he'd let a former inmate at Elmira escape.

More than anything else, he wished the boy well. The captain, Norwood by name, would not have caused any trouble if he rode on to a distant assignment, but the lieutenant might have sentenced him to lashes or even prison. If such brutal punishment was in the cards, Knight hoped the youngster deserted and made his way to safety somewhere farther south in the heart of Texas.

Knight suddenly stopped and stared. To the side of the road a battered wooden sign with crudely painted letters proclaimed to a weary traveler that he'd entered Pine Knob, Texas. Tears came to his eyes. He was home. After months hiking across country, getting rides when he could, stealing two horses and losing both, becoming a wanted fugitive, he had finally come home.

"Victoria." The name slipped unbidden

from his lips. He licked dried lips and knew he looked a fright. If he showed up on his own doorstep looking like this, he would give her the scare of her life. "But I want to see you. You're what's kept me alive all these years."

He started toward town when the rattle of a wagon behind him forced him to take cover. The reaction had become second nature to him over the past weeks, but he saw there wasn't any call to be that suspicious. He stepped back into the road and waved to the driver. "Joel! Joel Krauss! Hello!"

The driver drew back on the reins on his rig. Both horses gratefully stopped. Krauss stepped down hard on the brake and looped the reins around the handle. He bent forward, shielded his eyes, and then stood in the driver's box.

"Samuel? Is that you, Sam?"

"It's me, Joel, in the flesh. You're a sight for sore eyes." He went to the side of the wagon and held out his hand.

Krauss hesitated a moment, then shook. His grip was so firm that Knight winced.

"You're a wisp of your former self. What's happened?"

"It's a long story. All I want to do is go home, but it's good seeing you. Is Victoria at home or is she at church? This is Wednesday, isn't it?"

"Wednesday, ya, it is that." Krauss stared hard at him. "Have you lost track of the days?"

"It's been a long, hard journey. I don't want to frighten Victoria looking like this, but I want to see her. Truth to tell, I have no better clothing, though a bath and a shave would go a long way toward becoming more presentable in polite society." Knight tried to get everything square in his head as the words tumbled out. Plans jumbled, and seeing a neighbor brought back a flood of memories.

"You are skinny, you are. None of us here get enough of the food, but you —" Krauss took off his broad-brimmed black hat and wiped away sweat that had beaded under the band. Like a horse shooing away flies, he shook his shaggy head and settled the hat back down squarely so each side rested on his ears.

"Are you going into town? It's getting dark in a spell." Knight turned toward the town hidden in the pines when church bells began to ring. Wednesday evening service would begin in a few minutes.

"Things are changed, Samuel. You prepare

yourself for that. And the Yankees are here now."

"I expected carpetbaggers. Everywhere I have traveled, they are like a plague of locusts devouring everything around them with regulations and new taxes. Do you think they will let me practice medicine? Wait, no, never mind, Joel. There's too much crowding into my head right now. You go on into town, but don't tell anyone I'm back. I will go home and wait for Victoria to return from services. By the time I get there, she should return."

"Ya, you do that, Samuel. You heed what I said. Things are changed now." Krauss glanced uneasily at the six-shooter strapped to Knight's waist. "You do not be too quick with that gun, now, you hear? Everything's different in this town . . . different from when you left." With that, Krauss sank back down on the hard wood bench, slid the reins off the brake and got his team pulling again.

Knight almost called after him, wanting him to explain his curious comment. Of course things had changed. Texas had lost the war. Carpetbaggers had moved in, as they had throughout the South to suck the money and crops and vitality from their former enemy. President Johnson had reined in the worst of the calls for retribution by the most rabid Northerners, but Washington and the president were far away and the meddling carpetbaggers were everywhere, collecting what they considered their due as conquerors.

Knight touched the six-gun. Joel Krauss had seen it and worried that his old friend wouldn't understand that they had been reduced to second-class citizens. Knight had thought about that during the long hike home. If they let him practice medicine again, what did it matter? He was home and would see his wife in a few minutes.

He cut across a field growing a crop of yams, found a new road that hadn't existed when he went to war three years earlier and discovered it ran almost directly to his house. From the look of it, the new road carried considerable traffic. He wondered what that might mean and where it took wagons and riders. When he had built his house it had been on the edge of town away from such traffic.

His trek finally ended. He rubbed his eyes to be sure of what he saw. Things had changed, indeed. He stared at his house. A second story had been added. The yard was enclosed with a low white picket fence. Flowerbeds blazed with color. Victoria had always wanted to garden, but there had never been time. She'd acted as his nurse on many of the more difficult cases and had proven an excellent midwife when he had been out of town tending serious injuries on the outlying ranches and farms.

But the house. So prosperous, so neatly kept. He smiled in admiration. Victoria had not let the moss grow on her while he was gone. Such upkeep required a great amount of time, effort, and money.

He let the gate click shut behind him. Rather than going straight to the door, he circled the house. Nostalgia flooded through him when he saw the small vegetable patch out back. This had been the extent of her gardening before he left for Richmond. He stared at the neat rows and thought of her sitting on the front porch, carefully stitching at her needlework with precise movement. Everything about her had been that way. She had always attended to detail as he had taken in the larger picture.

They had made a great surgical team. She noticed things he did not and had always pointed out the small but crucial things he missed. Once a patient had been saved because he had closed off a big spurting artery and had entirely neglected a tiny one that bled slightly but constantly. If he had sewn up the patient, the abdominal cavity would have eventually filled with blood, causing extreme pain and eventual death. She had saved the man's life by pointing out the bleeder.

Victoria had saved his life, too, by marrying him. He had missed her terribly every day he had been gone.

He returned to the front porch, newly whitewashed and swept clean. He mounted the steps and started to open the front door. A colored woman beat him to it, pulling the door wide open and blocking any entry.

"You startled me," he said. "You must be a servant."

"You get on away from heah." She made shooing motions.

"I have come to see Victoria."

The woman glared hard at him. How could he blame her when he looked like a derelict?

"The lady of the house. I have returned and would see her. Or is she still at Wednesday church services?"

"Who are you? Do she know you?" The skeptical look froze him. He almost blurted out who he was. Then he decided surprising Victoria required some anonymity.

"She does. I have been back East and only returned to Pine Knob a few minutes ago. May I sit here and wait for her return?"

"No! You too filthy to go messin' up my clean porch."

"You have done a fine job keeping it spotless."

This mollified her a little. She motioned for him to go around back.

"You wait out by the toolshed. Who do I say you are?"

"I'd like to keep it a surprise. Tell her a . . . friend." Anything more would spoil the homecoming. He wanted to see the expression on her face when she realized her husband had returned, finally.

"Don't you go stealin' nothing. We got law in this heah town that don't take kindly to sneak thieves."

"I am sure. It's not possible for me to steal anything."

How could he steal from himself? All this was his, even if he scarcely recognized it. Three years had passed slowly for him but quickly for the old homestead with its additions, fresh paint, and landscaping.

He trudged around back, saw the toolshed some distance away and went to it. Sinking down with his back to one wall, he stared out over a pasture that had not been fenced when he left. Now wooden rails held in a half dozen fine horses dashing about. Victoria had never shown any interest in keeping animals. She must have fenced the meadow and rented it out to neighbors for their horses. Frederick Fitzsimmons had always wanted a breeding herd but his house in the center of town had not afforded space. If anyone came through the war richer than when it started, Fitzsimmons was the man. Knight looked down on the man's avaricious behavior as bank president, but he had advanced him a loan to keep the surgery open when all the patients could pay were eggs and pigs. Medical suppliers in New Orleans and St. Louis demanded cash, not a rasher of bacon or a bag of flour.

He remembered those days, struggling to get a foothold in the town. He had succeeded. He and Victoria had succeeded. His chin dropped to his chest and he dozed, only to awaken at the rattle of harness and chains when a buggy came up the road. Standing proved painful. Joints throbbing and muscles aching, he steadied himself against the shed. Before he went around the house to see his wife, the back door into the kitchen flew open. The maid spoke loudly, hands waving about. She pointed to the shed. The way she stood blocked any way out.

Then he saw *her* as she pushed past the maid.

Victoria was more beautiful than he remembered. She wore a simple white dress. On her it became a gown fit for the crowned heads of Europe. An intricate gold necklace caught what sunlight remained in the day. She pulled off gloves and handed them to the maid, who still chattered on. A stamp of the foot and an imperious gesture on Victoria's part silenced the maid and sent her back into the kitchen. Victoria smoothed her skirts and carefully descended the back stairs. Every movement etched into his mind. She walked so lithely, head high and confident.

He started to go to her, but his knees refused to bend. His feet had frozen to the ground. His heart hammered wildly, and breathing came in harsh gulps. He had no choice. Knight waited for her to come to him.

She peered at him in the gathering twilight and stopped a few paces away. "Sir? Matty said you wanted to speak with me."

"Victoria." The name came out in a croak, almost incomprehensible from the intense emotion welling inside him.

"Sir, really! It is improper to call me by

my Christian name. Please address me as
—"

"Mrs. Knight. Mrs. Victoria Knight, your husband has returned from the war." He held out his arms to her.

"Oh, dear, sweet Jesus, no! It can't be!" Victoria clutched at her throat, spun, and ran for the house.

CHAPTER 6

"Victoria! Wait! I'm sorry. I didn't mean to frighten you." He got to the back porch just as the maid stepped into the doorway to block his entry.

Knight grabbed for her, but he lost his balance. She added to his fall with a two-handed shove. Then she stood with her hands balled on her ample hips. If looks could have killed, Knight knew he would have been dead and buried out north of town in the Mount Pisgah Cemetery.

"Stand aside. I want to talk with my wife!"

"Yo wife? You crack that hard skull of yours? You git on outta heah 'fore I call the law."

"Victoria is my wife. I am Dr. Samuel Knight, and I demand to see her."

"You a doctor? That's rich. I won't call no law. I'll handle you myself and sweep you right on outta heah." She grabbed a broom and swung it at him.

Knight fended it off, ignoring the pain in his left forearm where the broom handle hit. He got to his feet, lowered his head, and charged like a bull. The broom landed hard on his back, but he had stopped reacting to simple pain. His arms circled the woman's waist. With a heave he lifted, got her off her feet, and swung her around. It was her turn to crash to the ground. This gave him the chance to burst through the door into the kitchen. Using his heel, he kicked shut the door and dropped a locking bar into place.

Outside, the maid screeched like a banshee and shouted for him to open the door. Then silence fell. She had given up using verbal intimidation to get him to let her in and rounded the house to enter from the front. Knight had only a few seconds before she rejoined the fight. He ducked into the dining room. Not seeing Victoria, he rushed into the sitting room and from there into a wood-paneled study dominated by a huge cherrywood desk. She sat behind the desk, frantically trying to open the center drawer.

"Stop it, Victoria. Stop it." He put enough snap of command into his voice that she looked up, eyes wide. Her mouth gaped.

"It's me. Your husband. Samuel."

"But you —"

"I'm a bit dirty, and for that I apologize, but it has been a long hard road."

"You're alive. You can't be."

"I sent you a letter whenever my guards allowed it. That has to be one a month for the past year."

"Guards?"

"The Yankees had me in their prison camp in upstate New York. Elmira. I was released after General Lee surrendered."

"You never wrote, not ever."

"Then the guards failed to post the letters. I wrote." His fury at them rose. They must have taken the letters and read them for their own amusement, never intending to send them along as they promised. It had been more than one making such a promise, too. Damn the entire lot of blue bellies!

"You can't be alive," she repeated in a voice so low he barely heard.

"You've done well keeping up the place. How did you decide to add the second story? It makes the house distinctive from the road. And that is quite a thoroughfare. I can't wait to see the rest of Pine Knob if such a large road goes right on by my house. *Our* house." He looked around the study that had been their bedroom before he had left. The desk stood where once their bed has stood. Their marriage bed.

"It's not our house, Samuel. It's mine. Mine and Gerald's."

"Gerald?"

"My husband. When I thought you were gone, I remarried. I am Mrs. Gerald Donnelly."

"No, you're not. You're my wife. Mrs. Samuel Knight."

The front door crashed open. Through an arched doorway a burly man with muttonchops and a florid face barreled in, the maid close behind.

"I fetched the mister. He's come to save you, Miz Donnelly." The maid swung the broom about, then subsided when the well-dressed man pushed her away.

"What the hell is this about, Victoria? I shall thrash this swine if he has touched one hair of your head."

"Gerald, I —"

"Leave my house this instant, you scalawag. Do it on your own feet or I shall have you removed feetfirst."

Too much had happened too fast for Knight. He looked from his wife to the intruder, then back. She sought help, all right, but not from him. His brain tumbled and words became difficult to form.

"You've got a Boston accent," he finally said.

"I am of the Boston Donnellys," the man said haughtily, as if that meant something. "The Boston Brahmins? The Blue Bloods? The Winslows, Saltonstalls, Winthrops?"

"This is a mighty far piece from Boston. What are you doing in Pine Knob, Texas?" Even as Knight asked, he knew the answer. Gerald Donnelly was a carpetbagger who intended to milk the cow until she came up dry and then move on, all with the power, authority, and approval of a Reconstruction Congress back in Washington.

"I have come here to marry the finest flower that ever bloomed in Texas. Now who are you?"

Knight rested his hand on the six-shooter holstered at his hip when Donnelly moved the tail of his coat back to reveal a gun under his left arm in a shoulder rig. The only men Knight had ever seen who sported such a holster were gamblers and pimps.

"I am quite adept at using my six-gun, you miserable piece of —"

"Gerald!"

They both looked at Victoria. She had finally pried open the center desk drawer and held a derringer taken from there. Knight turned faint when he realized she held the tiny gun in both hands — and pointed it at him.

"I'm your husband," he said, knowing this hadn't swayed her before. "Would you kill me?"

"I would. I will. You're dead to me. You've been dead to me for over a year. How dare you come back? *How dare you?*"

"What's he saying, Victoria? Tell me." Gerald Donnelly walked past Knight as if he didn't exist. He plucked the twin-barrel pistol from the woman's hands and tucked it into his coat pocket.

"She's saying that we are married. Since I'm alive, if you think you are married to her, you are wrong unless you want her branded as a bigamist."

Donnelly waved his hand about as if dismissing a trifle. He walked around to stand behind Victoria, his hands on her shoulders. In spite of himself, Knight had to admit they made a handsome couple. But she wasn't this man's wife. She was *his.*

"That's a technicality. I can deal with it in a day or two."

"You can't dissolve a marriage that has lasted six years!"

"A sham marriage, a fake. An annulment will be easily obtained since I know the judge well. I will give you, oh, say, one hundred dollars to be on your way and forget this whole sordid claim."

"Is this the kind of man you want, Victoria? He just placed a value on your marriage. One hundred dollars. Is that what it's worth to you? You're worth more than that to me. You're my life."

"If *that* is the price you want to pay, it can be arranged," Gerald Donnelly said coldly. "I have no doubt Captain Norwood can deal with you in such a way that you never bother me again." He coughed to clear his throat when he saw how Victoria responded. "Or my wife. You bother us any more and the army will deal with you severely."

"Captain Norwood?" Knight had to rest his hand against a table at hearing the name of the officer who had ordered him arrested for horse theft.

"I don't really know him, but he seems a good sort. Of a decent Ohio family. He's been in charge of the garrison here for the past ten days. Do you want me to send for him?"

Knight held his panic in check. He removed his hand from the pistol at his side and faced his wife. "You must choose. I don't think it is legal to cancel our marriage as if it never existed. Come with me, Victoria, come with me, and I promise we will be happy like we were before."

"You cannot erase the last three years,

Samuel. I . . . I have a life with Gerald that I never had with you." She shivered delicately. "I hated all that blood, the way you cut into people."

"He cut up people? I'll have him on trial for murder!"

"I'm a surgeon, damn your eyes," Knight snapped. "Of course I cut people open to heal them, not kill them."

"Some died," Victoria said in a tiny voice. "Too many did."

"I learned a great deal during the war. I — we — can save more patients now. There are innovative methods being taught in Europe. We can go to Paris and study them. There's no reason to stay in Pine Knob."

"Yes, Samuel, there is." Victoria sat straighter and looked ahead, not meeting his eyes. "I have a husband here. A lawyer who can take care of me in ways you were never able to."

"Get out or I shall summon my men to thrash you."

Knight put his hand back on his six-gun, then let his arm go limp. This wasn't the time or place to fight Gerald Donnelly. When that might be, and how, eluded him, but shooting it out in front of his wife deterred him. And Victoria was his wife, no matter what her so-called new husband claimed.

"This isn't over. Please, Victoria, don't make a mistake we'll both regret the rest of our lives."

Still not looking at him, she said tartly, "Good-bye, Samuel."

"You heard her. Get the hell out of my house." Gerald Donnelly moved to block his view of Victoria.

Knight started from the room but couldn't refrain from one last parting taunt. "You're wrong on both counts. She's my wife and this is my house." He looked at the stairs. "And there wasn't any call to build a second story. It ruins the look of the place."

Knight passed the maid, who held her broom like a soldier with a rifle at port arms. He politely touched the brim of his hat and stepped onto the porch. Night had come crashing down, isolating him and giving the sense that he had entered some alien world beyond his ken. He and Victoria had enjoyed sitting on the porch, sipping cool drinks, sometimes with alcohol in them, and watching the lightning bugs fluttering around the edge of the forest not fifty yards away. The trees had been cut down and the road put through.

Behind him he heard Victoria crying and Gerald Donnelly berating her. The tone of the man's voice almost caused Knight to go back in and give him what for. No one had the right to speak to Victoria that way. No one.

The maid closed the door. The metallic click as a key turned in the lock decided him. He had to find out what was necessary to put Donnelly in his place and regain everything that had been stolen from him. As he plodded along the road to Pine Knob, he realized this was a hard row to hoe. Fighting any carpetbagger was hard because they had the power of the Federal government behind them and were a law unto themselves. He shivered, wondering if Captain Norwood remembered him and would have him shot on sight. Avoiding the Yankee cavalry as he worked to pry Victoria loose from the Bostonian carpetbagger might prove difficult, but he had to do it.

A twenty-minute walk brought him to the middle of Pine Knob. He stood in the street and looked around, trying to remember who had owned which stores and why nothing was exactly right. If they had swept through town and torn down every other building to put up new ones he could not have been more disoriented. The courthouse had dominated the main street before. Now it was hardly noticeable next to a three-story hotel.

He pressed his hands against flat pockets, hunting for even a few coins. The hotel windows were brightly lit and showed a thriving restaurant. He didn't have enough money to stay in such a fine place, but even a nickel might buy him a cup of coffee or a dime a piece of pie. Living on small game and forage for the past two weeks had kept him from starving, but it also whetted his appetite for the things he missed most.

He inhaled deeply and remembered how that peach pie cooling on the window ledge had smelled. Peach wasn't his favorite; Victoria's cherry pie was. But he had done the right thing by not taking what belonged to the little girl, even if it had caused his belly to rub up against his spine.

A search of his pockets a second time produced no more money than the first had. Missing dessert was one thing. He needed money to hire a lawyer to challenge Gerald Donnelly.

The commotion down the street in front of a saloon that hadn't existed before the war caused him to freeze. Three soldiers poured from the swinging doors and into the street, shoving and shouting. One threw a punch at another. Drunker than a lord, he missed by a country mile. The second reared back to launch his blow, only to get sucker-punched by the third trooper. The trio piled into each other. Knight expected two of them to gang up on the third, but they kept the fight impartial, each fighting the other two equally.

He started away from them when one suddenly collapsed, clutching his belly. Knight was too far off to see the punch that did the dirty work, but the way the soldier lay unmoving meant a possibly serious injury. A lucky punch into a belly not properly tensed to take the impact ruptured internal organs.

Knight got halfway there and veered away. A mounted patrol trotted up. Two soldiers dismounted, one limping slightly. In the yellow light spilling from inside the saloon, the soldier whose leg he had tended and whose horse he had stolen went to pull the fighters apart. If anyone recognized him, this man would. He stepped onto a boardwalk, then pressed deeper into shadow as the soldiers dragged the unconscious private past him on their way to a wagon. Grunting, they heaved him into the bed.

"Thass two drunks tonight. The captain's not gonna be pleased."

The one with the limp replied, "He better

not declare the town off limits 'fore my leave in a couple days. My leg's hurtin' so bad I need a shot or two of rye to kill the pain."

"Thass one helluva excuse. Medicinal purposes rather than drinkin' just to get soused. I gotta hand it to you, Reilly, you're all the time comin' up with alibis for yer thirst. Me and the rest of this godforsaken company, we come off lookin' like drunks. Not you, no, sir. You need *meddysin.*" He laughed uproariously.

The two passed within ten feet of Knight and never saw him. He let out breath he hadn't known he held when they went back to talk to the remaining two fighters, who now clung to each other for support.

He walked on eggshells until he came to a cross street, then picked up his pace. He needed food and a place to stay for the night, the things he had been deprived of for so long and had expected to find when he returned to Pine Knob.

And Victoria. He had expected to have a wife when he returned, not a stranger intent on sleeping with another man.

"Hey, mister." The summons came from behind him. Knight glanced over his shoulder and saw a man moving fast. If the call hadn't gotten his attention, the ax handle swung at his head would have.

Knight instinctively ducked. The ax handle crashed into his shoulder, driving him to his knees. Then he found himself beset by two more men, using their fists on him. He curled up in a tight ball and let the blows rain down. He had endured this and more at the prison camp.

"You gettin' the message? Clear out of town. You ain't wanted here."

He shifted on the ground enough for the ax handle intended for his head to miss. Knight grabbed with both arms, circled the man's ankles and pulled hard, upending him. He received curses and more blows from the other two, but pain meant nothing to him now. With a hard kick, he scooted along the ground and grabbed for the fallen man's six-shooter. He fumbled and failed to get it from the holster but pulled back the hammer partway. When the man twisted away, Knight lost his grip. The hammer fell and the gun discharged.

His attacker yelped as the bullet tore into his leg. For a brief instant the other two stopped their pummeling to stare at their partner. Knight grabbed the ax handle and swung wildly. Luck finally rode with him. He connected with one man's knee, bringing him down in a pile of pain and curses.

Using the wood shaft, he levered himself to his feet.

"I'm gonna kill you!" The man who had shot himself pulled his six-shooter and pointed it at Knight.

With his feet under him and both hands on the ax handle, Knight swung for all he was worth. A stronger man might have done serious damage. As it was, he knocked the gun from the would-be killer's hand and broke a bone in his wrist.

"You're gonna pay!"

Knight went down again as the third man tackled him. Swinging an elbow caught the attacker in the nose. Blood spurted everywhere in a gory fountain that probably hurt worse than it looked — and it looked ferocious.

The few seconds of distraction let Knight pull himself upright using the ax handle that had been intended to break his bones. Awkwardly swinging it produced the right result. He smashed the ax handle into the man's face and across the eyes. Another bone broke, other than the already smashed cartilage in his nose. This put him out of the fight once and for all. With a surge, Knight got to his feet in time to kick the man who had shot himself. In spite of what had to be a painful wound in his leg, the gunman tried to get his pistol aimed to kill. Knight's kick deflected the gun again, and again the gun discharged. The man grunted. This time he had shot himself in the foot.

Loud voices in the distance warned that the army patrol had been alerted by the gunshots. Knight found a narrow space between two buildings most men could never squeeze through. Only his emaciated condition allowed him to scrape along. He saw flashes of horses riding past in the street behind him. He popped out into the next street over, got his bearings, and headed out of town.

He knew a spot near a spring not far away where avoiding any soldiers or lawmen would be easy. As a boy he had played in caves around the area and knew them like the back of his hand. Hobbling, every muscle aching, he left Pine Knob. He left the town but plotted how he would return and get some justice against Gerald Donnelly for sending men to beat him up.

He'd get justice for that and more. Much more.

CHAPTER 7

"He was here. You can see how he tried to erase his tracks." A corporal knelt beside the spring, using his rifle to support himself as he bent forward. A hesitant finger traced around the heel print that Knight had neglected to remove before hiding in the cave overlooking the springs.

"You're makin' that up." Private Reilly hobbled forward and looked around the banks. "Besides, how do you know it's the man we're huntin'? That could have been left by anybody stoppin' by to take a drink. As good as you are at trackin', it could be a hoofprint of some cow or horse."

"Ain't wrong. If you'd open your eyes, you'd see it, too." The corporal grunted as he got his feet under him. He didn't bother cleaning the mud from the butt of his carbine. "I grew up with a pa and two uncles who could track a snowflake through a blizzard. They taught me good."

Inside the cave, Knight cursed this unexpected turn of events. He had been dog tired when he had collapsed beside the springs the night before. A quick drink, then he had worked in the dark to remove any trace that he had been there. Bad luck had sent the soldier able to spy out the single boot print he had neglected. The private whose leg he had tended was also in the patrol. Whether that was good luck remained to be seen.

Flat on his belly, Knight peered past a stack of rocks blocking most of the cave mouth. This had been his favorite hiding place when he was a boy. No one had ever found it, no one he hadn't shown. The weeds grew up just right, and the way the cave mouth aimed more upward than out kept it from being immediately visible from the springs. He had almost fallen into it when he was eight. The best thing that had ever happened to him was when he was eleven and had seen Billy Yarrow kissing Marianne Suddereth down by the springs. He had snickered, but then he had clamped his hand over his mouth to keep from crying out when they got down to doing more than kissing. He had seen farm animals but never a boy and a girl doing what they did. Even as he remembered that late summer day, Knight blushed just a little.

Less than a week later Billy had been cut up bad by a scythe blade that broke. He had died from infection a few days later. Two months to the day after Billy's funeral, Marianne had upped and run off with a man twice her age who had been passing through town, peddling notions. There had been rumors that she had to get married. After going through medical school and learning what he had of human reproduction, Knight no longer disputed that gossip.

"Why not stretch out here and wait for him to get back? We can lay a trap."

"All you want to do," said Reilly, "is to goof off. The captain ordered us to cover as much territory as we can in a day's time, then report back."

"Screw him. He's as bossy as he can be. I don't think he knows what's goin' on half the time, so he covers it up with bluster."

"Bluster and makin' us walk extra sentry duty."

"You ought to know 'bout that. When you lost your horse to that drifter, you walked an extra ten thousand miles, I do declare."

"It felt like it. Still does." Reilly massaged his knee. "He told me to keep off it, and it'd heal just fine, but the captain wasn't havin' any of that. Maybe it was twenty thousand miles. That's a mighty long way."

"Who'll know if we take a short nap? It's another of them sultry days that drains the energy from you like water leakin' from a cracked jug. Not a whole lot at once, but little bits all the time till nothin's left." The corporal leaned his rifle against a rock and began digging in the soft dirt to hollow out space for his hip and shoulder. When he had made a comfortable contour, he settled down. In a minute he snored quietly.

Knight watched as Reilly limped about as if on patrol duty. More than once, the leg he favored caused him enough pain that he sat and rubbed it. After a complete circuit of the springs and the woods surrounding it, he returned and stretched out some distance from the corporal. He tipped his garrison cap down over his eyes and lay back. Like all good soldiers, he grabbed some sleep when he could, too.

Watching from the safety of his cave lulled Knight to drowsiness, too. He snapped awake at the sound of horses galloping toward the springs. Both soldiers jumped up.

"Who's that comin' like their horses' tails are on fire?" The corporal climbed onto a pile of rocks, shielded his eyes, and tried to make out the riders.

"Nobody we want findin' us snoozin' away the day. Let's ride."

"Might be the galoot we're searchin' for. If we let him slip past us, we're in for a court-martial."

"He didn't have a horse. Besides, mighty frontiersman, does that sound like a single horse or a whole danged herd of them?"

"We should go find out," the corporal said. "I heard tell that the town's lawyer had his own men out huntin'."

"Those were his men that got all beat up." Reilly shook his head. "It don't seem possible it's the same man that stole my horse, but it sounded like him. How could a scrawny, starved drifter shoot one man twice and beat up two men who could wrestle grizzlies and win?"

"If it had been a gang what beat them up, don't you think they'd be braggin' on how they run off a dozen men? Or a hundred?"

"Come on. Let's see who's ridin' across our patrol area." Private Reilly hobbled for his horse and swung into the saddle with more agility than likely from his injured leg. He didn't wait for his partner but turned his pony's face and galloped away.

"Slow down, damn you. Don't go leaving me behind like this." The corporal brushed himself off as he raced for his horse. The animal tried to buck and forced him to take extra time to mount. Then he galloped away.

Knight perked up when the soldiers vanished from sight. The corporal had left behind his carbine. With only two rounds left for his six-shooter, the rifle and loaded magazine jammed up into the stock would go a long way toward keeping him fed.

It might even go a ways toward settling the score with Gerald Donnelly. The longer Knight stewed about it, the more satisfying it became to think about getting the lawyer's head in his sights, then pulling the trigger.

He pushed rocks and weeds out of the way and slithered downhill on his belly like a snake. His fingers curled around the cool wood front grip. He hefted the rifle. The short barrel was intended for a horse soldier to draw it from the saddle scabbard and bring it around. While not as accurate as a rifle with a longer barrel, it was better than what he had now, which was almost nothing.

"You got two choices," came a cold voice. "You can either try to use it or you can leave it be. What's it going to be?"

Knight didn't release the rifle. He got to his feet and picked it up, his finger curling around the trigger. Before it could fire, he had to cock it, but there wasn't any call to do that.

"You're just as bossy as you were in Hell-mira." He turned slowly and faced the rider astride a paint. On horseback, he looked even more hulking and burly than he was, which was plenty.

The man hiked his leg up and curled it around the saddle horn. Leaning forward, he squinted the slightest bit as he studied Knight more closely.

"As I live and breathe, it is you, Doc. Isn't it?"

"Sure as summer rain, it is, Milo."

"You don't look like yourself." He un-hooked his leg and dropped to the ground. He grabbed Knight in a bear hug, then released him hurriedly when he felt nothing but bones. "The armistice surely did not treat you well. It doesn't look as if you've had a bite to eat since the blue bellies turned us loose up there in New York."

"Doesn't feel like I've had much to eat. There've been troubles along the way, but you're looking hale and hearty." Knight nervously shifted and looked past Milo Hannigan to his back trail.

"You on the run from them Yankees? Don't fret about them, Doc. My boys will take care of them, if that's what's needed."

"Your boys? Others from Elmira?"

"Some. You remember Ben Lunsford. Well, now, we picked up his younger brother, Seth. Seems after Sherman was done burning Atlanta, he set to stealing everything else in Georgia. Seth was the only Lunsford left alive, other'n his brother. Ben wanted to ride straight on down there and slaughter every last one of them baby killers, but I talked him out of it. We were outnumbered during the war. Now we're outnumbered and outgunned even more than before."

"Georgia must be a hellhole," Knight said.

Hannigan nodded sadly. "That's why I convinced the lot of them to ride on west. There's nowhere in particular we're going, but we'll know it when we get there."

"You've reached Pine Knob. This is where I grew up."

"Do tell? Are there jobs for the likes of us? Unreconstructed Johnny Rebs?" Milo Hannigan laughed with more than a hint of derision.

"I can't say. My welcome here wasn't what I expected."

"Your wife died? Them Yankees kill her? Or do worse to her? You always went on about how purty she was. I wouldn't put nothin' past them. They are the scum of the earth."

Knight had no stomach to let Hannigan know how unsettling the homecoming had been. Better that Victoria had died than be swept off her feet by a carpetbagger. Or had she decided to marry Gerald Donnelly because of what he had to offer her? That made her nothing but a cheap whore. Knight refused to believe that his wife hadn't been coerced into the marriage. She had to know he would come home, even if he had to crawl on his belly the whole way.

He rubbed the concave stretch under his ribs. That was almost exactly how he had returned home. "I've run afoul of the Yankees and a Bostonian carpetbagger." He wiped mud off the rifle butt. "I took this off a soldier who was hunting me."

"We ran into a pair of blue bellies." Hannigan took a deep breath, then let it out. "The boys handled them while I . . . scouted around."

Knight wondered what trouble Milo Hannigan found himself in. With soldiers everywhere and the iron fist of the Union smashing down all around, breaking the law wasn't hard. He had discovered that himself.

"You're safe enough here. At these springs." He kept from looking uphill at his secret cave. Letting anyone know — even a man whose life he had saved and who had likely saved his while in Elmira — bothered him. With nothing as it should be in Pine Knob and the world, he thought it was more sensible than needlessly suspicious.

"We're not going any particular place. I've heard tell of gold strikes in New Mexico Territory. And there's plenty to do in Colorado. Middle Park's got ranches aplenty for men willing to ride herd."

"What do you know about being a cowboy? You said your family were all storekeepers." Knight settled down, rested the stolen rifle against a rock beside him and felt more at peace than since returning home. Swapping lies with Hannigan had passed the time while they were locked up.

"What do I know about anything? If we find a mine, we can dig rock and get rich that way. Ben Lunsford wants to learn to be a tanner. He thinks stitching saddles and making holsters is a fit way to earn his supper and a shot of whiskey or two."

Knight looked at the way Hannigan carried his six-shooter slung low with a bit of rawhide strip holding it down in the fashion of a gunfighter.

Hannigan noticed his interest. "I've been practicing. The Yankees taught me to be a good shot. No sense wasting powder and lead, I say."

"During the war or after?"

Hannigan looked at him sharply, then laughed. He squared off, slipped the leather loop keeper off the hammer and drew. Knight had never seen a real gunfighter but doubted anyone could match Hannigan's speed. There had been nothing but a blur as he grabbed iron, pulled it free, and held the cocked pistol in a steady grip.

Knight froze. He didn't blink until Hannigan eased down the hammer and dropped the six-shooter back into his holster.

"I've practiced. I had to or I'd have been buried in some potter's field."

"You look well fed." Seeing how prickly Hannigan got at that, Knight eased the tension by rubbing his sunken belly and saying, "I wish I was." Punctuating his hunger, his belly rumbled ominously.

"Sounds like a thunderstorm building there. When the boys get rid of the Yankees, they'll whup you up enough food to put meat back on your bones." Hannigan dropped to the ground beside Knight and stretched out, staring up into the blue sky. "They're good boys."

"It's hard to know who to trust these days."

"Always watch your back," Hannigan opined, "because anyone might turn on you. Dangle a greenback in front of man these days and you have yourself a traitor."

"Or in front of a woman," Knight said, bitterness rising to burn his tongue.

As if he hadn't heard, Hannigan didn't even twitch at what his friend said. And he might not have. He stared at puffy white clouds drifting slowly across the sky and pointed. "You ever make pictures out of clouds, Sam? That one looks like a bronco rider. And just behind is a man fixin' to shoot him in the back."

"All I see are clouds."

"A storm's building. Mark my words. It's coming, and I don't mean up there. Chasing folks away from their farms and stealing their businesses is going to cause another uprising." His hand drifted to the gun at his side. His fingers curled, then relaxed.

"It didn't work the first time, trying to get free of politicians who wanted to meddle," Knight said. "Why should it a second, no matter how bad it gets?"

"After Atlanta, folks were stunned and the Yanks could push them around. More and more are realizing what's happening to them. Until then, me and the boys will drift around out west and wait until we're needed again."

"You're not going to join the Knights of the Golden Circle, are you?" Knight felt a tight knot forming in the middle of his chest. They didn't offer any good solution to the problems he faced . . . or those that Hannigan and everyone else did, as well.

"I'm tired of being bossed around. You remember the colonel who was in with us? The short one with the eye patch?"

"He was a bit touched in the head," Knight said. "He stood too close to his own artillery and the shock of so many cannonballs firing did something to his brain."

"That's one thing I like about you, Sam. You always have an explanation. Me, I just want a solution." Hannigan's fingers tapped on his gun. Then he sat upright. The six-shooter half came from the holster before he saw who trotted toward them.

"Ben!" Knight got to his feet and waved. For a moment the rider hesitated, then waved back. He galloped and came to a halt only a few feet away.

Ben Lunsford slid from the saddle and hit the ground running. He grabbed Knight in a hug that crushed the wind from his lungs.

"I thought you were dead. When they let the lot of us go, you weren't anywhere to be seen. What happened? How are you?"

"I couldn't wait to get home." Knight gave his best friend a slap on the shoulder and held him at arm's length to keep from getting another devastating bear hug. "I should have said good-bye." He looked up at a younger version of Ben Lunsford sitting astride a swaybacked horse. "That's got to be Seth."

"How'd you know that? You one of them gypsy mind readers?" The boy dismounted and came over. He hesitantly held out his hand.

"Your brother never stopped talking about you, not a single day we were in the Yankee prison camp." Knight shook the boy's hand. Other than the five years difference in age, Seth and Ben might have been twins.

Both stood close to five-foot-ten and were ruggedly built. Long hair poked out from under identical flat-brimmed hats, and eyes bluer than the sky above shined like gems. Ben had been a lady-killer. Seth had the same look that drew women in droves. Neither was handsome, but their confidence kept that from being noticeable.

"After I got out, I went and rescued Seth. The Federals had burned whatever they couldn't carry." Ben turned somber. "They killed damned near everyone in our town for no good reason."

"Ma and Pa died when they set fire to the house," Seth said. "I was in the outhouse and missed being killed alongside them." He shuddered. "I still hear their screams."

"Don't go exaggerating none, Seth. You heard your own screaming 'cuz you were so constipated," Milo Hannigan said, trying to lighten the mood and not succeeding. To Ben, he asked, "Where's the rest of the boys?"

"They're leading them two blue bellies on a chase, just for the fun of it. I told them not to kill anybody or we'd have a company of soldiers down on our ears." Ben Lunsford turned back and looked at Knight. He shook his head in wonder. "You're a sight for sore eyes, Doc."

"Splash some of that spring water onto your face if your eyes are that sore. I can't imagine anyone missing me."

"Always there with a joke. What are you doing out here and not with your missus?"

Knight fell silent. He was happy to see friends, comrades, those who'd shared his life for so long in Elmira, but sharing his heartbreak with them wasn't right. Taking care of Gerald Donnelly was his duty. He looked at the gun on Milo Hannigan's hip and knew all he had to do was ask. Hannigan would shoot down anyone Knight wanted dead. From the way the man acted now, he would enjoy it more than considering it a favor for a friend.

"We're not going to stay, Doc. Come with us. I've picked up a few others, besides these two owlhoots. It would be a pleasure, an honor to have you with us." Hannigan motioned. Seth took the horses to the spring to water them after Ben dutifully took off the saddles and dropped them on the grassy land away from the mud.

Knight considered the offer, then nodded slowly. "You have any food? I am famished. We can catch up on old times while we eat."

"And?" Milo Hannigan fixed him with a hard stare that drilled to his soul.

"I have some business to finish, then we can do some exploring. I hear Arizona's got some wide-open spaces where nobody tells you what to do."

"The kind of place we're all hunting for, Doc." Hannigan slapped him on the shoulder. "Now let's get to making a fire so Ben can show us some of the cooking skills he's learned."

"Ben? Cooking?" Knight laughed. "I'd better get down to remembering how to deal with food poisoning. You were the worst cook I'd ever seen, Ben."

The other four riding with Hannigan showed up, and dinner wasn't as bad as Knight expected. He found himself enjoying the company and even seriously considering Hannigan's offer to ride with them. But it had to wait until afterwards.

After he dealt with Gerald Donnelly.

CHAPTER 8

Ben Lunsford followed him around like a puppy dog. Knight wanted to get rid of him but had no idea how to do so without hurting the man's feelings. They had counted on each other in the prison camp. He still felt some of that bond between them but not to the extent that Lunsford did.

"You remember the time I got that cut on my leg? From the guard's bayonet while I was tryin' to get under the fence? See? I'm all healed now, and all I got's a tiny scar, hardly worth mentionin' compared to the one I got when that bull gored me when I was twelve and thinkin' I could outrun it."

"What're your plans, you and Seth?" Knight had no desire to talk about the prison camp or the crude doctoring he had done there. In the field, with men blown apart, he had let so many die. At least he'd had basic instruments and some supplies. Surgeon General Moore had been a wizard at getting medicines to his field hospitals. In Elmira, Knight had lacked even simple instruments, much less anything to disinfect. More than once he had used whiskey as both disinfectant and anesthetic after a battle. Liquor of any kind was banned from the prison camp, though many of the guards never had a sober day the whole time he, Lunsford, and the others were locked up. Some of that whiskey would have gone a long way toward relieving pain and suffering.

"Seth wants to get as far from home as possible. He'd jump aboard one of them clipper ships we hear about and go all the way to China, if he could. He's got this romantic vision of the world bein' different because it's on the other side of the ocean." Ben Lunsford shook his head sadly. "Me and you, we know different, don't we, Doc?"

"No matter where you are, there's trouble of some sort." He cleared his throat and looked toward town, hoping Ben got the message. He didn't.

"Things are better now, with you ridin' along with us. I don't have anything against Hannigan. He's taken charge, like he did in prison. Only he's different. We all are, but he's harder, if that's possible. Hell, I cut more'n one bluecoat's throat and never lost a minute of sleep. But Hannigan's worse now."

"How's that? He didn't strike me as being changed all that much."

"It's hard to say, Doc. He don't trust anyone. I understand that. I trust Seth. I for certain trust you. You're one of the few good men I've ever met who wasn't a blood relative."

Knight smiled grimly at that. If Lunsford thought Hannigan had changed, he had no idea what coming home to Pine Knob had done to this "one good man." Hatred boiled within him until he wanted to lash out. He held that anger in check. He saved it up for the man who deserved it most. How he would make Gerald Donnelly pay was still a mystery, but he would. His thoughts turned to stories he had heard of how the Comanche treated their prisoners, and it hadn't been charitably. The Comanches ranged far and wide throughout Texas and westward and had learned some nasty tricks from the Apaches. Before he died, Donnelly would sample the worst Knight could deliver, compliments of stories about the Indians and their enemy prisoners.

He sucked in a deep breath and held it until his lungs threatened to pop. While in Elmira, he had seen some inhuman acts that might be even more appropriate, considering Donnelly was a carpetbagger and likely to have approved of how the Union treated its prisoners.

"Don't go putting too much faith in me, Ben. Just take me at face value and don't worry about tomorrow while you're still living today."

"You always said the smartest thing, Doc. Live for the day, is that what you're sayin'?"

"I reckon it is. When did Hannigan say you were riding out? He and I had a long talk about any of you finding jobs in Pine Knob. Chances aren't all that good, not with a cavalry detachment here."

"They'd harass us for certain. We seen that in other places. It's bad enough bein' a native of a town, but a drifter comin' in, lookin' to settle down?" He shook his head sadly. "The carpetbaggers don't like that, and the townspeople don't much, either. Livin's hard enough for them without any drifter takin' jobs their menfolk need." He laughed without humor. "They get real protective of their women, too. *Real* protective."

Such a comment sent Knight's pulse rising. He felt his face flushing with anger. *Victoria. Gerald Donnelly.* His hand touched the butt of the Colt at his hip. Hannigan had plenty of ammo for a wide number of six-shooters his men didn't even carry. Never leave a gun or ammo behind, no matter what, had been the standing orders for every Confederate unit. Hannigan followed it, to Knight's benefit. He carried a loaded Colt Navy with three cylinders ready to swap out if the one in the gun came up empty. If Donnelly had been in his sights, all twenty-four rounds would have found targets in his vile heart.

"You feelin' all right, Doc? You got all red in the face and you're breathin' fast, too, like you run a footrace."

"When did Hannigan say you all were riding out?"

"Tomorrow morning, maybe hitting the road before sunup. We're headin' due west, no particular destination in mind, but soon enough we'll have to get some money. Our supplies are runnin' low, too. Not likely we'll get lucky like before, when we got most of it."

"You found someone to let you work?"

Lunsford looked sheepish. "Not exactly. We found a railroad car with its door unlocked. The supplies inside have kept us goin' for a couple weeks now. Stealin's not right, but we were mighty hungry." He looked at Knight's clothes hanging loose on his gaunt frame. "You'd never do a thing like that, would you, Doc?"

"Who's hungry and who's starving to death?" He patted his sunken belly. It had bloated for a while, before collapsing into its present state. "Hannigan's responsibility is to keep you and the others alive."

"I suppose so, but other'n Seth, I don't much like them. They and Hannigan get along good. Birds of a feather. But I think one of them — the small one with the oversized white hat — shot a man in the back at a saloon in Baton Rouge. Don't know for certain, but Johnny Nott's a tough character. I'm not even sure he was in the army, from what he says, but if he was, he deserted."

"We should have, too, rather than get captured and endure Elmira." Knight's patience had come to an end. "Tomorrow you're riding out? I'll catch up with you. I have some business in Pine Knob to take care of."

"Something about your wife, Doc? You've been avoidin' mention of her. Why'd you want to ride with us if she's in town?"

"Take care of Seth. I'll catch up before noon." He seethed with anger at Lunsford for asking such a question. It wasn't the young man's fault. There was no way he could know since he had just ridden in with the others and knew nothing about Gerald Donnelly or Victoria claiming she was married to that son of a bitch.

He forced himself to open his right hand. The Colt dropped back into the holster. He had unconsciously drawn it at the thought of Donnelly and Victoria together.

"You want somebody to watch your back?" Ben Lunsford shuffled his boots a mite, then looked Knight squarely in the eye. "Hannigan told us what happened to you, why you're out here hidin' from everyone in town."

"They got what they deserved. Donnelly might have set the soldiers on my trail, but they can't find me. Now you get on along."

"Me and Seth can —"

"Go."

Lunsford's hangdog look almost made Knight reconsider. They had been inseparable in the prison camp because they relied on each other. Of all the men he had known, Ben Lunsford was the most dependable, but this wasn't his fight. Knight heaved a deep breath and picked up the stolen rifle. He wanted it to be his fight and his alone. Justice demanded it.

Hannigan didn't have any spare horses, and Knight wasn't going to ask for one.

That might slow their departure in the morning. He glanced at the sun and estimated how long it took to hike into town — to his house. The night would keep him from being seen. After he finished with Gerald Donnelly, finding a horse to steal would be easy. He had done it twice before, after all. And that pasture out back likely wasn't Fred Fitzsimmons's at all but Donnelly's. The thought of stealing as many of those horses as possible gave him a warm feeling deep inside. More retribution.

Rifle in his right hand and swinging as he walked, he skirted Pine Knob and found the fancy new road leading to his house. The hour it took to walk in gave him plenty of time to think. What would Victoria decide if Donnelly was no longer in her life? At one time that would have been an easy question to answer, but Knight admitted he had no idea how his wife would react. She had made it clear where her sympathies lay. But did she love Donnelly? Knight knew she had loved *him,* and some tiny stirring of that soft emotion had to remain. Snuffing out the sun's heat would be easier than erasing her love for him.

Lights in the lower part of the house shined forth. Knight avoided them. He froze when he heard voices outside the house.

Two cowboys made their way toward a distant barn. From their banter they had finished the day's chores and intended to finish off a bottle of whiskey hidden in the hay. When they disappeared, Knight continued his approach to the house.

The light in the parlor winked out as he chanced a quick look inside. He ducked back and crouched on the porch. His hands shook as he lifted the rifle. Shooting blindly into a darkened room led to accidents. No matter what Victoria said or did, he loved her. She was his wife. He did this for her. Harming one hair on her head would make him the awful person she believed him to be. Worse, it would confirm Donnelly's opinion of him.

Knight came to a quick decision. Shooting Donnelly from ambush was wrong. Not only was it the mark of a coward to kill without facing his target, he wanted the carpetbagger to know who delivered divine justice.

A quick peek inside again told the story. The room was empty. Knight duckwalked around the porch as the next lighted window went dark. Rather than trail whoever extinguished the lamps, he went to the door and lightly tried the doorknob. It turned and the door swung inward on well-oiled hinges.

Coming out of his crouch, he went down the hall and peered into the kitchen. The maid bustled about, finished her day's chores. Her room just off the kitchen put her far enough away from those upstairs. Any ruckus might be ignored as being none of her business.

Knight tensed at the idea Donnelly and Victoria engaged in such noisy activities that the maid simply ignored their behavior.

He stepped onto the new staircase and put his weight down. A small creak hardly carried. He mounted the steps carefully, making almost no noise. Whatever carpenter had built the stairs had done an excellent job. At the top of the stairs ran a hallway from front to back with three doors on each side. A window directly ahead caught the lace curtains as it let in a humid night breeze. Two doors on the right stood open. A sewing room and a small library. The third door opened to storage. Boxes piled high and a wooden file cabinet with one drawer open had been pushed against the far wall.

Knight spun when sounds came from the room behind the middle door on the other side of the hall. He pressed his ear against the panel. His heart almost stopped beating when he recognized the unmistakable, well-remembered sounds Victoria uttered when they made love. He gripped the rifle so hard his hands shook. Rearing back, he kicked like a mule and knocked the door from its hinges. It slammed to the floor amid a rush of trapped air from beneath it.

The dark room prevented him from getting a clear view of those in the bed. He let out a choked cry of rage and lifted the rifle. His finger came back hard. Nothing happened. He hadn't levered a round into the firing chamber.

Then the cry turned into a loud moan that escaped unbidden from his lips. The dark shape he would have shot wasn't Donnelly but Victoria. His wife, astride the man under her, turned and shrieked. Then chaos turned everything upside down in the room.

Victoria flew from the bed, thrown to one side by Gerald Donnelly. He surged up, tangled himself in the bedclothes, then launched clumsily to crash into Knight. The two went down on the bedroom floor in a jumble.

"You! Why don't you die?" Donnelly tried to choke him. When he failed to get fingers around his assailant's neck, he began banging Knight's head against the hardwood floor.

His anger surging madly, Knight heaved

upward and dislodged Donnelly. They exchanged blows and finally came to their feet separated by the bed.

"Gerald, should I fetch the men?" Victoria clutched a sheet to her throat, hiding her nakedness. In the dark room, only flashes of white skin showed. It wasn't anything Knight hadn't seen and lusted after before, but now it infuriated him. She had been in his bed making love to this carpetbagger!

"Get an army, if you like, Victoria, nothing will save him." Knight clenched his hands into fists and dived across the bed. That was a mistake. He landed on the feather mattress and immediately bogged down.

"Got you!" Donnelly crashed down atop him, forcing his face into the mattress and suffocating him.

Knight rocked from side to side and clawed at the naked man to no avail. His starvation finally overrode his hate-fueled anger. Consciousness ebbed from him until darkness closed in.

He came to an instant later . . . or it seemed no more than that.

Knight quickly understood he had been unconscious for some time. Tied to a chair in the storage room, all he could do was struggle futilely. Again his weakened condition worked against him. He should have told Ben Lunsford to come along. He should have asked that Seth join them. He should have made sure the carbine had a round in the chamber, even though if it had, he would have murdered his own wife.

But the sick realization came to him that Victoria wasn't his wife any longer. As he and Donnelly had fought, she cheered on the carpetbagger. It had been a golden opportunity for her to be rid of the man, but she chose him over her real husband, her legal husband, returned from impossible hardship during the war.

Knight bounced up and down, taking the chair with him. His arms were tied with short lengths of rope. He couldn't see his feet, but from the way pain cut into his ankles, he had been secured there in the same fashion. Already his feet had turned numb from lack of circulation. Only a minute or two remained before his hands similarly died and his fingers became useless sausages.

The door opened and Donnelly entered. He had pulled a robe around his naked body. On bare feet he padded over and towered above Knight. Then he doubled his hand into a fist and struck out as hard as he could. The captive man lifted up and crashed to the floor, still bound to the chair. Donnelly righted him for another punch to the jaw.

"Damn, you got a bony chin." Donnelly rubbed his fist. "A hard head. It figures. You've done nothing but make the wrong decisions all your life."

"It looks that way," Knight said. "I married Victoria."

Donnelly hit him again, this time aiming for the middle of his chest. Air rushed from his lungs as the punch echoed into his body through his diaphragm.

"You don't mention her name. You left her to fight a war you knew you'd never win. You never wrote her. You abandoned her!"

"I wrote. I did," Knight gasped out. "The damned Yankee prison guards must never have sent along my letters. They never brought me any from her."

"She thought you were dead. Why write a dead man?" Donnelly walked around and punched him from behind. Knight's head snapped forward and lights exploded in front of him. "This time I'll make sure you're put in the ground to stay. Should I put you into a coffin alive and bury you? Would you like fighting for breath, knowing you were going to die? Might be better to see you hanged, though that would be a trial for her."

"Stop lying, Donnelly. Whatever you do to me is for your own sick gratification."

Another blow to his chest caused Knight to cough and spit blood.

"That's about the only smart thing you've said. Yeah, I want to torture you because of who you are. You're the past, Knight. You're a loser. Get rid of the past and losers like you and the future looks mighty good." He began punching methodically but after a minute stopped suddenly and stepped back. "Victoria insisted we store everything you left behind in here. I can use some of it to good effect."

Knight sagged forward. As he did, he felt the right chair arm break off. He hid how that arm was free and worked on the left. With his feet still bound to the chair legs, he was in dire straits, but he had a chance. One chance. He couldn't fail or his life was forfeit.

"Your old medical tools. I doubt you'll need this scalpel anymore." Donnelly held it up so it caught a ray of moonlight coming through a distant window. "I'm not trained, so I might get messy as I cut you up. Will it be painful? I hope so."

Gerald Donnelly stepped forward, the

razor-sharp tip of the scalpel moving about like the fangs of a striking snake coming for his face. Knight straightened and swung his right arm as hard as he could. The wooden chair arm connected with the side of Donnelly's head, but Knight was weaker than a kitten. The man staggered and fell to one knee, shook off the blow, and snarled as he stabbed out with the scalpel.

Knight swung again, using his left arm, which had come free as the chair arm broke. The length of wood caught Donnelly above the eye and opened a gash that spurted crimson. From the way he recoiled, he was blinded by his own blood. Knight knew what that was like. Blood made a darkness descend unlike anything else.

He kicked hard and felt the chair legs break away. Like a windmill he swung at the blinded Donnelly, hitting him first right and then left with the chair arms. A kick brought a bit of chair leg whipping around and drove the lawyer to the floor.

The scalpel clattered from his hand.

"I can't see. You've blinded me, you son of a bitch!"

Knight picked up the scalpel. With Donnelly in such a helpless condition, a single slice across his throat would end the fight. Severed carotid arteries would bring his miserable life to a bloody conclusion. Knight dropped, his knee smashing down onto Donnelly's diaphragm. Cartilage cracked under the pressure.

He pressed the cold surgical steel blade into the man's throat. "You wanted me dead. How's it feel to have the tables reversed?"

"I cuckolded you. I took your home and made it mine. Go on, murder me, you filthy Johnny Reb!"

Knight started to do as Donnelly demanded, but his oath came back. First, do no harm. Heal. Preserve life, not take it.

The hesitation gave Donnelly the time needed to lash out and unseat Knight, knocking him to one side. Blundering about, rubbing at his eyes in an attempt to see again, Donnelly swung around to hands and knees to scramble away.

Knight slashed with the scalpel. More luck than skill caused him to slice the man's Achilles tendon. Donnelly let out a shriek of pure agony and fell forward.

"I can't move my foot. You've crippled me."

"Good." Knight stood and watched as Gerald Donnelly thrashed about, covered in blood that was more his victim's than his own, but he had been hamstrung good and proper for all time. "You're going to remember me for the rest of your life, with every stumbling step you take."

Knight threw the scalpel into an open doctor's bag he had used when in medical school. He had forgotten the tools had been stored because he had a newer, better set when he'd joined the C.S.A. A bag of his old clothes had been stored alongside it. He made a pile, adding odds and ends from a previous life, then tied it all into a bundle. Picking it up, he stepped over Donnelly and went to the stairs.

He paused a moment. Victoria stood in the bedroom door, hand over her mouth. Without a word, Dr. Samuel Knight took the stairs down two at a time and burst into the darkness.

Killing Donnelly was the smartest thing he could have done. Now the carpetbagger would have Norwood's entire company on his trail. That was what he should have done.

Crippling him for life so he would always remember the man whose wife he had stolen felt like a better revenge.

Knight let the night swallow him as he headed for the fenced pasture and the horses there. Stealing a couple would be icing on the cake.

CHAPTER 9

Knight knew little about horses but was getting good at stealing them. He crawled over the rail fence into the pasture. Several horses came over to see if he had apples or sugar to offer. Taking a bridle from where tack had been stacked, he caught a fine-looking gelding and then led it over to the fence. Pressing against the horse forced it into the fence and gave him a chance to saddle it. Not content with one horse, he found two more bridles and finally mounted, leading his small remuda to a gate.

He thought he heard sounds coming from the barn. Two cowboys might give him trouble, but the real danger came from the main house. Gerald Donnelly would have bandaged his cut Achilles tendon and realized he was crippled for life. The man's fury showed every time he opened his mouth. Would he take out his rage on Victoria?

"You made your bed. Now lie in it." The bitterness welling up from inside Knight knew no limits. Her choice of a man, even if she thought he had died in the war, showed her true colors. What love he had felt for her curdled, like milk left in the hot summer sun. Hating her might come later, but for now all he felt was utter contempt.

Leaning out, he kicked at the gate with his toe and lifted the latch. If the other horses escaped, what did it matter to him? Let Donnelly do some work rounding them up. His damaged foot wouldn't keep him from riding.

Knight applied his heels to the horse's flanks and rocketed out of the pasture. A cry of elation escaped his lips, then he was galloping away to the road, almost dragged from the saddle by the reins leading the other two horses striving to keep up. He slowed his pace and settled down in the saddle, preparing for a long ride. Milo Hannigan and his gang — why did he think of them as a gang and not a footloose group of drifters? — would already be on the road heading west. If Knight kept riding in that direction, he had to pass through the middle of Pine Knob.

Rather than risk creating a stir by the sight of a decrepit, starved man riding a fine horse and leading others, he veered off the road. Smaller lanes criss-crossed the countryside. While he might not know them the way he had before the war, they provided more furtive ways out of town than the cavalry likely knew, having just arrived.

He passed Joel Krauss's house. The dawn light showed his old friend already up and doing chores. A moment or two would be all it took to greet him and bid him good-bye. Knight decided against it. Krauss had known of Victoria's betrayal and had said nothing. Perhaps he thought it wasn't his place to give such bad news to a returning army veteran, but Knight placed honesty above charity in this regard.

He sagged as he rode past. Blaming Krauss was no answer. Knight would not have believed him if he had told of Victoria and Donnelly, and possibly would have reacted badly. "Kill the messenger" echoed all the way through the South after Lee had surrendered. No one wanted to believe the conflict had ended so badly, and everyone needed to affix blame.

In a minute, Krauss and his home lay behind. In ten, Knight felt he had successfully skirted town and turned back westward along a path overgrown with weeds. At one time it had led to a small salt mine, but when that played out and other sources of salt were discovered, there was no longer any call to ride this way. He passed the small open pit, now a tiny lake of undrinkable water, and rode faster.

Knowing this road ran parallel to the main one to his right, he eventually cut across country until he found the deep ruts and potholes of the more heavily traveled road. He looked back toward Pine Knob, then westward. Not being a trails man, he got no information from the hoofprints in the dirt that might give a clue about Hannigan and his men already passing this way.

Knight shifted uncomfortably in the saddle, then moved the gun belt around his waist so the holster rested on his left hip, the butt of the Colt Navy facing forward. Having easier access to the weapon meant he could draw without standing in the stirrups. His right hip had burned from the weight of the six-shooter since he had left Donnelly. Now it rubbed his left. This warned him that becoming a gunfighter wasn't in the cards for him. He intended to take off the six-gun the first chance he got.

He rode another half hour without seeing any travelers. In a shady grove, he dismounted, let the horses graze, and began rummaging through the treasure trove he had taken from the upstairs storeroom. If he found a town needing a doctor, his equipment would come in handy. He placed the battered leather bag to one side. Cleaning the surgical tools was a chore for another time.

A smile lit his face when he held up the clothes. They had been work clothes, for the most part, but they might as well have been formal attire for a night at the opera when he compared them to what he wore. He stripped down, then slowly dressed in his discarded clothing, enjoying the feel of the untorn, clean cotton against his skin. No rents or holes let in a breeze, whether at the elbow of the shirt or the seat of his pants. His knees no longer poked through. The only thing missing was a pair of boots to replace the ones with the hole in the sole. Walking now, though, didn't bother him as much. He had fine horses to ride.

He saw they were getting decent forage, then led them to a small stream for watering. If he kept one and sold the other two, he would have more money in his pocket than any time since being released from Elmira. It was the least Donnelly could give him. The very least.

The rush of events had kept him on edge and alert. Now that danger had passed, he let the exhaustion wash over him like a muzzy blanket. He made certain the horses were securely tethered, then leaned back against a sweet gum tree intending only to rest. His eyelids sagged and within seconds he slept.

Knight came awake in a rush at the sound of horses along the road. Lots of horses. He reached for his six-shooter, panicked when it wasn't at his right hip, then remembered he had moved it. Drawing the Colt Navy from a sitting position proved easy. The pistol settled nicely into his hand as he waited to see who rode down on him.

"No need to get all antsy, Doc."

He twisted around and almost flopped onto the ground. Ben Lunsford loomed above him, arms crossed and looking pleased with himself.

"I snuck up on you real good, didn't I, Doc?"

"You scared the — yes, you did." He slid the Colt back into his holster and got to his feet.

"You got the look of a man who needs a noonday meal. I scouted ahead for a good place to stop." Lunsford pointed. "Them's the rest of the boys."

"There's good water here and plenty of grass for the horses."

"You're comin' up in the world. Those your mounts? Did Donnelly trade 'em for your wife?" Lunsford paled when he saw the reaction his joke caused. "Don't throw down on me, Doc. I didn't mean nuthin' by that. Honest. I was joshin' you."

"It was in poor taste. Don't mention it again. Ever." Knight relaxed. He had been ready to go for the six-shooter and shoot the only friend he had left in the world. The wound Victoria had caused in his soul had not begun to heal. Maybe it would never be right. "And I stole those horses, fair and square. Does that bother you?"

"Can't say that it does. Me and Seth have done worse 'n that since we came over from Georgia with Hannigan and the others. Hell, we've all done worse, but only when we have to." His eyes went to Milo Hannigan as he rode up. His expression told Knight everything he needed to know. Hannigan was the one committing the worst crimes. The Lunsford brothers and probably the rest just did what they had to for survival.

"Well, well, lookee what we got here. You beat us onto the road, Sam. We certainly haven't been dawdlin'." Hannigan glanced behind as if he expected to see someone riding down on him.

Knight suspected that might be the case. Ben Lunsford had hinted that breaking the law was less a consideration for Hannigan's gang than what they gained. Before the war, such behavior had been unacceptable. Now Knight engaged in it himself. Worse, he hardly considered horse thieving a crime if he stole from a Northerner.

"You sure nobody's on the trail behind you?" Knight asked.

"Now, Sam, who might you be worrying about? Could it be the blue bellies? Stealing a rifle from one of them isn't crime enough to call out the entire company."

"We ain't seen 'em," Ben Lunsford piped up. "Don't you go worryin' your head none 'bout them, Doc."

"I don't have the rifle any longer. I . . . dropped it."

"At the scene of some crime, I'd wager. No, Sam, don't worry. I'm not asking for an answer. What I don't know can't hurt me." Milo Hannigan swung down from his horse and handed the reins to Lunsford, as if he were nothing more than a stable hand. "We need to fix some food before we ride on."

Hannigan looked around and nodded

slowly. "You picked a fine spot for a rest. We can graze the horses a mite." He squinted at the three horses Knight had stolen. "Those make a fine addition to our herd. You mind if we let some of the others swap off as we ride? That gives us a chance to make fifty or more miles a day without killing our mounts. Ride some, switch to a fresh horse, keep going."

"I've got no objection, but I intend to sell two of them when we get to a town so I can have two nickels to rub together."

"I don't recognize the brands on their rumps. Looks like a G and a D all intertwined." Hannigan laughed and slapped Knight on the shoulder. "You got yourself some new duds, too. At least they look better than the rags you wore last time we talked."

"You said we were heading west. Do you have any particular destination in mind?"

Hannigan turned cagey. His eyes darted about, then fixed on Knight. Every time Knight had seen a man look like this, the next words out of his mouth were lies. For the love of him, he couldn't figure out why Hannigan would lie about a simple thing like this unless it was his nature. Some men found it impossible to tell the truth because lying was so much fun. It gave them a sense of pulling the wool over someone else's eyes and being superior as a result.

In the prison camp he had been closest to Ben Lunsford, but long nights spent swapping stories around the pitiful fire the Federals permitted them had forged a sense of camaraderie with Hannigan and a dozen others. He tried to remember something of Hannigan's history. It came to him that the man was closemouthed, which had prevented learning much at all. Hannigan had sported sergeant's stripes, but his blouse had been way too tight across the shoulders, hinting that he had taken it from a smaller man. Noncoms had been afforded more privileges, such as they were, than privates. Knight didn't remember Hannigan sharing much of his extra bounty. What extra rations Knight had received as an officer he had divvied up among all the men in his tent.

When the guards saw this, they had stopped giving him anything at all, forcing him to live off the largesse of the men he had helped. The best of times had been grim, indeed. Two privates had died, and he had left them in their bunks, not telling the guards. Their corpses had rotted, but he had collected two rations for almost a week. That had barely been enough to keep him alive, and the guards had locked him up in a hole as punishment for not reporting the deaths.

He had always thought they were put out, not because he collected the spare rations, but because they hadn't. Guards ate little better than the inmates, though somewhat more with each meal.

"I mentioned all the mining going on in Arizona. Might be work to be had there," Hannigan said.

"Stagecoaches carry the payrolls to the mines and gold and silver to the railroads," Knight said. "Enterprising men might find a way to make a living off that commerce."

"I do declare, Sam, me and you think alike on this matter. That surprises me just a tad, but then you've quite a career stealing horses since you left that hellhole in New York. What's a strongbox gone missing now and then, eh?" Hannigan laughed, confirming what Knight had thought. Hannigan rode at the head of an outlaw gang, not men hunting for real work and decent lives.

The others milled about until Hannigan gave orders as to what each was to do. He turned back to Knight. "They're good men, the lot of them, but they need a good leader to keep them on track."

"I know Ben and Seth, at least a little.

That one's familiar looking, too. Henry Lattimer, from somewhere in Tennessee." Knight watched the smallish Johnny Nott strutting around like a banty rooster. If anything happened to Hannigan, Nott would be the man taking over the gang — or trying to.

"Turning your back on Johnny, now, that's not a smart thing to do. No, sir, Sam, it's not." Hannigan laughed. "Get the joke? It's *not* a good thing to turn your back on *Nott.* Rumor has it that he shot a man in the back who made fun of him being short."

"I don't remember him from Elmira."

"He joined us after we drifted south, after we got out. I never heard that he served. Asking questions about his background never seemed a safe thing to do. I think it's about the same with Porkchop. We call him that because he always orders pork chops when we get food at a restaurant. Eats pigs' knuckles in a saloon, can't get enough bacon on the trail. The best I can tell, he served with a cavalry regiment, maybe Jeb Stuart's. He's a hell of a rider, knows everything there is to know about horses and can even shoe a horse using a bent tenpenny nail and spit."

The man Hannigan spoke of sat with his back to a tree, his eyes darting about suspiciously. He had the same look that Nott did. A bullet to the back was more likely than facing down an enemy. Hannigan had gathered a band of killers, other than Ben and his brother. Riding with them gave Knight a chance to leave behind all his crimes, but finding a place to settle down would be hard if Hannigan and the others robbed and killed as they went. It would be like pulling on a thread and hoping everything didn't unravel before the cloth vanished entirely.

"We lost one or two others. They kind of drifted away, not liking the way I did things. I don't hold that against them, and it might be for the best. We're a good size to ride fast, when necessary."

"I'm a bit sad leaving behind the Piney Woods, but doing it as fast as I can is good sense," Knight said. "I grew up there, but the rest of your gang's all far from their homes. All I need to do is get used to Pine Knob not being home anymore."

"While we were prisoners, you talked a blue streak about Pine Knob and your wife. Sorry that didn't work out for you." Hannigan spat, wiped his lips with his sleeve, and then asked, "You reckon the cavalry there will be on your trail for whatever you've done? Other than stealing some horses?"

Knight nodded glumly.

"Nott! Get your ass over here." Hannigan rested his hand on his six-gun. When the short man with the tall hat sauntered over, he said, "Watch our back trail for soldiers. Sam here thinks they might be comin' after him."

"What do you want me to do?"

"Use your judgment. You're the smartest one of all of us."

"Don't you forget it, Milo. Don't you ever damn forget it." Johnny Nott hitched up his gun belt and left.

"He shoots better than he carries a tune. We can take our time with Nott guarding our back trail."

"I need to rest up and get some food." Knight inhaled deeply. The smell of food cooking and coffee boiling made his mouth water.

"You're one of us now, Sam. Help yourself. Remember what I said about Nott. And Porkchop." Hannigan's laugh carried a note of pure evil with it.

"Thanks for the warning." Knight saw how Hannigan kept discipline in his ragtag band. Keeping them suspicious of one another worked so long as each depended on him to lead them.

Let one of them, Nott or Porkchop most

likely, make a bid to take over the gang and a stack of backshot bodies would feed the wolves for quite a while. Knight gave up speculating who would come out alive. By the time lead started to fly, he wanted to be far off and long gone.

The rest of the day was spent eating and lounging around, which made Knight increasingly uneasy. Donnelly wasn't the kind to let such an affront go unpunished. Trying to nap availed Knight little but a sore shoulder as he turned from one side to the other. Just before sundown he heard horses coming. He got to his feet and had his Colt out before anyone else noticed Nott returning.

Knight holstered his six-shooter and wondered where Nott had gotten another horse. As the man rode closer, Knight went cold inside. The horse trotted along without a rider and still sporting a McClellan saddle used by the cavalry, twin wood planks fit on either side of the horse's spine. Such a saddle was comfortable for the horse and hell for the rider, but this only spoke to which the US Army considered more valuable.

Johnny Nott drew rein and dropped to the ground. Knight thought he had shrunk another inch or just misremembered how short the man was.

Nott glared at him and pushed past to speak with Hannigan. "Got another horse for the remuda. The damn Yankee ain't gonna need it no longer." Nott patted his six-shooter. "Rode right up to me bold as brass and asked what I was doin' on the road. So I showed him. One shot. Right here." Nott pressed his index finger between his eyes. "Wasn't even much blood though it damn near blowed the back of his head off."

"You murdered a trooper?" Knight swallowed hard. "That's sure to stir up Captain Norwood and get the whole company on our tail."

"You worry too much, Sam," Hannigan said. "Nott made sure they weren't coming after us. Right, Johnny?"

"Sure as grits and gravy, boss."

"What's one more dead blue belly, anyway? From what you said, Sam, they're as likely to come after you for what you did as they are to get riled over Johnny taking a shot at a scout."

"He killed him."

"You don't like what I did?" Nott spun and thrust out his chin. A single step brought him within an inch of touching. He pushed out his chest and bumped into Knight. "You intend to call me out for doin' what the boss told me to do?"

"I heard what he said. There wasn't anything about murdering a soldier."

"Boss, can I —"

"Go grab some grub, Johnny. I'll talk to Sam. Good job." Hannigan spat. "Good-looking horse, too." He slapped the small man on the shoulder, then took Knight by the arm and guided him away from camp to where they spoke in private.

"Sam, you cannot go around telling Johnny he's done wrong. That man has a short fuse." Hannigan paused, then laughed. A touch of pure evil undercut any humor. "Don't tell him I said that. He's sensitive about how tall he is. But he has a hair-trigger temper and a mighty fast hand."

"The army will have every trooper in East Texas after us."

"Let them. We're going to be in West Texas, maybe New Mexico or even Arizona before they figure out their scout's gone missing. When they do, how're they to know he didn't run afoul of a Comanche war party? They're on the warpath all the time."

"When they find the body, they'll know it wasn't an Indian that killed the scout."

"Johnny's not a fool. He likely scalped the

bluecoat to throw suspicion onto the Injuns." Hannigan sounded downright cheerful at the prospect. "Now, go get some food. Talk to Johnny. Tell him how good he is."

"At what?"

"At everything. It's not true, but it keeps him all puffed up and in line." Hannigan slapped Knight on the shoulder and walked away.

Samuel Knight considered taking his horses and riding away then and there, but leaving Ben and Seth Lunsford behind with such cold-blooded killers didn't set right. Moreover, if Norwood came out on a sortie, he stood a better chance with Hannigan and his gang backing him up than he did on his own.

That didn't mean Knight liked his choice to stay. He made his way into their camp to find Ben and Seth. They had things to talk over before it was too late.

CHAPTER 10

Gerald Donnelly grimaced in pain as he lifted his right foot to an ottoman with a soft feather pillow atop it. He rubbed his leg briskly. Tingles danced from the tip of his toes all the way up to his hip. He leaned back in the chair when the tingling turned to throbbing pain again. Moving his injured foot reminded him of Samuel Knight and how much he hated the man.

"Victoria! Bring me something to drink. Lemonade. That would be good." He glowered when the maid came in.

"It'll be more than an hour to fix that, sir," Matty said. "I need to go fetch some of them lemons in town, if they have any."

"Where's my wife? Have her get it."

"Don't rightly know where she got off to. She left after she gave you breakfast."

"Find her!"

"Which you want? Your wife or the lemonade?"

Donnelly grabbed a book lying on a nearby table and flung it at the maid. Matty dodged easily, picked it up and leafed through it, finally stopping at the page where the book had been pressed open.

"You want to keep on readin' or should this go back to the liberry?"

"Out. Get out!" Donnelly groaned as he shifted. His foot flopped off the footstool onto the floor. The pain forced him to sit upright.

He rubbed his leg again, unable to reach all the way to his ankle. He grumbled when a touch of blood stained the bandages Victoria had applied only a few hours ago. Nothing had gone right the past week, nothing. That banker had balked when Donnelly demanded a loan to buy land adjoining their mutual farms. Fitzsimmons had shown nothing but animosity since Donnelly took the pastureland and horses on it for his own, using the law of eminent domain as his reason. The judge had not put up any argument, and Donnelly had made sure Fitzsimmons's lawyer put forth a weak argument for his client.

Donnelly had pointed out that one lawyer in town starved, two made a fortune. The lawyer — Donnelly couldn't even remember his name — had gone along with the scheme to take the banker's land and livestock. For his trouble, he got a lucrative job with the court preparing documents to foreclose on other property around Pine Knob.

"Matty, where's the list I was going over? The one with the land deed information in it?" He half rose, then sank back when no reply came. "Matty? Matty!"

For two cents he would fire her, but Victoria liked her for some reason. Donnelly settled back, trying to ignore the dull pain where Knight had cut his ankle tendon and concentrate on getting rid of the maid. A sharp knock at the door startled him.

"Who's there?"

"Captain Norwood, come to pay my respects."

"Respects," Donnelly muttered. Louder, "Come in, Captain. The door's not locked."

The cavalry officer came in as if on parade in front of the president. For a moment it seemed that a god had descended from Olympus. Boots polished like mirrors reflected light, and the brass caught sunbeams from outside and dazzled. Donnelly lifted his hand to shield his eyes. The officer's trousers had creases as sharp as the saber sheathed at his side, and his coat was spotless even after the ride from the Union encampment. Rigidly straight, Norwood

156

stared ahead. Donnelly wondered if he would salute as if reporting to a superior.

He didn't. That put Donnelly on guard. This petty officer was his pawn to move about. Military men didn't salute civilians, but Norwood should acknowledge his superior, at least with a nod of his head.

The captain took off his hat and tucked it under his left arm. Only then did he look directly at Donnelly. The flash of contempt disappeared quickly. Did that come from a military man looking down on a mere civilian or was it an acknowledgment that any physical disability was an unacceptable weakness? Either way, or some other reason, meant Donnelly had his work cut out getting the officer to heel like a proper cur.

"If you require further medical attention, my corpsman had extensive service during the war. He isn't a doctor but has seen debilitating injuries of many kinds. Treating them is a specialty of his."

"That's kind of you, Captain. The town's doctor is capable of dealing with my wound." Donnelly gritted his teeth. Moving his foot on the pillow sent lances of pain up his leg into his groin. That suggested what he would do to Knight when the damned rebel doctor was caught.

"I suppose you want a report on our hunt

157

for Knight."

"You haven't found him. Why the failure, Captain? I thought you were a capable officer." Donnelly saw the officer flush under his tanned, weathered skin. Such badgering only angered Norwood. Donnelly needed him cowed and obeying. Before Norwood responded, he hurried on. "Of course you are capable. I have seen your outstanding record and know you are saddled with lesser soldiers after your battlefield triumphs."

"How did you see my record?"

Donnelly shifted tactics another time. More compliments were necessary. "When I spoke with General Sherman about the military presence here, he bubbled over with praise. Perhaps he shouldn't have shown it to me, but his pride at having such an officer overwhelmed the tradition of keeping personnel files from civilian eyes." Donnelly almost smiled. Buttering up the officer by appealing to his vanity and conceit worked better than browbeating.

"General Sherman? You spoke directly to him?"

"I did, sir. He is a busy man, but he gave me a half hour of his valuable time to discuss plans for this region. Texas will be an important part of the Union one day. To reach that point, we need to keep the populace in check and to quash any rebellion until we achieve full potential."

"Keeping down the riffraff, such as Knight?"

"The son of a bitch maimed me!" Donnelly half rose and immediately regretted it. He collapsed back. "Such an assault cannot go unpunished."

"He's responsible for stealing a horse and possibly a carbine from a careless soldier. Those crimes deserve military justice. It will not do to let the civilians think they have free rein."

"You have disciplined those soldiers, of course."

Captain Norwood nodded curtly. Of course he had punished them.

"There isn't any report of finding him?"

"All scouts save one have reported back."

"Where was that man's territory?" Donnelly held his ire in check. Norwood ignored the obvious. If all the rest of his men reported back and one didn't, that was the direction Knight had most likely taken . . . and the scout was dead in a ditch alongside the road.

"To the west."

"Knight went west. If I were him, I would have gone south toward San Antonio. Are there others with him?"

"How should I know that, sir? The scout hasn't returned yet."

"Don't be an ass, Captain." Donnelly saw he had lost what goodwill and cooperation he had built with the officer. He softened his tone. "You are an experienced officer. Such a gap in your field intelligence means something. In this case it can only mean that . . ." Donnelly let his words trail off so Norwood finished the sentence and made it seem as if he had come to the proper conclusion.

". . . that Knight ambushed the soldier. Very well, I shall reconnoiter in force. To the west."

"Excellent, Captain. That is precisely what must be done. Good work. Bring him back."

"He will be captured and tried in a military court, not a civilian one. His crimes against the army take precedence over any slight he gave you."

"He crippled me for life! The doctor says I will need a cane to get around for the rest of my days. More than this, he stole horses. Three of them."

Captain Norwood chuckled. "I heard your hands were drunk in the barn when he stole the horses from your pasture."

"Don't you have a fugitive to catch, Captain? To the west?" Donnelly was tired of the officer. If brains were dynamite, Captain Norwood wouldn't be able to blow his nose. "Report back when you have news. Now go. I am tiring quickly." Donnelly rubbed his leg and winced. There was no need for him to feign that. His foot felt twice its proper size and throbbed with every beat of his heart.

"Sir." Norwood came even more to attention, if that were possible, did a sharp about-face and marched to the door. As he left, he put on his hat.

"Close the door, Captain. Were you raised in a barn?" Donnelly started to call for the maid to perform the small chore the officer hadn't, then he saw the reason Norwood had not fastened the door behind him.

A slender man had snaked between the door and jamb, looking more like a cat than a human with bones in his body. He wore a Stetson with a silver conch band. His fancy Kelly green brocade coat made him look like a tinhorn gambler. His vest gleamed in the sun, every ray catching another silver thread worked through the garment. A heavy gold watch chain dangled across a flat belly. Donnelly squinted to see if the fob really was a Masonic emblem. The gleam off the man's silver conch belt prevented him making out such detail. Sleek

161

black trousers tucked into the tops of fancy tooled boots tipped with silver caps strengthened the idea the man was an itinerant gambler, though he lacked a headlight diamond in his purple silk ascot.

He turned to face Donnelly. That small spin caused his coat to flare out, revealing a shoulder rig with a six-gun secured under his left arm. Seeing Donnelly's interest, he reached down and pulled back the coat on the right to reveal a second six-gun nestled in that armpit. "I've got more firepower than this."

"Can you use it?" Donnelly settled back. His question should have been taken as an insult. What fool carried two six-shooters like this who couldn't use them? He wanted to see what reaction he stirred.

It didn't surprise him when he failed to get any reaction. The man's cold dark eyes never blinked as they took in Donnelly from head to toe. His gaze lingered a moment on the ankle Knight had damaged, then went back to lock with Donnelly's.

"You don't want to find out. Not firsthand." The man kicked shut the door using the heel of a boot. As he moved Donnelly saw the pattern expertly cut into the leather. Skull and crossbones.

"You're here in response to my newspaper ad?"

"The one in the New Orleans *Times-Picayune,* yes, I am. You placed other ads?"

"Why is that important?"

"I don't audition for any job. I don't have to because I am that good. Either hire me or forget me. Whichever it is, you owe me one hundred dollars."

"For what?"

"Travel." The man shrugged. Somehow a small-caliber pistol appeared in his left hand. The heavier six-guns remained in their holsters.

"A parlor trick." Donnelly lifted his walking stick to point at the gunfighter. He yelped when a knife cartwheeled through the air and pinned the sleeve of his robe to the chair arm.

"That fancy walking stick of yours has a bullet and a firing mechanism in it. Don't think you can plug me with — what did you call it? A parlor trick."

Donnelly released his grip on the cane where a slender trigger had unfolded after he twisted the gold knob and cocked the hidden gun mechanism. He tried to pull the knife from the chair arm to free himself but couldn't.

He glared at the gunfighter. "Free me."

"In a moment. I certainly want my knife back before I leave. First I want to hear what gent is worth me killing in exchange for a thousand dollars."

"You saw the army officer who left? He's let this Johnny Reb slip through his fingers more times than I can count."

"This Johnny Reb, as you call him. He did that to you? Carved up your leg?"

"He cut my Achilles tendon. I will be a cripple for the rest of my life. Yes, dammit, Dr. Samuel Knight did this to me, and I want him brought to justice. *My* justice."

"Doctor? He was operating and slipped up? Drunk?"

"The circumstances don't matter. Yes, I will give you one thousand dollars to kill him. I will give you two thousand to bring him back alive so I can deal with him in my own fashion."

The gunfighter smiled thinly. Without any movement, the pistol in his left hand vanished. He walked over, pushed the cane-gun muzzle out of line with his leg and yanked the knife free. Again, he performed a sleight of hand that made the knife disappear to some hidden spot Donnelly could not find.

"Am I the only one hunting your Dr. Samuel Knight, other than the captain? I don't audition for jobs, and sure as the Mississippi's wide and muddy, I don't engage in a contest to beat out any other bounty hunter."

"Is that how you think of yourself?" Donnelly had no liking for this man, but he got the feeling that hiring him would mean hiring the best. "As a bounty hunter?"

"I consider myself a cold-blooded killer, but in polite society I refer to myself as someone who retrieves missing children. After all, every fugitive has a ma and a pa, whether they own up to producing such offspring as what requires my skills to fetch." He began to saunter around the room, examining the furnishings and contents of closed drawers. "Nice place. Expensive artwork and fancy furniture from where? Boston? There is a style about that seaport, and you do have a nice piece of scrimshaw on the mantel whittled by some sailor."

"Do you guarantee you will bring back Knight, dead or alive?"

"You insult me." Faster than thought, he drew both six-shooters. Both exploded at the same instant, startling Donnelly.

"You son of a bitch!" Donnelly craned around. The gunfighter had shot at the whale's-tooth scrimshaw. His eyes widened when he saw that one bullet had barely missed the carving on each side.

"I'll take the scrimshaw as a bonus when I return with your quarry. Alive." He tucked both pistols back into the shoulder holsters.

"You'll have earned it. Knight might not be traveling alone."

"What do you want done with his companions?"

"I don't care. Knight is the one who has to pay." Donnelly grasped the cane and tapped it loudly on the floor for emphasis.

"You carpetbaggers surely do know how to live high on the hog." The gunfighter gave a final appraising look and turned to leave. Facing away, he said, "Don't bother insulting the Confederacy anymore. I was on the staff of Jefferson Davis. In truth, it was I who found a place for him to live in the Garden District in New Orleans."

He opened the door. A cool puff of air stirred through the room.

"Wait," Donnelly called. "I haven't said I'd hire you."

"But you will. You'd rather pay me a thousand to kill than a hundred to just go away. Those are your only options. Either way, though, you will pay me."

He had started through the door again when Donnelly called once more to him.

"What's your name? You never told me

who it is I'm hiring."

"You can call me Hector Alton." He looked over his shoulder and smiled.

Donnelly went cold inside at the mirth he saw there.

"You can call me Hector Alton because that's my name. Good day, Mr. Donnelly."

When Alton left, it felt as if a weight had been lifted, an evil weight. Gerald Donnelly knew he had done well hiring the New Orleans gunman. Knight had no chance of escaping retribution now. None.

CHAPTER 11

"It's honest work," Ben Lunsford insisted. He looked around the circle. Most of Hannigan's men shook their heads. "You tell 'em, Doc. This isn't something to ignore. Those people need help. *Our* help."

Samuel Knight wanted nothing to do with deciding such an important change in the way they had lived for the past two weeks. Edging ever more to the west, they had hunted small game to stay alive and even done menial jobs in towns along the road to earn a few dollars. Some of the men had objected to that. Johnny Nott in particular disliked being a flunkey for any man, much less one who ran a store and asked that he sweep out the storeroom or a livery stable owner paying two bits to get the stalls mucked.

"We don't have much ammo, Ben." It was the only argument he could think of to keep Hannigan from signing them on as a private army for a group of ranchers tired of losing their beeves to marauding Indians.

"We won't need much. The sight of us whoopin' and hollerin' as we ride out will scare 'em off. The Injuns ain't expectin' to face more'n a cowboy or two with a six-gun or maybe a rifle. Faced with *us*, they'll turn tail and run. We're tough looking. We might not have to even empty our guns to scare the lot of them off."

"If we shoot up all our ammo charging them, where does that leave us if they counterattack?" Knight knew facts had nothing to do with the decision. Ben saw this as a chance to be a savior. Knight saw it as a chance for them to get shot up and maybe killed for little return.

"So hang back, Knight. Give me your six-shooter and I'll use it. I know how to use it." Nott puffed out his chest. "I don't cotton much to what Lunsford says usually, but this time he has the right idea. What are them cowpunchers willing to pay us?"

"A hundred dollars," Ben Lunsford said.

"That's all? For the lot of us risking our necks? Make it a thousand and it's worth my while to risk getting my scalp lifted." Nott did a quick draw, going into a gunfighter's crouch and swinging the six-gun around to cover each man in turn.

"Put that away before you make me mad, Johnny." Milo Hannigan lounged on his side by the fire, head supported on a hand with his elbow firmly pressed into the ground. "You know the rules. No pointing the gun 'less you mean to use it."

"Sorry, Milo." Nott didn't sound the least bit contrite. From the tiny smile on his face, he imagined fanning off six rounds and ending the lives of everyone in the gang.

"You don't reckon the ranchers would go more'n a hundred, Ben?" Hannigan looked thoughtful.

"They're almost at the end of their rope. Rustlers stole a lot of beeves earlier in the year and now the Comanche are on the warpath, raidin' from here all the way up to Adobe Walls."

"Don't suppose they'd let us have a night with their women, would they?" Henry Lattimer spoke softly. Whether he joked or not could be debated.

The entire time Knight had ridden with Hannigan and his gang, Lattimer hadn't said a dozen words but every time had carried a quiet menace with them. He had seen men like Lattimer in the prison camp and called them "not quite right." What they said and did wasn't outrageous, but they always looked at everything askew. Right now Knight was glad he wasn't a woman — and wondered if he ought to warn the ranchers.

"Don't think they would, Henry," said Hannigan, "but they might give us a few head of cattle. What we don't eat, we can sell at the next town."

"How about pigs? They got pigs? We can ask for a pig or two along with the money," said Porkchop.

This set off a round of argument over what animals to ask for. Payment in horses was out of the question. The ranchers needed all the horses they could round up for the cattle drive north to the railhead. During the year, Comanches and Lipan Apache raided for horses. Better to ignore such a demand and ask for cattle. Or pigs.

"What're your thoughts on this, Doc?" Ben Lunsford pushed his brother aside when he tried to whisper in his ear. "You always know the right thing to do."

Such a sentiment made Knight uneasy because of the way the rest of the men glared at him. He had the feeling they thought he was stuck up and superior to them because he had been an officer and a doctor. The more he tried to quell such animosity, the worse he made it. After all this time, he figured Captain Norwood had

171

given up pursuit. He wasn't sure about Donnelly, but no one coming up on them from the east had heard of Pine Knob, much less Gerald Donnelly. It might be time to leave Milo behind. Taking Ben and Seth with him would be fine, but he wasn't sure Hannigan would cotton much to losing half his gang that way.

This might be the way to get enough ahead on both food and money that Hannigan wouldn't mind three of them riding a different trail.

"I say we talk to the ranchers and make the best deal we can. They stand to lose more than a few head to the Indians if we don't agree to help."

"Let's do it!" Ben Lunsford slapped Seth on the back and jumped to his feet, doing an awkward dance that made Knight wonder if he had similar ideas about splitting with Hannigan after they had earned their keep with the ranchers.

That made life even easier. Afterwards. First, they had to drive off an entire Comanche nation with only a handful of bullets.

The rancher's gray hair fluttered in the cool breeze blowing from the north. He ran his hand through the thatch. From the lack of wrinkles on his forehead, he had turned prematurely gray. His hands shook, and he crow-hopped back and forth as nerves made his voice quaver. "We got word of them comin' fast. A dozen in the war party." He tried to spit and couldn't work up the gobbet. "Might be more. I moved my wife and children into town."

"How many hands can you put into the field?" Milo Hannigan pursed his lips as he considered this information.

"You askin' how many are still here? Most hightailed it. There are three left." The rancher made a sour face. "One thinks he can get hitched to my oldest girl if he shows some backbone."

Knight didn't bother asking. From how the rancher spoke, there wasn't a snowball's chance in hell of that ever happening. If the young cowboy was the only one left standing, he might have only the girl's reluctance to overcome to win the entire ranch.

"How sure are you there's only a dozen Indians?" Knight knew the rancher wouldn't be as upset as he was over such a small group of Comanches. There had to be more.

"Only twelve in that band." The rancher closed his eyes and made the decision to tell the entire truth. "Three more war parties have been sighted. All of them are joining up on my property."

"You've got the largest herd," Hannigan said. "To keep this from turning into a massacre, we have to stop them from uniting in one huge red-skinned army."

"Any chance the Federals will send reinforcements?" Knight had to ask. If bluecoats showed up, he would be at as big a risk from them as from a war-painted warrior out to scalp him.

"The mayor sent a request. The head of the cattle growers' association asked. They claim to be busy putting down revolts from here all the way to the Louisiana border. None of us believes that excuse for a minute. If we get ourselves killed, the land is open for them carpetbaggers to take."

"Might be you should reconsider that boy wanting to get hitched with your daughter." Hannigan laughed. The sound sent a chill up Knight's spine. "You and your men fortify the ranch house. We'll see what we can do to keep the Injuns from getting this far."

The rancher thrust out his hand. Hannigan hesitated a moment, then shook hard. With that, the rancher hurried back to his house to muster a defense, no matter how feeble.

"If the Comanches get past us, that fellow's going to lose his silver hair to the first brave who rides up." Hannigan motioned for his men to gather around. "We have enough ammunition for the first war party, then we'll have to use our fists."

"Don't pass by any dropped rifle. Take ammo off their bodies. We have to use their weapons against them," Knight said.

"Good advice, Sam. You listen to him, boys. He's got a good head on his shoulders. In spite of spending the war saving lives, he understands what we have to do to take them." Hannigan patted his six-shooter. "Let's mount and find ourselves somewhere to make a stand."

They stepped up. Hannigan, Nott, and Lattimer galloped off. Ben and Seth rode on either side of Knight. Porkchop brought up the rear as they trotted along, letting the others do the serious scouting.

"You all right shootin' at people, Doc?" Seth's voice almost broke with emotion.

"He's fine," Ben Lunsford cut in. "Have you seen how good a shot he is? He might be the best of all of us. Nott sprays bullets around like a dog shakin' off water."

"You'll be fine, Seth," Knight said, understanding what had actually been said. Seth had never faced anyone willing to kill him, not like his brother or any of the others in Hannigan's company. "Don't panic. Keep your wits about you."

"That's for sure," Ben said. "My first battle, I worried I was firing too slow. It took me forever to load my musket. I found out later most of the other soldiers either fired their ramming rod because they forgot to take it out or didn't load powder or lead or wadding. Getting off a shot mattered more than being the first to fire a round without any lead in it."

"You've told me that before, Ben. I don't have a musket to load." Seth drew his pistol and held it up. "Here's six rounds."

"Be sure to swap out the empty cylinder for one that you've loaded and you're golden. You're no coward, Seth. No, sir." Ben Lunsford dropped back to talk with Porkchop, leaving Seth and Knight alone.

When Ben Lunsford got out of earshot, Knight said, "If you're not scared, you're a damned fool. We don't know what we'll run into, but it's bound to be dangerous."

"Are you scared, Doc?" Seth turned his piercing blue eyes on Knight. "I can't believe it if you say you are. You look cool as a mint julep."

"What do you know about mint juleps? You ever had one?"

"Did. Once. It tasted terrible."

Knight kept Seth talking about inconsequential things to keep his mind off what they rode into. He wished he was as calm as Seth thought. Inside, his gut churned and the prospect of taking a life rather than saving it left him desolate. If things had gone differently in Pine Knob, he wouldn't be here, ready to shoot it out with an Indian he had never met before and had no grudge with.

"Curse you, Victoria." He spoke under his breath but Seth heard.

"You ever think about goin' home, Doc? To Pine Knob?"

"There's nothing for me there. Believing that there was got me through Hellmira, that and having Ben as a friend. Now? I don't have a wife, and a carpetbagger runs the town to suit himself. Because Donnelly says so, I can never practice medicine there and —" He cut off his words and held out his hand to alert Ben Lunsford and Porkchop. Seth already saw the warning that Lattimer had signaled from a low hill. It was time for them to earn their money.

"Stay with me or Ben. Don't go charging off by yourself."

"What if I can take me an Injun?"

"It'll be a trap. They're smart, Seth, real smart. This is how they live — and since all of them are fighting us, that means they've been good at it for every last day of their lives." Knight slid his six-shooter from its holster. His sweaty thumb slipped off the hammer. With a quick swipe, he dried it off, then put his heels to his horse and shot up the hill toward Lattimer. Seth and the others trailed him.

He never asked Lattimer what he had seen. The Comanches had half circled Hannigan and Nott, pinning them down. Nott's horse had been shot from under him. An arrow protruded from its shoulder. Nott knelt beside the carcass, his rifle resting on the horse as he fired methodically at the circling Indians. Hannigan remained in the saddle, getting off one shot after another from his revolver. When the hammer fell on an empty chamber, the *clack!* echoed all the way uphill.

"Divert them while Milo reloads." Knight doubted anyone heard his order, but it put everything into perspective on what he had to do. He charged downhill, firing at two Comanche braves on the flank as he went.

The sudden entry of another fighter unsettled them for a moment. One wheeled about, then fell from his horse as it reared. Nott fired into the horse's belly, bringing it down. The Indian scrambled to keep from being squashed. The horse neighed pitifully.

Without hesitation, the Comanche whipped out a knife and cut the horse's throat.

Knight appreciated the gesture. It was the rider's duty not to let the animal suffer. And it was his duty to keep the warriors from raiding the rancher's cattle. He fired twice, missed. As he galloped past, he swung his right hand over and aimed down on his left side. This time his bullet flew straight and true. The brave gasped and fell back, arms outstretched over his horse. Two bodies. Two corpses.

The impact of killing the Indian hit Knight as he plunged forward into a tight knot of three more warriors. Filling his field of vision were white and yellow streaks of war paint on their cheeks. One had outlined his eye in black. A red streak by it wasn't paint but blood from a cut. Knight fired and fired and fired. Another man grasped his chest and fell to the ground, dead.

He burst through the ring of fighters, leaving the two behind him in confusion. One called out in the Comanche tongue. More gunfire. Knight charged on, firing. It took several seconds for him to realize he had long since exhausted the rounds in his Colt Navy and dry-fired, the hammer falling on spent chambers.

Knowing his life was forfeit if he couldn't

shoot back, he fumbled to open the Colt, remove the cylinder, and slip in a fully loaded one. His fingers felt like they were numb with frostbite. His breathing came harsh and quick. When he drew back the hammer, a new round underneath, he hunted for a target.

He sat alone in the middle of a field. Not sure what had happened, he spun about. Three bodies lay on the ground. A sigh of relief escaped when he saw they were Comanches. When Seth waved to him and rode up, he lowered his gun.

"What happened? I don't hear any more gunfire."

"What happened? You're askin' that? Doc, you're a damn hero! You charged through and kilt dead their war chief. That mixed 'em all up. I got me two. Two! Sent another one skedaddlin' for the tall and uncut. Ben and Porkchop kept after them but gave up when they couldn't catch 'em."

"War chief?" Shock seized his arms and turned them leaden. He managed to move against the inertia and slide his Colt Navy into its holster. "We routed them? All of them?"

"Looks like," Seth said. He let out a whoop of glee. "We chased 'em off. *You* did it, Doc. If you hadn't charged in like that, they'd have cut us down."

"We need to get their weapons. Rifles. Ammo." Only things he had thought of before the skirmish rose in his head. Try as he might, figuring out what to say about their victory lay beyond his capacity.

"Nott's run himself down an Indian pony. Damn shame his horse got shot like that."

"It saved his life, Seth." Knight watched Hannigan, Lattimer, and Nott moving from one body to the next, stripping away anything of value. They took knives, beadwork, and buckskin pouches with whatever valuables a Comanche carried into battle.

"Got five rifles and enough ammunition to fight off the rest of those heathens!" Lattimer held one Winchester high over his head and waved it around the way the Comanche had when he prepared to attack.

Johnny Nott rode over, stared at Knight with his emotionless gaze, then touched the brim of his hat in mock salute and rode on. Familiar laughter caused Knight to turn in the saddle. Milo Hannigan gathered the reins of a half dozen ponies.

"You saved our bacon, Sam. If you hadn't opened fire when you did, the bastards would have killed me and Nott. Now, we turned the tables, got their guns and horses, and we're in position to hold off the rest of their war party. You done good, Sam. You done real good for a man who's never fought before."

"I've fought, just not like this."

"I saw the chief's body. One shot clean through the head. You're becoming quite a marksman. Now you need to put a little speed into a draw and you'll be the most feared gunman in the whole of Texas." Again Hannigan laughed, as if he thought the idea so absurd that it would become a standing joke.

Knight slipped his pistol from the holster and looked hard at it. He had hit the very spot where he aimed. Hunting rabbits and other small game, he only took one shot to bring them down. Something in his head made marksmanship easy. He had always been adept with his hand doing what his mind told. That made him a good surgeon. It could also turn him into a deadly killer. He wasn't sure such a skill should be nurtured.

He jerked his head up when Ben Lunsford shouted, "They've ridden around us. The lot of them other Injuns is headin' for the ranch house!"

CHAPTER 12

"See? See their dust? These were just a diversion." Ben Lunsford bounced in his saddle as he pointed.

"They're taking advantage of this fight," Knight said. "Do you think their war chief would be part of a diversion? He'd want to be in the thick of battle. Those braves are taking advantage of a loss to steal horses."

"And kill the rancher and whoever else is with him." Ben Lunsford wiped his mouth. His eyes were wide, and he hardly restrained himself. "We gotta get there pronto!"

"Slow down. We rush into a fight we know nothing about and it's us who'll get killed. You don't want that for Seth, do you?"

"Seth?" Lunsford looked ahead to where his brother rode with Hannigan and Nott. "They'll talk him into leading the attack. They don't care one whit for him."

"Whoa, hang on." Knight reached out and grabbed Lunsford's arm. "We need a plan.

Milo's not fool enough to rush in without having some kind of a plan. Seth's going to be in the middle of the fight, no matter what. We all are."

"The best way of not gettin' killed is to act like you can't. I heard a sergeant say that. I never believed it because he got himself shot to hell and gone not an hour later, but it makes sense. You get all timid and you make mistakes."

"React to what's facing you the best way you can and don't invent problems. Don't give up, no matter what. You might just be a better fighter." Knight kicked his horse to a gallop. "Come on. Let's see if Hannigan has any miracle to pull out of his sleeve."

Knight joined the others. Lattimer and Porkchop seemed not to know they rode toward the main band of Comanches. Nott looked ready to kill. The Lunsford brothers rode to one side, giving Knight the chance to speak with Hannigan.

"You saved us back there, Sam. Ready to do it again? This time we'll face three or four times as many Indians, if the early scouting's right."

"Can Nott count?"

"You don't like him much, do you, Sam? It's mutual. The two of you grate on one another, but I wouldn't trade either of you when the lead starts flying. The fight with the Indian chief showed that."

"He saved me. Or maybe I saved him. It got confusing."

"This can't be, if we're to get out of it alive. Truth is, I'm thinking of leaving those rancher fellas to their fate. Why get all shot up for people we don't know and who wouldn't give us the time of day if we ran into each other in town?"

"You promised to help. You said you'd take their money."

"Always the stickler for doing the honorable thing. Is that something doctors practice or did you grow up that way?" Hannigan gave a curt shake of his head. "Never mind. Just over the hill's one hell of a fight, if the gunfire means anything." Hannigan signaled the others to gather around. By the time they did, his words were almost drowned out by the rapid reports echoing to them.

"Here's the rub, boys. We don't have much in the way of ammo and there's no telling how many redskins we face. So we won't go charging in, not like Sam here did before. What we do is get on top of this ridge and find as many Indians as possible to take potshots at."

"Good idea, Hannigan." Nott stood in his

stirrups. "With all the shootin' goin' on, they won't know we're cuttin' 'em down until it's too late. Let's get to it!"

"Whoa, slow down. Who's the best shot? We only have a couple rifles able to knock the Indians off their horses at that distance."

"It'd be Doc. He's the best shot." Ben Lunsford thrust out his jaw belligerently, daring the others to contradict him.

"I'm not —" Knight was cut off when Hannigan tossed him a rifle.

"I've seen you hunting. You don't miss. Give him that box of ammunition, Lattimer."

"I'm a better shot," Lattimer protested. "I can take the eye out of a squirrel at a hundred yards."

"Good thing we're not huntin' squirrel. We don't need blind rodents runnin' around. Give him the ammo." Hannigan rapidly sketched out how the attack would go. When he finished, he turned back to Knight. "You have to take a half dozen or more out of commission before we can attack. If the ranch house is in danger of bein' set on fire, we have to go in quicklike. Otherwise, it's up to you, Sam."

"I'll do what's necessary." He stared at Seth and saw how the youngster studied him. He had given a fine speech about courage and honor. Now he had to demonstrate it. If he gave in to his urges and galloped away, Seth Lunsford would remember that until his dying day. Even worse, he might be scalped and dead before the sun set.

Dismounting and hiking to the top of the hill felt like mounting the gallows to be hanged. Knight dropped to his belly, opened the box of shells, and began loading the magazine until it wouldn't take another round. Wiggling forward, he slipped over the crest and studied the ranch house and the dangers there. Indians galloped around the house, occasionally firing into the building. They whooped and hollered to frighten the occupants. Knight didn't know how well it worked on the rancher and whoever remained of his cowboys, but it scared him spitless. No matter what Hannigan claimed, the instant he squeezed off a shot, the Indians would know they weren't being fired on by anyone inside the house.

He hesitated, trying to count the attacking Indians. After a dizzying minute, he gave up. More than thirty, that was for sure. Realizing Hannigan wouldn't launch his attack until that number had been reduced by a few, Knight put the front sight bead on an Indian and swung the rifle to take the motion into account. He fired. Nothing happened. The report sounded and the rifle kicked back against his shoulder, but nothing happened. And then the Indian he had targeted fell from his horse.

Knight bit his lip. He had forgotten the time it took for the bullet to cover the distance between him and his victim. As Hannigan had predicted, the Comanches rode past their fallen warrior. Knight fired again. A second rider flopped to the ground. This one was only winged and climbed to his feet, pointing toward the hill where Knight fired. Another shot ended that threat.

He wounded two more and then his luck ran out. Or his marksmanship suffered because he started thinking about the lives he took with every shot. Enough Comanches to overwhelm him started in his direction. Hannigan attacked then.

Firing slowly, Knight took out two more Comanches, but from the corner of his eye he saw Seth fling up his hands and tumble from the saddle. He hit the ground and lay still.

"No! You killers!" Knight got to his feet, snugged the rifle against his shoulder and fired like a machine. When the rifle came up empty, he tossed it to the ground and faced a warrior riding down fast on him.

He slapped leather, took the Colt in hand, drew and fired in a smooth motion. His aim was deadly. The bullet hit the brave in the middle of the chest. As he slumped forward, he exposed himself to Knight's second shot. This took the Comanche down.

Knight fired wildly into the seething battle below. As far as he could tell, he hit nothing else. He started to run down to join the fray, then good sense took control of his emotions. He took the time to load the last of the cartridges into the rifle and put in the last loaded cylinder in the six-shooter. Only then did he rush down to where Seth lay sprawled on the ground.

Astride the fallen youth to protect him, he kept two Indians from attacking. Then his rifle came up empty again. He slid his revolver from its holster, but he had to look around for someone to shoot. It took a second to realize the pressure in his ears came from sudden silence. No one fired. The distant thunder of receding hooves told the story.

The Comanches had been driven off.

He dropped to his knees and pressed his fingertips into Seth's throat. The pulse was strong. Eyelids fluttered, and Seth looked up. His eyes were glazed over but words formed easily. "I knew you'd keep me alive, Doc."

"You've been shot. A couple bullets are lodged in your chest."

"Get your medical bag and dig the lead out. You can do it. You can . . ." The youngster's voice trailed off. Horrified, Knight thought Seth had died, then realized that the youngster had lost consciousness.

"Doc!" Ben said as he rode up, reined to a skidding halt, and swung down from the saddle. "Is he —"

"He's passed out. I have to operate. Ben, get my bag."

"Seth'll be all right, won't he, Doc?"

"My bag. Now!"

He saw that Nott hobbled on a wounded leg. Lattimer sat on the ground, bent double and rocking back and forth. He looked up when he felt Knight's eyes on him.

"I'm next. Got gut shot. Hurry and get the boy fixed up so's you can get to me." Lattimer bent over again, always moving as if he could squeeze the bullet out of himself.

Porkchop and Hannigan stood at the foot of the steps leading into the ranch house, speaking with the rancher and one of the cowboys. Knight ignored them and ripped away Seth's vest and shirt. Using fabric from the shirt, he pressed hard on the worst of the wounds to stanch the bleeding until Ben returned with the medical bag.

When he did, Knight ignored simple surgical procedure and launched into cutting out the bullet. Antiseptic had been ignored, but he wanted the lead out before worrying about infection. After a few moments of frantic effort, he worked the bullet free from Seth's body.

The second slug hadn't penetrated too deeply. Knight plucked it out with his fingers. Only then did he hunt for antiseptic.

He didn't have any.

"I need —" He looked up. The ranch hand held a bottle of whiskey. Knight sprang to his feet and with a quick grab he snatched the bottle from the man. He poured a generous amount on Seth's wounds, then dribbled some into his open mouth. It was a good sign that Seth gagged and protested at the liquor's bite. He wasn't much of a drinker, or so Knight thought from the bragging the youngster had done. When a couple ounces drained down his gullet, Seth murmured and relaxed.

"How is he, Doc? He looks mighty pale."

"I'll drink to his recovery, Ben." Knight upended the bottle and knocked back a couple ounces of the fiery potion. He gagged, then took another drink before passing the bottle. "Help me get him into the house. Is there a blanket where we can lay him?"

"I'll see to it," the cowboy said. He started to ask for the bottle back, then thought better of it and ran for the house.

By the time they had carried Seth up the steps, a crude bed had been laid out for him in the parlor. Knight made sure he was resting easy, then said to his brother, "Watch over him. If he starts to thrash around, fetch me. I'll be looking after the others. Lattimer looked to be in a bad way."

"Thanks, Doc. I don't know how to repay you for savin' Seth like this."

He nodded, hefted the bottle with the few drops of whiskey sloshing in it, and headed out to look after Henry Lattimer.

Lattimer sucked down all the whiskey and let Knight stretch him out flat on the ground in spite of the pain.

"You're not in as bad a shape as it feels," Knight said. "One bullet grazed you. That's causing most of the bleeding. The other slug hit you in the diaphragm but didn't go too deep. You're going to feel a whale of a lot of pain if you try riding the next few days, but there's nothing that'll kill you."

"I just feel like I wanna be dead." Lattimer groaned and tried to curl up. Knight kept him flat.

"So we didn't lose anybody?" Milo Hannigan towered above Knight and Lattimer. "That's good."

"Seth and Lattimer are the worst. We gave better than we got."

"You deserve another medal, Sam. That's if I gave out medals. And I don't."

"Are there any wounded among the rancher and his men?"

"Nothing they can't take care of themselves." Hannigan looked around and shook his head. "We were lucky not to get our damn fool heads blown off. You killing their war chief kept us from getting shot up worse than we were, but they'll elect a new one and come back. The Comanche are known for carryin' grudges."

"I never heard that, but Pine Knob avoided the worst of the Comanche attacks when I was growing up. The Indians ranged farther south and west." Knight closed his medical kit and got to his feet. Every joint ached and his eyes blurred for a moment until he rubbed them. "I need a dozen hours of sleep."

"Do that and we all might get our scalps lifted. I sent Nott out after one band of Indians to find what they're up to. I'm after another. You have to track the third. I'm letting Ben stay with his brother and help out the rancher, if the Comanche come back quicker'n I think."

"I'm not much of a scout."

"But you've become a marksman. You might be a better shot than me, and that's saying something. Practice getting your iron out of the holster fast and you can be a real terror on the frontier, the best gunfighter around." Milo Hannigan smiled crookedly. "But you'd have to work at it to get better'n me."

"I'm no gunman." Knight rubbed his eyes again. "I can't even focus right now from shock at . . . at all this." He made a sweeping gesture to take in the half dozen dead Indians.

"Get on the trail. If you haven't found anything in a day, come on back. We'll regroup and make sure the rancher pays us so we can move on."

"Lattimer will take a few days to get into shape to ride. I'm not sure how long it will take Seth to get on his feet."

Hannigan didn't say anything more. He spun and went to strip the Indian bodies of any usable weapons and ammo. Knight watched and wondered when Hannigan picked up bows and arrows. They had gone through most of their ammunition. It might be necessary to fire arrows at any new war parties attacking.

In spite of his exhaustion, both physical and emotional, Knight secured his kit to his horse and stepped up. From his ghoulish thievery, Hannigan pointed east, then gestured for Knight to get on the trail. Every jolting step his horse took rattled Knight's teeth until he got into the rhythm. Then he conducted a quick inventory of his weapons. He had a rifle with a full magazine. His Colt Navy was loaded, but the spare cylinders were spent. Six rounds plus whatever rounds he had in the rifle. Hardly enough to hold off a real attack, but that wasn't what Hannigan wanted from him.

"Scouting," he muttered as he rode. "That's all. No shooting."

He rode to a rise a half mile from the ranch house and looked back. From there, everything seemed peaceful. Hannigan had dragged the dead bodies out of sight. The arrows stuck in the house walls and the windows shot out by Comanche bullets were invisible from a distance. He slowly surveyed the land around him. Rolling hills and heavy forest blotted out much of the territory, but he saw evidence of where the Indians had fled. A dead horse a ways to the east gave mute testimony to the deadly attack and the pell-mell retreat.

Making sure his rifle slipped freely in the saddle scabbard, he rode down the hillside to where the dead horse drew flies. Some scavengers had already picked at its bones. No sign of its rider remained, but tracks from several horses led directly to a wooded area farther east. Riding this way made him uneasy. It felt as if he erased the distance between him and Gerald Donnelly, him and Captain Norwood. Pine Knob was his past. He had no idea what lay in his future, but it had nothing to do with East Texas or un-faithful Victoria.

He argued with himself over following the trail. What he had learned so far amounted to nothing useful, but riding into an ambush doomed him and kept any real information from getting back to Milo Hannigan.

He walked his horse slowly. Every sense strained so he wouldn't fall easily into a trap. The soft wind blew cool and humid, a touch of fall in the air. Leaves whispered and in the distance a cattle egret let out a mournful call. He looked up. The few clouds in the sky occasionally outlined a turkey vulture. Nothing disturbed the peace. That struck him as odd — especially after the passage of a retreating Comanche war party — unless he'd followed the wrong trail.

Lungs expanding, he sucked in a deep breath. Nothing unusual carried on the wind. Whatever lay upwind didn't threaten him, not that he could tell. He continued to walk forward and entered the woods. Quiet descended around him. Only normal forest sounds continued until he had gone a half mile. He drew rein when he heard horses ahead. Knight started to reverse course and get away from what he suspected were the Comanches. He froze when he saw a rider behind him fade into shadows. Without being aware, he had been followed through the woods.

"Why don't you get your hands up, mister? I got a rifle trained on you."

The demand came from a thicket not far from the game trail he had been following. Since the demand had come in English, with a Yankee tang to it, he knew the Comanches hadn't gotten the drop on him. Without doubt, they would have shot him from ambush, not given him a chance to surrender.

"I'm looking for a war party that attacked a ranch a few miles away. There's no call for you to point a gun at me."

"I'm not so sure of that, Dr. Samuel

Knight." The hidden voice belonged to Private Reilly, Knight realized. "You've gotten me into so much trouble that my feet 'bout wore off with extra guard duty. Takin' you back's gonna win me a medal."

"More likely, Captain Norwood won't even tell you that you did good."

"You know him 'bout as much as I do, sir. Not havin' him on my neck all the time's good enough. Swing around and ride slow in the direction you were goin'."

"I am hunting for Comanches. A big party of them. Let me report back that —"

"We saw a passel of Indians ridin' hell-bent for leather to the north. Wasn't important, not when the corporal and me were sent to find you. I can't believe you just rode up and let me capture you."

"I've done what I can for you, Private. I think you might have let me sneak off before. Do it again."

"That's not so. I got careless."

"You're lying, Reilly. You know I don't deserve to be hanged, and that's why you let me go."

"You escaped, damn it. Anything else and the captain would have me in front of a firing squad. Now keep ridin'. Try to get away and I'll shoot, and it don't matter if I shoot you in the back. The captain gave orders."

"Dead or alive. Yes, sir, that's what he said." The corporal who partnered with Reilly stepped out of some brush on the other side of the trail, his carbine trained on Knight.

Caught in a crossfire, he stood no chance to escape now.

Knight's brain seized up. Arguments that might have gotten him free refused to surface. Too much had happened for him to be alert and able to react.

In that instant, he experienced something that he had never felt before. Giving up seemed like a decent alternative to fighting. Not once during the time spent in the Union prison camp had he considered giving up. Now? Now he did because his entire life had been twisted inside out. His home was gone. His wife was unfaithful. He was a criminal, wanted by both the marshal in the town where he had grown up and the military commander of the region.

Giving up was so easy.

"Climb on down. Keep them hands graspin' a piece of the sky." The corporal moved around to keep his rifle on Knight as he obeyed.

"He said he was lookin' for Comanches and that a ranch had been attacked." Reilly stood next to the corporal.

"He'd say whatever it takes to keep from gettin' arrested and taken back to camp. Get them shackles from my saddlebags, Reilly, and put them on our prisoner."

The private obeyed the order. He fished in the saddlebags of a horse tethered nearby and came out with two sets of shackles, one for Knight's wrists and the other to secure his ankles. The heavy iron links clanked as he returned with them, draped over his left forearm to keep the rifle ready for use.

"You tellin' the truth about them Indians?" Reilly stopped a few feet away so the corporal kept a clear line of fire.

"I am. The rancher needs help."

"So you gave it to him? Is that it? What a good Samaritan," scoffed the corporal. "We haven't seen so much as a feather off any Indian. He's lyin', Reilly. You fell for his line once. I'm orderin' you to get them cuffs on him. Now, Reilly, now!"

The private shrugged and stepped forward.

He hesitated and looked up. His mouth opened, then his head snapped back. A bullet tore through his forehead and knocked him flat on his back.

Knight stared at the body, stunned. He started to tell the corporal he had nothing to do with the killing when a second shot rang out. The other soldier jerked. His finger tightened on the trigger, but the shot went high. A final shot lifted the corporal from his feet and dropped him to the ground next to Private Reilly.

Knight turned and faced a man gripping a six-shooter. The still-smoking pistol swung about and centered on him.

CHAPTER 13

Knight dropped to his knees and checked Private Reilly. The man had died instantly from the bullet through his head. The corporal was equally as dead. Knight looked up as the killer strode forward, his pistol leveled.

"No need to see if they're dead. I don't miss."

The gun lifted so Knight looked down the barrel to the man clutching it. If Knight had seen the man walking along the street, he would have pegged him as a dandy, a ne'er-do-well out for a night on the town. As his fancy jade green brocade jacket flapped in the breeze, a second pistol was revealed in another shoulder holster. The man was a walking arsenal.

"Don't let the second six-gun fool you. I can whip that one out as fast as I can this one." He made a few quick moves, replaced the pistol in his right hand under his left armpit, then drew the iron under his right arm with his left hand. He did a border shift, tossing the revolver to his right hand in a display of extraordinary dexterity.

That left Knight with no doubt that he faced a gunslinger of great skill. "Why'd you kill them?"

"I couldn't have them taking you back. No, sir. I —"

The whistle of an arrow cut off his words. From the deep woods came another arrow to join the first in the dandy's right arm. Both arrows protruding from flesh, he dropped his pistol and half turned. Knight threw himself forward awkwardly, his arms wrapping around the man's knees to bring him down, saving the stranger's life. A dozen arrows whined through the air where his head and body had been an instant earlier.

"Comanches," Knight said. "I thought I trailed them into these woods. The two soldiers must have been here already."

The gunman's face was pale with pain. "Indians? They're after you, too?"

"I'm after them. We ran them off from an attack on a nearby ranch." Knight rolled over, pulled his rifle close, and ended up prone, studying the shadows dancing about. He squeezed off a shot and was rewarded with a grunt of pain.

"You've got better eyes than me. Where are they?"

"I can't see them. They had to be in those bushes yonder to put two arrows in your arm like they did." Knight shot again and again found human flesh. A brave half stood and toppled over a bush.

"How many are there?" The dandy moaned as he grasped both arrows in a powerful grip and began pulling with a slow, deliberate strength. As they came free, the bloody arrowheads showed how deeply the arrows had sunk into his arm. He threw them aside.

"No way of telling. There were four bands. We shot up one, the other three hightailed it. As many as forty braves might be out there."

"Not so many," the man declared with more confidence than Knight could muster. "They'd have rushed us if they saw how badly they outnumbered us. And they must have been watching."

"There might be more soldiers around," Knight said, a cold lump in the pit of his stomach.

"The shots would draw them like flies to honey. Whatever we face is out there and no more." The man rolled behind the corporal's body and peered over the top.

Knight fired twice more, the shots whining off into the forest. He heard one smash into a tree trunk. The other might have gone all the way back to the ranch house for all he knew.

"You saved my life," the man said. "Knocking me down got me out of the line of fire."

"We're even, then. You saved me from the soldiers."

"They were quite intent on haulin' you back to their camp. I heard that much. What've you done to merit such anger on their part? On the part of . . . who was it? Captain Norwood?"

"It's a misunderstanding."

The man chuckled. "Isn't it always that? Time to see what we're up against." He gathered his feet under him, stood, and drew his pistol with his left hand. With a deliberate stride he went directly toward the clump of bushes where the Indians had hidden.

"Wait!" Knight cursed under his breath, thinking the man had a few screws loose in his head to make an attack like that, standing upright and walking into the Indians as if he had nary a care in the world.

Knight rolled a couple times and ended

up resting his rifle on a rotten log. The first movement he saw in the brush where he had already hit two and the man had shot one Indian drew his fire. With methodical skill, he shot at anything that held even a faint human silhouette.

The man advanced and triggered off six rounds. He did the switch, clumsy now, got out his second pistol, did a border shift tossing the gun from his weak right hand to his left and shot twice more until his gun came up empty.

Knight thought that was the end of it. From some hideout the man produced another pistol and kept walking and firing. When the hammer fell on a spent chamber, he stopped. The gun disappeared as if he was a magician. A knife popped into his left hand an instant before he plunged into the brush.

The sounds of a struggle got Knight moving. He sprinted to the spot, saw an advancing Comanche and dropped him. That exhausted the magazine in his rifle. With a speed he hadn't known he possessed, he drew his Colt Navy and fanned off the rounds remaining. One hit the Indian grappling with the man. The Indian winced, grabbed for his thigh and gave all the opening necessary for the knife to rake across his throat. Wounded in leg and throat, the brave collapsed. He gurgled a few times as he drowned in his own blood, then died.

"We make a mighty good team, Dr. Samuel Knight." The dandy wiped off his blade in the grass.

Knight didn't see where it returned to a sheath. "How'd you know my name?"

"I listened a spell while the two blue bellies were goading you into doing something stupid."

"Goading?"

"The one with the stripes, the corporal, wanted you to go for your six-shooter in the worst way so he could cut you down. The private, now, he was actually looking like he would let you go. From what you said, he'd done that before, hadn't he?"

Knight didn't answer. He checked the bodies for ammunition and found nothing. These braves hunted with bow and arrow, not rifles, meaning he was in jeopardy. Any new gunfight would force him to throw rocks.

The man went on when Knight didn't answer. "Yes, that's the way I see it, and he would hang right alongside you. Two for the price of one. That's the way Captain Norwood would see it."

"You know him? Norwood?"

"Can't say I do, but aren't all the bluecoat officers the same? Give them a match, and they burn Atlanta."

Knight started back to where the two soldiers lay. They had rifles and ammo. He found his way blocked when the man rushed around and stood in front of him.

"What's got you in such a hurry? Can it be those two soldiers' rifles? You're out of ammo, aren't you?"

"So are you. You wouldn't have used your knife like that if you'd had any ammunition."

"You're a sharp gent, aren't you? You think things through." He held out his hand to push Knight back, only he missed, stumbled, and fell to his knees. He turned his face up and tried to speak. A slight twist from the waist caused him to crumple to the forest floor.

Knight bent and checked for a pulse. *Thready.* The man's complexion had turned pale, whether from lack of blood or shock hardly mattered. Fingers clutching the thick green coat's fabric on either shoulder, Knight heaved and began sliding the man along through the pine needles and detritus.

He let him drop when he got to where Reilly had hobbled the soldiers' horses. He didn't find any ammo for his six-shooter, but they had plenty for his rifle. Stealing the US Army–issue rifle proved to be the best theft he had made. Torn between priorities, he looked back at the dandy, then reloaded his rifle and both the dead soldiers' carbines before going to the wounded man. Peeling back the blood-soaked fabric revealed the full extent of the man's wounds.

Knight got his medical bag and started to work. Both arrows had gone clean through his arm and into his body. The wounds in his torso hadn't been apparent at first. When the man yanked out the arrows, he let otherwise-plugged blood flow freely. Knight moved the man's head to one side and pinched his nostrils, forcing him to gasp through his mouth. Not seeing any pink foam heartened him. Neither arrow had pierced a lung.

He found where the man had sheathed his knife at the small of his back. A quick move drew it. Knight went to Reilly's body and said softly, "They won't give you any more extra sentry duty for being out of uniform. Not now. Know your shirt's going for a good cause." He cut long, inch-wide strips for his makeshift bandages.

Returning to his patient, he poured the gunpowder from a Sharps cartridge into each wound and ignited it. The hiss caused him to look away, and the smell of burned flesh made his nose wrinkle. He ran his finger around each of the holes. Both had been sealed. Only a little more to go and he would have done all he could for his patient.

He rolled the dandy onto his side to press a patch down on the two cauterized wounds. When he thrashed around, Knight considered clubbing him to make him quiet, but the man settled down when the bandage circled his chest. Knight tightened it the best he could and tied it off with a surgeon's knot. If he had been in one of the Confederate field hospitals and this man had come in with his wounds, Knight would have sent him back to his unit when he regained consciousness. The loss of blood and shock were the only worrisome things. The injuries themselves were minor compared to a bullet wound.

Knight used the corporal's wool jacket to wipe as much blood from his hands as he considered the idea of leaving the dandy where he was but finally discarded it. Knight had no idea if the man would regain consciousness. If so, he could fend for himself. If he didn't, he needed water and whatever food could be forced down his gullet.

A new dilemma presented itself. If he

didn't leave the man, how did he get him back to the ranch house? The best he could do was throw him belly down over a saddle, but that was a treacherous way to travel. The wounds might begin to bleed again unless they were better tended.

Another problem nagged Knight. He didn't owe either soldier anything. They had wanted to take him back to Pine Knob to be hanged or put in front of a firing squad. Those were the best options facing him. He would never let himself be locked up again, as he had been in Elmira. *Ever.* Better to die than be penned up like an animal. All that had gotten him through that ordeal was the knowledge that Victoria waited for him at home. Now he had neither home nor loving wife.

Other than his hands, he had nothing to dig with. The next best thing was hardly a smart course of action, but he took it anyway. He pulled both men into a pile in a nearby clearing, then piled dried limbs and grass around the bodies until the kindling reached shoulder high. Then he set fire to the pyre. A huge roar forced him to step away as the wood caught. The greasy black smoke rising from the flames told him that the men were consigned properly to what he had read once about a Viking warrior's funeral. Or maybe it was more like an Indian funeral. More than once, he had seen the elevated platforms where intense fire had left a charred body behind. Either way kept them from having their bones picked by buzzards and carrion eaters.

"Come on," he said to the barely aware wounded man. "Can you ride?"

The dandy collapsed in his arms. Taking that to mean no, Knight heaved him up over the McClellan saddle of Reilly's horse and led the corporal's along until he found his own. The wounded man had ridden something, but listening failed to reveal a whinny for Knight to find it. Still, a horse was a valuable commodity. Being accused of stealing yet another horse rankled him, so he started a methodical search in the woods, trying to figure how far the man had walked to sneak up on the soldiers. After riding much longer than he anticipated, he finally heard a horse protesting loudly.

He turned toward the sound, then froze. His horse danced about. Knight tried to keep it silent and still. Ahead two braves examined a saddled horse. From the fancy silver conchas decorating the saddle, he knew whose horse it was. The dandy's hat and belt were adorned with similar silver-work. As quietly as possible he drew a rifle but did not cock it, fearing the sound would be heard by the sharp-eared Comanches.

Optimism soared when the two Indians began shoving each other. There wasn't any need to understand their language. They fought over the horse. Maybe one had found it and the other thought he, as a superior, deserved it. What the war paint smeared on their faces meant told him nothing, but he had heard it indicated one's standing within the tribe. The one with several white and yellow grease slashes on his cheek pounded on his chest and gestured grandly, making Knight figure he was of higher rank.

The other brave dived, arms circling his opponent's shoulders and pinning his arms to his sides. They rolled over and over on the ground until one kicked free and came up with a knife in his hand. The other circled warily. Knight found himself rooting for the one without a knife because the match seemed unfair. The situation changed in the blink of an eye. The one with the knife attacked, only to have his wrist bent around. He found his own knife buried in his gut.

The winner savagely turned the blade, completing the coup de grâce. He yanked his opponent's knife free and held the bloody blade high over his head. As he gave a whoop, he turned and saw Knight.

The doctor reacted rather than thought. The carbine came to his shoulder, and he levered a round into the chamber and drew back on the trigger in a single motion. The heavy rifle bucked against him, almost taking him out of the saddle. He worked to get control of his horse then saw that his marksmanship continued to be superb. The bullet had caught the Comanche warrior in the middle of his chest. He hadn't died instantly, but by the time Knight rode over, there was no need for his doctoring skills.

He replaced the rifle in its sheath, snared the reins of the dandy's horse, and secured them to his saddlebags. Not content, he started hunting for the Indians' horses. He found them tied to a tree not twenty yards away. He fastened their hackamores behind the other two riderless horses, then made sure his patient was securely tied down over the saddle. With five horses — and a patient — more than he had come with, Knight wheeled around and headed back for the ranch.

The going proved dicey, keeping the horses from trying to rear or jerk free, but if he rode slowly enough everything went smooth. As he topped the rise a quarter mile from the house, he drew rein and let out a low, heartfelt moan of despair. He hadn't found the main band of Comanches because they had gathered to attack the ranch once more.

Hannigan and the others were inside with the rancher. Rifle barrels stuck out from broken windows like spines on a porcupine. But Knight saw something those inside could not. An Indian prepared a kettle of pitch. He dipped his arrow in it, lit it, and let fly in a high arc. Wind caught the arrow and blew it away from the roof, but the brave already worked to prepare his next fire arrow. If he landed enough flaming arrows on the ranch roof, those inside would either be burned up or forced outside into the ring of Comanche braves. Either way meant their deaths.

CHAPTER 14

The Comanches circling the house, whooping and hollering, caused more panic than the lone brave shooting fire arrows toward the roof. Knight knew this was not something the Indians had concocted on the spur of the moment. It was a practiced, well-thought-out, deadly attack.

He pulled out two rifles, made sure he had loaded magazines in both, secured the horses, and settled down for serious shooting. Everyone told him he was a crack shot. It had never entered his mind, but he was beginning to think they might be right. His heart beat slowly, regularly, making it easier to aim. Whatever nerves he had were all soothed and quiet as he drew his finger back smoothly on the trigger. The rifle bucked. He missed the Comanche brave but hit the pitch pot and sent it skittering away.

For a moment, the Indian looked about, confused at the sudden turn of events. As he spun to face where Knight stretched out on the hill, a second shot drilled him in the leg. The impact knocked the leg out from under him and made him fall face forward. In the back of his mind Knight knew he had hit the femur. As the brave struggled to sit up, another shot ended his life.

Only then did Knight turn his attention to the Indians circling the house. Moving targets at this range proved more difficult to hit, so he shifted from aiming at the riders to taking out their horses. Killing the horses galled him, but human lives hung in the balance. Ben Lunsford and his sorely wounded brother were in the house. For all Knight knew the rest of Hannigan's men were, too.

He took down three horses before the Comanches realized they had two threats to deal with. Again, they acted as if they had faced similar situations. A quarter of the riders split off from the main attack and charged uphill toward Knight. His coolness surprised him. His accuracy devastated the attack. Again he aimed for the horses rather than the hunched-over riders, heads by their horses' necks to present as small a target as possible. Four horses stumbled and fell.

Knight put aside the two empty rifles and took up a third. He had Comanche warriors as targets. Somehow, this steadied his hand even more and let him get off one killing shot after another. Only one Indian remained when the rifle came up empty. The Comanche screeched and waved a knife high above his head as he charged.

Knight drew his Colt Navy and aimed it. The Indian skidded to a halt, stared wide-eyed at him, then turned and ran. Knight never cocked the gun or pulled the trigger. He knew the gun was empty. Two quick steps took him to the dandy draped over the saddle. Patting the man down for more weapons produced nothing but a pair of brass knuckles. They would be useless in the kind of fight offered by the Indians. Knight rummaged in saddlebags for the man's two spare six-shooters and returned to his spot on the hill, ready to add some lead to that still flying below.

Such a distance with a handgun defied the odds. He began firing, not so much hoping to hit anything as to add to the confusion. One Indian had run off due to a bluff. This was a more emphatic one.

It worked, too. Whether the Indians had taken enough punishment from those inside the house or thought they faced an entire army attacking from the rear didn't matter. They galloped away, leaving the dust to settle on their dead.

"Come on. Let's see if anyone's alive." Knight tried not to imagine what he would find in the house. Better to deal only with reality than conjure up death and destruction where none might exist.

He led his team of horses down the hill, going slow to give Hannigan or whoever remained inside the house a chance to identify him. When no bullet ripped toward him, he figured his approach worked. Either that or they had run out of ammunition. Almost to the house, he stopped to stamp out bits of tar that had dripped from an arrow to the ground and threatened to ignite a patch of weeds.

"Hello! I need some help. I have a wounded man."

Milo Hannigan came onto the porch, limping. He clutched a rifle in one hand and used the other to support himself against the railing. "You keep coming back like a bad penny. Every time you turn up, you're bringing another surprise. Who's that?"

"Don't rightly know, but he saved me from getting captured by two soldiers from Pine Knob."

"Do tell." Hannigan bellowed for help.

Sounds like rats scurrying turned into boots thudding on wood planking. Ben

Lunsford came out, six-shooter in his hand. Behind him stood Johnny Nott, covered in blood.

From a quick study, Knight decided none of that belonged to Nott. "How'd the fight go this time?" He didn't want to hear the casualties but asked anyway.

"The rancher's in bad shape. His future son-in-law is running things. Two of the cowboys?" Hannigan shook his head. "Porkchop caught one in his shoulder, but Ben fixed him up. No change in Lattimer or Seth." With some pain he thrust out his leg. "I stopped an arrow when they first attacked. Snuck up and fired from hiding."

"This job's costin' more'n anybody figgered," Porkchop said, collapsing into a chair behind Hannigan on the porch. "Worst part is, them Injuns stole all the cattle. I asked. The rancher only had a couple pigs. They're gone and all et up by now. Damned redskins." He coughed up some blood and spat.

"We going to get paid? The money, at least?" That hardly mattered to Knight but he had to ask. He wasn't sure why.

"We took what money he had. How do you want your ten dollars? In greenbacks or two-bit pieces?"

"I had my mouth all set to wrap around a

220

steak," Ben Lunsford said. "You need help with him, Doc?"

"I could use it." He began untying his patient. It took most of his strength to keep the dandy from slipping off and landing in a pile on the ground.

"The groom-to-be has sent for the army," Hannigan said. "One of the hands went off before the Comanches hit us again." He saw Knight's reaction. "It was blue bellies that caught you, wasn't it?"

"The dandy gunned them down and saved me from being dragged back in front of Captain Norwood. The soldiers recognized me."

"We got to ride before they come to fight off the Indians," Hannigan said. "We're in no shape to ride, but those spare horses you got will help since most of ours were stolen." He spat disgustedly. "Thievin' redskins."

"I'll see to Seth and the others. Are they inside?"

"Go on, Sam. There's plenty of tack to saddle up these nags you brought." Hannigan went to where the dandy lay. "What are we going to do with him?"

"Leave him." Knight remembered how easily he had gunned down the two soldiers, not knowing who he saved or anything about the situation with the Indians on the warpath. "He never told me his name."

"Alton." The stranger's voice was no more than a husky whisper.

"What's that?" Hannigan knelt and gripped the fancy lapels and lifted.

"My name's Hector Alton. You can't leave me. Not if the army's coming. I gunned down two blue bellies to save Knight."

"That so?" Hannigan looked up.

Knight only nodded. Something churned in his gut that told him it was wrong having anything to do with this man — with Hector Alton. Before he put his finger on it, Ben Lunsford called to him from the house. He abandoned Alton to Hannigan's custody and went inside, expecting the worst. To his surprise, Seth sat up, had color in his face, and grinned in recognition.

"Doc. You made it back in one piece."

"Barely. Let me check your bandages. We're going to hit the trail mighty soon."

"There's nothing keepin' us here," Ben Lunsford said. "The rancher died. All that one talks about is marryin' the girl and ownin' this place." He leaned over and whispered confidentially, "I don't think he loves her. He just wants the ranch."

"What there is left of it. Milo said all the cattle have been run off. Porkchop complained about no pigs. For defending them, all we got is ten dollars apiece."

"You know, Doc, you and the rancher are — were — are about the same size. Why don't you take some of his clothes as payment? That cowhand of his ain't goin' to wear his boss's clothes."

"Why not?"

"Because," Ben said, "his future wife would be reminded of her pa. That's not a wedding night fit for man nor beast."

"Get Seth out and help Milo get the horses ready." Knight heaved a sigh. "Looks like we have a new recruit by the name of Hector Alton."

"Alton?" Ben Lunsford scowled. "I've heard that name. Leastways, I think I have. Maybe the face will ring a bell."

"You watch your back. Just like you do with Johnny." Knight felt the jaws of a vise closing around him. He had to run because the cavalry had been called, and he didn't trust the men he rode with. His life had gone downhill fast after returning home.

"I gotcha." Ben Lunsford helped Seth to his feet and out the door.

Knight prowled through the house, opening drawers and feeling like he was a grave robber. In a way he was, but he told himself the rancher owed them for risking their lives. It wasn't their fault there had been so

223

many Comanches. It wasn't their fault, either, that the rancher had caught an arrow that took his life.

He made his way to the wardrobe in the bedroom. More than half was filled with women's clothing. Pushing that aside, he came to the rancher's duds. He took out a black Sunday-go-to-meeting suit. It was too formal for the trail but nothing else in the wardrobe was much better than the tatters he wore. Looking like an undertaker was the least of his worries, but best of all in the bottom of the cabinet stood a pair of boots. He kicked off his with holes worn through the soles and patched with old newspaper and tried on the rancher's boots.

A few steps convinced him they were a mite small but better than what he had worn since leaving New York. He rooted around a little more, then came upon the real find. A box with powder, slugs, percussion caps and wadding perfect for his Colt Navy. That weighed down his left pocket while he settled the holster and six-gun on his right hip. Facing a full-length mirror, he struck a pose. He looked downright prosperous. Then he squared off with his image, pulled back the black coattail and drew as fast as he could.

"That's mighty impressive."

He stepped to one side and saw Hannigan's reflection in the mirror.

"You practice more and you'll be the second fastest gunman in all of Texas."

"Second?"

"You'll never best me, Sam. Don't forget that. Get your ass out of here. We're ready to ride." Hannigan turned to leave, then said, over his shoulder, "That recruit you brought in . . . Hector Alton. He's going to work out just fine. He's got the right attitude, especially about the Federals and their carpetbagging ways."

Knight followed Hannigan and had gotten to the hallway when a gunshot rang out. Running, he burst onto the porch. Hector Alton stood propped against a railing, his six-gun held in his left hand. A cowboy lay dead on the porch.

"What happened?" Knight had to ask since Hannigan didn't. "Why'd you shoot him?"

"This is the kid who was goin' to marry the boss's daughter," Ben Lunsford said. "He was a snake but not dumb enough to throw down on any of us, not after we saved his worthless hide the way we did."

"He tried to stop us from leaving," Alton said, tucking his six-gun back under his right arm. "He wanted the army to arrest

us for not doing our job of protecting him."
Alton snorted. "I never agreed to protect
him from anything. Lifting that rifle in my
direction was a mistake."

Porkchop hobbled over and looked at the
body. "He wasn't inclined to pay us. I say,
good riddance. The girl's better off not
havin' to marry him. Which is my horse?"

Knight locked eyes with Alton. The faint
smile on the man's lips showed how much
he had enjoyed taking a life.

"Doc, come on. Mount up. We gotta ride!"
Lunsford said.

Knight silently mounted and followed the
others as they rode west once more, leaving
the carnage behind. He made sure to keep
Johnny Nott in front of him. Him and Hector Alton.

CHAPTER 15

Gerald Donnelly tried not to limp. It was unseemly for the man in charge of Reconstruction in the entire town. While he lacked a title, everyone knew he held the reins of power. No one in Pine Knob so much as sneezed without asking first — and paying for the privilege.

As he made his way down the main street, he passed in front of the bank. He balanced on his cane and touched the brim of his hat to acknowledge the banker, Frederick Fitzsimmons, sitting behind his big desk and looking important. The banker pointedly turned away, giving Donnelly cause to smile. Fitzsimmons had run things before the war, and maybe during, as well. While most of the men were in the CSA, he had taken advantage of the financial problems so many left behind had experienced by foreclosing and taking the deeds to many farms and a few surrounding ranches.

He had no love for Gerald Donnelly. Not when Donnelly told the circuit judge to seize all that property and put it up for sale. More than one prime farm had come his way as a result, much to Fitzsimmons's dismay. The banker had been the richest man in town. A few short months reduced him to just another business owner. Donnelly vowed it wouldn't be long before he took more than all the fine horses and their pasture behind his house from the corrupt banker. Fitzsimmons would be lucky if he didn't get his neck stretched for all the crimes he had committed.

Yes, sir, Reconstruction would put it all right.

Donnelly shot the banker one last sardonic smile, then hobbled on. His foot hurt like a million ants chewed on it. Knight had been expert in slicing the Achilles tendon. The fool of a doctor in town now said nothing could be done. He had tried to stitch up the wound and had let it get infected. Donnelly needed to find a way to get a new doctor in town and drive that one out.

When Dr. Samuel Knight had left, the city fathers had done what they could to replace him. All they had found was a first-year medical student with eyesight so bad the CSA refused to take him. For most things, his near blindness hardly mattered. Let him get his nose down into a wound to see what he stitched up, but Donnelly knew the infirmity had kept the man from doing a proper job.

Either that or he was in cahoots with Knight. That was a distinct possibility. Most of the town opposed Donnelly and were unrepentant rebels.

The whitewashed city hall rose to his left. He leaned against a post on the boardwalk and studied it. The mayor and three members of the town council had offices there, as well as Marshal Ike Putnam, when he wasn't in his tiny jail immediately to the north. The marshal hadn't cooperated with him. Losing his office space gave a subtle hint what else Donnelly could do with the power of Washington behind him. He had a couple men in mind to replace Putnam after he got rid of him. That was taking longer than he'd expected because the marshal was the mayor's brother.

The mayor had to go, too, for real peace to come to Pine Knob. But not today. The next election would be soon enough for the broom to sweep clean. Donnelly would see to that.

He made his way across the dusty street, dodging wagons and horsemen who had no respect for his infirmity. His cane clicked against the wood steps leading up to the city hall's double doors. Inside he heard a scurrying as if rats had taken over the building. His telltale cane alerted everyone in the town hall that their civic adviser was on the way.

"Good morning, Mr. Donnelly." A slight man with sandy hair, glasses and a perpetually frightened look opened the door for him.

"Is Captain Norwood here yet, Eustace?"

"He said he'd be late, sir. Something about losing a scouting party."

"If he's not here in fifteen minutes, ride out to the camp and tell him to get his ass here immediately."

"Uh, yes, sir. I, uh, I'll give him that message."

"Exactly as I told you. Don't weasel out and try to prettify it. He has to know who's in charge here."

"I know who's in charge, Donnelly." Captain Norwood came up from behind, his step surprisingly soft. "While you are in charge of civilian affairs, I am the district military commander. The *only* military commander, I might add. I answer to the War Department only."

"In my office, sir." Donnelly refused to

argue in front of underlings such as Leonard. Further, he knew ears were pressed to door panels around the small rotunda, all eagerly waiting for a fight between him and Norwood. Such gossip would cause tongues to wag for weeks. He would not give them the pleasure of such a fight. Moreover, arguing with Norwood made it seem as if he wasn't in control of everything to do with Pine Knob.

That had to be avoided or he would find the citizens of this sleepy little town taking up arms against him, the very thing he had been sent all the way from Boston to prevent. Any insurrection had to be snuffed out before it gathered fuel for fire that existed because of the war. Only if he failed to keep everyone in line would use of the military be required. And Gerald Donnelly never failed. Ever.

"Allow me." Captain Norwood held the door open. He made a sardonic half bow as Donnelly crowded past and went into what had been the mayor's office before he had appropriated it. The view of the piney woods was the only thing about it that Donnelly liked. He didn't care that the mayor ended up in a room hardly larger than a broom closet. The decisions required to keep Pine Knob a functioning town came from here, not the mayor's desk.

He hobbled around the desk and collapsed into the chair. It creaked under his weight. A new chair was necessary if he intended to keep decent office hours. His cane clicked down on the desk so the tip pointed toward the officer. He doubted Norwood noticed the thin metal tip covering the muzzle of the gun built into the walking stick.

"Captain, you have a wrongheaded idea about how things are decided around here. You do not tend to civilian affairs. I do. Your role is to keep the peace and do as I tell you."

"General Sherman disagrees. I have orders divorcing me from civilian control. With the Indian uprising gathering ferocity, my troopers must patrol farther afield every week to prevent massacres." He made a sour face. "A ranch not twenty miles away has been attacked. Drifters joined the ranch hands to fend off two attacks. With such persistence, the Indians are likely to commit to a third for revenge."

"Have you sent a squad out to support them?" Donnelly saw the answer in the man's face.

"A better use of my men's time is not to tidy up after an attack but to find the

Comanches' camp and deter them there. With force, if necessary, though I prefer to negotiate. Whatever their demands, they might be met and violence forestalled."

"You're a West Point graduate, aren't you?"

"A proud West Pointer, yes. What of it, sir?" Norwood drew himself to full attention. If his knees locked any harder he would faint and topple over — while still at attention.

"Nothing, just making an observation." Donnelly disliked seeking favors from a man he despised, but he lacked manpower to do it himself. Norwood wasn't committing his soldiers to field action, which meant any of several possibilities. They were ill-trained and vulnerable against braves tempered in the fires of a dozen raids. Equipment had yet to arrive. Norwood lacked sufficient officers to sortie. All might be true, but nothing of that mattered. The captain had sufficient manpower to find and bring in Samuel Knight. *That* took precedence.

"You are not inclined to idle speculation, sir. What is the reason you requested my presence this morning?"

"No need to be so stiff and formal, Captain. Please. Sit down."

"I will remain standing."

Such petty disobedience almost made Donnelly say something he would regret. If the officer sat with his trousers so sharply pressed, the pleats might cut into a good chair. Or —

He forced himself to smile and bow his head slightly. "As you wish. What have your scouts reported?"

"Pine Knob is in no danger from the Comanches."

"Have any of your scouts not returned? When you have expected them to do so?"

"West of town two were killed and their bodies burned. From what evidence remained, both were murdered. The fire proved a feeble attempt to hide the nature of the crime."

"West of town? The direction Dr. Samuel Knight rode when he left?"

"There is cause to believe he took part in the deaths of both soldiers. My tracker reported a second man present also participated, though what happened exactly will remain a mystery carried to the graves of my brave men. Since most Comanche attacks have been carried out using bow and arrow because we have so successfully prevented firearms from falling into their hands, we doubt the two were murdered by Indians. Both were shot. Other evidence indicates they were in the process of an arrest, shackles being dropped onto the ground before their horses were stolen."

"What are your plans to bring Knight to justice?"

"He will be captured. Rest assured, sir. When he is returned, he will be tried by a military court for crimes against the government. I expect nothing less than a conviction and death penalty."

Donnelly considered how he felt. Was such justice enough or should he pry Knight free and use the civilian courts to try him when the result would be the same? He needed revenge. By his hand, not this buffoon Norwood. But if Knight and those he rode with now gunned down soldiers with impunity, the chance to try him might evaporate in the first pitched gunfight with Norwood's soldiers.

"Keep me posted on your hunt for him." Donnelly cleared his throat and asked as Norwood left the room, "How many men do you have in the field hunting for him?"

"They all are, sir. As all are on the lookout for Comanches, members of the Knights of the Golden Circle, or those malcontents in the Ku Klux Klan founded by that devil, Nathan Bedford Forrest, or any other person or persons who might cause unrest.

Goodday."

Captain Norwood closed the door behind him. As angry as he remained about being called to account, he did not slam the door.

Donnelly found the controlled click of the lock snapping into place more unsettling. Opponents who ranted and raved had weaknesses to exploit. Norwood relied too much on regulations and orders, doing everything by the book, to be successful finding Knight, but Donnelly knew the soldiers weren't his only chance at bringing the errant doctor to justice. The second man prowling about where Norwood's soldiers had been killed had to be Hector Alton.

The gunfighter must have captured Knight by now. His return would be imminent. Donnelly took out a sheet of paper, ink, and a pen to begin the letter to Circuit Judge Thompson. When Knight was stuffed into a cell in the jail adjacent to the courthouse, he wanted the judge in town in two shakes of a lamb's tail to dispense justice. There would be no dispute over whose prisoner he was.

Donnelly moaned in pain as he shifted in his chair, his crippled foot a constant reminder of what Knight had done.

There would be no dispute whatsoever about who got to hang the son of a bitch.

CHAPTER 16

"They owe us. Why shouldn't we take what's our due?" Milo Hannigan looked around the campfire at his men.

"Ten dollars a head ain't much for what all was done to us," Porkchop said. "We was promised more'n that, anyway. Milo's right. We should swoop down on some o' them other ranchers, cut out a few head of cattle, and then sell them. There's plenty of buyers."

"Even the Indians might buy a cow or two," piped up Hector Alton. All heads turned toward him. "They swap for all kinds of guns. They want horses. Cattle to them is only something other white men want but are willing to pay top dollar for."

Knight stirred uneasily at all this talk of rustling. He felt the pressure of Captain Norwood breathing down his neck, even if there hadn't been any soldiers sighted in the area. If anything, the rancher's future son-in-law had made the call for help and had been ignored before Alton cut him down. That suited Knight just fine, but if the Comanches continued raiding, the army would eventually be forced to stop their depredations. When that happened, if he hadn't put a lot of miles between him and Pine Knob, he was likely going to get caught.

He ran his hand around his neck, as much from chafing due to the tight collar of the rancher's shirt he had taken as worry about a hemp noose dropped and tightened there. "We're better off moving west, as we planned. Sticking around here will only get the law on our trail."

Heads turned in his direction when he spoke. Staying quiet had given the others a chance to vent their anger at getting so little payment for fighting Indians. An opposing view brought out the sharp divisions among them.

"Now, now, Sam," said Hannigan. "We know why you're so all-fired anxious to get out of these parts. The rest of us don't have the cavalry hunting us for crimes and misdemeanors."

Knight looked sharply at Hector Alton. For a man who had murdered two soldiers, he looked innocent enough. He still used a sling on his right arm but had grown stronger over the past week. Knight had seen him practicing a quick draw. Even injured, he was fast. Real fast. Alton switched off between left and right hands and showed almost equal speed. Given that he was right-handed, he would be quicker with his right in a matter of days.

"I didn't sign on to steal cattle." Knight realized how sullen and petty that sounded. Before he could explain more, Hannigan cut him off.

"We're owed. They didn't pay. Most of the local ranchers don't have a problem like that. Any dispute could be settled between themselves or taken to a judge. We have no standing. We're not talking about making this a full-time job. The law might say it's rustling, but I say it's takin' what's ours."

A murmur of agreement went around the campfire. Knight felt deflated when even Ben Lunsford and his brother nodded. They avoided his direct gaze, staring into the crackling fire and watching embers twist into the night sky. If he felt more confident, he would have challenged Hannigan's leadership or at least demanded a vote. If the split had been big enough, the gang would see that and know trouble lay in breaking the law.

"How sure are you the Injuns'd want stolen beeves?" Johnny Nott stared straight at Hector Alton for an answer.

"Can't be for certain sure, but it makes sense, doesn't it? They steal from the white man all the time. They don't care for gold or silver. A pile of greenbacks doesn't mean anything more than a way for their squaws to start a cooking fire. All that's useless to them, but they know we — white men — crave it all. They get a meal or two out of the herd and swap the rest. They pay us in gold or silver for the cattle. Everybody comes out ahead."

"They'll trade those beeves for guns. Ask the farmers and ranchers if they think that's a good idea," Knight said.

"We don't know what they'd trade for. They don't have many rifles. Might be, they get more, they decide to become hunters and give up raiding. A deer's not as inclined to shoot back. We might be contributing to the peace by trading with the Comanches."

Knight knew a snake-oil salesman at work when he heard one. Everything Hector Alton said made sense as long as you didn't put it all together.

"We'll end up with rewards on our heads." That was the last card Knight had to play. He saw how this perked up Alton. The man looked eagerly around the campfire.

"Who all's got a price on their head right now?" Alton scooted closer to the fire and poked it with a branch to get more light. "A desperate bunch like this must have a few dollars of reward offered by the law."

"Not us. Not Seth and me," Ben Lunsford said.

Porkchop looked confused. Lattimer fell silent. Johnny Nott looked defiant. Of them all, Knight suspected the back-shooting Nott was a wanted man.

Milo Hannigan waved it aside as if it meant nothing. "Leave it up to the carpet-baggers and we're all wanted men. They hate Southerners. All the more reason for us to settle accounts on our own without relying on the authorities."

"Then we're decided? All of us? We take what beeves are owed us and sell them to whoever's willing to pay the most, even if it is an Indian." Hector Alton sounded far too eager to engage in cattle theft for Knight's liking.

None of the others saw what he did. They all agreed.

"What'll it be, Sam? You in or you out?" Hannigan touched the butt of his six-shooter suggestively.

"I'm in." It felt as if the words were ripped

from his throat, almost choking him. "But it's only this one time, to get what we earned."

"That's agreeable," Hannigan said, his hand slipping away from his gun. "That's mighty agreeable."

Knight turned in, his sleep plagued with nightmares of cattle stampedes and Milo Hannigan on a hill, silhouetted by lightning, firing his six-shooter in the air and laughing.

"We got good steaks," Ben Lunsford said. "What more should we have done than rustle the cattle?" He lifted a fork filled with prime beef, savored it for a moment, and then chomped down on it. Eyes closed, he chewed with appreciation.

"We didn't get anywhere near what we were owed." Nott spun the cylinder in his pistol until Knight wanted to tell him to stop. If he did, Nott would open fire. The man had been edgy ever since they sold the cattle they hadn't kept for themselves to a Comanchero. "The trader rooked us. We're owed. We deserve more."

"I'm new to this wild bunch, but I have to agree with Mr. Nott." Hector Alton looked earnest. "Y'all risked your lives and most of you got shot up real bad. Ten dollars and a steak, even if it is a good one, doesn't come close to paying you for your trouble. You're owed. You're owed lots more."

Knight felt the tension and knew how most of the men felt. Even Ben Lunsford agreed that they should have been given more. Rather than stifle the unrest, Milo Hannigan had remained silent and let the restlessness grow. He used this to secure his position as leader, though neither Knight nor any of the others had ever voted him into that role.

"What would make it right?" Hannigan poked the fire and got everyone's attention. "If we all end up each with a hundred dollars, how's that sound?"

"You have an idea how to get such a princely sum, Mr. Hannigan?" Alton poked the fire, too, but it had nothing to do with the one in front of them.

"The stagecoach carries money all the time. Enough to give us the money to ride on in style. But I see that Sam doesn't like the idea of us taking that. What's your idea, Sam? How do you think we should get paid?"

Knight took a deep breath. Hannigan ought to be a politician. He knew the exact moment to engage and when to ask questions of the opposition that fed those supporting him. Whatever he said wouldn't be received well by the others.

"Yeah, Doc, we want to know what you have to say." Seth Lunsford's confusion was apparent. "You always have a level head."

"That's why I want to hear his opinion." Hannigan smiled crookedly.

"Stealing's not the way to live. The more trouble we cause, the more the law will come after us."

"It's not like we're stealing horses. That's a bad crime." Hector Alton spoke in a level tone, but Hannigan laughed. The others snickered, even Ben Lunsford. They all knew his trouble with the army. "Unless you're taking horses from the Yankees."

"Hardly stealin'," grumbled Porkchop. "Not if them bluecoats are forced to walk. Serves 'em right after all they done to us."

That sentiment carried the decision. Knight could never argue with it.

"The war's over. Our side lost, and we have to get on with our lives the best we can. The cattle weren't taken from any Yankee."

"The rancher owed us. He got killed. The boy who wanted to be owner refused to pay us and he got killed." Nott slammed his pistol into his holster to emphasize his point. He looked significantly at Hector Alton.

"Sam's got a point," Ben said. "If we take something that's not ours, it should be from Yankees, not the folks we went to war to defend. It might be too much holding up a stagecoach because we don't know who's riding along, not before we shove a gun into their faces."

"There's a trading post north of here. The three men there are all from Ohio. They're come to Texas to exploit us." Johnny Nott shot to his feet and stabbed a finger into the night as if he were a moral compass pointing to evil. "We can send them back to where they came from."

"And take whatever they leave behind," Alton said just loud enough for the others to hear and agree.

"In the morning, we run some carpetbaggers out of Texas!" Porkchop said.

"You'd think they had done this before," Hector Alton said. Hands on the horn, he leaned forward in the saddle and raised in the stirrups to get a better view. "Do you know if they've held up a store before today? Any of them?"

"Why not ask if I have?" Knight said, his temper short.

The rest of those following Hannigan had fanned out to approach the isolated trading post from four different directions. Knight and Alton hung back to provide any support necessary, no matter which point of the compass required it. Nott and Hannigan went to the front door while the Lunsfords secured the corral with a dozen horses in it. Porkchop came in from the north and Lattimer advanced from the south. Knight cast a critical eye on those two. Porkchop rode easily, but Lattimer clutched his side as if his belly wounds still bothered him. Without real medicines, his wounds might have gotten infected. Telling Hannigan had gotten him slapped down.

"You steal horses." Alton held up his hand as if to ward off a blow. "Just joshing you. You aren't the kind to shove a six-shooter under someone's nose and ask for their money."

"I'd do it if I had to."

"Do tell?" Alton's complete attention focused on him.

"If medical supplies were being held back for no reason and a patient needed it, I would do whatever it took."

"I'm right glad you're my sawbones. Hannigan likes that you ride with him, too. I can tell. You two must go way back."

Knight winced as gunshots echoed to him. A few seconds passed, then came another

246

volley. Without waiting for Hector Alton, he snapped the reins and brought his horse to a canter to get to the store. One shot cowed potential victims to make them surrender without a fight. Many shots meant a fight had broken out. He hoped his medical expertise wasn't needed — then he mentally changed that to hoping it was. Nott was likely to kill and not leave wounded needing attention.

"You goin' in, Doc?" Ben Lunsford ran up with his gun drawn. "Better let me."

"Stay outside. Keep Seth from getting into too much trouble." Knight knew appealing to the man's protectiveness for his younger brother kept them both safe. He had nothing to lose.

Hitting the ground running, he had his six-shooter out when he burst through the door. A quick look around confirmed his suspicions. Nott waved his smoking gun around wildly. Two men lay dead on the floor. A third sprawled over the counter, a sawed-off shotgun still clutched in his hands.

"Anybody injured?"

"Johnny took good care of them," Hannigan said from the back room. He came out dragging a pile of buffalo hides. "They got a ton of these things stored there."

"What the hell do we want skins for?" Nott prodded each of the men in turn to be sure they were dead. Only when he was satisfied did he thrust his six-gun into its holster and see what Hannigan had discovered. "Damn me if you're not right, Hannigan. Hides and not much else. Not even much in the way of food."

Hannigan let Johnny Nott poke through the piles of smelly, badly cured buffalo hides as he searched for money. He dropped a cigar box onto the counter, frowned and shoved the body away to the floor, and finally opened the box. Out spilled a handful of coins and a few greenbacks. "There's not more'n twenty dollars here. They must have spent all their money buying those skins. We got here a few days too late."

"That means whatever hider sold the skins is rollin' in the money. How hard is it to track them down?" Nott kicked one body and set to rummaging through the store, hunting for ammunition and anything valuable to him.

"Neither of you hit?" Knight ignored Nott and locked eyes with Hannigan. He didn't like his expression. It mirrored Nott's too closely.

"They cheated us, Sam. They don't have enough to make it worth our time to rob this place, unless you know a market for buffalo hides."

"They got others back there, too. Some fox, from the smell," said Nott. He finished his search and piled what he was taking in the middle of a blanket. Four quick moves caught up everything into a bundle he fastened with secure knots before slinging it over his shoulder.

"How much cash was there, Milo?" Knight pointed to the pitiful pile on the counter. "Can't be more than twenty dollars."

"Less. We should have hit this place earlier, or maybe later after they sold the hides." He pushed back his hat and scratched his head. "Who's got money out here for buffalo? These were getting shipped back east. Maybe moved to a train and sent up to St. Louis or even Chicago."

"They died for no reason," Knight said.

"No reason? No reason? What's wrong with you, Knight? They resisted. Tried to keep us from robbin' them. *That's* reason enough. Get the money, Hannigan, and let's get out of here. The place stinks to high heaven." Nott pushed past Knight.

Hector Alton stood in the doorway, but he made way, only to enter after Nott was mounted and riding away.

"Other than what you'd give a buffalo hunter, what's in here?" The dandy poked about but took nothing.

"There's enough beans and oatmeal to keep us on the trail for a month," Knight said. "We can be in West Texas on it, without having to stop and hunt or scrounge whatever grows that's edible."

"You're in a powerful hurry to be gone, Sam. You having nightmares about the army coming for you?" Hannigan laughed.

Knight forced himself to keep his hand at his side and not throw down on him. Hannigan never noticed, but Alton did.

He laid a hand on Knight's shoulder. "You hold your temper in check, sir. Don't go shooting anybody, especially him, unless you want to lead this outfit." Alton studied him.

Knight pulled free.

"I didn't think you had it in you to lead such a dangerous group. Now, you want to help me paw through the booty to see what'll keep us going for another week or two?"

"I'm no thief." Knight stormed from the trading post.

He heard Hector Alton's mocking, "Not a thief, except for a few horses and an entire set of clothes off a dead rancher. And I do wonder where that six-gun came from."

Knight swung into the saddle and rode off, the words ringing in his ears. Alton was right. He wasn't any better than Nott or any other petty thief, except stealing bothered him.

CHAPTER 17

"Why can't we move on?" Samuel Knight put the question to Milo Hannigan and did not try to sugarcoat the tone. "Robbing the trading post didn't get us anything worth mentioning, and three men died."

"Wasn't anybody who mattered," Johnny Nott said. He cleaned his fingernails with a large knife and never bothered looking in Knight's direction. "Not all of us are squeamish about folks dyin'."

"I saw more die than you'll ever kill," Knight snapped. "Too many of them died under my knife. It wasn't possible to save all of them. Or even many of them."

"The difference, Doc, is that you didn't put 'em on your table 'fore you killed them. Yankees did. Me, I make sure it's *my* lead in their black hearts. There wasn't a one of the men at the trading post what wasn't a Yankee. You're not tellin' me to save a Yankee, any Yankee. Ever. Not a one of 'em

252

is worth savin'."

"We didn't have a quarrel with them, and they didn't owe us a cent."

"They were Northerners," Nott said, flicking dirt from the knife tip and swinging around to squint hard at Knight. "You sound like you're turnin' soft on them, Knight. You don't care to kill Yankees anymore?"

"I took a vow to save lives, not take them. And we're not at war. They won, Nott. The Federals won, in spite of anything we did then or can do now."

"And you're fine with what they're doin'? You're fine with that carpetbagger in bed with your wife and the two of 'em —" Nott went for his six-shooter as he saw Knight's reaction. He was too slow by half.

Knight's revolver was already coming up fast, his thumb on the hammer.

"Wait, Doc." Ben Lunsford grabbed Knight's arm and held on to keep the six-gun from rising to center on Johnny Nott's chest. "You don't want to do this. We're all friends here, partners. If there's one thing them Yankees would want, it's for us to be fightin' amongst ourselves."

Knight pulled free and slammed his pistol back into the holster. Without a word, he walked away. Behind him he heard the low murmur as Nott protested being thrown down on like that when he didn't expect it. Knight and Nott had never gotten along, but now he had created a real enemy. Watching his back became a priority anytime he and Nott were together, and maybe especially when Nott was out of sight.

"I saw what you did, Dr. Knight. You've got a fast hand. About the fastest I've seen."

"Other than your own, Alton?"

"There's no call for us to brag on ourselves. We're both mighty quick with a gun."

Knight spun on the dandy and shoved his face within inches. "Why are you here, Alton? I patched you up, and your arm and side are all healed. You attached yourself to Hannigan like a horsefly to a rump."

"That's mighty graphic. I can see it now, only instead of one of those black horseflies, it's a fly with my face buzzing around before coming down to suck some blood. Is that what you meant?"

"You're not mad at what I said. Any other man would be."

"Might be your speed with that Colt scares me."

Knight edged away. Hector Alton never moved a muscle. Whatever he felt, it wasn't fear. The harder Knight tried to figure out the man, the muddier the picture became.

Saving him from the two soldiers had been too coincidental to believe, and now he rode with them for no reason Knight could fathom. Killing traders and gaining nothing from it hardly squared with the way Alton acted and spoke. Everything he did furthered his personal plans.

Knight had no idea what those plans might be.

"If you want to hold up banks like Nott keeps saying, why not team up with him? Partners splitting the take two ways is better than spreading around twenty dollars among eight of us."

"Well, sir, I've taken a fancy to riding with Milo Hannigan. It can't be that a man as smart as him doesn't have a stack of wanted posters following him around."

"You talk like a bounty hunter."

"A bounty hunter? Not that, Doctor. I want to ride with real outlaws. Anyone who can plan a daring theft is someone I support. My gun will back up the man with a stagecoach to rob. So far, all we've stolen have been those beeves and a herd of horses."

Knight felt the sting. Other than the rancher's horses, he was the only one bringing in stolen mounts. "You ought to be afraid of the army finding out who gunned down their two soldiers."

Alton grinned crookedly and shook his head. "We know what happened. You'd be swinging from a gallows if I hadn't shot them boys, but as far as the Federals know, you're the one who killed the pair. What was the one's name? Reilly? Him and you were acquaintances? Don't you think Captain Norwood knows that? It's your name on any arrest warrant, not mine. Nobody in these parts knows me."

"Why did you come here, Alton? It's a long way from New Orleans. We don't have the whorehouses or gambling or much else to appeal to a sophisticated man about town like you." The man looked for all the world like a riverboat gambler. Or a gunman, with his two pistols in shoulder rigs and another pistol hidden away.

"A change of scenery is always good for a man. You realize this now that you've tried to go home to Pine Knob and found it wasn't as you . . . left it."

"A better question is why do you stay? Hannigan isn't offering anything but trouble. Nott is killing men and not gaining anything but the sick personal thrill of it. Is that what you want to do? Kill people like you did the two soldiers?"

"You are a troubled man, Dr. Samuel

Knight. A troubled man. Settle down some and we can talk again." Alton went off, whistling tunelessly.

Knight's hand twitched. It was so easy to draw and fire.

But that's what Nott would do. Shooting a man in the back wasn't an honorable thing. Murdering a man went against everything Knight believed. He was better than Nott, and he was better than Hector Alton. But the questions about the dandy festered like a burr under a toenail. Why had he come? Why'd he stay and what had provoked him to shoot the two soldiers? No answers came.

That told Knight as much as he needed to know. Suddenly, getting away from the gang mattered most. If he rode with Hannigan much longer, the law would catch up with him. The law or the army, Captain Norwood riding at the head of the column as bugles blew and cavalry sabers flashed in the bright Texas sun.

He had to part ways but felt an obligation to the Lunsfords. The two weren't outlaws, not like Nott or even Milo Hannigan. If he got them to ride with him, he would feel better. And to hell with the rest of the gang.

"What's wrong, Doc?" Hector Alton levered

a round into his rifle. He should have been watching the road but kept a hawklike gaze on Knight.

"This is wrong. For two weeks we haven't done anything right. We should be in El Paso del Norte by now. Farther west. In New Mexico. Anywhere but here."

"You stayed and you didn't put up much protest when Hannigan suggested robbing this stagecoach. It's been a week since word of the gold shipment got out. Don't you think he's been careful?"

Hannigan had scouted along the stage-coach route to find the perfect place for the robbery. Asking around the town — Knight couldn't even remember the name — had brought assurances that the gold shipment was real and significant. The raid on the trading post had been spontaneous and that lack of planning had shown, in both the bodies piled up and the lack of money stolen. Hannigan did everything right this time to make sure nobody got shot and that they would ride away with saddlebags full of gold coin.

"I can't fault him except on one point. What's the gold for?"

"I don't follow you." Alton shifted to aim the rifle down the road toward the spot where the stage slowed on a steep incline.

"What do you mean?"

"Gold coins? A stagecoach carrying a strongbox crammed full? The bank in that town is tiny."

"That's why we aren't robbing the bank. There's nothing there."

"Who gets the gold? There aren't cattle markets around. Farmers won't bring in their crop for another month. Who's sending the gold and where's it going?"

"You worry too much, Doc."

"Don't call me that."

"Ben Lunsford does, and you don't mind. We're an informal bunch. I told you. Call me Heck. You want me to call you Sam, like Hannigan does?"

Knight ignored that and said, "There's the stage. I see the dust cloud its wheels kick up."

"Time to get rich."

Knight's gut churned. His objection to the robbery had been ignored. Becoming an outlaw didn't set well with him, no matter who that gold might belong to. After this, even if the Lunsfords refused to join him, he planned to leave the gang.

Alton's rifle barked. Knight jumped, though he expected it. He swung his own rifle around and tracked the driver. If the stagecoach didn't stop at the top of the incline, he was supposed to shoot the driver. He drew a bead, then moved it away from the bulky man's midriff. For him, now that he had spent so much time shooting at game, this was an easy shot. The difference was that a human life hung in the balance, not a deer's or rabbit's.

The driver looped his reins around the brake and stood in the box, hands high. Knight straightened, then blurted, "Where's the shotgun messenger? There's no guard in the box with the driver."

"So what?"

"The gold, the gold! Who sends that much gold without a guard?"

"Might be they thought to sneak it past. We don't see a guard, we don't think anything there's worth stealing." Hector Alton sounded pleased at his conclusion.

Knight jumped to his feet, shielded his eyes, and made a slow turn, taking in the entire terrain. He spun back and saw Hannigan, Nott, and Lattimer riding toward the stage, bandannas up over their noses and six-shooters drawn. Every instinct in Knight's body told him something was wrong, and a second later he saw what it was.

Bluecoats boiled from inside the stage-coach.

Knight lowered his rifle and fired. The slug took off the lead horse's ear, causing enough of a ruckus to give Hannigan and the others a chance to react to the soldiers. Two men had even ridden in the boot. They threw back the canvas flap and tumbled out, carbines blazing.

The sudden noise, the commotion, and so many horses rearing in fright turned the robbery into chaos. That was all that saved Milo Hannigan from being shot from the saddle by the hard-riding Captain Norwood. The officer and a squad of men had hidden in some nearby trees and charged the robbers.

Knight settled his nerves, took a breath, and started shooting. To kill another man, even a Yankee soldier, turned his stomach. He did his best to send his rounds into the side of the stage. The sound of a bullet ripping through wood added to the confusion. When the team hitched to the stage pulled free and raced away, even more dust clouded the scene.

"They'd better get away now while they can. Did they see the soldiers coming at them?" Knight spoke to empty air. Hector Alton had vanished along with his horse.

Realizing he had been given silent advice, Knight backed away, found his horse, and galloped away. Letting the others fight their way free of the ambush didn't set well with him, but if he was caught, he would hang. Norwood would take a single look at him and order his men to tie a noose and find a tree tall enough for an execution. The only solace Knight took in his retreat came with the knowledge that none of the others had a reward on his head. If they were caught, it would go easier on them than if they were wanted for a dozen other crimes.

At least he *didn't think* anyone else had a wanted poster following them around. Nott might. Knight had no good feelings for the back shooter, but the others deserved better than to be locked up in a federal jail, probably all the way north in Detroit, for such a poorly planned and executed robbery.

He reached the edge of a forest and plunged into the shade. It felt as if he'd entered a different world. More than once he changed direction to lay a false trail. His horse's hooves crushed pine needles and twigs as he rode but with enough backtracking and riding along game trails to find creeks to follow, he stood a good chance of becoming impossible to track.

By the time the sun dipped low, he approached their camp. Two horses stood off to one side where a rope had been strung to use as a tether. He recognized Hector Alton sitting on a stump. The other man had his back to him and vanished into shadow. Knight made a circuit of the camp and got a better look at the man with Alton.

He rode in and dismounted. "Are you all right, Porkchop?"

"Doc, they shot me up. I can't keep all the holes plugged." The man tried to stand, wobbled, and collapsed.

Knight grabbed his medical bag and went to the fallen outlaw. He ripped open Porkchop's shirt.

"My good shirt, Doc. You tore it."

"That's the least of your worries. You have any whiskey? This is going to hurt like hell." He took out a thin flexible probe and forceps. Porkchop had taken no fewer than five slugs. Dismissing the two in his arms as minor, Knight concentrated on the three in Porkchop's chest and belly. The thin rod snaked down into the wound until resistance betrayed the depth of the bullet. He used the forceps to pull out the first slug, tossed it into the dirt, and worked to stop the bleeding.

"Here's all the liquor I got."

He glanced up. Alton held out a pint bottle. Keeping his hands on the wound, Knight said, "Pour a little in this wound.

Then give a healthy swig to Porkchop."

By the time the whiskey was gone and Porkchop had passed out, Knight had pulled all five bullets from his body. His hands were covered in blood up to his elbows and so much had leaked from the patient that the ground had turned to bloody muck.

"He got shot up bad. Is he going to make it?" Alton peered over the doctor's shoulder.

"Get a fire started. I need boiling water to clean up the wounds."

"Is that smart? The blue bellies must be out there hunting for us."

Knight wasn't in a mood to argue. He stabbed out with the forceps as if they were a knife. "Do it." He put enough menace in his words to make Alton obey automatically.

The man caught himself, then said, "You got a temper, Doc. A real temper. You are going to get in big trouble if you don't keep it under your hat."

Knight almost came to his feet to drive the forceps into Alton's back, then caught himself. The dandy meant to fuel that anger, but Knight took it as a warning and something to be aware of. Going off half-cocked benefitted no one and only got him deeper in trouble. He settled down and worked on the wounds, taking a heated pebble with his forceps to cauterize the worst of the wounds to be sure all bleeding had stopped. By the time he finished, Porkchop had even stopped moaning. He looked up to see Milo Hannigan and the others slowly making their way into the camp.

From the bloody arms and faces, the rest of them hadn't escaped untouched. A quick count showed that no one had been left behind — or killed.

Knight went to Ben Lunsford. "You and Seth all right?"

Ben painfully dismounted and turned to him, nodding slowly.

A quick check assured Knight the wounds were superficial. "You get yourself cleaned up. I'll see to the others."

"Lattimer took a bullet in the shoulder. That man's gonna have more scars than you can shake a stick at," Seth Lunsford said. He held up his arms and spun about to show he had escaped unwounded. "It was pretty terrible, Doc. We got away, though."

"This time." Knight failed to hold down his complaint.

Hannigan went over. Every line in his face blazed anger. He hunted for someone to take it out on, and Knight had given him the target. "You weren't anywhere to be seen. You have something to do with them

Federals coming at us from all directions?"

"Nobody warned them," Knight said. "They set us up. What happened at the trading post told them we were in the area, and asking about gold shipments the way you did sent some townsman running to Norwood. The ambush had to happen, if you believe the army's here to keep the peace."

"Peace, my ass! They're here to enslave us. They —"

"Admit it, Hannigan. You made a mistake, and we all paid for it. Porkchop's going to live, but only because Alton and I took care of him."

"Alton. Where is that popinjay? I should never have trusted a man who dresses like that."

"We should have been in Arizona by now. Or Paso del Norte or anywhere that's not the Piney Woods. There's nothing here for us."

"Speak for yourself, Sam. You're the one who's burned all his bridges. We can live off the banks and stages, and there's got to be an army post or two we can rob."

Knight saw Lattimer sink to the ground and flop back. Seth had said it was only a shoulder wound, but the man had lost blood and might be going into shock. Without so much as a fare-thee-well to Hannigan,

Knight went to the fallen man and began working on the wound. The bullet had buried itself in deep and stopped only when it hit bone. For the time and effort he expended on Lattimer's wounds, he could have fixed Porkchop twice over.

The stars hid behind swiftly moving storm clouds well past midnight by the time he finished bandaging everyone. Exhausted, he stretched out on the ground and tried to sleep. He kept thinking of the trap and how close a call it had been. They all might have ended up in a Federal prison — or worse. If Hannigan or Nott or any of the others had killed another soldier, Captain Norwood would never rest until they were all caught or killed.

He finally drifted off to sleep with a single thought in his head. It was time to part company with Milo Hannigan and the gang.

CHAPTER 18

For three days Knight squirreled away food for the trail. The others paid him no heed since he drifted from one to the next, checking their wounds, changing bandages, and being almost invisible. He noticed he was excluded from the council Hannigan assembled around him. Lattimer and Nott became his close comrades in arms. That suited Knight fine because the food and other supplies he slipped into his saddlebags were intended to get him as far from everyone as possible.

In too many ways it had become an outlaw gang. He saw how easily he had gone along with the notion that they were owed the cattle after defending the rancher and getting almost nothing for their blood and sweat. The killings at the trading post had put him on alert, but he still hadn't seen the full meaning of what Hannigan said until the disastrous stagecoach robbery.

That drove home that what they were doing mattered — and law-abiding people who had once been his neighbors considered them thieves, outlaws, and killers to be arrested.

Or cut down like mad dogs.

He slipped a handful of beans into his coat pocket. Fixed up with some greens, that made a meal or two out on the trail. Stealing the food from the others rankled, but he hadn't been able to talk to the Lunsfords about his plans. He wanted Ben and Seth to ride with him. They lacked the killing fervor of the others. Even Porkchop showed a ruthless streak now and then, making him a better partner for Hannigan than Knight and the Lunsfords.

It almost seemed that Hannigan knew what he planned, at least as far as Ben and Seth went, since he kept the two of them away from camp, on patrol and hunting for any soldiers who might be sneaking up. Knight realized those two were in the best shape of any of the gang and most able to spend long hours in the saddle. The only other one of their number who had escaped the robbery unscathed was Hector Alton, and he spent a great deal of time with Hannigan. Knight saw how Alton never took part in serious strategy talks, but the dandy didn't seem to take notice of that.

With a bit of sleight of hand, he added a small bag of gunpowder to his stash, giving him enough to reload his Colt Navy several times, should the need arise. He hoped to sneak off one night, ride like the wind, and be so far away when Hannigan noticed he had left that he wouldn't have to use the six-shooter to gain his freedom. More than once, Hannigan had made it clear no one left without his approval — and that permission would never be granted. The only way out was feetfirst.

That only strengthened Knight's resolve to clear out.

"Your pockets bulge when you put too much in them."

His hand dropped to the Colt on his right hip. He didn't draw. Hector Alton stood over him, feet squared off, his green brocade coattails pulled back so both six-guns were exposed in their shoulder holsters. Knight had watched Alton practice. Any stiffness he had once shown in his right hand or weakness in his arm from the arrows had passed. The man was as quick on the draw as anyone Knight had ever seen, not that he had ever really known a gunfighter. Growing up in Pine Knob had been dull. Even the saloon fights were bare-knuckled brawls that ended fast because everyone involved tended to be falling-down drunk. Other than the town marshal and deputies, men with six-shooters never walked the streets. At least, not that he knew.

"Don't worry your head none, Doc. I'm not going to say anything to Milo." Alton looked over his shoulder to where a new powwow with Lattimer and Nott was getting started. "He might not believe me even if I said you were leaving."

"I haven't decided."

"You've made up your mind." Alton came over and squatted beside him. "I want to go with you. There's nothing keeping me here."

That startled Knight. He tried to find words and failed.

"They think they're rough-and-tumble outlaws. They aren't. Nott's the only one who might have a reward on his head, and I wonder about that. I heard him talking about the man he shot in Baton Rouge."

"In the back."

"Yeah, he shot him in the back after a poker game. None of the players knew any of the others, so the law had no idea who gunned down the tinhorn who had been cheating. Any of them might have pulled the trigger."

"Only it was Nott." Knight wondered how

such details had been pried loose from Nott when he had been so tight-lipped about the killing. It wasn't that Alton was an easy man to talk to or that they had all gotten drunk. What whiskey they had was long used up for medicinal purposes.

"I want more excitement in my life."

"Coming with me's not the way to get it. If your complaint is that none of them is a wanted outlaw, sticking with me will be worse."

"You stole horses from the army. They want you for killing two soldiers."

"You gunned them down."

"You've never thanked me for that kindness, either. If I hadn't come by when I did, you'd be buried in some unmarked grave, rope burns around your broken neck. The way I see it, you need me to look out for your back."

Knight trusted Hector Alton less than he did Nott or Lattimer, but he said nothing. The man held a winning hand. All he had to do was let it slip how Knight intended to sneak away and all hell would be out for lunch.

"When are you leaving? I can be ready any time." Alton cocked his ear expectantly, waiting to hear the precise time and details.

"I haven't decided yet."

"You want to see if the Lunsford boys will come along. Is that it? Don't look so surprised. They don't fit in any more than you do with this amateur outlaw gang."

Knight only nodded, not trusting himself. The sooner he talked to Ben, the better. He had no intention of letting Alton ride with them, but if they told him tomorrow at dawn was the time and rode out after midnight, that gave them a six-hour head start. If Ben went, he knew Seth would come along, too.

"Hannigan's sent them into Pine Knob. They left a couple hours ago."

"What? Why?"

Alton shook his head. "Don't have any idea, unless he wants them to scout out the bank there." Alton put his hand on Knight's shoulder. "Don't look so distraught, Doc. This works out just fine. They're already away from camp, and Hannigan won't miss them. We sneak into town, team up with them, and the four of us head out and never look back."

"That makes sense." And it did, even if it meant that Alton rode with them.

"Let's think on leaving around midnight. That'll give us a few hours before Hannigan figures out we're gone. Chances are real good he won't do anything about finding us, so we'll be away and free as the wind."

Knight nodded. It was as if the other man read his mind as to timetables and what Hannigan would do when he discovered the defection. But why had he sent the Lunsford brothers into Pine Knob? That made no sense.

"We've got a few extra hours. I took Nott's turn as guard until two. You were supposed to take over until four, then my regular time was up till dawn. We've got six hours before anybody wonders where we've gone."

"Thanks, Alton. You've taken care of everything." Knight patted the bulging saddlebags filled with food Alton had swiped from the others. They had enough food for four on the trail until they got beyond the reach of Hannigan or Captain Norwood or anyone else. By the time they were scraping the bottom of their food, they could settle down, get jobs, and live peaceable lives away from outlaw gangs and cavalry troops.

"Lead your horse out, but not in the direction of Pine Knob. Hannigan will try to track us. We want to confuse the trail as much as possible. That'll give us extra time."

"Do you know where Ben and Seth are in Pine Knob?"

"Not exactly. Being sent to scout Fitzsimmons's bank tells me they'll be easy enough to find. On a rooftop across the street watching or sitting in a chair on the boardwalk where they can count the coins in the pockets of depositors. How much time they need to case the bank I don't know. How smart are they?"

"Clever enough, but if Hannigan gave them specific instructions, they might take a few days — or be back before we get to the outskirts of town."

"They'll be in town. That bank's a tough nut to crack." Hector Alton swung into the saddle and looked around the quiet camp. Fires had died down, casting eerie shadows behind the sleeping men. "That way's best."

Knight said nothing. He stepped up and walked his horse behind Alton. Something the man had said gnawed at him, and he couldn't think what it was. He worried too much about the Lunsfords and what trouble they might get into if they weren't circumspect poking around the bank. The citizens in Pine Knob were friendly, but any behavior that struck them as odd got gossiped about. Ben and Seth were outsiders and likely to draw attention for that reason alone, though the rush of Northerners because of Reconstruction might blunt curiosity about them.

Or not. They were Southerners. Nothing hid that the instant they opened their mouths. In Texas a Georgia accent bored into the ears like a worm because it was so much more pronounced than local speech. Carpetbaggers were tolerated. Other Southerners were noticed.

Knight followed Alton single file so the tracks might appear as only one horse. Closer examination would reveal the truth, but to do that Hannigan would have to wait for the sun to get up into the sky. They played for time. Causing confusion at the start might turn into an hour in town to find the Lunsford brothers. After a mile north, Alton cut toward a stream and turned to go north.

"Town's in the other direction," Knight said.

"Wait and see how this covers our tracks. This isn't the first time I've laid a false trail."

Knight rode along, vowing to change direction unless a reason appeared for the misdirection. It did within a few minutes. Alton crossed from one creek to another that ran toward Pine Knob. Knight pictured the landscape in his head. The stream passed within a couple miles of the town. He had played in it when he was a tadpole.

"See? Even if Hannigan finds our tracks,

he'll be confused which direction we actually went."

"How'd you get to be such a trails man? You dress like a tinhorn gambler."

Alton chuckled. "A childhood spent on the run. My old man was crooked as a dog's hind leg. He never did anything honestly to earn a dollar if he could steal a dime instead. The thrill was always in outsmarting the other poor sucker."

"So you learned all this from him?"

"Mostly. He got lynched when I was eight. That might have been the best thing that ever happened to me. A gambler took me under his wing and I learned poker and a dozen other games."

"Is he the one who taught you to use those six-shooters?"

Hector Alton fell silent for so long Knight wondered if he had even heard. After a considerable time he said in a voice so low as to be almost inaudible, "I taught myself. Either learn or die."

Knight had no response for that. Alton folded into himself and rode in silence. For that, Knight was grateful. He needed a chance to consider how mad Milo Hannigan would be. They had been friends in Elmira, taking each other's part, but they had never been friends like he was with Ben

Lunsford. How much of a betrayal would Hannigan feel when he found that in one night, he had lost half his gang to defection? The man had a fiery temper. He usually held it in check, but when that fury exploded, people died. A prison guard had pushed Hannigan too far and had lost an ear, a nose, and an eye.

Beyond that, Knight wondered what it would take to convince Alton to ride on alone, letting him and the Lunsfords follow their own trail. Hector Alton fit better with the gang than he did with men seeking to settle down and avoid the law. That put Knight's thoughts on a different path. Where should they head after leaving Pine Knob? West took them past San Antonio and across desert sure to take its toll on them. Better to angle up toward the Staked Plains and Adobe Walls, heading more northward. From all he had heard, that was lonely country, but rich with cattle roaming the prairie. Like most of West Texas, rainfall might be sparse some years, making life hard, but when it did rain, there wasn't a better place to live. A man had elbow room. An ambitious, hard-working man could prosper.

His medical skills would be in demand, and the Lunsford brothers could find work easily. That sounded better to Knight with every mile he rode. All he needed to do was convince Alton not to tag along. His background ensured trouble, no matter how he professed to want to walk the straight and narrow.

"There's a house. You recognize it, Doc?"

Knight tugged on the reins, stood in the stirrups to look around and got his bearings. The first pink fingers of dawn poked at the sky, giving an unearthly tint to trees and buildings.

"Old Lady Rawlins's house. Her husband died ten years back. All three of her children followed him into the grave. Diphtheria. Worst outbreak we ever had, unless they had another while I was gone. She tended them and others and never got sick, not a day. I'm not sure that was a good thing for her."

"Went a little loco?"

"We can pick up a road not a hundred yards farther in that direction that will take us into town."

"We need to be careful. You need to be especially careful since that army captain has it in for you. Gerald Donnelly, too, from what I hear."

"You certainly have your ear to the ground for a man who's ridden with Hannigan for only a month or so." Knight thought furiously. "You aren't well-known in town, are you? You should check the bank and see if you can flush Ben and Seth."

"What'll you be doing?"

Something in Alton's tone put Knight on guard. "I'll scout the area to be sure it's clear of soldiers. We wouldn't want to hit the trail and find we were riding into a Federal camp, would we?"

"No, sir, Doc. That we wouldn't. Where do we meet up? After everyone's rounded up?"

"The post road going north is our best bet. You, Ben, and Seth start along it, and I'll watch for you. I know the area like the back of my hand."

"See you real soon." Hector Alton trotted off. Knight watched him uneasily. The man's tone had been mocking, sardonic, and there wasn't any reason for that.

He waited for him to vanish around a bend in the road before making a beeline for his old house. It was a foolish thing to do, returning to see Victoria just one more time, but he couldn't restrain himself. His feelings for her mixed utter contempt with love that had endured anything the Yankee guards could do to him in a prison camp. Hatred was too strong, and that told him he was getting over her. His passion was muted when he thought of her. He no longer cared.

And yet he did. One more time. There was no call to speak to her, but he wanted to see her flowing brunette hair and even look into those soft, wonderful brown eyes that carried so much emotion.

He shook himself out of the reminiscence. She had chosen a carpetbagger over him, and the only way she could legally marry was for him to be dead or for Gerald Donnelly to pull legal shenanigans with his carpetbagger cronies. He touched the Colt holstered at his hip and considered another way for this tragedy to end, possibly with a happy ending.

If Donnelly was out of the way, would Victoria come back to him? He doubted she would if it were obvious he had killed her ersatz husband, but if he was shot and killed from ambush, and no one was ever brought to justice for the crime, would she consider how wrong she had been with Donnelly?

Knight shook off such terrible thoughts. He was a doctor, not a gunman like Johnny Nott, content to shoot men in the back. Would he even want Victoria back under those circumstances? He had never been good at keeping secrets. Somehow, some-where, sometime he would blurt out his deed. He knew her well enough to know her killing him as he slept would not be too far-fetched an end.

There wasn't any way to get back with her, even with Donnelly dead. He still had to see her once more before riding away from town.

He tethered his horse a ways down the road, then advanced on foot. The sun had poked above the pines to the east, giving the house a bright coat of sunlight. Two stories. He shook his head. That looked so wrong. It was wrong because Donnelly had built it. He heard the maid bustling about at the rear of the house, but he didn't see Victoria anywhere. Surely, the lady of the house was up with the sun to oversee her servants?

Knight knew he should turn and leave. Instead, he silently mounted the steps to the front porch and turned the cut-glass doorknob. The door opened on silent hinges to show the stairway leading up. Another Samuel Knight would have left then. He closed the door behind him to avoid a betraying draft and carefully placed each foot on the stairs leading to the second story.

At the head of the stairs he paused. He went cold inside when he heard the sounds coming from the big bedroom. Again a different Samuel Knight would have fled. He opened the door a few inches and looked in where Donnelly and his wife were locked together in the throes of passion.

Knight drew his pistol but did not cock it. He sighted along the barrel, lined up the bead on the front sight and mentally pulled the trigger. As quietly as he had opened the door, he closed it and went downstairs and outside.

All the way he wondered who would have been the target if he had actually fired. By the time he mounted and rode away, he realized it no longer mattered.

CHAPTER 19

Knight felt curiously hollow inside. Being so devoid of emotion, either love or hate, made him wonder if he still lived. He pinched himself. The tiny jolt of pain convinced him this wasn't a dream where he did strange things and nothing mattered. The real world surrounded him . . . and everything mattered.

He rode down Pine Knob's main street. The town council had argued over giving it a name ever since he could remember. They wanted to hang some meaningless name on it like Main Street. Everyone called it that already, but the mayor had demanded that it be named after Sam Houston. That had caused a new round of discussion. Those favoring Main Street had slowly worked around to supporting Goliad Avenue. Or even San Jacinto Street. By the time he had left for Richmond and the war, everyone on the council had laid claim to a different name and they had a new mayor who wanted it named after himself. Putnam Street.

Knight would miss such useless argument. During the town meetings, passions had flared and the arguments had meant something. The war changed their importance. Left to a man like Donnelly, Lincoln Boulevard was as likely as Fremont Street.

Amid his memories came a different idea. If he found the Lunsfords before Hector Alton, he could get them to leave with him. Alton could search till the cows came home and never find them. That took care of what he saw as the worst situation. Something about the dandy made him uneasy. It had to be the way the man watched him, a predatory snake following a bird. His insistence on finding out if Hannigan or any of the others had rewards on their heads warned Knight, too, that he likely dealt with a bounty hunter.

But if that were so, why hadn't he just turned the lot of them over to Captain Norwood and let the officer sort through stacks of wanted posters before giving him his reward?

Other than Nott, the only one with a possible reward on his head was riding into Pine Knob to hunt for the Lunsford brothers. The petty crimes Milo Hannigan and the rest had committed along the way from Elmira had never risen to the level of a judge posting a reward for their arrest. Stealing eggs and a cow now and then had hardly alerted the law to a gang of desperadoes rampaging through the countryside. With the South in as poor a shape as it was, such thieving had to be commonplace for men to simply survive.

The town came alive around him as he went from one end of the main street to the other, hunting for any sign of Ben and Seth. Their horses weren't tied at any of the hitch rails, and when he approached the bank, he kept an eye peeled for the two spying on Frederick Fitzsimmons and his customers. The bank hadn't opened yet and wouldn't until ten o'clock, another three hours. He pulled his hat down and turned up his collar a mite to hide his face. The dust on the rancher's black coat and boots gave him the look of a stranger, someone passing through. In Pine Knob that had once been something worth commenting on.

Now, Northerners drifted through on their way to run small towns throughout Texas. He might be misidentified as a Yankee, but if it kept people who had been his friends and neighbors at bay, that mistaken identity was worth it. He wheeled about at the end of town and headed for the livery stables, hoping to catch sight of the Lunsfords' horses.

The few nags in the stalls were all unknown to him. He rode back halfway down the street and stopped in front of the restaurant. The plate-glass window had been broken in places by tiny rocks, giving a star pattern difficult to peer through. Only four customers made it easier to eliminate the Lunsfords as being inside. He passed a small saloon. The barkeep swept the front steps and never looked up as Knight rode past.

He knew Ben and Seth. They might drink a beer, but it would be to get a free meal along with it. Seth had gone on and on about taking his first drink of whiskey and how he hadn't liked it. Riding with the Hannigan gang hadn't given any of them the chance to practice knocking back shots of rotgut. All the whiskey they had went for antiseptic and anesthetic as he repaired the gunshot wounds.

A complete trip down and back hadn't flushed his quarry. He wondered where the two might be. They weren't inclined to slack off from a job, even one they didn't care for. He tried to imagine their reaction when

Hannigan ordered them to town to find out the best time and methods of robbing the bank. Ben might have thought it was thrilling, but Seth would have argued against it.

Why had they come to Pine Knob? That didn't make sense.

Knight was thinking so hard that it almost did him in. The clop of hoofbeats meant nothing with the town alive for another day's commerce, but five horses together should have alerted him sooner. He jerked around in surprise, then averted his eyes to keep from staring at the sergeant leading a patrol down the main street. Knight always felt it when someone stared at him. He expected others to have the same unnerving feeling of someone walking on his grave.

The sergeant halted a few yards away and pointed at him. "You. Where's the city hall?"

Twisting around, Knight pushed his coat back to expose the handle of his Colt. Shooting it out wasn't going to end well for him. A dozen schemes flashed through his head. Shoot the sergeant, cause their horses to rear, ride like hell. That was the best he could hope for.

Instead, he jerked his left thumb over his shoulder in the direction of the whitewashed building.

"That where Mr. Donnelly has his office?"

Knight shrugged, still not trusting himself. Seeing the sergeant wasn't satisfied with that, he nodded. He hadn't known Gerald Donnelly had staked out a claim to the town hall, but it made sense. The carpetbagger wanted to be the spider in the middle of the web, feeling every twitch along the strands.

"Talkative cuss, ain't you?"

Knight nodded again.

The sergeant snorted in disgust, lifted his gloved hand, and motioned his squad on. They trotted past Knight, eyes forward. He tried not to stare at any one of them, but he worried a trooper might recognize him. Only Private Reilly had seen him up close, and he wore different clothing, but luck was running out for him. Luck and time. Reilly was already dead, and Knight might join the unfortunate soldier soon.

That thought caused him to sit upright in the saddle. Alton had cut down Reilly. How far away was the dandy from doing the same to him? Knight shook his head to clear it. When he operated on a patient, he trusted his instincts. Those same instincts hadn't been too reliable in his life, but Hector Alton . . .

He tapped his heels against his horse's flanks and headed for the marshal's office. Scurrying about, being afraid of his own shadow, had to end. Going around back of the office to the side of the town hall, he dismounted. The soldiers had stopped in front, out of sight. Showing more bravado than he felt, he went to the door leading into the jail. Before he could back out, he opened the battered wood door and looked in. Deserted. Marshal Putnam and his deputies were out and the cells stood empty.

He angled in and pressed his back against the wall, just to be sure. All he heard were rats rustling around in the back of the office. Using his heel, he kicked shut the door and went to the stack of wanted posters on the marshal's desk. Flipping through them quickly, he hunted for any with Alton's likeness on it. His heart skipped a beat when he saw the reward on his own head. He was worth a hundred dollars to the army for horse theft and suspected murder.

Knight stuffed the poster into his coat pocket and kept looking for anything indicting Alton. He fingered a faded wanted poster with a description that might be Johnny Nott. A man from Baton Rouge was wanted for murder, but the reward was only fifty dollars. The authorities thought more of bringing Dr. Samuel Knight to justice than they did a back shooter. No one else in Hannigan's gang looked back at him from the wanted posters. With a quick shuffle, he put the notice for the killer who might be Nott back into the pile.

He had started for the door when he heard voices outside. Knight froze. The marshal and a deputy had returned.

Ike Putnam knew him and would turn him over to the army in a heartbeat. He slipped his six-gun from the holster, ready to shoot it out. The door opened halfway. He lifted his pistol.

"What's that?" The marshal's gruff voice echoed through the office. "Who's he to order me around like one of his toadies?"

Knight didn't hear the reply.

"If he wants someone to apple polish, let him pay for it. I got work to do. Hell, I got a desk to put my boots up on so I can take a nap before lunch."

The door opened another few inches, then stopped. Knight held his breath.

"Oh, hell. If I tell Donnelly off now, do you reckon he'll leave me alone the rest of the day?"

The door closed. After a moment, Knight gripped the latch and carefully opened the door to peer out. Putnam and his deputy trudged up the steps into the city hall. Without a wasted movement, Knight left the jail and hurried around to the rear where he had left his horse.

It was time to get out of town. Finding the Lunsfords hadn't worked for him. As much as he hated the idea, meeting up with Hector Alton was all that remained. Maybe the dandy had found the brothers, but Knight doubted it. He mounted and considered leaving Ben and Seth to their own devices. The poster crumpled in his pocket warned him how dangerous staying in Pine Knob had become for him. They were still safe, at least from the law, unless Hannigan tried another ill-advised robbery.

The bank? Knight couldn't believe even Milo Hannigan thought that was a good idea. It was just past the first of the month. The army paid once a month. Any money coming in to cover Captain Norwood's payroll was weeks away.

He rode around the jail and was headed directly out of town when a familiar voice called to him.

"Don't go rushing off on our account, Sam."

Knight felt no surprise when he turned and saw Hector Alton on the city hall steps, Gerald Donnelly leaning heavily on a cane next to him.

"You get on down off that horse, why don't you, Dr. Knight?" Alton walked down slowly, pulling back his green jacket to show the butts of both pistols hung under his arms.

"Am I worth it for you, Alton?" Knight pulled the wanted poster from his pocket and held it up. Then he crushed it and tossed it aside. "A hundred dollars?"

"A hundred? Is that what the army's paying for you? My employer's giving me ten times that. Isn't that right, Mr. Donnelly?"

"Gun him down. Go on." Donnelly hobbled forward, eagerness etched on his beefy face. "Do it, Alton. That's what I'm paying you for."

"You're not letting the marshal or the army do your work for you, Alton?" Knight said.

"They all got sent off on wild-goose chases. I saw you go into the jail and knew the charade was over. You were going to leave the Lunsford boys behind, weren't you?" Alton shook his head. "What kind of friend does that make you, abandoning them like that?"

"They aren't in town, are they?"

"Hannigan is a fool, but he's not stupid enough to think robbing this bank would be worth the effort. I was surprised you believed me when I said Ben and Seth were scouting it for Hannigan."

"You've got a silver tongue. Your lies sound mighty good."

"Get off the horse, Sam. Do it or I'll shoot you out of the saddle."

Knight dismounted. As he did, he looked around. Alton had told the truth about the marshal and the soldiers. They were nowhere to be seen.

"Finally getting some good sense, Sam? Mr. Donnelly sent the soldiers off on a wild-goose chase, and he ordered the damn fool marshal to the other end of town."

"Quit talking. Kill him. I'll give you two thousand if he suffers before he dies." Gerald Donnelly balanced on his good leg and lifted his cane, twisting the gold knob.

Knight had seen canes with rifle mechanisms. It figured that Donnelly carried such a weapon.

But his attention was fixed on Alton. "You are a bounty hunter. That's why you stayed with the gang. You wanted more than me. You wanted to turn the lot of them in for a reward, only there wasn't one."

"Amateurs. The whole herd of them aren't even dangerous enough to be wanted men. Even you aren't desperate enough for a good reward. A hundred dollars." Alton spat. "It's good that Mr. Donnelly thinks you are worth more."

Knight saw Donnelly lifting his cane, ready to take the single shot while Hector Alton distracted him.

Knight caught movement out of the corner of his eye as skirts swirled and quick, light steps passed him. "Hold your fire for a minute, Donnelly. She's not got a good view yet."

Donnelly's eyes got big with surprise as Victoria stepped up behind him. "Victoria, get out of here. It's dangerous."

"Gerald, what's going on?" The woman clung to her carpetbagger husband, causing him to wobble. He had to lower his cane-gun and use it to keep from stumbling.

"Drop the gun belt, Sam. Go on or I'll be forced to make you." Alton widened his stance and took a deep breath, expanding his chest to bring the pistol butts out from under his coat.

Knight experienced a curious stillness settle over him. He had never faced a man in a gunfight before. There wasn't any doubt this was to the death. He might die in the flash of a six-gun, but that never entered his mind. Cold calculation filled him as he watched Alton suck in the air. A thousand details came together, and his hand moved like lightning.

As fast as he was, Alton was faster. He

grabbed the six-gun under his left armpit and had it out before Knight leveled his pistol. Alton even got off the shot before Knight, but he rushed it. His bullet tore past Knight's ear. The whine deafened him in that left ear. Then both ears rang as he fired.

Accurately.

His bullet caught Hector Alton in the middle of the chest. The man staggered back, tried to lift his six-shooter but dropped it. His left hand reached for the gun in the other shoulder holster. When his arm refused to move, shock washed over his face. Then he crashed onto his back and died.

Victoria screamed. Donnelly tried to get free of her clinging hands and bring his own weapon up. Knight had plenty of time to aim. His shot ripped the cane from Donnelly's hand and unbalanced him. He sat heavily, Victoria following him down. She knelt beside him, holding his arm and sobbing. Blood spurted everywhere. Knight's accurate shot had blown off Donnelly's index finger as it wrapped around the folding trigger on the side of the cane.

Gerald Donnelly's mouth opened and closed like a fish out of water. In his fear, he wet himself, the spot spreading from his crotch down his leg and onto the city hall steps.

"I'm not going to kill you," Knight said. He didn't bother mentioning that he had passed up that chance earlier, too. "Consider me letting you live as your wedding gift. From me to you, a future of hobbling about, jumping at shadows wondering if I'm watching." He took a step forward. Donnelly recoiled. "I hope your children aren't missing a finger or born with your limp."

He made a show of lowering the hammer and returning his six-shooter to his holster. With a smooth motion, he vaulted into the saddle and galloped away from Pine Knob and his past.

CHAPTER 20

"Stop him. Get him. He shot my husband!"
Victoria's words floated behind Knight like
a swarm of angry bees trying to sting him.

They missed their target. He no longer
cared. What did worry him was the sound
of the marshal shouting at the top of his
lungs for his deputies to saddle up and get
after the killer. From the jumble of voices, a
dozen responded.

It took him a second to realize he was the
killer and Marshal Putnam meant to capture
him — or have a posse do the deed. He had
faced down Hector Alton and put a bullet
through the man with no more thought than
if he had been plinking at an old bottle.
Alton's speed had been better, but the
rushed shot left him dead on the ground,
not his intended victim. Knight tried to feel
something about that. Pride? Satisfaction?
Horror that he had taken a life? Nothing
came to fill the void inside.

He bent low with his head alongside the horse's neck and rode like the demons of hell nipped at his heels. From the direction of town came tiny pops. It took him a few seconds to realize the marshal was shooting at him. At this range, hitting anything with a handgun amounted to luck. A long gun could have taken him out of the saddle. Then even that possibility disappeared as he took the bend in the road, cutting himself off from direct view of town entirely. The horse began to strain under him. If it died from exhaustion, he was a goner. He reined in slowly and brought the horse to a brisk walk to give it a chance to rest. Its sides were lathered up, its gait uneven.

Luck had ridden with him when Hector Alton missed with his faster draw. Luck again favored Knight as he caught sight of a blue uniform in the bushes along the road ahead. A soldier stood facing away, relieving himself. Although he couldn't see it, Knight heard the soldier's horse thrashing about in the bushes just off the road. Whether the Federal stood guard alone or only represented the final element of a bigger patrol didn't matter. Knight dared not engage the soldier in either case.

Riding past put him in even more danger if the rest of a patrol waited. He veered away, cutting across a field. More than once he glanced over his shoulder to see if his detour drew unwanted attention. The best he could tell, the soldier had never even noticed him. Knight rode a couple miles farther, then came to a broad new road. He started to wheel around and ride away because the road led to Donnelly's house.

Then a slow smile came to his lips. Gunning down Hector Alton had started new ways of thinking. Before, he had been hesitant to do anything out of the ordinary. Doctors lost patients trying innovative techniques.

Dr. Samuel Knight was coming around to thinking those were patients he would have lost no matter what. Trying something new had to give better results.

He rode directly for the Donnelly house. The maid bustled about in the parlor, cleaning and tidying up. He averted his eyes from her, not wanting to stare and draw her attention. As quietly as he could, he rode past the house to the barn, jumped down, and led his horse inside.

He inhaled deeply. Fresh paint. Clean stalls. New hay. This wasn't a barn used very much, but why should it be? Donnelly stole whatever he wanted. Horses taken from other ranchers went into the pastureland seized from the banker using legal niceties or outright intimidation. The only horses likely to be put in this immaculate barn were those pulling Donnelly's buggy.

"You deserve a rest," he told his horse, giving it a pat on the neck. His hand came away lathered. He stripped off the tack, then brushed and curried the horse as he let it work on a nosebag of oats. The horse's hunger sated, he removed the bag and let the horse graze on the hay in front of it while he soaped and waxed the saddle and cleaned the bridle.

Not content, he wandered about, poking into crates and hinged boxes. He found some old bread and a half bottle of whiskey. The bread tasted better than the tenderest steak. Knowing he was sorely out of practice with the vice of drinking alcohol, he only sipped at the bottle before stashing it in his saddlebags. The vile taste told him the tarantula juice was better suited for medicinal purposes rather than drinking.

"Popskull, that's what it is," he said, licking the last drop from his lips. Further searching gave him enough gunpowder to load a dozen cylinders. Nowhere did he find bullets or wadding. As he climbed to the loft to explore there, he saw a buggy rattling along the road. He slipped his Colt from its holster.

Victoria drove the buggy. Gerald Donnelly sat beside her, hunched over, holding his hand. Knight smiled. Better to leave the man with a limp and no index finger than to kill him. Every day of his life he would think of the man responsible for his infirmities. That punished him more than being laid in his grave ever could.

Knight leaned against the side of the loft, watching Victoria help Donnelly from the buggy. At one time, the flow of her lustrous brown hair caught on the breeze would have excited him. Her trim figure and smart good looks would have made him love her all the more. Now she was just another woman. Less. She let Donnelly lean on her as she helped him to the house.

She called for the maid to help. Knight noticed that the cane was nowhere to be seen. That pleased him. His bullet had smashed the weapon along with Donnelly's finger. He stood straighter when Captain Norwood and three soldiers galloped up. The officer ordered his men to wait while he went to the porch where Donnelly sat on the bottom step, being fussed over by Victoria and the maid.

Knight was too far away to hear what was

said. The angle of the barn to the house cut off his view of two of the three soldiers, but they had no reason to search the house or grounds. The marshal's bragging about running off a desperate killer meant nothing to the captain, but not even Norwood thought his quarry lingered in the victim's barn, tending his horse and stealing whatever he found in old boxes.

A few minutes later, Victoria walked with the captain to his horse. Knight imagined all that was said. A reward was offered. The desperado had to be stopped before he killed and maimed again. And the officer agreed since Knight had become such a thorn in his side. Norwood stepped back, gave Victoria a half salute, mounted and bellowed for his men to follow him as he galloped away.

Knight sagged a little. He had been tense and hadn't known it until knotted muscles tried to relax. He forced himself to calm down. There wasn't a safer place in the entire county than where he stood. The only question lay in how long to remain. Donnelly didn't know his nose was being shoved into his mortal enemy hiding out not fifty yards away from where he nursed his maimed hand.

Another buggy rattled up. Victoria went to

greet the man and they exchanged a few terse words. She stabbed her finger into his chest, pointed at Donnelly, then tapped the newcomer again for emphasis.

Knight guessed correctly. The man took a doctor's bag from the back of the buggy and went to tend his patient.

Somehow, seeing the man who had replaced him in Pine Knob affected Knight more than killing Alton or dodging Norwood and the cavalry patrols. It drove home that he was no longer necessary to anyone in town. If he had returned to Victoria and a one-story house, what he would have done lay unknown to him. The other doctor giving up a practice built while Knight was at war didn't seem to be in the cards. A small town with two doctors? They'd both starve in short order, just as a single lawyer did until a second hung out his shingle. Different professions, different clientele.

There were only so many ways a doctor can be paid in eggs and bales of hay. Two doctors splitting that meant trouble for them both.

He rummaged around in the loft and found nothing more worth stealing. Not hurrying, he dropped to the barn floor, saddled his horse, led it from the barn, and mounted. The pasture Donnelly had stolen from Fitzsimmons beckoned because it took him away from the house unseen. Instead, he rode past the house. The maid scrubbed at blood Donnelly had left on the lowest step leading to the porch.

She looked up, her eyes went wide, and she started to cry out.

"Matty, have a good day." His words caused her to swallow her clamor. He touched the brim of his hat and continued to the road, not hurrying. When he reached it, he considered going back toward town, then knew such arrogance tempted fate. He went to the end of the road just past Donnelly's house, then cut across country, heading back in the direction of Hannigan's camp.

The closer he got to the camp — or where it had been when he left only the night before — the less confident he felt about the direction his life had taken. Returning to an outlaw gang went against everything he believed, but he had shot down a man in a gunfight. What was the difference between holding up a stagecoach and stealing horses from the army? Of those in the camp, he was the worst outlaw and the most notorious.

At the edge of the clearing, he drew rein and watched the men moving about as they prepared the evening meal. Ben and Seth did most of the work cooking. Porkchop lay sleeping off to one side. Lattimer, Nott, and Hannigan huddled by another fire discussing what Knight believed to be future robberies. No one noticed him sitting in the shadows. He could fade back into the pines and be gone, rid of the men whose only connection with him was incarceration in Elmira.

He rode into camp. Hannigan and the two with him never looked up. Seth came over and laid a hand on his horse's bridle.

"Where have you been, Doc? Me and Ben have been worried sick. Not sick enough to need you. I mean need your medicine. Aw, shucks. Are you all right?"

Knight dismounted and let Seth hang on to the reins.

"It's been a crazy day."

"You smell of gunpowder. You been practicin'? Ben says you're 'bout the fastest with a six-gun that he's ever seen, but he ain't seen that many, if you ask me. That's not sayin' you're slow or —"

"Seth. Stake out my horse, then come on back. I want a word with you and your brother."

"Sure, Doc, glad to help out."

He sat on a stump near the fire where a

stewpot leaked out a mouthwatering aroma. Somewhere along the trail, Ben had turned into a decent cook.

"Milo wondered where you and Heck got off to. Is he with you?"

"He won't be coming back, Ben. Ever." Knight touched the butt of his Colt to give the reason.

"I worried about that, Doc. I really did. There was somethin' wrong 'bout that gent. I couldn't put it into words, but . . . wrong."

"He wanted to bring the whole gang in to collect a reward."

"He was a bounty hunter? I knew it!" Ben slapped his thigh so hard it sounded like a gunshot.

That attracted Hannigan's attention and he motioned for his two partners to stay where they were. He went over to tower above Knight. For a moment, he simply stared. Then he said, "Where'd you get off to, Sam? You had us worried."

"I followed Alton into town. He was a hired gun working for Gerald Donnelly. They wanted to arrest us all for the reward, only you and the others disappointed him. There's not a price on your heads."

"There is on yours?"

"A hundred dollars." Knight looked through the gathering dankness at Nott.

"Alton thought there was a fifty-dollar reward out on Nott, but he couldn't be sure."

"Hardly seems worth the effort to nuzzle up to us. What aren't you telling me?"

"Well, Milo, he worked for Donnelly. Donnelly had put a thousand-dollar bounty on me, and that kept Alton sniffing around to collect the money."

"You don't sound too worried."

"I'm not worried about him now. At all."

Hannigan frowned, started to say something, then thought better of it. He took a deep breath and finally said, "Is there any chance you have the soldiers on your trail?"

"I don't think so." Knight held back his suspicion that the marshal had gathered a posse and the town's citizens might be coming for him. If he wanted to get away from the gang, he needed a diversion. By the time the posse found this camp, he intended to be gone. Dealing with the law would take the wind out of Hannigan if he intended to fetch his errant outlaw back.

Hannigan nodded curtly and returned to huddle with Nott and Lattimer. Those two occasionally looked toward Knight. He ignored them.

"They're afraid you're plotting something, Doc." Ben looked pained. "Are you?"

"I'm riding out as soon as I get the chance. I want you and Seth to come with me. This isn't any life for you, all the robbing and killing."

"I worry about Seth. I do." Ben sampled the stew, made a face, then added more than a pinch of salt to season it. "He's growed up physically but he's never lived nowhere but in that small town we were born in. The war changed everything. We lost our family, our town, and all we've got is each other."

"That might make him a tad wild," Knight said. "He's like any other boy who wants to cut the cord and make his own decisions, even if they are dangerous."

"He'd listen to you. He respects you, Doc. So do I. We got through the prison camp together dependin' on each other. I don't see no reason to forsake that now." Ben stirred the stew a bit more and said in a voice almost drowned out by the crackling fire, "I don't want Seth havin' a price on his head. Hell, I don't want one on mine, neither."

Seth staked Knight's horse away from camp, then returned to the fire, settled down, and looked from his brother to Knight and back. He took a plate of stew but didn't start spooning it into his mouth.

He stared at the two and finally said, "When are we leaving'? I know that's what you two have been chewin' on."

"You'd go? Leave behind all this glory?" Knight didn't try to keep the sarcasm from his tone.

"If we stay, we'll end up dead. What? It surprises you that I see that? It's as plain as the nose on your face. We ain't outlaws. Not Ben and me. Not you, Doc. Why pretend to be and get ourselves all shot up?" He ate a spoonful of the stew. "This is real good, Ben. Now when are we sneakin' away?"

The three of them quietly left the camp a little after midnight, just minutes before the Pine Knob posse swooped down on the camp.

CHAPTER 21

"I feel kinda bad about sneakin' away like we did, Doc." Ben Lunsford kept looking over his shoulder in the direction of the camp. "That was a posse. I heard one of them sayin' he was a deputy and in charge. He got into a powerful argument with somebody who musta been the Pine Knob blacksmith from the way he talked."

Knight knew both the deputy and the blacksmith. Alvin Williams had worked iron and made horseshoes in Pine Knob for as long as he could remember. The smithy was a crotchety old man, sure he knew everything better than anyone else. If he had joined the posse, even as a favor to Marshal Putnam, it meant he needed the money.

Like too many towns where Reconstruction ruined businesses rather than getting them upright and profitable, Pine Knob and its people suffered under the carpetbaggers. Now that Gerald Donnelly had a limp and a missing finger, he would take out his anger on everyone more than he had before and call it retribution for the part Texas had played in the war.

The cavalry detachment would keep civil uprising from getting too bad, but Knight knew those who had remained in town — or who had survived the war and returned — were in for a trying time. A touch of guilt turned him sad. What he had done to Donnelly sparked much of the man's wrath that would be taken out on the Pine Knob citizens. But it was only a light touch.

"Good riddance."

"What's that, Doc? You sayin' it's not wrong leaving Milo and the others to fight the posse on their own, not even warnin' them what was comin'?"

"Hannigan hasn't got a reward on his head. None of them do, except possibly Nott. I saw the poster and matching his likeness with the smeary description isn't too likely, even if Donnelly has ordered the posse to bring in anyone not living in Pine Knob."

"You sure about that?" Seth drew even with Knight and rode almost knee to knee. "Milo took us in when we didn't have nowhere else to go."

"You do now." Knight pointed into the

night. "That's where we are heading."

"Uh, Doc, where's that?" Seth sounded uneasy. "Ben and me have never been to Texas before, so we don't know where *that* is."

"I don't, either, but it's got to be better than where we've been. We're riding into the future."

"If you say so." Seth slowed and rode with his brother, letting Knight choose the road they took.

He had no idea where they went, only that it was into a part of Texas where they were unknown and had a chance to start over. Keeping to the countryside and away from the main roads struck him as the best plan. He knew many of the men in the posse. Riding across country wouldn't set well with them. They chose the easiest road. If he and the Lunsford brothers kept away from such obvious ways of escape, he knew they would be fine.

In spite of what he told Seth, he worried a bit over Milo Hannigan confronting the lawmen. If Nott got a bee in his bonnet, lead would fly. Hannigan had a tight rein on Lattimer, but Nott always showed that uncontrollable wild streak. Violence and gunplay ran just under his exterior all the time.

■ ■ ■ ■

It was past noon several days later when Knight began to get antsy. The weather changed from showing a bright, clear blue sky to one littered with lead-bellied clouds promising rain or worse. But the impending storm meant less than the feeling in his gut that they were being followed. He slowed their steady pace and finally signaled for them to halt. "You pitch camp."

Ben looked at the sky and nodded. "I've seen clouds like that open up and soak everything."

"A real frog strangler," Seth agreed.

Ben said, "The chance of hail is worse. Some of them hailstones get to be the size of your fist. Get hit in the head with one of them and it'll knock you into next week."

"We'll need some branches to make a lean-to," Seth said. "Wish we had an ax. All I've got is this puny ole knife." He drew a knife from a sheath in his boot and shook his head. "It's not up to the task. You got anything better, Doc?"

"What? No, nothing." Knight hadn't been listening too closely. His attention was focused on their back trail. Something definitely was not right. "Go on and start some shelter for us. I want to be sure we're alone out here."

"Alone?" Ben Lunsford laughed. "I never felt more alone. We haven't seen hide nor hair of a livin' soul all day. For a couple days, come to think of it. You see something that passed us by, Doc?"

"Be sure to pitch camp on higher ground." He looked into the branches of the trees around them and considered telling them to make a nest between a trunk and limb to get off the ground. It wasn't the possible torrential rain or hail that worried him as much as being found out.

But by whom?

They had been on the trail for almost a week. The Pine Knob posse wouldn't pursue them that long. Once they had questioned Hannigan, chances were good they had given up. A dollar a day or maybe the promise of a shot of whiskey wasn't enough to keep them away from their work in town. If Donnelly had offered a sizable reward for him, that might keep a few in the saddle, but the marshal had to tell them the most offered for their quarry was one hundred dollars. Split ten ways, that hardly made it worthwhile to saddle up.

He smiled a little at the idea of Gerald Donnelly offering a real reward for his scalp.

Donnelly might have paid off Hector Alton if the bounty hunter had succeeded, but the carpetbagger wasn't the kind to post a public reward of a thousand dollars. Or even five hundred if it came out of his own pocket.

Victoria's approval had to be considered, as well. She had abandoned Knight for Donnelly, but unlike him, some feelings had to remain in the woman. She wasn't the kind to carry a grudge, though she might because her new husband had been hamstrung with the cut to his Achilles tendon and then had his trigger finger shot off.

Those iniquities went a long way toward changing the way she thought about her first — and legally, still only — husband.

All this tumbled around in his head as he retraced their trail, meandering through the forest and paying attention to the tracks left on the ground. Even a blind man would have no trouble following them. There had not been any reason to hide their passage, though now he wished they had taken to a creek every so often to erase their tracks for a short while.

He tugged on the reins to halt his horse when sounds filtered through the trees. He canted his head to one side. At least three men came toward him. Rather than face them, Knight cut off at an angle, went down a draw, and slipped his six-shooter from its holster.

He waited only a few minutes before the riders made their way above him. One tall-crowned hat poked up above the vegetation hiding Knight from their sight. It took no imagination to guess where the other two rode — they trailed the man with the hat, making him either their leader or a trusted scout.

If they were a posse, it also put the man at risk of being ambushed first. Knight decided the lead rider ordered the others around. A posse. But not one from Pine Knob. No one in town wore such a fancy, expensive hat. They weren't soldiers, either, so Captain Norwood had not sent them to find his elusive escaped prisoner.

He let the riders get a ways along the path before urging his horse up the slope and onto their trail. His hope that they merely passed the same way and weren't tracking renegades died when the one wearing the big hat jumped to the ground and ran his fingers around a slight depression. The man's words were muffled by distance, but Knight made out their intent.

"— within a day. Can't rightly tell what went on here. Looks as if one doubled back.

Three horses went on, one returned."

"Maybe they dropped something and he rode back to find it?"

"He rode back to see how close we're gettin'," said the third. "We better speed up to catch them. They'll light out and make us work to find them."

"You're right about that, Custis. The one coming back's not good news for us. They're suspicious."

"Well and good. They oughta be, after what all they done."

"That storm's fixin' to erase the tracks. Let's get to work."

Knight tried to come up with a plan that offered success for him and the Lunsford brothers. The riders knew he wasn't with the other two, but who were *they*? Bounty hunters? Owlhoots sent by Donnelly? It hardly mattered if all they wanted were dead bodies to take back to Pine Knob.

If they tried that, there'd be more corpses — and not the ones the riders figured on. He pulled out a small chamois bag with the two spare cylinders for his Colt Navy. Eighteen rounds went a ways toward staying alive, if Ben and Seth also opened fire. Neither was as good a shot as he had become, but trapping the riders in a crossfire improved the odds. If they had no idea how many they really faced, giving up made more sense than fighting it out, especially with a storm coming and night making any arrest chancy. From what he had overheard, these men took few chances. Stack the odds against them and they'd cut and run.

He wished that were so, but if Donnelly had bought and paid for a man like Hector Alton, these would be no less skilled with six-guns.

Knowing where the trio headed helped. He didn't have to get too close. Being discovered meant death for them all, the three being able to pick him off and then have a numerical advantage over the Lunsford brothers. When he got within a quarter mile of the camp, Knight dismounted, made sure his spare ammo was handy in his coat pocket, then drew the rifle from the saddle sheath. How good — how ruthless — the three men were dictated the result of a protracted fight. Knight vowed they would suffer. If they won, they would know they had been up against worthy enemies.

His long stride slowed as the woods turned into a pitch-black morass. Night made the approach more difficult than he'd anticipated, but when he got within earshot, he hesitated. What he had expected wasn't happening. Advancing to the edge of the clearing where they camped, he took the measure of the three. He swallowed hard when he saw firelight glinting off badges pinned to their chests as they confronted the Lunsford brothers.

"I don't suppose you've ever heard of the Texas State Police," the man in the tall hat said. "It's brand spanking new. The governor empowered us to make sure there's no discrimination going on anywhere in the state."

Ben looked at Seth, then shrugged.

"We're not discriminatin' 'gainst no one."

"You don't feel a mite uneasy that my boy here, Custis, is black?" The man wearing the fancy hat bent over so the Lunsfords got a good look at him. The firelight turned him demonic.

Knight rested his rifle on a fallen log and sighted in on the one speaking. That had to be the leader.

"He's your friend. Reckon you can be friends with anybody you like now." Seth shifted so that his hand came closer to his six-shooter.

That made all three of the policemen yank their guns out with considerable speed, but only Fancy Hat spoke.

"You just stay where you are. Don't resist

or we'll gun you down."

The second man plucked pistols from Ben and Seth's holsters and passed them to the man in the hat standing beside him. Custis remained in the saddle, looking down on them.

"These ain't much in the way of six-shooters," the policeman said. "They ain't even been fired in a day or two."

"We use rifles when we hunt, and there's not been much game," Seth said. "Fall's makin' even the rabbits hide away in their holes."

"So you're not much in the way of hunters? Where's the other owlhoot riding with you? Can't be out hunting, not in the dark 'less he's hunting snipe."

"You ought to know all about that," Ben Lunsford said.

"What do you mean by that?"

"You're on a snipe hunt if you think we're crooks. We're just brothers lookin' for a place to put down roots."

"Where's your partner? There was three of you what rode into this camp."

Knight held his breath. If Ben lied, he and Seth were dead.

"Well, now, there was another pilgrim what rode a ways with us, but we went to ground early since we didn't like the chances

321

of bein' caught in a big rainstorm. He decided to keep travelin' and outrun it."

"The strange thing was, he went back the way we came," Seth piped up. "Never did get a name, but then we never asked."

The three policemen put their heads together and discussed the matter. The man in the hat straightened and said, "You boys spread out everything from your saddlebags on the ground where we can see it all."

"Who are you lookin' for? Whoever it is, he ain't in our gear."

Knight saw how one policeman reacted. Ben was lucky he didn't get a pistol barrel laid alongside his head. Instead, the man shoved Ben toward his tack. Knight forced himself to take his finger off the trigger. Tension rippled through him. If he didn't relax, he was likely to make matters worse taking a shot into the trio of lawmen.

The two policemen on the ground poked through the strewn belongings, taking what they wanted. When one kicked at the pile remaining, Fancy Hat went back to Ben and Seth.

"You ever see him?" He held out a wanted poster.

Knight knew it carried his likeness.

Ben and Seth both reacted and looked at each other. School was fixing to be out for lunch. Knight put his finger back on the trigger, intending to take out the man closest to Ben before moving on, but again he had underestimated the Lunsfords.

"That's him!" Seth cried. "That's the man what rode with us but left. Ain't that so, Ben?"

"It is. This picture's not the best, but my brother's right. He rode with us for the day and then skedaddled when we said we were pitchin' camp early for the night."

"Where'd he go?"

Both of them shook their heads and tried to look innocent. Knight hoped they succeeded. Too much depended on convincing the Texas State Police that their quarry had already fled.

"Custis, you got the memory for how men look. You went through that stack o' wanted posters. Did either of these two show up?"

Custis shook his head. "Nope, neither of 'em. I don't remember seeing them on any other reward poster, either."

"You boys might be what you claim." The two policemen on the ground exchanged looks. "You got any money on you?"

"You took what we had. It was in our saddlebags." Ben reached to his vest pocket.

This spurred both policemen to reach for their six-shooters again.

He froze, then moved even slower to turn out the pocket. "I got a watch my pa left me, but it doesn't run. He always told me it was gold but he lied. See? The paint's scraped off. Don't know what it's really made of, but it's not gold." He held up the watch, letting it spin slowly.

One man snatched it and examined it. He gave the stem a few turns, held it to his ear, then tossed it back. "Don't work."

"Just like my pa."

This made the trio laugh, and Knight knew the police would believe their story and leave the Lunsfords alone. When the two mounted, conferred, and pointed in his direction, he snaked back on his belly a few feet, stood behind a tree to avoid being seen, and then made his way back to his horse as fast as he could walk. The Texas State Police would be coming this way in an attempt to pick up his trail. Ben and Seth had sold them a fib, and it was up to him to keep from getting trapped in their lie.

Knowing he had to cover his tracks, Knight cut off a length of rope, tied it to thick bushes and dragged the bundle behind him as he rode at an angle away from the trail he had left. Then it became a moot point. At first only a few drops of rain fell, then the heavens opened and any hoofprints he left would be obliterated.

Even so, he rode on for another hour before curving back toward the camp and didn't rejoin Ben and Seth until just before sunrise.

CHAPTER 22

"Buffalo Springs," Ben Lunsford said. "Never heard of the place. It doesn't look like a whole lot."

To Sam Knight it looked like paradise. The quiet town showed plenty of activity, and it all went on peaceably. The jailhouse at the edge of town was tiny. If it held two cells inside, they had to be the size of coffins. His guess was that the jail only held drunks on Saturday night and not many other criminals. Those drunks would be flushed out, hungover, and returned to where they belonged before Sunday services. Even a quick ride through town revealed more churches than saloons. A few men walking around wore six-guns at their hips, but nowhere near as many as in Pine Knob, and that had been a quiet town before the war.

Buffalo Springs whispered to him. *Settle here. This is the right place.*

"It's more like home than anywhere else I've been," said Seth. "What do you think, Doc? Do we ride on?"

"Folks watched us mighty careful-like," Ben said. "That's goin' to be a problem if the marshal has a poster with your moniker on it, Doc."

"You're right," Knight said. "That's why I'll find somewhere outside of town to camp while you and Seth find jobs and see what the people are like."

"They look mighty good from here," Seth said, eyeing a young lady walking arm in arm with an older woman, perhaps her mother. The girl and Seth both smiled. The woman jerked on the arm she held trapped and herded the girl into the general store.

"If she has a boyfriend or a protective father, you might find yourself in a world of trouble," Ben said. "We don't need that."

"You're just sour because your girlfriend upped and married Jed Pendergast. She'd have done better with you, Ben. I ain't sayin' different, but you were off to war. When we heard you'd been put in the Yankee prison, Ruby gave up hope. And Jed was there, if you know what I mean."

"Shut your mouth." Ben Lunsford scowled and looked down the main street. "It's only common sense for us to scout this place and see if anyone's ever heard of Doc. Or us."

"Nobody's heard of us, not out here in West Texas," Seth said. "I want to find a hotel and sleep in a real bed again."

"Go ask about prices," Ben said. "Me and Doc will hash this out."

Seth Lunsford trotted off, grinning from ear to ear.

"He's happy as a clam," Knight said.

"I envy the boy, I do, but goin' along with that happiness is a touch of green. All Seth's ever seen of the world is wherever we went after we left Georgia. Even ridin' with desperados like Milo Hannigan and Johnny Nott didn't sink into his thick head."

"He's a good boy."

"I didn't say he wasn't. He needs to be more careful, or he'll find himself in a tangle he can't get free of. Mark my words, he'll be in trouble before the end of the week, if we stay that long."

"I'm in no hurry," said Knight. "Don't rush things. We talked about the need to find a town and settle down. I've never heard of Buffalo Springs before we saw the signpost along the road. That might mean nobody here's heard of me — and certainly not the Lunsford brothers."

"I'm tired of being on the trail," Ben

admitted. His butt hurt and more than one saddle sore kept him squirming every time the horse broke into a gallop. "And being away from Hannigan and the others in his gang gives a chance for me to avoid being locked up again." He stared at the tiny calaboose. Never again after being prisoner for so long in Elmira would anyone lock him up.

What worried him was the chance that living a good life, a law-abiding one, was all it took to avoid being stuffed into a cage. It had been so long he wasn't sure he remembered what do and how to behave in polite society. Before the war he had worked on the family farm and hadn't gotten into town too often. The war put him in the front line with a rifle, shooting anybody wearing a blue uniform. That had been his world for three years until he and Dr. Knight and a passel of others found themselves captives of a fast-riding, straight-shooting ranger unit from upstate Pennsylvania.

"We rode past a stock pond. You remember me pointing it out, Doc?"

Knight nodded.

"You find yourself a place to camp near it. You can water your horse there, and maybe set traps for small animals come to drink. That'll keep you from wastin' ammunition and makin' a whole lot of noise."

"I can be almost invisible."

"While you're there, me and Seth'll find out everything about Buffalo Springs. You want to know if they have a doctor, I reckon."

"If you and Seth decide to stay, I can move on if there is a doctor here. No town this size needs more'n one sawbones."

"Don't talk like that. If you leave here, so do we. I owe you more'n I can ever repay for what you done in the Yankee prison. I'd be dead and covered with their damned quicklime if it wasn't for you."

"Consider the debt repaid, Ben. We have to move on from what happened during the war. You and Seth, do what is best for you. I have a reward on my head, but it's back in East Texas in the Piney Woods and it's not all that much to draw bounty hunters."

"People are starin', Doc. You get on outta town. And Seth's ridin' back like his horse's tail is on fire. Whatever he discovered is powerful important."

"I'll give you a week, Ben. You and Seth do a good job scouting. And I don't just mean the ladies." He saw how another young lady wearing an apron had come out from the bakery and was sweeping the same spot on the sidewalk over and over because she had eyes for Ben. Knight wheeled about and rode off.

Ben Lunsford watched him leave and felt all hollow inside. Doc had saved him too many times to remember. He had done the same, but somehow he always felt obligated, as if he were the youngster and Dr. Samuel Knight was the father, the old-timer with the experience and advice he needed to keep going. Doc wasn't five years older, but the gap in how he experienced that difference ran to decades. Ben smiled ruefully. He felt as young compared to Doc as Seth did to him.

"Is he off already? I wanted to say goodbye to him." Seth stared after Knight.

"What'd you find out?"

"Without a nickel between us, stayin' in the hotel's not gonna happen. The sour old woman who runs the place wouldn't even talk to me about repair work or cleanin' up to earn our keep."

"But? You're too happy lookin' not to have somethin' more to say."

"Seems a goodly number of the men in Buffalo Springs left in the past month or two. They all lit out to be gold prospectors in the Guadalupe Mountains, wherever that is, so there're jobs goin' beggin' all over town."

"Did she happen to mention where these might be?"

"She rattled off a bunch of names. I tried to remember what she was sayin' but didn't come close, not by half. But the gunsmith's apprentice took off. He's got more work than he can handle in a month of Sundays. I was always pretty good with my hands, especially fixin' tiny stuff."

"Pa said you should have been a pick-pocket with your light touch."

"He never said that, Ben. You take that back!" Seth leaned over and tried to grapple with his brother. Ben avoided him.

"Simmer down. What else did this sour old woman who wouldn't give you the time of day have to say?"

"The auburn-haired filly we saw goin' into the general store? That's Marianne Yarrow. Her pa owns —"

"Don't go gettin' ideas. You know why we're here. It's to find out if Doc is able to settle down. I don't know if this is the kind of place I want to call home. The dust looks like it gets kinda fierce. I don't like places without hills covered with trees. If you haven't looked, this land is sparse when it comes to growin' things."

"They run water in acequias, she called 'em. That's canals, I reckon."

"You certainly learned more in a few minutes from a woman who wouldn't hire you than I expected to find out in a week of pokin' around."

Ben had to shake his brother to get his attention. The girl and her mother had stepped from the store. Marianne Yarrow, Seth had said. With so many of the town's eligible bachelors off hunting gold to become millionaires, husband material might be slim pickings. He needed to warn his brother about getting trapped by a girl with feminine wiles and obvious good looks foraging about for a man to support her.

"You want I go with you to talk to the gunsmith about a job?"

"What? No need, Ben. If I can't convince him, there's no way you could. That's what Doc says."

Such confidence rocked Ben back on his heels. Seth hadn't shown much in the way of gumption before.

"You go on and see to it by yourself, then. I'll see what I can find to keep body and soul together while we're in town."

"The Golden Gate Drinking Emporium," Seth suggested.

"You thinkin' on a shot of whiskey? We don't have any money."

Seth heaved a sigh when Marianne and

Mrs. Yarrow disappeared around a corner. He made a dismissive motion and said, "They need a barkeep. You know how to make drinks and draw beer. And you wouldn't drink up the saloon's profits."

Ben Lunsford had never been much of a drinker. He didn't know much about fixing the more exotic drinks that might be ordered, either. The few times he had hung out in a saloon, he had been surprised at the knowledge the bartenders showed. One gent on a riverboat had worked for over an hour and not once repeated a drink ordered by the patrons. They were mostly soldiers on their way north to join their units but had to avoid blockades at Vicksburg and other ports along the river. The barkeep might have taken advantage of the soldiers' ignorance if they ordered drinks they'd never tried. Who was to say that a claret sangaree, an Allston cocktail, or a champagne flip served up on the riverboat matched anything ever before concocted in the history of man?

Most patrons wanted a shot of coffin varnish and a chance to brag until he got too drunk to stand up. Ben had never considered a job in a bar. He had always thought he would end up working his pa's farm and only going into town for supplies.

He let Seth hurry off to the gunsmithy and turned toward the Golden Gate, a ramshackle place owing its name to the yellow-painted batwing doors leading in.

It took a considerable amount of courage for him to go through those swinging doors. The typical odors hit him like a blow to the head. Cigar smoke. Spilled beer. A sharp tang of something like acid in his nostrils.

"Come on in, mister, and find yourself a spot at the bar. I don't reckon you'll have trouble staking out a claim." The woman speaking to him had her gray-streaked brown hair pulled back in a severe bun. She worked to wipe clean a shot glass and almost dropped it. Her gnarled fingers were so crippled with arthritis that Ben wondered how she even held the glass, much less polished it. Too much makeup turned her face into something he expected to see in a mortuary. If she smiled, cracks had to appear. In spite of her advancing age and lack of skill applying cosmetics, Ben thought she was strangely handsome — in her day he might even have called her beautiful.

"I'm lookin' for the owner."

"Look no more. I'm Hattie Malone. I inherited the Golden Gate and have been running it for a spell now. What's your pleasure?"

"A job."

"Do tell?" Sharp brown eyes fixed on him.

He felt like a bug being studied under a magnifying glass.

"What do you drink? There's no reason not to be friendly while we talk this over."

"I'm not much of a drinker. Water's good."

"Water's good if you don't have a nickel for a glass of beer, which I think's the case. Is that it?"

Ben nodded, hardly trusting his voice. He felt as if she bored into his skull and read everything as plain as if it had been printed in a newspaper. It wasn't a pleasant sensation. She drew two beers, then came around the bar to set them on a nearby table. She sank into a chair and pointed to the one across from her. Ben took it. He cradled the beer in both hands, hardly daring to take a sip.

"Go on, drink up. It's not gonna kill you. Not today." She drained half her glass, smacked her lips, and put the glass onto the table with a distinct click.

Ben hesitantly tried the beer, then drank more. "That's good. I expected it to be bitter."

"I make my own beer. I mix my own whiskey, too, even if I serve it in bottles with labels saying it came from Kentucky. The brandy is harder to make, so I charge more for it. It's hard to get nitric acid to give it the right kick."

He wondered if she was joking, then decided she wasn't.

"You're mighty open about your business, Miss Malone."

"It's Mrs. Malone, and my old man took off for the goldfields. He left me with the Golden Gate and more debt than any two men could pay off."

Ben smiled a little. "Good thing two men weren't runnin' this place. I'd lay odds that debt wasn't more'n one woman could pay off."

"You're a smart one, aren't you?"

"Ben Lunsford." He considered for a moment, then half rose and thrust out his hand.

She shook, but the grip was weak from the malformed fingers. "I've found the smart ones try to steal me blind."

"Then I'm not a smart one." He sipped at his beer. "I'm a real smart one who knows better than to steal."

She gave him an appraising look. Hattie raised her glass and held it out. It took him a second to realize she wanted to propose a toast. He lifted his glass and waited.

"To the Golden Gate's newest employee."

She clinked glasses with him and drained hers.

He was slower to follow.

"You really aren't much of a drinker, are you?"

"Never had the chance, not on the farm, nor during the war."

"Don't get started. It's a vice that will rot your liver and give you the collywobbles. A dollar a day, meals, and a cot in the back room. There's a scattergun under the bar. Any damn fool tries to break in, I expect you to use it. If another damn fool tries to start a fight, use the bung starter on his head to end it real quick. No killing unless it's required." She gave him another hard look. "You've killed men?"

"During the war." Ben felt a momentary surprise that he had never thought before that the Yankees he had shot could be considered as having been killed. Looking down the barrel and pulling the trigger, there had been a detachment that had escaped him. If he had ever run a bluecoat through with a fixed bayonet and felt the blood squirt all over him, maybe the death would have meant something different, something less detached.

"Working as a barkeep might seem like being in a war on the bad nights. There's a canvas apron behind the bar. Put it on and learn where everything is. The rush starts in a couple hours."

"Where are you going to be?"

"With you tending bar, I can finally grab a little sleep. Be here when I get back or I swear I will track you to the ends of the earth and make you wish your mama had strangled you at birth." With that, Hattie left.

Ben Lunsford felt a little lost in the cavernous saloon all by himself. Then he set to work, doing what he knew was necessary. Sweeping, getting fresh sawdust on the floor, polishing glasses, trying to read the smeared labels on the liquor bottles. Since most of the contents looked and smelled the same, he doubted there was much variation. For all he knew, it all came from the same keg. He hesitated sampling each bottle to see if the taste from one matched that in all the others. To do so meant he'd be drunker than a lord by the time Hattie returned.

He found himself liking the physical work. Being by himself helped his spirits, too. Taking care of himself was a chore at the best of times but continually watching to be sure Seth didn't get himself in trouble — or worse — weighed more on him than he realized. The responsibility was gone, for a while.

"How do you do it, Doc? You're always there for me. For Seth. It must —" He broke off his self-lecture when a definite rap-rap-rap came at the back door.

He grabbed the sawed-off shotgun, went into the storeroom, and carefully slid the locking bar away. A swift kick moved it out of the way so the door opened fast and quiet. He wasn't sure who was more startled by the pointed shotgun, him or the young woman in a caramel brown gingham dress and pert yellow bonnet. She stood with her hands clutched in front of her. The sight of the shotgun made her bite her lower lip, but she never retreated.

"Please, sir, I expected Hattie to answer as she always does. This *is* Thursday, isn't it?"

"I can't rightly say, ma'am. One day's like another to me." He shifted the shotgun away from her. "Sorry. I didn't know who'd be poundin' on the door like you was."

"You are new? Hattie's just hired you?"

"That's right." Ben tried to get his wits about him. The woman's dark hair poked out from under the bonnet and haloed her perfect face. Her cheeks weren't rouged but naturally red. Eyes bluer than the sky fixed

340

on him. Considering the fright he must have given her, she recovered fast.

"Has she mentioned to you my, uh, my purchase every Thursday afternoon about this time?"

"She neglected that, ma'am."

"Please. I am Amelia Parker."

Ben introduced himself, put the shotgun just inside the door, and wiped his hands on the apron. He licked his lips and finally realized he was staring.

"Sorry, Miz Parker. You want to step in? There ain't nobody in the saloon. Or did you want to wait for Hattie? She went out to get some sleep 'fore things got busy tonight."

"She must trust you, if she left you in charge. Even if there aren't any customers right now." It was the lovely woman's turn to shift about nervously. "I . . . I came by to pick up a special package."

Ben said nothing. He wondered what Amelia Parker might get from a saloon that required her to sneak about. No respectable woman entered any saloon. The Golden Gate likely had the same penalty to a God-fearing woman's reputation that others did elsewhere. But why had she come around like this? He didn't smell alcohol on her, and she looked the picture of health. Ben

341

doubted anyone patronizing a saloon on a regular basis was half as hale and hearty.

"I . . . Hattie sells me a bottle of whiskey. A full quart. It's always wrapped in brown paper and tied with string. She keeps it by the door until I come for it."

"Every Thursday."

"Yes, every Thursday. The whiskey lasts a week."

Ben Lunsford stepped back and looked around. A crate near the door held the package as Amelia Parker described it. He picked it up and shook it. The sloshing sound told him it was likely the whiskey the woman sought. He held it out.

She silently took it, tucked it under her left arm and fumbled about in a pocket. As if it might burn her fingers, she thrust out a greenback for him to take.

"Do you get change? Look, if you want to wait for Hattie, I can —"

"No. This is the price I agreed upon after it . . . after it happened."

Ben held his tongue. If she wanted to lift the veil on her mysterious need to buy whiskey out the back door of the Golden Gate, she would do it on her own.

"It's for my father," she blurted. "He was hurt badly a month ago. A wagon rolled over both his legs and left him an invalid."

She cradled the wrapped bottle as if it were a baby. "This is the only way to kill the pain, at least for a short while."

"What's the doctor have to say?"

She laughed with a harshness that shocked him. "The doctor left to find gold. Fixing up people with broken bones or sick from the grippe wasn't good enough for him anymore." She looked down and went on in a low voice. "Thank you. I shouldn't burden you with my troubles."

"I know a doctor. A good one. He might be able to help out."

Ben Lunsford felt as if the sun had come out from behind a dark cloud as Amelia's face lit up with hope.

CHAPTER 23

Milo Hannigan started to speak up, then took a drink of the bitter beer so he wouldn't make a spectacle of himself. The last thing he wanted was to be center of attention in the bar when everyone else wanted to run their mouths off about Samuel Knight. He had come into Pine Knob wondering if he could find out how Knight had convinced the Lunsfords to hightail it. The story of how Knight had gunned down Hector Alton grew with every telling. The best Hannigan figured, none of the men doing the boasting about Knight's speed had seen the gunfight.

What he wondered most about was if Knight had shot Alton in the back. That was the way most disputes were settled. Squaring off, pulling iron, firing — that proved too dangerous for most men to tolerate. The idea wasn't to outdraw and outgun your opponent but to be the one who walked away from the fight. That usually meant an ambush of some kind, but that didn't seem to be the case. Not if so many believed the two men had faced each other and Knight had beaten Alton to his six-shooter.

Hannigan worked on his beer, turned warm since he had nursed it for almost an hour as he listened to the stories.

"You mean to tell me the man who used to be a doctor beat a gun slick to the draw?" He had to throw the question out to see who answered.

"I was there at the city hall a few seconds after the killing," spoke up a man with a deputy's badge pinned on his vest. "I didn't see it, but from the way Gerald Donnelly blubbered on and on, Alton drew first. At least he cleared leather and shot first. Dr. Knight was slower but more accurate."

"That makes the killing self-defense. Why's the law after him then?" Hannigan watched the lawman closely for any hint that he had been identified as an outlaw — and one with whom the killer had ridden. As far as the deputy was concerned, Hannigan was another drifter coming through Pine Knob trying to find a place to make a stand in the Reconstructed South.

"Oh, Dr. Knight's done too many people wrong. He shot off Donnelly's finger out of pure spite." The deputy grinned crookedly, showing a missing front tooth and another that had almost rotted from his head. "I wouldn't throw him in the hoosegow for that. It ought to be open season on all carpetbaggers, but Donnelly calls the shots in town now. He says jump and the mayor asks how high on the way up."

"Because of the Union soldiers?"

The deputy made a sour face. Hannigan motioned for the barkeep to bring over another shot of whiskey for the man. It took a couple minutes for the bartender to work his way down the length of the bar and refill the shot glass. The deputy held his own counsel the whole while, but the instant his tongue licked at the rim of the glass and he tasted the whiskey, he got mighty talkative again.

"That's got to be the answer. The threat of them blue bellies pouring into town and making life hell for us keeps the mayor in line. The marshal don't much care, but then he don't much care about anything these days. Him and the mayor — they're brothers — don't get on too well anymore."

"Why's that?"

"Marshal's wife upped and died a few months back. Took the life right out of him." The deputy looked around. "I've been angling to get his job. Let him retire, me, I pin on his badge. I'd double my pay all the way to thirty dollars a month."

"With the doc gone, there doesn't seem to be much call for a marshal, much less a marshal and a deputy."

"Two deputies," the man said. "Rory's the marshal's nephew. No way could he hold a job doing anything else. He's not right in the head, not since he got a fever when he was fourteen." The deputy sighed. "I suppose I'd have to keep him on if I got to be marshal. I'd as soon keep for myself what he's getting paid, but it's not too much since Rory lives with his ma — the marshal's sister. She takes good care of him. I surely would not mind her takin' good care of me, if you follow my meanin'."

"So Doc Knight is a wanted man but nobody from this town's on the trail after him."

"We got up a posse a while back, but all we found was a bunch of drifters outside of town. We chased them off."

Hannigan tensed. He hadn't realized the deputy was in the posse, but if he had been, the huge amount of whiskey fogged his memory.

"Drifters, eh?"

"That's the way it'll go around here, until them carpet-baggers steal all they can carry

347

and go on their way." The deputy looked sharply at Hannigan. He sucked in his breath and slipped his hand down to the pistol at his side. "You're not one of them, are you? Naw, the only Northerners are Donnelly and the Federal soldiers. I can tell by your accent you're from Georgia."

"North Carolina." Hannigan had no desire to get into a "Where are you from?" discussion with the lawman. "You're a Pine Knob man, born and bred, aren't you?"

"Naw, I came up from the Hill Country. Don't know why I left. Just a change of scenery appealed to me, I suppose. It's quieter here, that's for sure."

"Nothing ever gets stored in that bank, does it? No big shipments of gold or anything important."

"Nope, nothing like that. Not until . . ." The deputy's words trailed off as he stared into his empty glass.

Hannigan gestured for the barkeep to pour another, then leave the half bottle. He waited for the deputy to help himself to another shot of the popskull before edging him back toward discussing what might be stored in the bank's safe.

"You're going to be standing guard by your lonesome, I take it. Rory's not up for it and everything you say about the marshal, well, he's too despondent to do a good job. That'll be a real chore."

"Could be. The captain's not said how much money'll be moving through town. It's not real money, though. Just green-backs."

"Issued on the local bank?"

"The Federals want their bills to be uniform. All these are from a St. Louis bank, or so they say. I've never seen one of them greenbacks."

"With so much responsibility, you might want to cut back on the liquor. It wouldn't do showing up to stand guard if you have a snootful of tarantula juice."

"The money's not coming in until tomorrow sometime." The deputy almost fell as he turned to point toward the bank. His voice was clear and the words weren't slurred, but he had knocked back a drink or two more than his body could handle. Hannigan helped him to a chair before his legs gave out under him.

"That much money'll be guarded by the army. How many men's Captain Norwood assigning to help you?" Such a direct question ought to have caused a suspicious man to clam up.

The deputy was past controlling his mouth. "Only a couple. They don't want to make it look like any kind of big deal, not after they laid that trap in the stagecoach and didn't catch a single robber. The captain's still a mite touchy about that. Donnelly doesn't josh him, but the junior officers all make snide remarks. Nothing the captain can bring them up on charges over, but he's a laughingstock because of it. Not that he wasn't before. You ever see how he goes around lookin' like he's headin' for the parade grounds?"

"Do tell." Hannigan felt a mite better that the captain had paid some price for the ambuscade. Having his gang all shot up had almost cost him their leadership.

Lattimer was back in the saddle, Nott wanted to kill rather than rob, and Porkchop might never be healed enough to sit up straight. The bullets in the man's gut had taken a lot of years off his life, but he hadn't lit out like Knight and the Lunsfords. That showed some loyalty. What Hannigan needed to cement his control was a big holdup. Enough time had passed that nobody who wasn't in the posse even remembered the attempted stagecoach robbery.

Hannigan appreciated how Knight had erased a failed robbery from the town's memory and replaced it with talk about a doctor turned gunfighter. Hector Alton hadn't died in vain.

"Have another drink," Hannigan offered, pouring a fresh shot into the glass. "And then you can tell me about the women in this here town. What are they like? What do they like? What would it take to get them to like me?"

This set off the deputy on a wild tale-telling session that lasted until he passed out a half hour later. Hannigan stared at the unconscious lawman, sipped at his own whiskey, then left to return to his camp. He had a bank robbery to discuss with his men. Stealing paper money wasn't as good as having a few gold coins jingling together in his vest pocket, but it went a long way toward keeping his men happy and making their stay in Pine Knob worthwhile.

"We're all gonna get rich?" Porkchop licked his lips. "I like that. I'm gettin' sick of eatin' nuthin' but beans. I want a good meal."

"Pork loin?" Johnny Nott mocked the man, but Porkchop either ignored his attitude or didn't notice.

"That'd be good. Ham steak. If I get enough money from this bank, I'll pay to have a piece of pineapple put on it. You ever had pineapple, Nott? You don't strike me as the kind what enjoys food."

"Shut up."

They were just outside of town, waiting where they had drawn their horses to a stop in the shade of a tree.

Hannigan looked around at his companions. "All right, men. Everyone shut up. You've seen the bank. In the past couple days, everyone's ridden past at least once, looking for places where we might run into trouble. Give me a report on what you saw."

Nott and Porkchop shrugged. They hadn't seen anything to trouble them. Lattimer frowned and started to speak, then clamped his mouth shut.

Hannigan said, "Go on, Henry. Spit it out. What's eating you about the job?"

Henry Lattimer scratched his chin and finally got his words all in a row. "We go in guns blazin' and get the money. We load up our saddlebags with the greenbacks."

"Yeah, that's it. I scouted the inside of the bank. That's a safe, not a vault. The president just closes the door and never locks it since he's such a lazy bastard." Hannigan grew anxious. He wanted to get the robbery done with.

Lattimer scratched his chin again. "What if the safe's not open?"

Nott and Porkchop listened as Hannigan gave answer. "I told you already. I stick a gun in the president's ear. His name's Fitzsimmons. He opens the safe, and we're out of there."

"Where?"

"What do you mean 'where'?"

"If we come back this way, we ride past the bluecoats in the camp. There's not much of a road north. They can track us real easy across such soft earth."

"So we ride south. Or east. I don't care if we head back toward Louisiana. It might be fun to get onboard one of them side-wheeler boats and spend our money going down to New Orleans."

"So which is it? We get the money and ride south along that road or do we head back east?" Lattimer wrestled with this decision to the point that Hannigan wanted to pistol-whip him and leave his writhing body in the middle of the road.

"Don't make me mad," Hannigan said. "We come out, might be good to split up. You choose whether you want to go south or east. Or ride through the damn Yankee soldier camp hurrahin' them. It doesn't matter."

"He's right, Milo," said Porkchop. "We need a getaway plan. It can't hurt to have a place all picked out where we'll regroup."

Hannigan wanted to add another of his

men to the pile of bodies in the middle of the road. This kind of questioning amounted to insubordination. They asked the questions but didn't trust him. That worried him. Would they question his decisions during the robbery or would they obey?

"Nothing's going to go wrong. But if you want a rendezvous, you boys remember that hilltop where we camped on our way into Pine Knob."

"That's been a while, Milo," said Porkchop. "You mean the spot where we camped that Doc found for us?"

"That's the one. We stayed a couple days because the hunting was good. It was the first decent meal we'd had since riding into Texas."

They all nodded, remembering. Hannigan hated mentioning Knight. It gave them someone else who had left without so much as a word — a traitor — and the traitor had taken the Lunsford brothers with him. Right now he could use a man like Ben Lunsford backing him up. Seth lacked the spine to ever be a reliable outlaw, but Ben had the makings of a man with a quick gun and no morals.

"We rob the bank, we hightail it out of town, and meet up on that hilltop. It's got a clear view of the land around so we can tell if a posse's after us. Is there anything else? No? Good. Now let's go get rich." Hannigan pulled up his bandanna and drew his six-shooter.

Without waiting to see if the rest followed him, he galloped down the main street and brought his horse to a dusty, abrupt stop in front of the bank. He jumped to the ground and kicked open the door. Two tellers looked up, surprised. Three customers looked over their shoulders to see what the commotion was.

"This is a stickup. Reach for the sky!" He fired a round into the ceiling. Plaster came crashing down in a large lump that caused a billow of dust to momentarily hide the tellers and customers.

Hannigan felt the hot sting of a bullet before he heard the report. Then he realized it was a second shot fired at him that he heard. The small lobby echoed with gunfire, all of it directed at him. Both tellers and at least one of the customers had opened fire.

He shot through the dust. A grunt told him a customer had been hit, but the tellers crouched behind the counter, shooting over it. His three men crowded in close behind.

"Fill the counter with lead. Smoke 'em out!"

Both Lattimer and Nott fanned their six-shooters until their guns emptied. Twelve slugs tore through the thin wood. One teller stopped shooting. Hannigan figured he was either severely wounded or dead. He hadn't expected any resistance, much less men dying.

"There's one left," Porkchop said. As cool as could be, he walked around the end of the counter, aimed and fired three times. He motioned to Hannigan to join him. "Ain't nobody left now, 'less you want them dead, too?" Porkchop aimed at the two surviving customers.

"No need if they don't move. Keep 'em covered."

Hannigan kicked his way through a flimsy railing separating the president's desk from the lobby. It took a second for him to realize Fitzsimmons was nowhere to be seen. He circled the desk, thinking the coward had ducked into the knee well. Empty. Spinning around, he hunted for the bank officer. The only two standing, other than his own men, were the customers.

He cursed under his breath, but he didn't need the president. Two quick steps brought him to the safe. The handle refused to turn. The door didn't budge. The safe was securely locked. Suddenly angry, he fired at the door. His bullet ricocheted off and broke the Regulator clock on the far wall.

He spun on the customers. "Where is he? Fitzsimmons?"

The two looked fearfully at each other, then one summoned enough courage to say, "He's not here."

"I know that, you fool." He pointed his pistol at the man and fired. The hammer fell on a spent chamber. "What's the combination to the safe?"

"The tellers might know," Porkchop said. "Only I kilt them. Well, one of 'em, anyway. You filled the other with ten pounds of lead."

"Lattimer, you still got the shotgun?"

"It's with my horse."

"Get it. Blow open the safe."

"But all the gunfire'll bring the marshal runnin'."

"Get the damned shotgun. Do it!" Hannigan's fury exploded. He started firing his six-shooter, every time the hammer falling on a spent chamber. Only a rising panic wiped away his anger. Their time in the bank before the law arrived was running out. "Get the shotgun," he said in a more controlled voice.

Lattimer ducked out and returned with his sawed-off shotgun. Four times he fired at the safe, denting the door. All he accomplished beyond this was blowing off the handle. Unless they used a chisel to remove the hinge pins, the door was permanently frozen shut.

"Ain't workin', Milo. I don't have any more shells." Lattimer futilely hammered at the safe with the butt.

"Forget it. Get what you can out of the tellers' cages and take everything of value off these gents." He pointed his empty gun at the two customers.

Hannigan realized his mistake in that instant. The pair came to a conclusion that they were goners. Both went for their six-guns. Hannigan dived behind the counter as bullets tore past him. He felt a sharp sting as one customer's bullet almost took off his right ear. Then came more gunfire. Not being able to see what happened magnified his imagination. A loud crash confused him. Hannigan popped up like a prairie dog. The front door had been knocked out of its frame by a retreating customer. The other lay dead on the lobby floor, filled with lead from Nott and Porkchop.

"Get the cash. Come on. Hurry it up." Hannigan pulled himself to his feet, took a second to get his senses about him, then ran for the destroyed door.

Outside he faced a dozen men coming

toward the bank, all with their six-shooters drawn. He yanked down his bandanna and waved his pistol around.

"I tried to stop them. They're getting away!" he shouted. "A dozen men. They rode west!"

He vaulted into the saddle and headed west, only cutting down a side street to the south when he was out of sight of the mob forming outside the bank. Whether his men escaped mattered less than getting away himself.

He rode until his horse began to collapse under him. Then he got off and walked.

CHAPTER 24

"I'm tellin' you, Doc, she's in need of your skills. At least her pa is. From what she told me, he's in a bad way, and the old town doctor lit out for the goldfields with the rest of the men in Buffalo Springs." Ben Lunsford idly wiped rings off the bar, tossed the rag aside, and began rearranging glasses.

"You like working here?" Knight looked around. The empty saloon mocked him even as it suited him. Being around too many people worried him that they might recognize him off a wanted poster. He had learned from Ben that the town marshal, by the name of Hightower, wasn't very efficient, but he didn't have to be because most of the troublemakers had rushed away to the goldfields. Knight wanted to avoid coming face-to-face with the lawman as long as possible, though it struck him as unlikely that a wanted poster had come to West Texas so fast.

"Not a whole lot," Ben said in answer to Knight's question. "I was gettin' to like ridin' with Hannigan and the others. And you, Doc. I enjoyed bein' out on the trail where there wasn't nobody tellin' me what to do."

"Is that your problem working in the Golden Gate?"

"The owner's a real harridan. She hired me and then watches me like a hawk, thinkin' I'm stealin' from the till. Hell, there's hardly any till to steal from. A good night's a half dozen men comin' in for a single drink before goin' home. 'Course, I haven't been here long enough to see what a Saturday night's like, but the land's so poor here, all desert sand and dry, that cowboys 'd have to ride a lot of miles to get in here for that drink."

Knight saw this as a benefit for him, not a detriment. The fewer people to ask questions, the better.

"Where's she live? This Amelia Parker with the banged-up father?"

"Not far outside town. They got a small place from what she says. The only medicine her pa gets is a quart of whiskey a week."

"That might be good enough, depending on his injury. I should go see."

"Are you sure that's a good idea, Doc? If

you set up shop, all informal and out of the way, here in town, you can see what demand for your medical skills might be."

"If the former doctor's gone, I can guess. Amelia Parker? I'll go make a house call."

"He's been in a bad way for a spell. You sure this is a good idea?" Ben Lunsford belligerently leaned onto the bar as if challenging Knight.

"Don't get your dander up. Is there a reason you don't want me going there? You were the one who mentioned how bad off he is."

"I was just blowin' off steam. You know how it is." Lunsford poured a shot glass of whiskey and downed it. He choked, then chased it with another.

"I never knew you were much of a drinker, Ben. Don't swallow all the profits." Knight looked around the empty saloon again. "If there even are any profits."

"You don't — aw, hell. Do what you want, Doc."

"Yeah, thanks. I will. I took an oath to mend people who need it." Knight gave Ben Lunsford one last speculative look and left.

The day had turned stormy. Dust clouds whirled about with no hint of rain to hold down the sand cutting at his face. He pulled up his bandanna and tugged at his hat to protect his forehead. From what Ben had said, he knew where the Parker spread was. He kept his horse moving into the teeth of the storm for several miles until he saw the sandblasted sign directing him to the simple whitewashed house.

Leading his horse to the barn, he put it into a stall next to a frisky colt. It was the only other animal in the barn. Head down, he made his way to the front porch and knocked on the door. A woman opened it. His eyes watered from the dust and grit caked his mouth, turning his words indistinct.

"I'm a doctor. Heard in town 'bout a man needing help."

"A doctor? You're a doctor?" She eyed his dusty black coat and the six-gun he wore slung low on his hip. He looked more like a gunfighter — or an undertaker — than a doctor. "Who told you?" She shrank into herself, arms hugging her body and her foot tapping nervously. Then she opened up like a blossoming flower and stepped forward so he got a better look at her.

"Ben Lunsford, the new barkeep at the Golden Gate." Knight wiped at his eyes. He blinked hard, not believing what he saw.

"Is something wrong? You look surprised."

"Miss Parker? Amelia Parker?"

"Yes."

"Ben never told me you were so good-looking."

"He's a kind man. I think he's a bit sweet on me." She pursed her lips as if this thought just occurred to her.

"I can see why. I mean, I think I can see. My eyes are watering from all this dust."

"You're not from around here, are you?"

"I hail from . . . the Piney Woods. East Texas."

"Oh, forgive me. Please come in out of the dust storm. It's one of those things people who live out here get used to. Well, not used to, but we can tolerate it better than folks used to a storm being rain and hail." Amelia Parker had to use her shoulder to close the door against the gusting wind. "You're a doctor? That's your medical bag?"

"I've had it since I was a medical student. It's seen better days." He placed his battered bag on a table.

"Haven't we all?"

"You look to be in fine shape. I mean physically. No infirmities." Knight bit his lip to keep from babbling. The woman was pretty as a picture, something Ben had neglected to tell him. Her appraisal that Ben was sweet on her explained a lot about him not wanting Knight to go out to the farm.

"Why, yes, thank you. It is my father who requires a doctor's attention." She glanced toward a door off the parlor.

"Ben said he was run over by a wagon and it broke both legs."

"Crushed them. Even if there had been a doctor to tend him, I doubt he would ever walk again. And lately, something awful is happening to his legs."

"Are they turning black?"

She nodded. "And the smell is overpowering. I can barely change the bandages without, well, without becoming sick to my stomach."

Knight sucked in his breath and held it. He had seen too many cases of gangrene during the war. Never had he gotten used to the injury or what had to be done.

"You look concerned, Doctor. I know I have been, but there's nothing I have been able to do other than make him comfortable."

"I need to examine him." He picked up his bag, aware how little it contained. "Do you have any laudanum?" He knew asking for chloroform would gain him nothing. During the war, he had never been given an adequate supply of the anesthetic. The lack only increased the pain of his patients and led to more deaths.

"I don't think so. What is that?"

Knight ignored the question and said, "I'll need boiling water and that whiskey Ben sold you."

"He said he wouldn't tell anyone."

"Don't think poorly of him. He understood how serious your need was — how seriously your pa needed surgery." Knight smiled just a little. "He wondered why a proper young lady wanted an entire quart and came to the proper conclusion."

"I'm glad, but he promised not to tell anyone. *Anyone.*"

"I'm a doctor. Your secret is safe."

"Don't I have to be your patient first?" She flashed him a small smile. "That would mean you have to examine me." She turned and hurried away after such boldness. He heard her rattling pots and pans, then pumping water from a well.

He closed his eyes and tried to settle down before examining her father. He knew what he would find. After pulling back the sheets covering the unconscious man's legs, his worst suspicion was confirmed.

"Where do you want the water?" Amelia Parker turned her face away from the sight of her father's mutilated, decaying legs.

"There. Then you should leave. This is not going to be pleasant."

"You . . . you have to amputate, don't you?" She turned pale, and her hands shook as she put the kettle down on a bedside table.

"I do, but that's not the worst news. He is so weak he might not survive the operation."

"You've done this before? This isn't the first time you have operated to . . . to cut off a man's legs?"

"The war left many men in worse condition who lived, but you should leave in case the operation isn't successful."

"I'll stay. He is my father."

"Once I begin, I have to continue or certainly lose him. If you faint, I cannot tend you without neglecting him." Knight saw resolve harden in her.

"I won't faint. What do you want me to do?"

"I need a tarp or blanket for the legs once I remove them. Put it there on the floor." He turned his full attention to the man on the bed. He had been robust once. Now he lay a skeleton. However, his condition wasn't as bad as many Knight had seen. Amelia had kept him clean and had given him water when possible.

He wasn't sure she had done him any favors. Knight used the hot water to sterilize the bone saw. This wasn't as good as using carbolic acid, and he wished he had chloroform to take away any remaining feeling. *If wishes were horses, beggars would ride.* He began sawing.

Now and then he felt Amelia Parker swiping sweat from his forehead and keeping it from blurring his vision as he worked. The horrendous odor of decayed flesh quickly paralyzed his sense of smell; he no longer noticed. The sight of the broken legs would haunt him forever, though. Now and again he ordered the woman to give her father as much whiskey as he could drink. It was little enough until the man passed out.

After an hour, he finished. The last of the small arteries had been cauterized, preserving what blood the man had left. He stepped away and looked at his handiwork. During the war some amputations had been measured in minutes — even less. The numbers of soldiers waiting for surgical care had been over whelming. Taking his time with Amelia's father hadn't been any less monumental. If anything, he felt a more personal pressure to do well for the woman's sake. Never during the war had a son or daughter, a father or mother, been watching his every move.

"I'll dispose of the legs," he told her.

"I . . . thank you. I wouldn't know what to do. Bury them? Or save them and bury them with him."

"He made it through the amputations. He's stronger than I thought."

"My pa isn't one to give up or give in."

"I know. You're the same way."

She started to protest, then turned away. "I'll boil more water. I need to clean up all this blood. His bed."

"It should be burned. He'll be all right on a pad on the floor."

"My bed. I'll move him to my bed in the other room."

Knight didn't argue with her or point out that her pa might die in that bed. He rolled the legs into the blanket and lugged them out back. He found a shovel and dug a shallow hole for them. What she said about burial of the body with the amputated limbs stuck with him. He saw no way for the man to live, but miracles happened. If Amos Parker lived, it wouldn't have much to do with the operation or anything his doctor did.

He returned to the house to find Amelia dithering about in what he thought was an uncharacteristic fashion.

She looked up, distraught. "I don't know how to move him. Even . . . even so much lighter, he's too heavy for me."

"I'll show you how we transported patients during the war."

Together, each grabbing a corner of the blood-soaked sheet, they heaved Parker off the bed and jockeyed him to Amelia's bedroom. As gently as possible, they lowered him to the small bed. Knight stepped away and looked around. The Spartan room had a few personal touches. He noticed a faded photograph on a table. "Your ma?"

Amelia nodded. She picked up the picture and ran her finger around the wooden frame. "She died a few years ago. Pa insisted that she have this picture taken right after we moved to Buffalo Springs. It was expensive, and the photographer looked to be a fraud who only wanted to take our money and run off." She replaced the frame on the table, then used a clean bit of her skirt to wipe away blood she had transferred with the brief, loving touch. "He did a good job, in spite of charging so much. I'm glad Pa paid for the best because it's about all but memories I have of her."

Knight turned from the woman, checked her father, then herded her from the room.

"It's best to let him rest now. I poured enough whiskey into him to take away some of the shock, but his body has to adapt."

"What about infection? Shouldn't we

watch over him? I mean, shouldn't I stay with him?" She stood on tiptoe to look past Knight.

"There's nothing you can do for a spell." He didn't add there was nothing anyone could do, this side of heaven. "Let's sit in the parlor."

She laughed without real humor. "You call this a parlor? That sounds so elegant. One day I hope I can have a real parlor, a sitting room, a kitchen big enough to work in. Why, I couldn't swing a cat without hitting the walls here, but it was all we could afford. After Ma died, it was hard enough just to keep up with the chores. Then Pa . . ."

"Sit down here," Knight said, guiding her to a short divan with well-worn cushions. "I'll be back in a minute." He went into the kitchen, heated water, got clean rags, then returned to sit beside her. He started cleaning off the blood staining her face and hands with gentle strokes.

"Whatever are you doing, Doctor?"

"Taking care of a patient. Or should I say nurse? You held up well in a difficult situation."

"You just want to . . . examine me." Again the tiny smile darted across her ruby lips.

"Do you mind?"

For an answer, she moved closer. Her

body pressed into his as she laid her head on his shoulder. Knight held her, wondering what he should do. Then he realized from her slow, regular breathing that she had fallen asleep. Somehow, he didn't mind being used as her pillow.

CHAPTER 25

"It's a grand job, Ben. I've learned a whole lot, and I don't mind smellin' like gun oil all the time. Not a bit." Seth Lunsford bent over a worktable and lowered a jeweler's loupe to better see the burr on a sear taken from a S&W break-top pistol. He took a small file and worked to get rid of the offending scratch of metal, then buffed it smooth and put a drop of oil on it. He looked up at his brother and smiled. "All ready to be put back into a pistol. It'll work just fine now, and I figured it all out myself."

"Yeah, good," Ben Lunsford said glumly. "I'm glad you like what you're doin'. Does it pay worth beans?"

"Well, no, but I'm only an apprentice. Mr. Yarrow says I can work up to assistant in about a year. There's a lot to learn about guns. There's so many different kinds, and the new ones are better'n anything else. The six-guns with cartridges are a lot more

373

complicated, but then they're easier to load and fire. I'm learning how to load shells, too."

Ben Lunsford looked around. He picked up a Remington and cocked it. With a smooth move, he lowered it and pointed it straight at the door as it opened and a man swung in. For a moment, they stood frozen, then the newcomer pushed back his coat and laid his hand on his iron. Sunlight shone off the worn thumb rest on the hammer . . . and the star pinned on his chest.

Ben lowered the pistol and laid it back on the table. "Sorry. I didn't know anyone was comin' in."

"That's a relief. I'd hate to start the day flinging around lead in a gunfight I didn't even start." The marshal closed the door behind him. He eyed Ben critically, then turned to Seth and asked, "Is my new Winchester all fixed up?"

"Yes, sir, Marshal Hightower. I got it right here. It's a beauty, too. They're calling it a Yellow Boy, or so Mr. Yarrow told me. I sighted it in. It's got that octagonal twenty-four-inch barrel and a full magazine. I polished up the wood till it looks like a mirror. And whoever engraved it did a right fine job."

Seth Lunsford pulled the rifle from under

the table and laid it across a pad. He stroked it as if it would purr. Ben stepped back and kept his eyes on the lawman. It had been bad luck to point the pistol at the door just as he came in, and now the marshal was suspicious of him. That might be enough to make him move on. He was sure he could get Doc Knight to agree. The man hadn't shown his face in town over the past week, since he told the surgeon about Amos Parker being all busted up.

He frowned as he wondered if Knight had kept riding after tending to the injured man. If so, good. Amelia Parker was a fine-looking filly and one he could snuggle up against all night long. He had seen her first, and it wasn't right if Doc tried to snake her away from him.

"You're Seth's brother."

"What?" Ben Lunsford jumped, pulled from his reverie by the unexpected question.

"Yeah, Marshal, that's my brother Ben. He gets all dreamy now and again."

"It's good to have dreams. Is that what brought you to Buffalo Springs?"

Ben Lunsford cut off his brother before he responded. "We're just passin' through, but we needed to make a little money before ridin' on." Anything said to the marshal counted against them in the long run. Worse, Knight might be the reason they all got thrown into jail. If the army caught up with them, he and Seth might share Knight's fate.

"Hattie says you're doing a good job for her at the Golden Gate." The marshal smirked. "Of course, her idea of doing a good job is salted with enough cursing to burn the ears of a lop-eared mule. And from the look of the work you do, Seth, you're turning into a damned good gunsmith." He held up the Winchester and ran his fingers over the elaborate etching on the side. "If it shoots half as good as it looks, this is the best rifle I've ever owned." He laid it back down. "And your friend. He's fitting into Buffalo Springs better than anybody has in years. We don't usually take to strangers so quick."

"Friend?" Ben looked at Seth, whose eyes had gone wide. "Who do you mean?"

"The doctor fellow. Dr. Samuel Knight. It's nothing less than a miracle the way he saved Amos Parker. Poor Amos isn't out of the woods yet, from all accounts, but he's not fixing to up and die like he was." Hightower fished out a ten-dollar piece and dropped it onto the table for the rifle. "You might pass on a word of advice to the doctor, though. Tongues are wagging about him staying out at the Parker farm, just him and Amelia and her papa, who can't properly chaperone them." He grabbed the rifle and went to the door. Over his shoulder Marshal Hightower said, "When Amos is better, there's plenty of work for a good doctor right here in town. Doc Sparkman took off to the gold mines to make his fortune. He wasn't bright enough to realize he had a gold mine right here in town. Good day, boys."

Ben Lunsford sagged when the lawman left, shuffling because of a gimpy leg and arthritis.

"How'd he know Doc was with us? Did you tell him, Seth? That was a damn fool thing to say."

"I poked around and asked about wanted posters. Oh, don't look like that, Ben. I told a fib about being robbed by a highwayman. Not a one of the posters carried Doc's likeness."

"It was still wrong to link him and us. What if there had been a poster? Or what if Captain Norwood comes this way? The Comanches are kickin' up a fuss all over Texas. There's no way to know where that blue belly will show up."

"I didn't mean to. He mentioned as to

377

how it was a coincidence Doc and us showed up in Buffalo Springs at the same time. I didn't say we knew him, but then again I didn't say we didn't. The marshal's not a stupid man."

"Not as stupid as my brother."

"Ben, I'm sorry, but I can't unsay what I did. And you just confirmed that we know Doc."

"Doc, Doc, Doc. Always goin' on about Dr. Samuel Knight, like he's some kind of hero."

"He got you through Elmira. You and him —"

"I got *him* through that damned prison camp." Ben Lunsford left his brother protesting. He stomped outside and looked around. For two cents, he'd get his horse and leave Buffalo Springs.

Amelia Parker had come to town a couple times and had even bought a bottle of popskull for her pa. She had hardly remembered Ben's name. And she had thanked him for sending Dr. Knight out to save her pa. All she wanted was to take the whiskey and rush on back to the farm, no matter that he offered her a free drink. Talking to him had become a chore compared to bragging on Doc Knight.

"I saw her first, damn your eyes." Lunsford

went to the Golden Gate Drinking Emporium, paused a moment, then pushed through the yellow-painted doors.

It looked no different from when he had left. Echoes sounded in the empty saloon as the swinging double doors flapped back and forth. Hattie Malone sat at a table just inside the door, a bottle of Billy Taylor's in front of her. She got soused earlier every day now that he worked behind the bar.

"Glad to see you decided to show up. There's plenty of glasses to clean. And you're doing a piss-poor job of wiping the foam off the beer glasses. When you got 'em all spotless, refill the whiskey bottles."

"We don't have any more whiskey mixed up." He ducked behind the bar and put on the canvas apron. It felt more like slave's chains than a way of protecting his clothes from spills and stains.

"Then get to mixing up some. There's plenty of rusty nails to give it body. Must be ten gallons of pure alky back there somewhere. Mix that with enough water and throw in a horseshoe and some nitric acid and you got prime whiskey."

"Trade whiskey," he muttered. "Trade whiskey that'll burn out your guts and leave you mewling like a baby."

"I heard that. You whump up a batch that

can do that, and I'll think about paying you this week." Hattie Malone laughed and downed another shot of whiskey. She let out a belch and closed her eyes. For a moment Ben thought she had passed out, but no such luck. Her eyelids flickered open. "Don't forget to sweep out the back room after you mix the whiskey."

"Are you going to pay me?"

"Oh, don't make it sound so terrible. It could be worse. I could pay you with shares of the Golden Gate. This albatross hardly brings in enough to pay me. We can split the profits. If there ever are profits." She belched again and laughed like a cackling crow.

"Where do the cowboys go to get drunk? This is the only saloon in town. They ought to be crowdin' in here shoulder to shoulder."

"A whole passel of Baptists settled the place. Dancing and drinking are ag'in their beliefs. The ones what don't cleave to that mostly left to dig their fortune out of the ground. Gold mines." Hattie spat and missed the cuspidor by a foot. "Danged fools. The only ones who get rich off gold rushes are the shopkeepers what sell them the picks and shovels."

Ben Lunsford began his chores but

stopped when two customers came in to break the monotony. Hattie had laid her head on crossed arms and snored loudly.

"Welcome to the Golden Gate, gents. Name your poison." Ben waited to hear what the two cowboys wanted. From the condition of their clothing, they had been on the trail a long time. Every move caused tiny dust clouds to form.

"What can we get for a dime?" The two exchanged a look that told Ben even this much would tap them out.

"A beer for each of you." He snared the coin and dropped it in the till. "That'll cut the dust on your palate. Where you from?"

"We're on our way to the Guadalupe Mountains. Heard tell of a gold strike there." The shorter of the two sipped carefully at his beer, nursing it so it would last a spell.

His partner gulped his down in one long swallow, belched, and clicked the glass down on the bar. Using the back of his sleeve, he wiped foam from his lips. He left muddy tracks.

"We were over in Louisiana when we heard of the tons of gold bein' hauled out of the ground. How can we pass that up?"

"You come through Pine Knob? Over in the Piney Woods?" Ben knew the question lacked subtlety, but he wasn't up to teasing the information from the two.

"I reckon we passed through. If it's the town I'm thinkin', wasn't too hospitable a place."

"Why's that?" Ben perked up, wanting to hear the reason. It took some discipline on his part not to laugh aloud when he heard the answer.

"Damned carpetbaggers run the place. One's seized all the land and is givin' it out to his cronies, declarin' a state of emergency. He's got an entire detachment of Union soldiers under his thumb. Believe me, it was a good day when we rode through that place."

"What caused the emergency?"

"No tellin'. There're Texas State Police swarmin' all over, but they're at odds with the fellow. What's his name?" The cowboy turned to his partner.

But Ben Lunsford answered before he thought better. "Gerald Donnelly."

"Yup, that's the owlhoot. You been there?"

"A while back. I didn't cotton much to the way he ran things, either."

"This place — Buffalo Springs — looks like a nice place, but it's kinda quiet." The one who had been sipping at his beer downed the half glass remaining. He stared at the foam inside the glass rim with some longing.

Lunsford put his finger to his lips, cautioning them to be quiet, got on tiptoes and looked out past the bar. Hattie snored peacefully. He ducked back and gave the two pilgrims fresh glasses of beer.

"Much obliged, mister."

"Don't mention it. Ever." He jerked his thumb in Hattie's direction. "She finds out I'm givin' away the product, I'm kicked out on my ass."

"Then we're toastin' you." They lifted their glasses in silent salute and worked on the new glasses of brew.

"You saw that there's not a whole lot goin' on in town. I'm hungry for word of what's happenin' anywhere else. Since I left Pine Knob, I ain't heard squat about it. What else can you tell me?"

"Is that your hometown?" The shorter of the pair leaned closer, as if sharing a deep, dark secret. "You done good leavin' that place. The carpetbagger has recruited hisself a gunfighter to be his private bodyguard. That didn't set well with the army officer, so they're always squabblin'. You know who gets hurt in a case like that."

"Neither of them," opined Ben Lunsford. "Is the marshal still there or have the bluecoats run him off?"

"We didn't stick around long enough to ask."

"I saw a deputy," the other cowboy said. "Didn't look like he had the sense God gave a goose. There's no way he could be the only lawman in that town."

"So the soldiers and the marshal are stickin' close to Pine Knob? They aren't castin' about to find any outlaws that have been bedevilin' them?" Ben waited for the answer since it would help him decide whether to ride on or stick it out a while longer in Buffalo Springs. The longer he stayed, the less he liked it, but Seth had taken a fancy to the place.

He felt his belly tensing up at the thought of how Doc had gotten on with Amelia Parker. Ben had seen her first. Just because Doc patched up her pa wasn't any reason for her to ignore a real man.

"You're lookin' kinda tense. Can we buy you a drink?" The cowboy winked broadly, meaning he wanted someone else to drink with but couldn't pay for it.

"Why not?" Ben poured himself a shot of whiskey and upended it. He licked off the rim of the glass and put it down on the bar. The two cowboys drained their glasses and looked expectantly at him.

Hattie still snored away and nobody else had come into the Golden Gate. He fixed up the two with fresh glasses of beer and poured himself another shot. Life in Buffalo Springs looked secure. For a while. Until he got tired of it and decided to move on.

The whiskey surely did go down his gullet smooth and warm to a puddle in his stomach. The alcohol relaxed him and gave him a better outlook on life. How could Hattie Malone ever deny him that?

CHAPTER 26

Milo Hannigan kept his head low as he urged his new horse, one he'd stolen after the bank robbery, to even greater speed. The horse's flanks heaved and lather flew. The entire town of Pine Knob had turned out, armed and angry, when it became obvious the bank was being robbed. Hannigan blamed Fitzsimmons for rallying them as fast as they had gathered. The damned president ought to have been in the bank. If he had been doing his job, he should have been at his desk and forcing him to open the safe would have saved lives.

"Come on, you worthless nag." Hannigan raked the horse's flanks with his heels. The more distance he put between him and Pine Knob, the better.

Then he was sailing through the air, staring at the sky only to land hard on his back. He hit with such force that the air rushed from his lungs. Gasping, hurting, he tried to sit up and failed. Hannigan finally rolled to his side and used an elbow to get out of the dirt. His lungs hurt so bad breath refused to enter his chest. He tried to curse his horse, then saw there was no need. The horse had stepped into a badger hole and broken its leg. If Hannigan couldn't even make tiny mewling sounds, the horse made up for it with a keening that rose until Hannigan thought his eardrums would explode.

He kicked around, got his feet under him and stood on shaky legs. Air came slowly. Each breath hurt like fire filled his body. He stumbled over to the horse. Its nostrils flared as it thrashed about, eyes so wide white showed around the brown irises. Hannigan drew his six-gun and fired once, putting the horse out of its misery. The recoil caused him to stagger. He spun around and headed for a stand of pines off the road. His horse was gone, but that said nothing about those the posse rode.

There had to be a posse. Fitzsimmons offering a reward was the least of his worries now. If Captain Norwood got on the trail, Hannigan's crimes became federal. Running across a county line wouldn't be good enough to escape robbery and murder charges. He had to outrun the whole damned Union army.

He flopped onto the ground when he heard hooves thundering along the road. Squirming around, he saw a half dozen riders draw rein and circle his dead horse. One rider jumped down and examined the horse, reporting to a deputy. After exchanging a few more words, he struggled to pull the saddlebags from under the horse's carcass. The deputy rummaged through them, grumbled and tossed them back to the man on the ground. Hannigan froze like a deer when the deputy turned slowly in the saddle to take in the terrain. The lawman's scrutiny passed over Hannigan and centered on a patch of forest twenty yards back toward town.

Hannigan wanted to run but knew any motion would pull the posse's attention to him. He lay facedown and slowly recovered from having the wind knocked from him. His entire body hurt like demons poked him with pitchforks. As the pain faded, he looked back toward the road. A smile came to his lips. He recovered, and his luck soared. The deputy ordered had half his men on down the road. The rest he took back in the direction of Pine Knob. With only half the original number of deputized citizens hunting for him, he had a better chance of getting away.

Shooting one of them from the saddle and stealing his horse crossed Hannigan's mind, but he discarded that unless the theft happened away from the others. Why let them know he was nearby? Let them think he was all the way back to Georgia and beyond their law.

Slowly moving backwards on his belly, he got up so the thicket hid him from chance view from the road. He brushed himself off, turned, and faced a leveled shotgun.

"Howdy," Marshal Ike Putnam said. "If you want to keep on livin', get them hands up high and don't even think on doin' anything dumb." The marshal chuckled. "That might not be possible, I know, considerin' how that bank robbery went for you."

"You got the wrong man, Marshal. I didn't hold up a bank or kill anybody."

The lawman's smile faded. "Good of you to remind me how you flung lead around and left so many dead. None of them dead folks voted for me, but that don't mean them dyin' ain't a loss. I grew up with them. Why me and Lester, we soaked Miss Marley's chalk in ink so it turned black and when she tried writin' on the blackboard with it, nuthin' showed."

Hannigan lowered his hands a fraction of

an inch. If the garrulous marshal kept on, his attention would drift for a moment, giving an opening to —

"I got orders to bring you in alive, but nuthin 'd please me more than to drag your lifeless body back to town just to spite him."

"What are you saying?"

"I'm sayin' you use your left hand to take out your iron and drop it. Then strip off the gun belt. If you don't give me no trouble, I'll let you keep your boots on. Now do it!"

Hannigan had no choice. At this range, even the marshal wasn't going to miss with a shotgun. He dropped his six-gun, then let his holster fall to the ground.

"Let's start on back. I reckon we can make it by sundown. A pity you had to shoot your horse. It looked like a noble steed, not unlike one me and Lester stole from a drifter passin' through town. We was ten or eleven, so we didn't actually steal it. More like we borrowed it to see how such a fine horse rode 'cuz neither of us had ever seen one like it. Lester thought it was a Tennessee walker, but I knew better."

Hannigan considered making a break for it so the lawman would kill him. Dancing with the devil had to be better than listening to Marshal Putnam all the way back to

Pine Knob. Then he discovered something worse.

"You're not taking me to the jailhouse?"

"After all that walkin', you still got the energy to ask dumb questions? Might be I run you around town a couple times to burn off that curiosity?" Marshal Putnam hefted the shotgun resting across the saddle. "Go on up to the porch."

Hannigan knew who lived in the two-story house, and not being taken to the town's hoosegow gave him a surge of hope he might escape. The marshal had kept up a steady stream of personal stories of his days growing up in this hick town, but he had also been keen-eyed and alert. If Hannigan had tried to run, he would have filled his hide with buckshot. Now he had a chance to overpower Gerald Donnelly and get away.

Hannigan tromped up the steps. A black maid opened the door and silently ushered him inside. He sized up the place and made his plans. Try to get away now or later? If he waited, the marshal's attention would waver. That would be a better time than immediately.

The *click-click* of a cane tip against the wood floor brought him around.

Donnelly hobbled out, a black-gloved

hand gripping the cane's knob. "You didn't run too far." He pointed with the cane to a hard wooden chair.

"My horse stepped into a gopher hole and broke his leg." Hannigan sank into the chair, trying not to slouch. He had to remain alert. A quick sprint out the back meant freedom for him, but he had to avoid the marshal.

Donnelly snorted. He used the cane to lower himself into an overstuffed chair. He thrust out his injured foot and rested the cane on the toe of his boot. Seeing Hannigan's interest, he lifted the cane and pointed it at his heart. "It's a rifle, it's loaded, and it is quite accurate, especially at this range." Donnelly turned the golden knob on the end of the cane. A dull click warned that a trigger had sprouted on the underside and that a hammer was prepared to fall on a cartridge.

"Should I worry? You don't have a trigger finger. Heard tell it got shot off." Hannigan risked getting shot, but he wanted to see Donnelly's reaction.

Only a few reasons existed for Hannigan to be brought to the carpetbagger's house rather than thrown in jail — or left alongside the road, swinging from a tree with a rope around his neck. He had to find out what

Donnelly wanted before moving a muscle.

"Don't think you can anger me, Mr. Hannigan. Yes, I know your name. I know that Samuel Knight rode with you. Why did you part company?"

"He thought he was better than the rest of us."

"I detect a hint of bitterness in your words. It's easy to understand that he would leave you, but the rest of your men stayed with you. Where are they? After any robbery, even one as piss-poor as your attempted bank holdup, a rendezvous point would be part of the robbery."

The front door slammed open, interrupting Donnelly. He swung his cane gun around to center on Captain Norwood.

The army officer stalked over and with his back to Donnelly, faced Hannigan. "On your feet, sir! You are under arrest!"

"Norwood! Your lack of manners is appalling. Your tone is insulting, and my guest will not be badgered. I will not permit it under my roof!"

"Your guest? Are you confessing you took part in the bank robbery, too?"

"Your accusations fall on deaf ears, Captain. I have been appointed to administer civil law in Pine Knob and see that Reconstruction proceeds properly. As that administrator, I have authority to order the army to carry out my desires."

"You're not my superior, Donnelly. I take orders from the Secretary of War, not you. I —"

"I can get official orders here in a day, Captain. The telegraph is a great invention, and one which has connected Pine Knob with Washington, D.C. Secretary Stanton — you know Edwin Stanton, personally? I do — will respond quickly to my query as to whose wishes are to be followed here. I understand there is an opening for a junior lieutenant in Indian Territory. Are you willing to take a reduction in rank to assume a trivial command there, or would you prefer to be mustered out of the army entirely, Captain Norwood?"

Hannigan smirked at the officer's fury. Norwood turned red in the face and balled his fists, ready to strike out. Hannigan hoped he would try. He believed Donnelly would cut down the man should he attack either of them. That told Hannigan his position was more secure than he thought. He began to enjoy the bluecoat's discomfort.

"This man is a murderer. He and his gang killed four men and tried to rob the bank of an army payroll."

"Your money is intact, Captain, and the

death of any citizen of this fine town is unfortunate, but you are jumping to conclusions if you think Mr. Hannigan is responsible. Didn't the robbers wear disguises?"

"They had bandannas pulled up to hide their faces. But we got good descriptions of their clothes, and several witnesses overheard them calling each other by name."

"I have faith in the marshal to maintain order. There's no crime here to interest the military. Why, Pine Knob hasn't even tried to pass a Black Code or otherwise deny Negroes of their civil rights. That should interest you as it does me, showing our intense desire to maintain the rights of *all* citizens. That includes falsely accusing citizens of serious crimes. Now, Captain, I have business matters to discuss with Mr. Hannigan."

"Yeah, Norwood. Business," Hannigan said, feeling ten feet tall. He now held the winning hand, no matter that Donnelly pointed a rifle at him. He knew the man's weak points. All it took to get what he wanted was to mention Knight.

"I'll get evidence. When I arrest him, it won't matter if you are sleeping with Edwin Stanton's wife. You will watch Hannigan's execution, Donnelly. I promise." Norwood executed a right face, clicked his heels, and marched out, slamming the door behind him.

Donnelly turned back to Harrigan. "I will need to rehang the door. He needs to make more sedate exits."

"You surely did tell him off."

"I can get him back in a heartbeat, Hannigan. If you are not able to give me what I want, it will be amazing how quickly I can discover you were the leader of the gang cutting down locals."

Hannigan said nothing. The cane rifle pointed at him again, balanced on Donnelly's bad foot.

"Where is the rendezvous point for your gang? Tell me. I'll have them arrested and you will not be charged."

Hannigan never hesitated describing the hill where they had agreed to meet. "You'll have to approach from the north since even those fools will see you approaching from any other direction. There's heavy forest to the north, so sneaking up on them will be easy."

"You give them up so easily?"

Hannigan shrugged. What did it matter to him if Nott and the others were arrested?

"You are as much of a scoundrel as I hoped. Will you testify against them in court?"

"Not if it means I have to admit I was their leader. A lynch mob would string me up alongside them if I testified I was inside that bank."

"That won't be necessary. What will it take for you to track down Knight?"

Hannigan considered his options. "You're offering me a job?"

"Hector Alton did a poor job of bringing Knight to justice. Can you do better?"

Knight's betrayal showed on Hannigan's face, much to Donnelly's approval.

Hannigan settled down and chose his words carefully. "I'll find him. I know what he looks like, after all. How far could he have run?"

"I want you to go to the ends of the earth, if that's what it takes to drag him back here. Alive. He has to be alive."

"Does it matter if his health isn't all that good?"

Donnelly laughed harshly. He moved the rifle cane away from its target in the middle of Hannigan's chest, turned the knob, and retracted the trigger.

"I don't care. Bringing him to justice is my only concern. Alton failed. You will succeed, Mr. Hannigan, or I will find someone else who can."

"It's sure not going to be Captain Norwood. He's not willing to do what it takes to find Knight, much less arrest him."

"We agree on this, too. Good."

"It'd be easier if the rest of my men rode with me. They all know Knight and his ways. Four of us stand a better chance of getting him soon."

"Four?" Donnelly pursued his lips. "That's all in your gang?"

Hannigan restrained himself. Let Donnelly come to whatever conclusion he wanted. Knight and the Lunsford brothers would all pay for deserting. If Knight had to be alive, so be it. Nothing had been said about the two brothers.

"Do we have a deal, Mr. Donnelly?"

Gerald Donnelly stood, met Hannigan halfway, and thrust out his hand. Hannigan made no comment about the missing finger. This fool was going to help him run down Samuel Knight. After that, maybe Donnelly might suffer an accident and someone like Milo Hannigan might move up to replace him in Pine Knob as head of Reconstruction.

Someone *exactly* like Milo Hannigan.

CHAPTER 27

"It's pretty bad, isn't it?" Amos Parker pulled himself erect in bed and held up the blanket over his midsection for a quick look.

"You're not going to walk again, if that's what you mean." Samuel Knight closed his medical bag. "No more kicking dogs and other small animals."

"You got a mouth on you, Doctor." Amos dropped the blanket back. "Might be that's what she sees in you."

Knight perked up. He looked at the man, who fixed him with a steely look. Amos had improved dramatically in the past week. Once the threat of infection passed, his recovery had been nothing less than a miracle.

"That got your attention, didn't it? You know she's taken a shine to you. I'm not dead, either. I see the way you look at her." The man harrumphed. "She could do worse. Hell, 'fore he lit out for the goldfields intending to get rich without working, her boyfriend *was* worse. Never saw what she did in that Chisolm boy. A lazy lout who lived off his pa and second wife."

"But he was a handsome lazy lout, Papa," Amelia Parker said from the doorway, "and he had hidden talents."

"You hush up, girl. That's more'n I want to know. It's likely more'n the doc wants to know, too. Isn't that so, Dr. Knight?"

"You rest, Amos. You've got a bottle of whiskey if the pain gets to be too much, but I predict you'll be out of bed by this time next week. We'll see about getting you outfitted with crutches."

"Samuel's asked around town and gotten Mr. Orr to fix you up. You know how good he is making furniture. He said it would be a challenge to carve you a set of crutches that wouldn't break under your, uh —"

"Bullshit. That's what Grayson Orr would say, isn't it?"

"Rest, Amos. I've got to drive your daughter back to town. Other people get sick, too."

"And, Papa, I took a job as bookkeeper at the bank. It doesn't pay much but it'll keep us going." Amelia Parker looked smug at her triumph, getting her father's full attention.

"Thanks for not saying until I get back on

my feet." Amos heaved a sigh. "I suppose we need the extra money to pay off the doctor."

"I work cheap." Knight looked at Amelia. She blushed. He wondered what went through her mind in that instant and how close it was to what he was thinking.

"Nobody with good sense thinks that the price you're likely to pay is cheap," Amos said. "You two, get out of here and let a man get his beauty sleep."

"Papa, there aren't enough hours in the day for that to do much good." She bent and kissed him on the forehead, tucked the blanket around what remained of his legs, and hurried away to the front room.

Knight trailed her out, appreciating the view from behind as she bent to pick up her purse and a large ledger.

She looked back without straightening and gave him a smile that could only be described as lascivious. "For my entries," she said.

It was his turn to blush.

She stood up and held out the ledger. "For my *bank* entries. I do declare, Dr. Knight, you seem to have developed quite a sunburn. How did you do that with all the time you spend indoors?"

He went to her. His arm circled her trim

waist and pulled her close for a kiss. She didn't resist. If anything, she melted even closer as she returned the affection, but she pushed back too soon.

"I do have to get to work in town." She looked up at him, her expression unreadable. In a whisper she asked, "Is that payment for what you did for my pa?"

"Not even close. Now, let's go. My horse isn't used to pulling a buggy."

Arm in arm they went to the buggy. He helped her up, then hopped in to snap the reins. The horse protested, shook its head and finally decided to begin pulling.

"I get off work at five this evening," she said. "May I expect an escort home? So you can be certain Papa is following your orders?"

"It depends on how many people need my services. How Buffalo Springs survived without a doctor is beyond me. Some are in serious condition, but the ones who just want to look me over are lined up like I was giving away free money."

"I am sure they all find you perfectly acceptable. I do." Amelia Parker looked ahead, her hands demurely folded in her lap. "You and the Lunsford boys? Have you been friends long? You seem like an unlikely trio."

Knight wondered how clever it was to tell

her of their background, but his story of being in Elmira with Ben came out in bits and dabs. As it did, he had to ask her about how well Ben Lunsford was fitting into town.

"I don't socialize with anyone who frequents the saloon, but more than one who comes to the bank has mentioned how Seth Lunsford is quite personable and has favorably impressed Mr. Yarrow. Don't tell Seth that, though," she cautioned. "Mr. Yarrow likes to pretend he's an old meanie. He's not any of that and has been saying nice things about Seth's determination and work ethic." She swiveled a little to half face him. "This is especially consequential because Seth and Mr. Yarrow's daughter have been seeing a great deal of one another."

"So he has a girlfriend?" Knight had to smile. Buffalo Springs was kinder to them than he had expected.

"You make it sound as if such a thing never happened. We are very friendly in town." When he laughed, she hastily added, "Not *that* friendly, but friendly. Treat us well and reap the rewards."

"I'm certainly not reaping rewards for treating the Buffalo Springs citizens as patients. No one has money to pay me. Mr. Hesseltine offered me five acres of his farm in return for treating his boy."

403

"And you turned him down. Why is that? West Texas is dry, and growing anything in this alkali soil is difficult, but five acres is still valuable."

"What's his son going to inherit when he gets older if I take his pa's land? I'll take a bale or two of hay. I can trade that for a place to sleep in the stables."

"I've meant to ask about that. Do you like sleeping in a horse stall? Does your horse pine away without your presence all night long?"

"Nothing like that. Without money, I can't even rent the smallest room at Miz Dennison's boarding house. This way, I have a roof over my head and get out of those dust storms."

"If you let me use your horse to pull my buggy to get home this evening, and you don't come along, how am I supposed to return the horse for your night of bliss together?"

"You'll bring it back tomorrow. All my patients today are in town."

"I . . . I have a better idea. We, I mean Papa, has a spare room in the house. There's no way I, we, *he* can ever repay you for your work keeping him alive. It's not much, but the straw is cleaner than in a livery stable."

"Are you angling for me to be able to look

in on my patient anytime during the night?" Knight grinned when he saw her blush.

"Consider the offer. Here's the bank. Leave the buggy and horse around back. There's a watering trough and a post where you can tether the horse." She stepped down and stopped for a moment, still looking into the bank. "Good-bye, Samuel."

"See you tomorrow, Amelia."

She pulled back her shoulders and walked proudly into the bank. Knight watched and waited. She hesitated, shot a quick look back, blew him a kiss, and hurried inside.

He heaved a sigh. Life always got more complicated. Buffalo Springs had been a stopover, a place to get supplies before moving on, and now he considered settling here. The idea of finding a woman who made him forget Victoria startled him, but being able to outrun everything else that had happened in Pine Knob had to be a miracle. Gerald Donnelly and Captain Norwood and Milo Hannigan, all in the past.

He hefted his medical bag and started toward the Golden Gate Saloon but hesitated when he reached the gunsmith's shop. Seth Lunsford sat at a table, peering closely at a trigger mechanism he had disassembled. Knight went in. His shadow crossed the table and made Seth look up.

The boy blinked, rubbed his eyes and said, "How're you doin', Doc? I've got a broken spring I can't seem to reach, not with my clumsy fingers." He held up the trigger assembly. "I told Mr. Yarrow I'd finish it before lunch but I'm no closer to getting it done than I was an hour ago."

"Let me see." Knight held it up, scowled, then handed the trigger back. "I bent a pair of forceps and the instrument's not worth a whole bunch to me now." He rummaged about until he found the damaged forceps and handed them to Seth. "Try this. See if you can hook the spring and pull it taut."

Seth Lunsford chewed his tongue as he worked, then sat back with a surprised look on his face. "You saved me, Doc. I can't believe it was so easy."

"Use the right tool and all things are possible." He held up his hand when Seth held out the forceps. "I've got a good pair. Keep those. You might need them again."

"I can think of a couple different ways to use them. Thanks, Doc. Thanks! What can I do to pay you back?"

Knight knew he had to say something or get into an endless argument. He took off his gunbelt and laid it on the table. "Cleaning and oiling take time, and with all the patients lining up, I haven't had a chance to get rid of the grit."

"This place does kick up a passel of dust." Seth slipped the Colt Navy from the holster. "This is one fine six-gun, Doc. I'll get it all fixed up proper for you. I might even get to use this." He held up the forceps.

"Don't work too many hours. I heard tell you've got better things to do with your time off from the shop. What's her name?"

"Aw, Doc, you're gossipin'. I didn't think you were the kind. There's nuthin' goin' on between me and Marianne — Miss Yarrow."

"Good luck with that 'nothing.' I was on my way to see if anybody had shown up for my office hours at the saloon. Is Ben working right now?"

"He's always workin'. Miss Hattie's a real slave driver. He doesn't complain much, but I can tell he doesn't like her or the job."

"There're plenty of other jobs. Amos Parker needs a spare hand on his farm until he learns how to get around without legs. Ben can help out." Even after Amos got up and around, there'd be much he couldn't do.

Knight knew the farm was prosperous enough to support the Parkers, but if Ben added his strong back to the mix, it could be the best within twenty miles of Buffalo Springs.

"I dunno 'bout that, Doc. He said he'd

never do any farmin' again. He sounded mighty sure of that, but it's got to be better than puttin' up with all those drunks every night."

"All?" Knight shook his head in wonder. The Golden Gate hardly counted as a ghost town with its few customers, yet Seth thought it was crowded with drunks.

"I'll have your Colt all fixed up and ready to go by the end of the day."

"Thanks, Seth." Knight looked around the gunsmith shop, then left. He needed ammunition for the six-gun, but in Buffalo Springs spending what little money he earned for powder and bullets was an extravagance. The town was peaceful. He liked that.

He walked slowly down the boardwalk, greeting people as he went. Hardly a one hadn't been helped by him in some way. They were friendly once the notion settled into their heads that he was capable and not some snake-oil salesman. He pushed through the colorful swinging doors into the Golden Gate. Two men already sat at his "examination" table in the back. He stopped at the bar first.

"Not many customers today, or did you poison the rest with your rotgut, Ben?" He tried to joke, but the sour expression told him Ben Lunsford wasn't in the mood. "Anything I can do?"

"Doc, you can take your gun, shoot me, and put me out of my misery." Ben looked around, hunting for Hattie Malone. Not seeing her, he didn't bother keeping his voice low. "She docked me a week's wages for breaking too many bottles."

"Seems there's bound to be some breakage. That's not fair to you."

"It ain't fair at all. The longer I work, the deeper I get in debt to her. I can't see the end of the tunnel, and she's got me workin' double shifts. Double shifts! And I always do somethin' wrong and owe even more."

"Working more and owing more's no good," Knight agreed. "Do you want me to talk to her? I can reason with her."

"Don't bother. She's suspicious of doctors and damned near everyone else. It would only make things worse for me."

"Other than that, how are the people in Buffalo Springs treating you? Seth's got himself a lady friend. Do you have any prospects?" Knight sucked in his breath when he saw the flash of anger in Ben's eyes.

"I did, but she found somebody else."

"There are plenty of women in Buffalo Springs. If you promise not to run off to prospect for gold, you can have your pick."

"Yeah, my pick. You want a bottle for your customers? You're the best business this place has, Doc."

"I wish I collected as much as Hattie does for me bringing in business."

"You need an office of your own. A surgery. There's an empty place down by the gunsmith shop. Seth can show you. He mentioned it to me yesterday."

"I'm not sure I could afford it, but maybe the landlord there would cut me a deal."

"Sure, Doc, why not? Ain't nobody in town what don't like you like a brother."

Knight wanted to find out what was eating away at Ben, but a low moan from the rear of the saloon caught his attention. From the way the man held his gut and doubled over, he was in serious need of medical attention.

"Got to operate, I'm afraid. That looks like a case of bad indigestion or appendicitis. Considering old Quinton can eat a work glove and think it needed salt, you'd better get the sheets out and hang up some curtains so I can work."

"Why bother? The customers would take bets on whether he'd bite the dust. Oh, all right. I'll hang up the sheets." Ben left his place behind the bar and vanished into the back room.

Knight set about getting enough whiskey into Quinton to dull his senses, then began cutting. He'd been right about the ailment. By the end of the day, people came in to congratulate him for saving Quinton's life. He had, but his modesty kept him from taking too much credit.

Besides, he was kept humble by the disapproving looks that Ben Lunsford gave him from behind the bar.

CHAPTER 28

Ben Lunsford looked around the empty saloon, spat toward a cuspidor and missed, and finally dug around under the bar until he found his special bottle. The amber liquor tasted good and wouldn't rot his belly like the trade whiskey he concocted and sold to the few customers foolish enough to come into the Golden Gate. He sloshed an inch of whiskey around in the bottle, pulled the cork and took a healthy swig. The whiskey burned all the way down and puddled in his stomach. The warmth spread and chased away some of the discontent he felt. A second gulp drained the bottle.

His tippling had increased to outright guzzling. It took more booze to have any effect, but he switched bottles in the back room, filled some with water and others with the grain alcohol to improve the kick, and Hattie Malone never noticed her stock was being drained by a nonpaying customer.

"She owes me," he said, bending down behind the bar to take out another full bottle from a case that had come all the way from Kentucky. "She owes me big-time. Won't pay me what I'm worth." He had started to break the seal and pull the cork when a customer at the bar cleared his throat.

"You think that, Ben, then I got a job for you. Leave Hattie and come to work for me over at the livery." Jacob Stevenson put his elbows on the bar and leaned over to stare at him.

"Doing what? Mucking stalls?"

"That," the man said. "And I'm getting in a dozen mares for breeding. I decided I can raise them and sell to the army. Heard they're going to build a post near Buffalo Springs."

"Do tell. Where's this?"

"Can't be too far. They need to store their payroll in the bank. Now are you going to draw me a beer? And I want some of that free lunch mentioned on the sign out front."

"I haven't had time to do up a sandwich. The beer's on the house." Ben worked the cork out of the bottle, considered taking a draw from it, then settled for a shot glass since he had a customer who might bad-mouth him for putting his lips to whiskey intended for others.

Clifton Stevenson frowned when he saw the calculation going on, but he plowed ahead with his offer.

"A partner's what I need when I get the ranch working. A dozen horses to start and I can expand it to ten times that."

"You'd take me on as a partner? You offerin' me half?"

"You can work up to that. Right now I'm raising the money. If you know anything about raising horses, that'd go a ways toward becoming a full partner in a year or two."

"Sounds like a lot of work."

"It would be," said Stevenson, "and there wouldn't be any hitting the bottle while you work for me."

"Where's the money comin' from? The livery's not makin' much. Not enough for this kind of dream to come true."

Stevenson took a big drink of the beer and leaned forward to conspiratorially whisper, "I got a ton of money sitting in the bank right now from an uncle what died back East."

"The money's burnin' a hole in your pocket? Why not give me some of it?" Ben Lunsford laughed at that.

Stevenson nodded. "That's what I'm doing, wanting you to come work for me. Two years is what I figure before you'd be a full partner."

"Tell you what, Jacob, let me think on it. Then maybe we can drink on it." Ben knocked back a shot and poured himself another.

"Don't get too far into that bottle, Ben. Liquor's a cruel master." Stevenson finished his beer. "Thanks. Let me know soon on my offer. I need to get started with that herd before winter sets in."

Ben Lunsford watched the livery stable owner push through the swinging doors. He took another shot of whiskey and lifted it in mock salute. The liquor hardly burned now. He had deadened his innards. Another shot tasted good to him, and another until he decided another customer wasn't coming in. Maybe after the workday ended. Ben closed the outer doors and turned around the CLOSED sign.

Bottle in hand, he made his way on unsteady legs down the main street. "Buffalo Springs," he muttered. "What a dump." He stopped in front of the bank and thought about what Stevenson said about a large inheritance sitting in there.

He had seen the vault. The door couldn't be opened, but brick walls surrounded the metal cage where the money had to be stacked. Pull those bricks out and he knew he could reach in through the metal strips and take the money. If he had any skill with a lariat, he could toss a loop into the cage and rope anything there. He reenacted a sudden pull that would drag money and boxes where he could grab it. He lost his balance and sat hard.

That let him see into the bank lobby. Anger built when Amelia Parker walked across his field of vision. She had strung him along until Doc Knight stole her from him. From the way she talked with the bank president, she worked there now. He hadn't heard and Knight sure as hell hadn't mentioned it. Breaking into that vault would show them all. Knight and Amelia Parker and everybody in Buffalo Springs.

Ben pushed himself to his feet, made sure the bottle was intact, and continued to the edge of town. Empty stores and houses gave mute testimony to how the population had been decimated by the lure of gold strikes farther west. He kicked in a door and staggered in. To his surprise, a man cloaked in shadow sat at the dusty table.

"Never thought to see you here, Ben. And you brought me a bottle. I don't have any glasses so we'll have to take turns drinking straight from the bottle."

"Milo?" Ben Lunsford stared at the shadowy figure, then at the bottle. He had been hitting the booze hard all day, but he'd never experienced hallucinations before. Some of the men who frequented the Golden Gate complained of seeing mirages and hearing voices. He thought that meant they were weak-minded, not like him.

"You're a hard man to find, Ben."

Ben Lunsford tried to back up and flee, but Hannigan drew his six-shooter and laid it on the table. To make sure Ben got the idea, he shifted in his chair and pointed the muzzle straight at him without picking up the gun.

"It was Doc. He talked me into leavin'. I didn't want to. Honest."

"Now, why do I think there's only a hint of truth in what you're saying? You aren't the type of fellow to be swayed. Seth, now, Seth is another matter. That boy's got no willpower. Tell him to eat a bug and he'd gobble it right on up. Ain't that so?"

Ben nodded. He took a quick drink to steady his nerves. His heart threatened to explode in his chest. "I never thought I'd see you again, Milo."

"Things change all the time, Ben. Sit. And put the bottle where I can get to it. You *are*

417

offering me a drink, aren't you?" He slid the gun to one side and made room for the bottle between them on the table.

"Sure thing, Milo." Ben pulled up a rickety chair across from the gang's leader. With a shaking hand, he pushed the bottle closer. Hannigan made no move to drink, so Ben took a long swig to steady his nerves. It didn't help.

"Is Sam here? In Buffalo Springs? That's the name of this dusty hellhole, isn't it?"

"Yes." Ben made no effort to keep the contempt and outright anger from his voice. The single word came out more like a cussword than a simple answer.

"Well, well, you two have had a falling-out? Is that it?"

"We don't see eye to eye on some things." Fury that Knight had taken up with Amelia Parker when he'd seen her first burned away some of the drunkenness. He took another drink and lowered the level in the bottle by a finger.

"Would you see eye to eye with coming back to my gang?"

"All of you? Nott, Lattimer, and Porkchop?" Ben looked around, expecting them to pop up like Hannigan had.

"I came into town by myself. A scouting expedition. They're outside of town. We've got regular jobs now working for Gerald Donnelly."

"The carpetbagger? How'd that happen?"

"We got into a mess in Pine Knob, and he vouched for us, let's say. In return for not locking us up, we work for him. Like Hector Alton."

"Alton?"

"He's dead, Ben. Your good friend Sam cut him down."

"Yeah, right, I knew that." The alcoholic haze made thinking — remembering — hard. "It's somethin' he'd do. Did he shoot him in the back?"

"Might as well have. Tell me about Buffalo Springs and everything that's going on here."

"For Donnelly?"

"For me, Ben. For us. For all of us. That bank looks attractive, but half of Buffalo Springs has turned into a ghost town."

"There's plenny of money in the bank, Milo." Ben Lunsford gushed out what he had just heard from Jacob Stevenson. "And word is that the army's puttin' in a post not far out of town. They'll keep their payroll here until they finish buildin' their fort."

"It's a fool's errand robbing an army post," Hannigan said. "They have sentries with rifles and enough firepower to make it downright dangerous if anything went wrong. No, I prefer to grab the money before it reaches the quartermaster's hands."

"It'll be months 'fore they get troops moved in, but the money Stevenson inherited. That's in the bank."

"How much?"

"Can't rightly say, but it's enough to start a horse ranch. Breedin' stock and land and all."

"You're winning me over to thinking you can fit back into the gang, Ben. What more is there if we swooped down on a town all unexpectedlike? Other businesses with money to steal?"

"I think the Golden Gate's owner has a stack of greenbacks hidden somewhere. She must. Business is terrible, but she always has money to buy supplies. She musta made it 'fore most of the men hied off to find gold."

"A bank brimming with money, a saloon where there must be sacks of money, a town without many men. Ben, I'm beginning to feel a plan forming. Let's drink to a profitable reunion, you and me and the rest of the boys." Milo Hannigan took the bottle from Ben's hands and sampled the liquor. He made an appreciative nod and handed the bottle back.

Ben's thirst required him to drink twice what Hannigan had. He wiped his lips on his sleeve, then started to speak. He caught himself. Hannigan saw the hesitation.

"Spit it out, Ben. If we're riding together again, we're partners. Partners share whatever's on their mind."

"I want Seth to get back with you. And the rest of the gang."

"Just your brother? Not Sam, too? It's good to have a doctor along to patch us up when we run into a bullet or two."

"If you want him. But Seth's my brother. I gotta take care of him."

"How noble of you. Of course you can invite him to ride with us again. Just be sure he doesn't go blabbin' to the law. There is a marshal in town, isn't there?"

"He's old and crippled up with arthritis."

"I'm liking what I hear more by the minute. You talk to Seth. Then the two of you meet up with us south of town a couple miles. There's a stock pond near the road. We're camping there. You come on out before dawn and then we'll take this town apart."

"Take it apart," Ben whispered. He liked the sound of that. He owed nobody nothing in Buffalo Springs.

"And you be sure Sam rides out with you. There's no call to tell him you and Seth have joined up with us again. He might not believe you. Tell him whatever it takes, but bring him to camp and let me convince him it's the right thing to do to ride with the Hannigan gang again."

"Right, Milo." Ben took another stiff drink. He pushed the bottle toward Hannigan, but the outlaw leader pushed it back.

"I've got to tell the others what's happening. Dawn tomorrow. And get Sam to join you." Hannigan grabbed his gun with impressive speed, spun it around, finger in the trigger guard, and slid the six-gun into his holster as he stood. He touched the brim of his hat in a mocking salute and left through the back door.

Ben sat shaking as he worked on the bottle. Hannigan had been the last man on earth he'd expected to see in Buffalo Springs. Knight had promised that nobody was on their trail, not the army and certainly not Milo Hannigan and his gang. Ben snorted in disgust. That showed what Dr. Samuel Knight knew. Nothing. He didn't know squat.

Purpose came back to him. He had drifted along, not going anywhere and seeing no future working as barkeep in Hattie Malone's saloon. Riding with a smart man like Milo Hannigan changed things. They'd crack this town like a walnut. They'd ride out of Buffalo Springs with saddlebags crammed full of money.

And maybe he could sample a bit of what Knight did with Amelia Parker. That'd be retribution for her getting stolen away. It'd show her what she missed by taking up with Knight. Hannigan was all het up to get Knight to rejoin the gang, but Ben had other ideas. If he forced Knight to watch while him and Amelia —

"Ben! Ben! I was lookin' for you and I saw Hannigan. Milo Hannigan. He was ridin' out of town like he owned the place." Seth Lunsford stood outlined in the doorway. "Are you all right?"

"Come on in and have a drink. I got a proposition for you, Seth. It's what we've been waitin' for ever since we blowed into this town."

"You talked with Milo? Ben, he's poison. You know what Doc said about him."

"Have a drink, and I'll explain it all to you, boy. You've got enough wrong to confuse you. I'll set you straight about the way it's gonna be."

Seth silently entered and sank into the chair Hannigan had occupied only minutes earlier. It took Ben longer to lay it all out because his words slurred, but he sobered as he talked. Excitement burned away the fog. And determination grew, along with plans of his own. Plans for Dr. Samuel Knight.

CHAPTER 29

"That'll fix you up," Samuel Knight said, wiping the blood off his hands. "I've sewed up the cut. Keep it washed now and then with whiskey and you'll be right as rain in a week or two."

The cowboy pushed up off the table at the rear of the Golden Gate saloon, winced, and put his hand over the sutures. "Poured on the stitches or poured down my gullet to kill the pain?"

Knight laughed. It was too common a sentiment when he finished.

"If you ask real sweet, Hattie will give you a discount. For a week."

"Doc, you ought to get a cut of all the booze sold here. Everybody I know likes the idea of you perscribblin' whiskey for what ails us." The cowboy gingerly took a step. The next came with more confidence. He smiled. "This ain't so bad. I'll be back in the saddle 'fore I know it."

"You tell your boss I want you with both feet on the ground for a week. Don't go riding or the wound'll rip open and your guts will spill out."

"That'd prove I got guts. Some of the others on the spread don't think I do."

"Is that why you got gored by a bull? You tried to show them you weren't afraid and waved a red flag in front of a mountain of gristle and mean?"

The cowboy looked sheepish and nodded.

"Get on out of here. And don't ride until this time next week."

The cowboy shuffled away. Knight settled down into a chair. The saloon was empty except for him and Ben Lunsford.

"Hey, Ben, can I have a beer? Doing all this doctoring has given me quite a thirst."

"Sure, Doc, why not? You ought to get paid something, and that deadbeat ain't gonna pay you a dime."

"I'll get a cow from his boss. Maybe a few steaks to keep me going this winter."

Ben Lunsford sat beside Knight and slid a beer across the bloodstained table used for his operations. Knight wondered what was eating his friend. He asked. "You look like someone's walking on your grave. What's wrong?"

"Everything, Doc. Ever damned thing in

this town. Look, I need for you to come with me tonight."

"What's up?" Knight saw a subtle change in the man's demeanor. Ben had gone from nervous to cagey.

"I got something to show you. It'll be worth your time."

"Should I bring my medical bag?"

That took Ben by surprise. He opened his mouth, closed it, then said, "That'd be a good idea, I reckon. Your doctoring skills won't be needed, leastways I don't think so. But you will enjoy it. Meet me outside the livery after I close up here."

"All right, Ben. I have to admit you're piquing my curiosity."

"Yeah, I'm pickin' it, Doc." He stood abruptly and almost ran back behind the bar as if he was a little boy caught doing something naughty.

Knight had no idea what was going on, but he'd find out soon enough. The saloon would close in a couple hours. He had time to make a quick circuit of town to see if anyone else needed medical attention. He finished his beer, bid Ben good-bye, and stepped out into the cool afternoon.

Sometimes he only helped the town's residents with small chores, just to keep busy. They appreciated it, and it gave him a sense of belonging to the community, no matter that he had just arrived. He sauntered along, greeting those out and about. As he walked past the gunsmith shop, Seth Lunsford waved to him to come in.

"Evening, Seth. How's everything?"

"Fine, Doc. Just fine."

"You did a good job cleaning and oiling my Colt. I've never felt it work better. With the ammo and powder you gave me, all of it right here in my bag, I can go plink at cans to keep my marksmanship sharp when I get a break."

"Doc, has Ben said anything to you about . . . about him?"

"Him? You mean Ben or someone else? I just left your brother over at the saloon and when he closes up, we're riding out."

Seth turned white. "Doc, I don't want to go."

"What are you talking about? What's anybody talking about? Ben wouldn't say where we were going, just that it was a surprise I would enjoy."

"I don't think so, Doc. I really don't think you will enjoy it. If he didn't tell you, that means they're layin' an ambush for you."

Knight pulled up a chair and sank into it. He had never seen Seth Lunsford this agitated. "Give it all to me. The whole story.

Where don't you want to go and how's this tie in with Ben and me going off to some secret rendezvous?"

"Ben talked with him, and they want me to ride with them again. I like Buffalo Springs, Doc. I got a good job, and then there's me and . . ."

"The boss's daughter." Knight had to smile. He understood how this anchored Seth to the town. He felt the same weight with Amelia Parker holding him, and he found himself enjoying it.

"Yeah, that. I don't want to leave."

"Then don't." Knight went cold inside when he finally understood Seth's dilemma. "It's loyalty to your brother and —"

"And Milo Hannigan. Him and Ben got together. I saw them in a deserted house on the edge of town sharin' a bottle and talkin' like they were partners and he'd never rode off without so much as a fare-thee-well."

"Hannigan's in town?"

"Down the road a few miles at a stock pond. I didn't hear what he said to Ben, but gettin' you to ride with him again isn't what he wants. Ben hinted that Hannigan is workin' for that carpetbagger back in Pine Knob. Donnelly has sent Hannigan and his entire gang out to catch you and take you back."

Knight's mind spun in crazy circles. He had always thought it was possible for Donnelly to send a posse after him, but it had been long enough that even the carpet-bagger should have given up. Cutting his Achilles tendon and shooting off his finger ought to have alerted Knight that Donnelly would never quit hunting for him. After he'd shot down Hector Alton the doctor foolishly thought he was safe and that Donnelly would creep away in fear and shame.

"All of them are after my scalp?"

"Doc, it must be worse than that."

Knight had no idea how it could get worse. Everything he had done in Buffalo Springs lay in jeopardy of being destroyed.

"They're goin' to hurrah the town. I heard rumors that Jacob Stevenson's got a pile of money sittin' in the bank. If Ben mentioned that, Hannigan won't be able to keep his hands off it." Seth Lunsford picked up an oily rag and began twisting it around his hand, first in one direction and then in the other. His agitation was contagious.

Knight began fidgeting as he tried to work out something that preserved the good work he had done so far and didn't endanger anyone in town.

That included Amelia Parker.

"Do you think Hannigan has told Donnelly he's found me? Us?" He saw that Seth had no idea. Everything Seth had learned came from his brother, and Knight doubted Hannigan trusted Ben anymore. He played on Ben's discontent to do Donnelly's bidding.

If Hannigan had stumbled across Buffalo Springs and found where Knight had gone to ground, he would be safe if Hannigan died — Hannigan and the rest of his gang. That was a tall order and one Knight wasn't sure he cared to consider as a solution.

"Have you told anyone else?"

"No one, Doc. Nary a soul. What are we goin' to do? If Ben's throwed in with Hannigan again, nothin' either of us say will sway him."

"I can go along with him and maybe get the drop on Hannigan." Knight experienced a second's dizziness. That was no solution. He had to kill not only Hannigan and the three riding with him but also Ben Lunsford to keep them from reporting back to Donnelly where his pigeon had come to roost. Ben turning on him cut Knight to the quick. Seth might be wrong about his brother's intentions, but the setup smacked of betrayal. Ben had sold him out to Hannigan. And Gerald Donnelly.

"What if I try to talk him out of it? He's

my brother. He should listen to me."

Knight doubted that would happen, but Seth's idea was the best of any he came up with.

"I'll stay out of sight and back you up. If he tries to hurt you, I'll —" Knight thought what he would do but his lips refused to put the rest of it into words. *Shoot him down like a mad dog.*

"Strap on your six-shooter, Doc. Catch up."

"Wait, Seth. Don't go on alone." Knight tried to grab the boy, but he slipped through his fingers like a greased pig and looked around. Somehow he knew his brother waited at the stables and took off at a run.

Knight pulled his gun belt from the medical bag, closed the bag, and stashed it under the table Seth had used to work on the six-shooter. He settled the gun belt around his waist, tied down the holster with a rawhide thong, and went after Seth. His steps faltered when he passed the bank. If Ben Lunsford was stopped, there'd be no need for anyone in the bank to know the danger they might have faced. When Ben never showed, Hannigan had to realize his plans had fallen apart and leave.

Knight knew he kidded himself. Hannigan didn't have sense enough to ride away.

Besides, with the object of Donnelly's hatred still in Buffalo Springs, Hannigan had a mission beyond robbing the bank and shooting up the town.

Knight pushed open the door and looked around the small lobby. Amelia Parker looked up from her desk, smiled, and motioned him over. Time pressed in on him. He had to be sure Ben's anger didn't overflow and drown his brother. But he went in.

"Are you coming out to the farm tonight for dinner? Papa wants . . . What's wrong, Samuel?" Even worried, Amelia Parker was beautiful.

"Close and lock the vault. Tell everyone you can find there's likely to be a raid on Buffalo Springs. It's the Hannigan gang. The marshal won't have wanted posters on them, but that doesn't mean they're not all vicious killers."

"Wait, Samuel, where are you going? You put on your gun. You're not taking them on all by yourself!"

"Amelia, spread the word. Barricade everything and then get to safety. Leave right away for the farm and keep your pa safe."

"You want me out of the way. Who are these men, Samuel? Who?"

433

He grabbed her, pulled her close, and planted a frantic kiss on her ruby lips. She gasped for air and started to ask more questions. He left before she had the chance. Twilight moved swiftly through the streets, turning every alley into a potential ambush and sending ghosts flitting about behind unlit windows. Here and there oil lamps flared, but he worried that Amelia's alert would go unheeded. Buffalo Springs was too peaceable a town for its own good, and it was going to pay for that.

Turning the corner, he saw the corral behind the livery stable. Several horses swayed, preparing to go to sleep. He approached slowly, hand on his six-shooter. Loud voices echoed from inside. Pressing against the wall, he slipped his six-gun out, cocked it, and spun through the opening, hunting for a target.

"Looks like a Mexican standoff, Doc." Ben Lunsford stood with one arm around his brother's neck. In his other hand he held a six-gun.

"Let Seth go. This is between us, isn't it? Did Hannigan offer reward money for me?"

"Something like that, but I got a beef with you that money won't settle."

"I never did anything to you. You're my friend. We survived Elmira by depending on each other."

"You changed, Doc. You turned into a lowdown snake. Everyone in this damned town thinks you're a saint. Me, they wouldn't wet their whistle to spit on me."

Seth tried to speak, but Ben tightened his grip and choked off the words.

"Me and my brother'll go join up with Hannigan. He wants you alive to give over to Gerald Donnelly, but I think I'll just shoot you."

"He doesn't want to ride with the gang anymore, Ben. Seth has a life here. He's got a girl and —"

Knight dived and rolled when Ben Lunsford opened fire. Bullets kicked up straw and muck inches away. He found shelter behind a bale of hay.

"What's eating you, Ben?" he called as he stayed low, out of the line of fire.

"You took her! You stole her away from me. *I saw her first.* I was the one givin' her pa his painkiller, but you chopped off his legs so he wouldn't be hurtin' no more. Why'd she want a barkeep when she can have a doctor?"

Three more rounds tore into the hay bale. Knight tried to remember how many shots Ben had already fired. Two? Or was it three and he had to reload? He took the chance and stood, his pistol held stiff-armed and pointed straight at Ben Lunsford. His luck held. Ben tried to reload and hang on to Seth at the same time.

Seth dropped to his knees, then threw himself forward so Knight had a clear shot. His finger came back slowly. The front sight centered on Ben's chest.

He couldn't shoot. Not after all they had been through.

"I knew you was a coward, Doc. You're a coward!" Ben Lunsford kicked at his brother, then ducked into a stall.

"Get out of there," Knight yelled at the younger Lunsford.

"He's reloaded, Doc. He's gonna shoot you."

Knight waited for Ben to pop up. Such a shot came easily, but his qualms about hurting a onetime friend made his bullet go wide, tearing away a big bright splinter from the partition between stalls. Then Knight had to duck as Ben sent a flurry of lead in his direction. He waited for the shooting to stop to try again. Seth Lunsford hunkered down on the far side of the door, safe.

A million things confused Knight. He was a doctor pledged to save lives, not take them. Ben Lunsford wanted to bring Hannigan and his cutthroats to Buffalo Springs to shoot up the town and rob the bank. What Ben had in mind for Amelia Parker if no one stopped him drove all the good sense from Knight's brain and forced him to act.

"Doc, no!" Seth Lunsford cried out to stop him.

Knight hopped over the bale of hay, his six-shooter leading the way as he charged forward to end this. Ben Lunsford would never get his filthy hands on Amelia. Ever.

He fired twice as he rounded the end of the stall. The bullets tore into wood. The stall stood empty, mocking him. Ben Lunsford had hightailed it. He had left to report to Milo Hannigan. It was only a matter of time before the Hannigan gang swooped down on Buffalo Springs and the real fight began.

CHAPTER 30

"I knew he was a scoundrel. Never shoulda hired him." Hattie Malone slammed her fist down on the bar so hard glasses rattled the entire length. She picked up the shotgun and waved it around. "When I get Ben Lunsford in my sights, I'll blow him to kingdom come!"

Knight glanced at Seth, sitting in a chair at the edge of the crowd. It had taken several hours to get the townspeople assembled in the Golden Gate saloon, but Seth hadn't recovered from the shock of seeing how his brother behaved, how he had threatened to kill him, and then shot at a man who hadn't done him any harm.

Knight moved so he put some space between himself and Amelia Parker. She had insisted on attending, claiming Buffalo Springs was as much her home as any of the others. He had failed to get her to ride back to the farm and guard her father. Her thinking on the matter made sense. Hannigan and the rest likely wanted whatever they could steal in town. The outlying farms and ranches were too scattered for easy plundering. That left her pa high and dry and safer than if he were in town armed with a rifle.

Knight still wished she would leave for her pa's farm. Hannigan showed a vicious streak, and Knight hadn't told her what Ben Lunsford had said about wanting her for his own. If nothing else, with her beside him, Knight could keep her safe. He had the option of trading his life for hers. Of everything in Buffalo Springs, that deal made the best sense if Hannigan rode triumphantly through the streets.

He wanted Dr. Samuel Knight. Gerald Donnelly wanted him. The bluecoats wanted him. There wasn't hardly anyone in East Texas who didn't want a piece of Knight's hide to nail up on their wall.

"Where's Marshal Hightower? Didn't you send for him?" He looked over his shoulder and saw the answer in Seth's expression. So much had swirled around the young man, he had forgotten to get word to the lawman. "Never mind. I'll fetch him."

"I'll go with you, Samuel." Amelia Parker locked her arm through his so escape without her was nigh on impossible.

The short distance down to the marshal's office gave him a chance to try again to persuade her to leave town.

"I refuse. These are my friends, my neighbors." She tightened her grip on his arm. "Friends, neighbors, and more. I love you, Samuel, in case you haven't figured that out."

"Then do as I say and get to safety. I know Milo Hannigan." He sucked in a deep breath and let the truth rush forth. "I rode with him and his outlaw gang. Ben, Seth, and I left when it got too much for us to stand."

"You were a robber?" Amelia walked a few paces, never letting loose of her grip on his arm. "Then you must have been forced into such a life of crime."

"I patched them up after more than one robbery went wrong. Hannigan isn't a very good highwayman."

"See. I knew it. You were there to save people, not kill them."

"I've killed men." Knight went cold inside remembering how he had faced down Hector Alton, and it hadn't stirred him at all. Stone killer, he had heard it called. All emotion drained when he went for his six-shooter. Alton had been quicker to clear leather, but his aim had been shaky.

Knight's hand had been steady and his aim precise.

"Of course you have. You can't save everyone, as you did Papa. And during the war. You said conditions in your surgery were deplorable. Most surgeons lost more patients than they saved. I am sure your record was better."

He wanted to contradict her, but they had reached the jailhouse and the conversation had drifted from persuading her to leave town.

"Marshal? Marshal Hightower? Are you asleep?" She turned to Knight. "He's such an old dear, but I swear that he sleeps eighteen hours a day."

Knight opened the door, started to let Amelia enter first, then jerked her back.

"Samuel, that hurt!"

"Stay here." He pushed past her and went to the marshal. The man sprawled back in his chair. His hat had fallen to the floor, showing the fringe of gray hair on his bald head. Smack in the middle of his forehead a tiny dark hole showed where a bullet had entered. Knight had seen wounds like this during the war and felt a knot in his belly as he rocked the dead lawman forward. A piece of skull the size of his fist had been blown out the back. He glanced down.

There wasn't any blood on the floor because it had all drained into the marshal's fallen hat.

"Oh, no, what happened?"

"Ben must have stopped by to pay his respects as he left town. Or Milo Hannigan decided to remove any opposition when he returned with the rest of his men. Does it matter?"

"He's dead." Her voice came out low and tortured. "The only other time I ever saw a dead man was when Bobby Lee Banfield was killed by his mule. H-his chest had been crushed. He d-died almost instantly."

"So did Marshal Hightower. He probably died while he was snoring and never even woke up to see who killed him." Knight took the man's coat from a rack and draped it over him, then went to the gun case. A chain kept casual thieves from making off with the rifles.

A savage yank tore the chain loose. He scooped up the five rifles and piled them into Amelia's arms. Finding the drawers with boxes of cartridges for the weapons took a minute longer, but he herded her out and back toward the saloon.

"These won't go far in arming the men, but it's better than nothing. We have plenty of ammo. Our best tactic is to outlast Hannigan. He can't have that much ammunition with him. At least we never had enough when I rode with him."

"Is he as terrible as you make him out, Samuel? Really?"

"You don't want to find out. He'd sell his own mother into slavery if he ever had one."

Amelia laughed uneasily. "That's a joke, isn't it?"

"Yeah, a joke." He stopped her and said urgently, "Go back to your pa. Take a rifle and a couple boxes of ammunition. Keep him safe."

"He's a better shot than I am."

"Then give him the gun, and you reload for him. But leave town while you can."

They had reached the saloon. Anxious eyes turned toward them as they came in.

"Doc Knight, you got us some rifles. Where's Hightower? He hasn't lit out for the tall grass, has he?" Hattie Malone spat and reached for the rifles cradled in Amelia Parker's arms. Amelia let her take them, but she looked to Knight.

"The marshal's not going to join us."

The Golden Gate's owner looked hard at him. "It's like that, is it?"

"We can arrange a funeral afterwards." Knight knew better than to add, "If any of us are still alive."

Hattie understood. From Amelia's tiny gasp, he thought she finally realized how serious a threat Hannigan posed to everyone in Buffalo Springs, even after seeing Hightower's dead body. Knight knew some things took a while to percolate down so people accepted emotionally what they knew intellectually.

"How're we defendin' ourselves, Doc?" Hattie worked the rifle lever.

He handed her a box of cartridges. "I'm not the mayor. I'm certainly not the marshal. Pick somebody else to lead you."

Hattie whistled. Everyone inside the saloon crowded out into the street.

"You got elected while you were gone. You oughta know how that works, Doc. If you don't stick around to turn down a chore, you get to do it. Ain't that so?"

Knight shuddered as the citizens let loose with a cheer of support. He had no idea what to do. Working as a surgeon and not an officer in the heat of battle was poor training for what was to be done. He looked around. Dawn threatened the eastern horizon.

"We don't have much time. Hannigan will go for the bank."

"So we all crowd in and defend it!" Hattie started off.

He grabbed the woman's arm and swung her around. "We'd be trapped inside. Better to turn the tables. Let Hannigan and the rest of his men go in. If we're all outside, we can trap them."

"That's a good plan, Doc." Seth Lunsford hefted a rifle and began loading it. "We have resources outside as well as outnumbering them. If they try to shoot their way out, they'll run out of ammo." He exchanged a look with Knight. They both knew keeping his guns loaded had been a problem for Milo Hannigan.

"Spread out, circle the bank, then hide. Wait for the outlaws to break in and then we've got them."

"But they'll blow open the safe and take the money." Jacob Stevenson tried to protest. Hattie took him aside to explain the trap for him. Having his money in jeopardy didn't set well with him.

Knight hoped Hannigan stayed trapped and never got away with it. Then again, letting the outlaw go with the money had a chance of ending the threat. Hannigan had no loyalty to Donnelly. The lure of getting rich drew him to Buffalo Springs. Having money from the bank vault gave Hannigan reason to keep on riding.

Then Knight remembered Ben Lunsford

and the way he had gone plumb loco. Hannigan galloping away did nothing to stop Ben's hatred. Money wouldn't quench his anger, and chances were good that Marshal Hightower had died from a bullet fired by Lunsford.

"What do you want me to do, Samuel?" Amelia Parker moved closer, holding a box of cartridges and a rifle. She thrust it out for him to take.

Knight had decided to order out of town anyone incapable of fighting. Tying Amelia up and sending her along presented the only path to safety for her. She would hate it, but he couldn't bear the thought of anything happening to her.

"I want you out of town. If I hog-tie you and —"

A bullet came whistling down the main street, derailing his intentions.

"They're comin' hard!"

Knight tried to find who'd shouted the warning. Then the world exploded all around him. Following the single shot came a fusillade. Hooves thundered toward him and the Hannigan gang fired at anything moving. When the saloon erupted in flame, Knight staggered away. Johnny Nott had tossed a lighted kerosene lamp through the open doors. When the bottled alcohol

446

caught fire, the inferno forced Knight away.

He heard Hattie wailing about her destroyed saloon. Then Knight saw Ben Lunsford gallop past, firing at the woman. She threw up her hands, rifle cartwheeling in the air. When she collapsed to the street, there wasn't any question she was dead. Ben had taken the first of his revenge against his former employer.

Knight levered a round into his rifle and tracked Ben, only to lose his target when the killer ducked low, using his horse as a shield.

"The town'll burn down," Amelia said. "We have to put out the fire before it spreads."

"That's what Hannigan intended. If everyone's on a bucket line fighting the blaze he started, no one's guarding the bank."

Amelia Parker seemed caught between getting a firefighting effort started and going to the bank.

Knight grabbed her shoulder and turned her around. "Fight the fire. I'll take care of the bank robbers." He started to kiss her, but she'd already called out to the others and rushed off.

"I'll help you, Doc. We both got a score to settle. I still can't believe Ben used me as a shield." Seth Lunsford looked so young. His face flickered with shadows and flames, turning him into something demonic. Or was he only determined?

Knight wanted to send him away, too.

Since it was Knight who was responsible for Hannigan's blood feud, he knew he had to stop the attack. "We can stop them, Seth."

Knight gripped the rifle stock so hard his hands shook. He forced himself to relax. This was no different from facing Hector Alton. "Try to get them in a crossfire. And" — he struggled to word it right — "and Ben is willing to kill both of us. Remember that. If it comes down to you or him, make your first shot count."

Seth Lunsford swallowed hard and nodded once. He said nothing as he started walking fast toward the far end of town and the bank. Knight ran to catch up. A few words of encouragement buoyed courage. He had seen it work during the war as he listened to the best of the CSA officers talking to their troops before a battle. Jeb Stuart had been a master at finding just the right thing to say. Knight hunted for words and failed to find them. He was no Stuart, and he was no officer deploying his troops.

The only things he had in common with so many of the Confederate officers were that he was outgunned and outmanned.

He held out his arm and slowed Seth's headlong rush. Four horses shifted about nervously in front of the bank, mesmerized by the fire burning on the other side of town.

"One's missing," Knight warned. "Check around back. I'll make sure to keep Hannigan bottled up in the bank."

"What do I do if I find him, Doc?"

"Anybody sees you first, you're dead. Does that answer your question?"

Seth turned pale but gamely dodged around, keeping hidden from the bank as he made his way to the back. Knight settled down behind a water barrel, rifle resting on top so he could cover the door. A single lamp flared inside the bank, causing Knight to half rise. He settled back when he realized the robbers needed light to work on the vault and hadn't set fire to the building as Nott did to the saloon.

Patience wore thin as he waited. Then he jumped to his feet, ready to charge when gunfire sounded from the rear of the bank. He had gotten halfway to the front door when Johnny Nott popped out, his six-gun in hand.

"Knight!" The outlaw lifted his six-shooter. He was a heartbeat too late. Knight pulled the trigger of the already aimed rifle. Nott let out a curious sound like a stepped-on puppy, threw up his hands, and fell backwards.

The shock of seeing the outlaw die so fast almost caused Knight's own death. Both Porkchop and Lattimer boiled out, guns blazing in the weak dawn. Knight grunted and spun, falling to one knee as a bullet hit him in the side. It tore through his black coat but only creased his left side. Sluggish blood oozed from the wound. It burned like hell, but he knew he had to ignore it if he was to live.

He swung around and fell facedown. His finger drew back and the rifle bucked. Porkchop doubled over as he fired into the ground in front of him. Knight got off a second shot that tore straight through the dust cloud. Porkchop stopped firing. A quick survey showed that Lattimer hobbled toward the skittish horses. The outlaw had never recovered from all his prior wounds. Knight took out Lattimer's legs. The man thrashed about, screaming curses. He fired at Knight until his pistol came up empty, then he tried to crawl away.

Knight scrambled to his feet and drew a bead on Lattimer. "Give up or I'll shoot you down like a dog."

Lattimer sat up, hands reaching over his head. He jerked and fell back when a shot rang out.

Knight looked at his rifle in shock. He hadn't fired.

"Drop the rifle, Sam. Drop it or I'll drop you." Milo Hannigan had come up behind him.

"Why'd you shoot Lattimer?"

"I told him never to surrender. If he shows a yellow streak, then he'd spill his guts about me and the rest of the boys when it came to a trial."

"There's something else, Hannigan. This way, you get a bigger cut of the loot from the bank," Knight said.

"That, too." Milo Hannigan laughed. "You always were a clever fellow, Sam. Too bad it never got you anywhere."

"Are you going to take me back to Donnelly?" Knight still held the rifle. From reflections in the bank windows, he got an idea where Hannigan stood. Steeling himself for the attempt, he tensed to spin and fire. If luck rode with him, he'd come close enough to ruin Hannigan's aim.

"I considered it, but being under his thumb don't set well with me. It's personal between you and him, but it's *real* personal between us, isn't it, Sam?"

451

"So you'll just shoot me in the back?" He got ready to feint right, move left and fire until the rifle came up empty.

"Donnelly said you shot Hector Alton in the back, but he's the only one saying that. Everyone else in Pine Knob brags on how fast you were. I never liked Alton, but he was fast. Before long, I'd have taken him on just to see which of us was best. You outdrew him, so you'll make a good stand-in for him. Drop the rifle. You're wearing your iron. I see the bulge under your coat. Drop the rifle and face me."

Knight took a final look in the window and realized his wild scheme would end in his death. He bent, laid down the rifle, then turned, slowly straightening. He faced Hannigan and his drawn six-shooter.

"You got stones, Sam. I'll give you that. Let's see if you got speed." Hannigan returned his pistol to his holster, but he never took his hand off the butt.

Seeing this and knowing he was at an immediate disadvantage, Knight went for his Colt. Never had he moved faster. He heard a distant gunshot. His side ached where he had been shot, but nothing new tormented him. His six-shooter still leveled, he swiped sweat from his eyes. Milo Hannigan lay on the ground, kicking feebly.

Knight advanced slowly, keeping his six-gun aimed at Hannigan. The outlaw tried to lift his gun hand, but when he succeeded, his fingers lacked the strength to hold the six-shooter.

A mocking laugh greeted Knight. "You're faster'n I thought. Hell, Sam, you're faster'n anybody in Pine Knob said." Life left the man. He collapsed into a pile.

"Milo. Milo!" Knight rolled the man over. They had been friends once. More. They had survived the Union prison camp against all odds. He ripped open Hannigan's shirt. The accuracy of his shot astounded him. He had drilled the outlaw through the heart. He had outdrawn him and shot with impossible accuracy.

He stood, his Colt dangling in his hand. He swung around, bringing up the gun when shots sounded from behind the bank.

"Seth!"

Knight lit out running, hoping he wasn't too late to save the boy from his own brother.

CHAPTER 31

Samuel Knight threw caution to the winds.
He rounded the bank and waved his six-
shooter around . . . as if Ben Lunsford cared
about such a clumsy display. It took a
second for him to understand what he saw.
Seth lay curled up in a ball. From the way
he shook, he was a ways from dying.

"Ben? Where are you, Ben?"

Seth grated out, "Behind the pile of
garbage. Where he belongs."

Such venom from an obviously wounded
man — and Ben Lunsford's doting brother
— shook Knight into crystal clarity. He
rounded the heap of trash. For a moment
he stood with his six-gun pointing at the
man laid out on the ground. Then he holstered his Colt. It wouldn't be needed. He
turned away from the obviously dead man
with the bullet ole in his forehead and
returned to Seth Lunsford. He knelt and
gently unfolded the young man.

"Is it that bad, Doc? I never seen you grimace like that before."

"I see four holes leaking out your blood. Are there any more?" He probed gently. Seth gasped and passed out. Those four wounds showed how much punishment Seth had taken from his brother before plugging him.

He wondered if Seth had gotten in a lucky shot or if he had taken enough time to accurately fire. Ben had come apart in so many ways after arriving in Buffalo Springs. Knight looked up to see the reason. Amelia Parker stood over him and Seth. Her dress was partly burned off, and her face had turned to a splotchy, sooty gray from smoke. She held her right hand in her left.

"You've been burned," Knight said.

"It's not bad. We put out the fire and kept it from spreading. How's Seth? He looks to be in a terrible way."

"I need my bag and surgical instruments. And whiskey. Did any survive the fire?"

"None of it. Hattie's dead. So are a half dozen others, but we kept the fire from spreading. The town didn't burn down." Amelia stared at Seth as if she hardly believed anyone in such terrible condition still lived. "We can take him to the hotel. We can set up a hospital there since several others are burned and were hit by splinters when the saloon blew up."

"Take him to my house," came a high-pitched voice.

"Is it closer than the hotel, Mr. Yarrow?" Knight recognized the gunsmith's voice and never took his eyes off Seth. His breathing had turned shallow and ragged. "He needs immediate attention."

"He'll get the best damn nurse in town. My Marianne — his Marianne now, I reckon — won't leave his side. Let me help, Dr. Knight."

The two of them hoisted Seth. Amelia cleared the way and retrieved his medical bag from the smithy's. They laid Seth on the kitchen table and Knight set to work. Time ceased to have any meaning but eventually all four slugs lay in a saucer half-filled with blood, and Seth was sewed up good and proper. His breathing had evened out and some color returned to his face.

"It'll be a week before he can do more than sit up. I don't recommend letting him do that for the next few days." He spoke to a girl who looked too young to have a boyfriend, but then Seth was young.

Marianne Yarrow solemnly nodded and even wrote a few notes to herself to make sure her Seth pulled through.

Only then did Knight turn to applying a makeshift salve on Amelia's hand and tending the rest of the town's injuries. It was past noon when he sat at the table and simply stared straight ahead without any idea what went on around him. As if in the distance, he heard Amelia and Marianne talking.

"Take him to your farm. There's no reason for him to stay in town. Besides, with your hands, your pa might need him."

Amelia Parker answered, but Knight had lowered his head to the table and fell asleep amid terrible dreams of Ben Lunsford and Milo Hannigan and Hector Alton. Worst of all was Gerald Donnelly laughing at him. He kept trying to see around the carpetbagger for one last look at Victoria. He failed every time.

"There, there," he heard. "I'll dry those tears. You're safe now. Safe, Samuel. Safe."

He felt angel wings fluttering on his cheeks, brushing away tears. Then he fell into a dreamless state akin to death.

"I wish you would rest more, Samuel. That bullet wound in your side's not healing properly." Amelia Parker pulled his coat away and ran her finger through the hole in the fabric. "I need to mend that, too. You need a new coat, but no one will notice the hole if I work closely."

"The only thing that's changed is getting the outlaws buried. I wanted to be at their funerals," Knight said as they walked along the street.

"I can't believe you when you said they shot each other. Their leader, the one you called Milo Hannigan, looked as if he had been in a gunfight. Did you shoot him?"

Knight ignored that and said, "Let's get some dinner after I check on Seth."

"Miss Yarrow says he is doing well. She doesn't leave his side. I know she's thinking about churches, but not for his funeral. For their wedding." Amelia moved a little closer to him to give him a nudge.

Knight stopped abruptly, causing Amelia to stumble. She caught herself and frowned. Then she saw what he already had. Three riders came down Buffalo Springs' main street looking for trouble. They carried rifles across the saddles in front of them. He had seen their look before. They swivelled from side to side, heads always moving, eyes darting about hunting for anything — anyone — threatening them.

"Who're they?" Amelia moved closer to him and held his arm. He wished he had his six-shooter strapped on instead of riding in his medical bag.

The burly black man in the lead guided his horse to them. He touched the brim of his hat. As he moved, his duster opened enough for Knight to see the badge pinned on the man's coat. The glimpse was all he got. The rider wanted to conceal his identity.

"Howdy, ma'am. Sir. What sort of trouble have you had in town? The saloon's burned to the ground, and one of my boys says the bank's got more holes in it than a piece of wormwood."

"Outlaws held up the bank a few days back," Knight said. "It got shot up then, along with the owlhoots trying to steal the money."

"Do tell?" The black man squinted a bit at Knight. "You remind me of someone." He snapped his fingers. The rider to his right edged closer and held out a wanted poster.

Knight almost panicked. With his six-shooter in the bag, he was at a disadvantage shooting it out with three lawmen with their rifles ready for action. He recognized them now from back outside Pine Knob when they had braced Ben and Seth. He had watched from hiding, a rifle trained on the three policemen. Only Amelia's grip steadied him.

The lawman held up the wanted poster and looked from it to Knight and back.

"If I didn't know better, I'd say this was your picture on the wanted poster. And that didn't happen to be the Hannigan gang sticking up the bank, now would it?"

The two deputies swung their rifles around to cover Knight. With Amelia beside him, he dared not move for fear that they would open fire and shoot her, too. They had the look of desperados, in spite of their leader wearing a badge.

"Is that the name of the criminal you're hunting?" Amelia asked. "Hannigan?"

"He's the leader, but this galoot looks like Dr. Samuel Knight, wanted for more crimes than can be put on a poster. You happen to be this Knight fellow?"

"Don't be absurd. This is my husband. He is a doctor, but his name's Amos Parker. I must ask you to prove *your* identity. You can't ride into a town and accuse a pillar of the community of being this . . . this outlaw."

"Me and my men are duly deputized by the state of Texas. We ride for the Texas State Police."

"I've never heard of such an organization." Amelia stamped her foot. "You need more proof than that."

"These rifles are all the proof we need. I reckon we found ourselves Samuel Knight, and we're takin' him in."

"What's going on? Hold down the ruckus." Marianne Yarrow came from the gunsmith shop. Knight caught his breath, but Amelia headed off trouble.

"Miss Yarrow, tell these men they have made a mistake. They have mistaken my husband, Amos Parker, for some common criminal."

"A killer, ma'am. His picture on this here poster matches what we see in front of us."

"Then you've made a mistake. Amos has lived here for . . ." Marianne hesitated. When Amelia made no effort to fill in the gap, she hurried on with her tall tale. "He has lived here for the last three years. He and Amelia married soon after he set up his practice."

"That's the only detail in common, Marshal. The man you seek and my husband are both doctors. I am sure *mine* is much better than any fugitive from the law."

"The picture is a bit smudged, Custis," one of the other riders said. "This gent's a lot heavier and his hair don't look a thing like the picture."

"Hair's easy enough to change. Hell, you been scalped. Your hair's not the way it was 'fore that Comanche took a knife to your head."

"My husband has not been scalped, thank you. Now, we must be on our way."

"You were coming in to look at Seth," Marianne said.

Knight almost dropped his bag to fetch the gun in it. All three Texas State Police officers reacted as one.

"Would that last name be Lunsford, ma'am?"

"Seth Yarrow," came a querulous voice from inside the shop. "He's my son-in-law." Mr. Yarrow came out, limping. He had injured himself fighting the saloon fire, and Knight had patched him up.

"What's wrong with him? Hell, we'll just take a gander for ourselves. You got that other wanted poster?" Custis motioned for the one who had held up the first poster to pass over a second. "We got a better picture of one Seth Lunsford, wanted for running with the Hannigan gang."

"Well, it's not my son-in-law. He's a hard worker and doesn't go gallivanting off to do — what? What's this Seth Lunsford supposed to have done?"

"I'll have a look at him for myself." Custis pushed past Yarrow and went into the shop. "Where is he?"

"In the back, in the bedroom," Knight said. He motioned Amelia to silence. "You might want to wear a mask before you go there."

"What are you saying?" Custis came back, the rifle riding in the crook of his left arm.

"He's got scarlet fever and is still contagious. Have you had it? Most folks here are immune after an epidemic two years ago."

"A year after he came to Buffalo Springs," Amelia added, if the policeman couldn't figure that out for himself. Knight wished she would stay quiet and let him talk. He'd seen the fear on Custis's face at mention of the disease.

"I never had it." He looked at his two deputies. They edged away on their horses, ready to take flight. "My duty's clear. I got to see him."

"Look in on him, then," Knight said. "I'll help you get a look at his face, but I'll need to scrub down after I go in."

Custis hung back, letting Knight go into the bedroom. Seth Lunsford slept heavily, still recuperating from his wounds. Knight held up the sheet to reveal Seth's face. No matter what the poster's picture was, Seth looked worlds different. He had lost weight and, while his color was good, he was pale enough to be mistaken for a corpse. To add to the tableau, he moaned softly and stirred. Before Custis got too good a look, Knight dropped the sheet back.

"He's not the man you want. Now, if you want to be on the safe side, scrub down real good with lye soap. You won't have to burn your clothes but —"

Knight held back his merriment at the way the policeman backtracked from the room, fearing some horrible contamination. Before he followed, Knight made sure Seth rested easily. He had run a fever for a day, but that had broken. He was on the mend. With the Texas State Police chased off, Seth had a good life ahead of him in town.

He looked back at his sleeping patient, wondering if Seth would adopt the nom de guerre Mr. Yarrow had given him as his "son-in-law." After the way his brother had turned on him, Seth might not mind being Seth Yarrow if it meant settling down peacefully, though it might bother him not passing his name along to any children with Marianne.

"Sir, this is a wanted poster for *Ben* Lunsford." Amelia looked around at the crowd that had gathered to see what the fuss was about. "Do any of you know Ben Lunsford?"

"Was he one of them outlaws that shot up

the town? May he burn in hell."

The murmur passed through the crowd. The three policemen huddled, passing the wanted posters around and arguing. Finally coming to a conclusion, they mounted.

The black policeman tipped his hat to Amelia. "Sorry to have troubled you, but we wanted to beat the soldiers here, if these men were the outlaws we're all chasing."

"Soldiers?" Knight knew holding his tongue was the smart thing to do, but this offhanded comment worried him more than facing down Milo Hannigan. "What soldiers? The ones building a fort outside town?"

"A roving patrol. The captain's got a bug up his ass to catch Samuel Knight." The man stared hard at Knight, then shrugged. "Expect him to show up in a few days. Leastways, we were only a couple days ahead of him." With that, the Texas State Police wheeled around and trotted from town.

The crowd slowly dispersed, leaving Knight and Amelia alone in front of the gunsmith shop.

"You didn't have to lie for me," Knight said.

"I did. Those men have no idea what you mean to this town." She looked up at him, her bright eyes filled with love. "Or to me."

"Living is never easy."

"It can be better. You finish your rounds and come out to the farm for dinner. I am fixing an apple pie to celebrate."

"Celebrate what?" Knight looked around. The stench of the burned saloon filled the air and more than one building had windows shot out or bullet holes in the walls. Men and women had died, and the law was still hunting him down . . . Milo Hannigan and his gang, too.

"Surviving. Us. Think of all we have. Now, I must go. I have to buy a few things for dinner." She stood on tiptoe and gave him a quick kiss, smiled, and hurried off.

He watched her go, wishing he felt as confident about the future. Knight turned when the woman who ran the bookstore called to him from across the street. Her husband had been the most severely burned of any who had fought the saloon fire, but he was on the mend. Everyone in Buffalo Springs was on the mend. Things looked brighter now that the outlaws were dead and life had returned to normal.

Knight spent the rest of the day sitting on the boardwalk, talking with the good people of Buffalo Springs, hearing what they thought lay ahead for him — for him and

Amelia Parker — and promising no Texas State Policeman or other lawman would ever trip them up to turn him over. He had been accepted as one of them.

Twilight turned shadows into black curtains and lights popped up in windows throughout town. He made a quick visit to Seth Lunsford. Marianne sat beside his bed, reading a book. Seth slept without any sign of distress.

Knight stepped out into the cool evening as stars began winking into the night sky. "Starlight, star bright, first star I see tonight," he said, remembering the old rhyme from his childhood. "May I have this wish I make tonight."

He mounted and rode to the Parker farm. Through the side window he saw Amelia bustling about, laying out the china service that had belonged to her mother. It would be hers when she married. He felt a lump form in his throat. She would lie when Captain Norwood rode into town, but the officer knew his quarry. One glance at "Amos Parker" and hell would break loose. No matter how many others in Buffalo Springs made the claim he wasn't the outlaw Norwood chased down, the Union officer would not be deterred. It was personal for him and doubly so for Gerald

Donnelly.

Dr. Samuel Knight turned his horse's face and rode into the night, not knowing where he went and not caring, as long as it was far away from Buffalo Springs.

ABOUT THE AUTHORS

William W. Johnstone has written nearly three hundred novels of western adventure, military action, chilling suspense, and survival. His bestselling books include *The Family Jensen; The Mountain Man; Flintlock; MacCallister; Savage Texas; Luke Jensen, Bounty Hunter;* and the thrillers *Black Friday, The Doomsday Bunker,* and *Trigger Warning.*

J. A. Johnstone learned to write from the master himself, Uncle William W. Johnstone, with whom J. A. has co-written numerous bestselling series including *The Mountain Man; Those Jensen Boys;* and *Preacher, The First Mountain Man.*

The employees of Thorndike Press hope you have enjoyed this Large Print book. All our Thorndike, Wheeler, and Kennebec Large Print titles are designed for easy reading, and all our books are made to last. Other Thorndike Press Large Print books are available at your library, through selected bookstores, or directly from us.

For information about titles, please call:
(800) 223-1244

or visit our website at:
gale.com/thorndike

To share your comments, please write:
Publisher
Thorndike Press
10 Water St., Suite 310
Waterville, ME 04901